Joseph's Visions

AKA

"Hawk"

By

Shelby Jean Roukoski-Clark

AKA

"Mary-Eagle-East"

LaVa Publication
Webb, AL

Joseph's Visions
AKA
"Hawk"
By
Shelby Jean Roukoski-Clark
AKA
"Mary-Eagle-East"

About the Book, "Joseph's Visions": It was an era before DNA, Luminol, cell-phones, P.C.'s, 'chat rooms', Fax machines, E-mail and 'global village'. It was the late 1960's or early 1970's when a war-weary Native American Army Ranger, Captain Joseph Winterhawk, retired from the military and came home to what he hoped would be 'life as it once was'. However, his personal dream of peaceful, quiet days was short-lived. He'd not even set foot on reservation land before his mentor and friend, Dr. Jerrold O'Barr, offered him a ride home. Then God, fate or destiny had other ideas, so instead of going home, 'Doc' turned the truck around, taking the newly retired officer with him as he paid a call on one of his patients. The front door of that house opened and Hawk's life was changed---forever. If he'd had any inkling of all that lay ahead of him for the next several months, he might've been tempted to refuse what he came to call 'the last ride' and prudently hiked on to the Rez and his mother's home. But yet again, had he done so---he never would've had that second vision and he would've missed the mystical 'dance', as well as the future that eons ago, had been planned for him. More importantly, he would have missed saving the life of one who, in turn, would make his own life complete.

Shelby Clark
June 25, 2002

"There is great honor in knowing and proving you can kill your enemy yet have chosen not to do so."

Unknown

About the author, Shelby Jean Roukoski-Clark

Born of immigrant grandparents in north Georgia's foothills at a time when 'the great depression', although far past, was still very much 'alive and well' in the mind-set, lives and environment of poor people in that area who eked out an existence from the stony, red clay land. This was an era when actual cash money was scarce as hens-teeth and a nickel was to be treasured. Although many residents owned land, the majority worked either as cotton mill hands, sharecroppers, or during WWII at 'sewing plants' where uniforms were made. At that time, many country folks' entire livelihood depended upon what they themselves raised then canned, dried, preserved or harvested from the red dirt soil---thus early on, their children learned about reality and the meaning of 'responsibility'.

Not fortunate enough to attend college, the author became a wife and subsequent mother of two uniquely special daughters---'beautiful girls with generous spirits, kind and loving hearts'. In 1996, when unusual events began bringing changes in her life, the author wrote her first book---'The Post Oak Tree', followed by a three-part novel that has not as yet been titled. If, as a reader, you find moments of peace reading of earlier times---then by all means, read this tale. Set in the late 60's and early 70's, it begins with a mystical shock for the hero and continues as the suspense mounts. There is an attempted murder, an effort to 'bend the law' and the evolving of a gentle, 'soul-mate' love story.

Shelby Clark
July 2, 2002

INTRODUCTION

"JOSEPH'S VISIONS"

Book and cover by

Shelby Clark aka Mary-Eagle-East

Initially, this book was God's idea so I credit Him as
desiring it to be written. But among humanity, I wish to
dedicate "Joseph's Visions" to the exceptional Native
American Indian actor, Mr. Rodney Arnold Grant of the
Omaha Tribe. Rarely attending movies, I'd not taken note
of Mr. Grant's work until fall of 2001 when in a television
movie, I saw him in his 'Bucky Miller' role. His work so
inspired me that I rented all available videos in which he'd
previously appeared and after viewing them, concluded he
must have a vast audience as he not only is blessed with
acting abilities but a powerful screen presence as well. He
brings strength, character, realism plus a subtle, quiet
dignity to his roles. Early on, Mr. Grant draws his audience
into the film with him, then we hope his character will
appear in every possible scene---finally at 'the end', he
leaves us not only impressed but pondering as to what his
'character' might be doing the next day. To me, his
outstanding talent certainly meets 'the standard' and towers
over much of what passes today as 'star-quality', statue-
names and box-office 'bally-hoo'---many times followed by
general disappointment in those who hope for a higher level
of entertainment. Although I've never had the honor of
meeting Mr. Grant, I wish him to know that countless
people eagerly await more of his fine work. His role as
'Bucky Miller"--- (the loyal friend-to-the–end in spite of

hard work, hell and high-water) opened my spirit to that of Mr. Grant—and Mr. Grant IS the heart of my character-hero, 'Captain Joseph Winterhawk'!

With Grateful Spirit
Shelby Clark
2002

Shelby Jean Roukoski Clark

"JOSEPH'S VISIONS"

Chapter One

As though determined to hold back fall's arrival, a fiery late summer sun beat down upon the land which, in turn, gave birth to heat waves which shimmered and danced like vague, distant, watery mirages. As the army ranger hiked north toward his mother's home, each military cadence stirred a film of hot powdery dust spoiling the usual 'spit-shine' on his heavy paratrooper boots. Heat soothed his cramped travel-weary muscles, perspiration passing thru his jungle fatigues quickly evaporated in the arid atmosphere surrounding him. Off in the distance, he welcomed the sight of his favorite mountain range. Then pausing momentarily, he removed his beret---his keen dark eyes swept over the countryside---his country---the land of his ancestors! He smiled as peaceful look came over his face--- once again, he was 'home'---alive and in one piece.

Taking time to breathe in the clean warm air, his keen olfactory noted familiar scents blending with the ever-present aroma of dust. Beside the highway, some dry withered grass baked in the sun, exhuding a scent not unlike fodder when gathered in the fields and scattered over the terrain, a few struggling clumps of wildflowers hinted a faint fragrance that reminded him of funeral flowers. The faded, heat-damaged leaves on bushes bordering the roadside could no longer hide a few yellowish-brown 'age spots' and offered yet one more whiff of dying greenery--- another sure sign of summer's demise and the onset of fall. He closed his eyes and stood motionless while antiphon choruses of insects shrilling out their hearty song in post-noon heat seemed to magnify, growing ever louder---filling his entire being. Once again, he was 'one' with the land.

Suddenly, amidst his 'glorying-in' life as he'd always known it, a refreshing, gentle breeze blew in from beyond the hills. Turning to face it, he closed his eyes to enjoy this short-lived pleasure---and caught the scent of freshly mown hay! There'd be plenty of time for curing-out before baling---he knew there'd be no rains arriving anytime soon.

Picking up his bag, he moved on. He'd hiked about two miles out of town when a fourth vehicle approached from the rear. Never losing pace, he stepped off onto the dusty wilted grass and was surprised when this driver slowed to a stop then gave a sudden wheazy blast on the horn. Shifting his large OD duffel, the soldier glanced toward a familiar dust covered, rust-brown truck now halted on the road beside him.

"HEY! HAWK!! That really you!!?"---a gravely male voice shouted out through an open window! A pleased grin spread over Hawk's smooth, dark-caramel features as he shouted back over the noisy engine---"Hey, Doctor-man! Is that really YOU?!" Dr. Jerold O'Barr leaned over forcing open the obstinate passenger door---"Get yourself in here! Looks t'me like you might be needin' a ride before you get t'your stoppin' place!!"

Hawk easily tossed his heavy discharge duffel into the truck bed then slid onto a dusty front truck seat and slammed the creaky door shut behind him. Taking the right hand offered him, he gripped it between both his own. All the while Doc was rattling away---"Lord above---where'd you come from?? We haven't seen YOU in awhile!! You ride th' bus into town? Didn't anybody come in t'pick you up?" Hawk held up one strong brown hand---"Slow down, Doc, you never change---'poor Indian' can only answer one question at the time! I hitched a ride to Offutt on a C-130---and from there, I did indeed ride the bus---and no, nobody came in for me. Actually,"—Hawk leaned back against the seat, took a clean handkerchief and blotted his damp face and neck---"I never told anyone I was coming."

O'Barr stared at the handsome Native American 'warrior' beside him---"You do beat all, boy! I can understand why maybe you never asked anyone t'come an' pick you up--- probably wanted t'surprise th' family an' all that. But I'd hoped after thirty years, that you knew ME well enough t'at least ASKED me t'drive you home! Damnation! You fly from God-knows-where in one of those roarin', ear-splittin', military cargo planes---ride hours on a bus t'get here---then take off like Moody's Goose hikin' all th' way in! You forget how many miles THAT includes?"

Doc sounded a little 'put-out' with him, so Hawk grinned--- "Now, now. Don't get all jazzed-up, Doc! I'm accustomed to hiking and running full-pack for a mighty long way! AND...", Hawk held up his hand---"...just for the record, I DID come by your office but was told you'd most likely be out all afternoon! Having said all that, it's my turn to ask a question of my mentor. How've YOU been since I last saw you? You taking care of yourself? After all you're pushing 60, I should think----,." Breaking in, Doc snorted---"I'm fine, dammit!! An' while we're about it, you're no spring biddy yourself, Captain Joseph Winterhawk!" Glaring over at his passenger who pressed his lips to keep from smiling, Doc went on---"Why you're not even a young rooster, anymore!" "Nonsense, Doc--,"—Hawk protested—".. you know I'm just hitting my prime! I got lotsa juice left!" "Hitting your 'prime', my hind-end!"---Doc shot back--- "Fact of th' matter is---one o'these days, you'll wake up t'find yourself a de-feathered, practically useless old turkey! How old ARE you anyway?! When I come here t'the reservation, you were just a snot-nose little brat!!"

3

Doc momentarily turned his attention to a dirt and gravel turnoff leading to the Winterhawk home then after correcting his steering---he gunned the old engine into unaccustomed speed! Just getting wound-up, O'Barr continued his 'tirade' as dust billowed through the open truck windows settling over the captain's camouflages. "Humph! I remember now! You're thirty-eight years old!"---Doc shook a short stubby forefinger---"I gave you your first smallpox vaccination---an' you screeched like some varmint caught in a trap! Almost bit off my finger t'boot! An' you can bet I wanted t'put my belt on your skinny little butt---however I figured I might get scalped as I was not only a green-horn doctor, but ignorant of any culture west or north of th' Mississippi! Didn't know whether your tribe had accepted they weren't supposed t'be scalping 'white eyes' anymore or not! 'Specially Irish 'white-eyes'!" He paused then stated---"Twas a point t'ponder for th'boy I was back then!"

Suddenly Hawk could hold it in no longer and let loose with hoots of laughter. Doc chuckled, soon both men roared with old familiar camaraderie until Doc almost ran off the road again! "Please, Doc!!"---Hawk groaned as he wiped at his eyes---"No more---I'm not accustomed to this much fun, the army doesn't approve of over-doses of levity and after all these years---it might kill me! Besides, I can see your driving hasn't improved any---so I'd best not distract you until the wheels stop rolling!"

After clearing his sinus' then spitting expertly out the open window, Doc drove on in silence for a few minutes. Suddenly, he whacked the steering wheel with one hand--- "Uh oh! I clean forgot something, Hawk! You got a time schedule? I mean you wantin' to see th' family any particular time?" "No sir! Got all the time in the world. I signed out, Doc,---retired myself. My first twenty years are in---and now, I'm just your average 'no-account' Native American male."

The battered but reliable truck screeched to a dusty, gritty halt---after the mechanics of turning around, Doc ignored Hawk's bit of 'red-man' sarcasm and headed back toward the highway. "Aww, I really didn't have a call or anythin'---it's just that last year some new folks moved-in up th' road---remember th' old Sanderson place?" Hawk nodded as Doc continued---"Well, th' husband fell off th' barn roof several months back, cracked some ribs, hurt his back, can't walk---confined t' bed. After th' fall he was hospitalized an' soon as he was 'able', I recommended physical therapy teach his wife some exercises that might help him. He hated exercise an' cussed so when it was time t'do em, I just told th' therapist t'forget it! Talk about your 'hard cases'---this one's a prize Missouri mule! Uncooperative, cold, nasty-tempered---unless, of course, he's criticizin' somebody or makin' an obtuse remark. Personal opinion---he's plain 'mean'! Why SHE got mixed up with th' likes of him! Anyhow, whenever I'm out this way---I drive by an' see how th' hateful coyote is gettin' on! If he has a problem, she calls but---well, I reckon I kinda enjoy her company so I use him as an excuse t'drop in."

O'Barr became quiet, warm air whipped thru the open windows filling his truck with the smell of dust, hot vegetation and creek water flowing nearby. Realizing Hawk might've misunderstood his last statement, he turned slightly to the right and hastened to clear up any confusion---"Not that SHE suspects that, Hawk!! Lord no, she's a fine Southern lady, real 'quality'---what folks might call 'genteel', I guess. Why, a body feels like 'royalty' when visitin' her---th' way she carries on over you! She has this soft accented voice that sounds like it's comin' from deep in her chest. An' looks?" Doc paused slightly then went on---

"Got this most peculiar shade of streaky reddish blonde hair, fine smooth fair skin with blue/green eyes---I believe she once said that three of her grandparents were European immigrants and one was part Cherokee Indian!"

Hawk rubbed his ear, cleared his throat, cast his dark eyes sidelong at the admiring man behind the wheel and asked--- "And how old is this paragon of beauty, virtue and southern culture?" "Old? Oh,"---Doc mused---"...around thirty, maybe thirty-two. Why?" The captain shrugged---"Just wondered. You better not let Mrs. Doc find out about this little side-jaunt you enjoy so much. You'll be in big trouble!" Doc bristled---"Get this straight, boy! This is a LADY we're talkin' about---an admirable woman who puts up with a lot. B'sides,"---he grinned—"...Ida adores her, th' same as me!"

Slowing his rattling truck, Doc turned on a white sandy driveway leading up to the Sanderson place. "What th' woman needs,"---he continued---"..is a good man to 'do' for her---th' way she hasta 'do' for him---'cause he certainly shows her no appreciation. More to th' story but---well, maybe later---we're here now! Hop out---you goin' in with me." Hawk groaned softly---"But why? They aren't expecting company, Doc! Besides, I might 'insult' them by crossing the threshold---or has the social climate around here changed that much during the past twenty years? I've always heard Southerners were an especially 'class-conscious' bunch---not to mention 'race-conscious'!"

Now standing outside the closed truck door, Doc stared back inside at his 'adopted' god-son and younger friend. "Just do what I tell you. I think you'll be pleasantly surprised---at least by her---tho 'pleasant' ain't exactly a word I'd use t'describe him! B'sides, I wanta show you off---I'm proud of you, m'boy!" Hawk sighed as he exited the truck and stood rubbing his boots against the back of his pants-leg. Finally he beat the dust off his uniform as best he could, slapped his beret across his palm a couple of times then setting it properly on his head, he followed Doc toward the house.

Taking in the outside appearance of the house, he saw it had been cleverly renovated with weather-worn notched wood-logs, perhaps from abandoned old barns in the area. Even the stones had been hauled in from some closed quarries in the general vicinity. "Why,"---he thought admiringly--"...it looks wonderful! A house whose inhabitants SHOULD be happily enjoying the fruits of their 'repair & remodeling' labors!" Then he recalled Doc's litany of reasons as to why those living inside may not be quite so happy. "A shame"-- sighing he followed Doc up the stone steps.

Taking hold of a specially ordered heavy brass knocker fashioned in the shape of an Indian bow and hanging on a brass chain, Doc rapped it sharply against the longer arrow part which was fastened stationary to the old wood door. Soon, the doorknob turned and a soft, soothing feminine voice like warm honey flowed toward them. "Doctah O'Bahrr! Ah do d'claire!! Such a lovely s'prise---do come in!!" Doc reached behind him, took Hawk's arm and pulled him along thru the open door. Stopping just inside, Doc turned to the woman while innocently remarking--- "Uh...Mrs. McDougal, I was just in th'area an' thought I'd check in on your husband. How's our patient this week?" Doc's hand gripped Hawk's arm as the latter blinked, adjusting his eyes from brilliant outer sunlight to the dim, quiet inner foyer. As they'd entered and Doc asked his question, the woman had turned away and was still looking toward another area of the house, finally her gaze returned to Doc as she replied---"He's just about th' same. Now,"---

she said briskly after glancing Hawk's way,---"Who is this you've brought along?"

And for the first time she actually raised her eyes and looked at Hawk's face, at once their eyes met because he'd been staring at her since the moment he could clearly focus again. Already, he'd politely removed his beret. "Uh, Mrs. McDougal,"---Doc offered---"Captain Joseph Winterhawk, Army Rangers---we're old friends, he's out with me t'day." Hawk didn't exactly hear when Doc's introduction speech ended---neither did Mrs. McDougal. On first eye contact, neither could free their gaze from the other. Suddenly he realized Doc was no longer just holding his arm but was giving it a healthy pinch---he must say something---but what!?

Left hand tucking his cap beneath his left arm, he swallowed hard, inclined his head slightly toward her--- cleared his throat and croaked---"Mrs. McDougal." Then, he extended his right hand. Was he supposed to? Inexplicably, he couldn't recall if a man offered to shake hands with a woman first or not---all social military protocol had vanished---utterly! "Oh God!"---he prayed--- "Please don't let me make a complete ass of myself!" He found his voice but it sounded foreign to him, like someone else--- he struggled on---"It's—uh--a pleasure to meet you. Doc's been telling me how you folks had fixed up this place---and how much improved---it looked. I must say, even with that, uh--I--I wasn't prepared to find such outstanding work---not to mention your excellent use of natural---er, available resources. Very nice, indeed."

A modicum of caution returned to him as he forced himself to cease blathering. Graciously, she'd taken his hand, held it for a short moment then finally released it.

The minute his eyes lit on her---something had begun stirring deep inside him---something from long ago and far away. He'd seen her before!! And he knew at once where and when he'd seen her---there was absolutely NO doubt! Now, in order to appear 'himself' and get thru the visit without embarrassing her ---he went into what he called 'a military mode'! Dear God, how could such a thing happen at this point in time---and without any warning whatsoever?! It had been---how long---26, 27 years ago?

"Captain Wintahhawk."---she was saying softly---"Ah'm honored t'have you heah!" Doc thought she looked strangely pale but she continued---"Doctah, let's all go in so you can speak t'Mac". She turned and led them to a large bedroom just past the living area. "Mac,"—she announced at the doorway--"..we have company! Doctah O'Bahrr dropped by t'see how yoah doin'---an' this gentleman with him is Captain Wintahhawk of th' U. S. Ahrmy Rangers." Winterhawk put out his hand but the invalid pointedly ignored it and instead snapped---"Dammit, I need a couple of pillows to prop myself up!"

Staring at the two men---he barked at his wife---"Get a move on, woman!! An extra pillow under my shoulders and head?! How can I entertain our 'honored' guests here if I'm flat on my back?" Dutifully she propped him up---then backed away from the bed as McDougal's cold eyes took in Hawk's uniform, the bone structure of his face---and the color of his skin. Just as the mixed-blood Omaha/Sioux had seen humiliation rise in the woman's beautiful face, he detected a sneer just barely hidden on her husband's lips as the man continued in a sarcastic tone---"So, we got 'Tonto and Kemosobe' over to visit---well, sit down, men! Take a chair! Let's hear what the two of you are doing away from town---out here in the wilds! You chasing bank robbers, marauding Indians or something?" After a short silence, he

9

let out a harsh bark of laughter---"...Or has the U.S. been invaded and sent our red soldier brothers to come and rescue all of us 'pore white landowners frum a fate worse than death'?"

Her face now highly flushed, Mrs. McDougal turned to Doc and spoke quietly---"Pull up a chair an' converse with Mac while Ah take th' Captain with me. We'll make coffee an' bring some refreshments." Face pointed straight ahead, she left the room---Hawk followed in her wake.

Once in the kitchen, she remained silent while staring out a window over the sink---he guessed she was 'counting to ten and gathering herself together'. Finally, she turned toward her guest as a tight little smile lifted the corners of her mouth---"Captain? If you'd like t'wash up while Ah begin ouah coffee..."---she pointed---"...theah's a half-bath thru that doah." "Thank you, Mrs. McDougal, I believe I'll take you up on that offer---Doc and his pick-up truck pretty well dusted me out!"

Soon, he returned---his thick, shiny, black hair combed carefully into place. Checking the coffee that by now was dripping into a carafe, she gestured toward a chair behind her and spoke quietly---"Please, do be seated, Captain." Her hands were gripping the sink so hard he could see her white knuckles, suddenly she turned to Hawk---"Are you hungry? Ah'll bet Doc's had you s'busy that you haven't had a bite since early mornin'! If you don't mind lunch left-ovahs, theah's some eggs an' really good country ham with two homemade biscuits." Without waiting for a reply, she began warming the left-overs in a small kind of electric oven and before long the food was before him.

"Oh—an' heah's some homemade fig preserves,"---she brought him a jar---"Straight from Georgia." "Figs." ---

Hawk commented as he held the jar up toward light coming thru the window. Her face softened---"A kind of fruit. You know, like in th' Bible? Try them---honestly, they're quite wondahful." Handing him a covered dish, she commented gently---"…And put some buttah on those biscuits! You can stand th' extra calories!"

Watching him start to eat, she sighed then asked pardon for her ill-tempered husband---"Ah do apologize t'you foah Mr. McDougal. Ah want you t'know that yoah most welcome in this house." "No apology necessary, Ma'am, Doc warned me on the way out---and, too, I've seen men like that in army hospitals." Catching her eyes, he assured softly---"No offense taken." Looking as tho a weight had lifted from her shoulders, she was quiet for a minute before replying almost wistfully---"Then Ah hope, perhaps you'll accompany Doc back t'visit us again---we don't have many guests." Hawk didn't have to guess at the reason for THAT!

By now his heart was pounding like a drum during a pow-wow gathering---"Are you from Georgia, Ma'am?" She nodded and smiled. Still speaking in his newly acquired alien-sounding voice, he continued---"Over the past twenty years wherever I was stationed—when I had weekend leave I'd drive off base to take in the countryside. I've been to Fort Benning, Georgia---several times!" She nodded, waiting for him to go on.

Swallowing a bite of food, he exclaimed---"Mrs. McDougal! Your 'left-overs' are better than most meals---this is delicious! But back to the subject, while at Benning, I went to Atlanta and saw the Cyclorama---you know, that circular civil war theatre?" Her eyes brightened as she lowered herself into a chair across from him then leaned up against the table like a child---"Oh yes, Ah do know! Saw

11

it once mahself! As school kids, we made up money all
yeah then took a school bus t'Atlanta. We spent th' entiah
day takin' in sights of th' big city---plus the Cyclorama. Ah
was so excited that Ah finally got sick, threw up in th'
restaurant ladies room---then went right on!" Laughing
softly, her eyes shining, she almost whispered---"An' Ah
remembah that th' last thing we did befoah goin' home was
attend a movie at th' old Fox Theatre! It was Doris Day
starrin' in "Mah Dream Is Youahs"! Ah nevah forgot how
beautiful she was---such a singin' voice. From then on,
each time Ah heard her on th' radio---I'd think of th' Fox
Theatre in Atlanta!"

She paused for a moment then looked at him, asking---"Did
you happen t'know that th' ceiling in th' Fox was made up
t'look like th' night sky?" He watched transfixed as she
went on, her fingers waggling around in the air---"Bright,
twinkly little stars strewn all across th' darkest blue sky you
evah saw while these thin whispy breaths of white clouds
honestly seemed t'float along. Th' carpet felt six inches
thick and all around were hangin' these heavy velvet drapes
with gold fringes and twisted satiny ropes! Such
unbelieveable gilded, ornate décor---an' now,"---she sighed,
looking down at the table---"...Ah heah it's all fell into
ruin." She tilted her head to one side, looking back into his
eyes---"Guess back then we poah Georgia folk believed
goin' to a movie at th' famous Fox Theatre in Atlanta was
real 'uptown'---that was wheah "Gone With Th' Wind"
premiered, y'know!"

Putting her hands on top of the table, she clasped them
tightly together before asking in an odd hesitant tone---"Do
you evah ....read? I mean, do you have time foah...uh,
novels an' such?" He looked at her for a few seconds then
replied gently---"Well, to be truthful, there's not a lot of
time for an Army Ranger to read for entertainment. Not

with continual textbooks to study, field films and maps to view, paperwork, traveling, training maneuvers and orders overflowing the desk---not to mention what I'm now hearing referred to as 'warmongering'! Anyway...,"---he picked up the final remaining tidbit of his food---"...now, I'll most likely have a bit of time to read, maybe even a novel or two!" His smile and deep quiet slightly accented voice comforted her---he sounded like Jesus must have sounded. "An' did you evah see 'Gone With Th' Wind?" Swallowing the last bite of buttered biscuit with Georgia fig preserves, he nodded and told her he had.

Regretfully he downed the final sip of his coffee while wishing she'd never stop talking. As she reminisced a bit more on her past life, he was fascinated at how alive and animated she'd become. Suddenly her dramatic, lovely eyes had a far away look as she spoke softly---"But all that was a long time ago..." Then she became quiet, temporarily lost in a time that he figured didn't include him. Hawk concluded Doc had definitely 'understated' when he described her beauty and charm. She was from another world---not exactly angelic perhaps---but not entirely human either---and after nearly thirty years, she remained just exactly as he remembered her!

Unobtrusively, he slid two fingers between two shirt buttons, pressing them against the crucifix he always wore around his neck. Just as soon as they were on the way back---he'd have to tell Doc. Silently he considered Doc's reaction ---he just hoped the old guy wouldn't be so shocked that they'd hit a pole or end up in a ditch!

Hawk's dark eyes followed her as she walked to a cupboard, took out a sealed container and set it on the table. He watched her remove the lid, take out several flattish 'cakes' resembling his mother's corncakes, she then stacked them on a china platter. Still chatting to him, she reached for a fairly large tray and set an entire 'coffee' with all the trimmings. "Ah guess this is everything!"---he felt hypnotized by the sound of her voice and her warm, genuine smile---"Dr. O'Bahrr loves 'dried-fruit pies', that's what we call them back home---all fried an' full of calories! Come along, Captain, let's join th' doctor an' Mr. McDougal." "I'll take this,"---he said softly then took the tray from her---"Lead the way, Ma'am."

Later, after enduring McDougal's unfit company for another 20 minutes, Doc rose from his chair---"Mrs. McDougal, we thank you for th' conversation, th' coffee plus your delectable pies! Seein' as we've managed t'clean up this whole platter---reckon Hawk an' I best be on our way. As always, stoppin' by t'see you folks is th' high point of a body's day, no doubt about it." Hawk stood, nodded briefly at McDougal whose hostile eyes still glared pointedly at him. The uniformed man politely thanked the couple for allowing him to be a part of this impromptu visit. Then turning directly to the lady, his body a wall between her and the man in the bed---his black eyes held her sea-colored ones as he spoke---"Doc's absolutely correct. My compliments, I've never had better food---or company. Thank you for being so gracious----Mrs. McDougal."

The sun had begun to drop somewhat closer to the mountain range just west of the old Sanderson homeplace as Doc cranked the truck and began rattling down the sandy drive carrying them back the same way they'd come in only an hour ago. "One hour!"---thought Hawk---"And I feel like somebody pushed me out of a Huey---without a rappel rope!" Looking back to gaze toward the house, his eye caught a slight movement in the sheer panel covering a long narrow glass beside the front door. He prayed it was her--- hopefully catching one last glimpse of him as he rode away from her---perhaps forever. After reaching the highway, Doc turned left and headed back toward Hawk's family home----both men unusually quiet.

Presently Doc glanced over at the retired 'warrior' and asked---"So, now what's this business of your retirin'? You tired of 'Nam as well as other secret covert action in exotic places? Or you got something else in mind? You're not old enough for 'retirement'! Why, good Lord---man, you'll die of boredom around here!"

His mind still filled with the sight and sound of Mrs. McDougal, Hawk shook his head and muttered at the open window---"Not so sure it's 'boredom' that'll cause my death!" Then he turned to Doc, picking up what he hoped was a 'normal' tone---"At this point, I got nothing concrete in mind but after a year of considering it, for some unknown reason, I had a strong feeling this was the right time for me to make a home for myself." Exhaling, he stared at the road ahead---"And if 'retirement' doesn't work out, I can always rejoin. God knows, we're never going to win this Asian war, I'm afraid we got another 'Korea' on our hands---only the terrain is worse! 'Nam is a hot, stinking, fungus-ridden hell---with certain areas nothing more than a dope and whore paradise---drugs and humans sold both day and night---kids and all. The entire scene is an oriental nightmare---you can't tell the enemy from the citizenry---or your allies. What is it they say—'rich men plan wars and poor men fight them'? Sane civilized people go crazy over there, Doc----Americans aren't prepared for what they find in that place. Only God and my Indian blood saved my life many times over then brought me safely back home...and in my right mind." With Mrs. McDougal still looming large in every part of him, he thought---"Hopefully I'll be able to STAY in my right mind!"

"But..."---he went on---"...back to the subject of 'retirement', twenty years of being away from home was long enough for me." Quickly he looked over and lay a hand briefly on the older man's arm---"But the best thing I EVER did was take your advice about joining up! Instead of staying here and maybe becoming ---well, the service made a man out of me! And I saw places I never would've seen had it not been for meeting your friend, the retired Colonel, when he visited you---then deciding I wanted to be 'like him'. I know I've thanked you before for all the time you spent with me during my growing-up years when I needed a lot of male guidance and discipline---but I want to say it again. I'm grateful to you from the bottom of my heart."

"Between you and Father Murphy, I grew up with the best male counselors a kid could've had and I wouldn't be the person I am today without the two of you! You showed me how to get along in the real world, make something of myself and have a future when I was older. Father Murphy worked on my miserable 'heathen' soul until he got me faithfully confirmed to the Church. Of course, that included years of countless 'penances'!" Hawk chuckled then went on in his serious tone---"And Mama? Well, Mama is a rare treasure---a loving soul who tried her very best with all us kids, but after Dad passed---she had a lot to handle. However, by raising most of our own food, plus her sitting with the sick---then 'doing' for Father Murphy---it got us by in fair shape---and thank God for what He sent our way because---as I said, it did 'get us by."

"As it now stands, I'll have a nice army check coming in every month and if I get to ailing, I can rattle your cage or go to the army doctors!!" Hawk paused, laughing---"And yes, I'll pay you each time I call!" Doc snorted but said nothing giving Hawk time to say more. From past experience, Doc knew when any hidden streams in this man's psyche might be exposed---the adult soldier always clammed up. But right now Doc had a feeling that for once, Captain Joseph 'Hawk' Winterhawk had an unusual 'mind to talk'---and he wanted to hear everything the man had to say!

"You got an hour or so to drive up to the picnic grounds on South Mountain, Doc? It's on the way and I haven't been there in years." Inwardly, Doc congratulated himself on his hunch---"Sure. Got nothing but time! I've had m'southern-fried pies an' two cups of coffee---it may be a stretch f'the gut here, but that oughta hold me till supper!"

Chapter Two

Parking in the shade, Doc shut off the engine and glanced at his passenger---"Wanta walk about an' stretch your legs?" "Good idea."---Hawk wrestled the passenger door open--- "Believe me, other than hiking from town earlier---I haven't had much physical activity during the past 48 hours!" Silently they began walking toward the water spigot----and after a long refreshing drink, they ambled off for a side-trip in the direction of two wooden outhouses.

Later on, halfway up the mountain, Hawk concluded Doc shouldn't climb farther so he chose an open spot, collapsed onto a carpet of brown pine needles covering the ground and announced---"Man, I'm ready to sit for awhile." Taking off the beret, he peered up at Doc and asked---"You don't mind if we don't go up any farther do you?" Doc paused, took in a deep breath then answered stoutly---"Naww. We may as well take some time right here t'smell th' roses." Gratefully, he sat down, leaned against a fallen tree---and waited.

17

"Doc,"—Hawk began---"...you remember years back when I was a kid and we'd gather for pow-wows?" "You mean when other tribes would show up for th' gatherings?"---Doc questioned? "Yes."—Joseph went on. "It was great when the pow-wow was held here on our reservation! I looked forward to that more than Christmas." His eyes gazed dreamily off in the distance as a soft golden afternoon mist began sifting over the valley below---"I was taught to dance----and I could dance with the best of them!" He was silent before continuing in an almost inaudible tone---"I can still hear and feel the pounding of our drums as I danced and chanted----it never leaves you, Doc."

He turned to look at his mentor---"I mean, I've been a Catholic for decades---but what I've come to accept is that it's a cultural thing---not a religious thing. Somebody said that once about Jews---that their 'Hebrew-ishness' wasn't a 'religious' thing but a 'cultural' thing. Don't know how true that is for them---but I know what it means to me as an Indian. Once while getting ready for an assignment, I researched the Hebrew language---I was astounded as to how many of their words were similar to our Native American languages, right down to the pronunciation! Even more amazing, the word-meanings were nearly the same. I do wish you could visit their 'Wailing Wall' in Jerusalem to watch and listen to them pray---you'd never forget it! Anyway, back to the subject---I don't worship any other gods, Doc, I want you to KNOW that. I just feel that since Almighty God created all things---when I feel the need, I can thank Him for the trees, the animals, the birds, the hills and plains, the water, a beautiful day, etc. But if I want to REALLY get into the 'thanking Him'---I can dance and chant to Him. Each time I've come home during the past twenty years, I've gone to a special mountain top on the Rez, built a fire, played my flute and my drum---I've prayed, sang and chanted while I danced before God---then I'd spend the rest of the night there."

Hawk turned away looking back below then in a soft voice, he asked---"How do you feel about that, Doc? Do you think what I've said makes me a pagan or a heretic?" Doc rubbed his forehead, took a deep breath then exhaled. "Joseph, I know you t' be one of th' finest men I've ever had th' good fortune t'know! You're a 'good Catholic', a good son, a good friend, an honorable, educated and loyal man---you're a seasoned military officer. Of course there's nothing heretical or pagan about you! Now, what's this all about? I mean, what is it you're really trying to say? Did McDougal upset you back there with his black-hearted oafishness?" Doc flung out a hand and spat---"Don't bother yourself with people like him---they're not worth the brain-cell burn!"

Hawk smiled, looked down at the ground where he sat--- "Doc. Remember when I told you about my dream---or 'vision'? Lord, I've never quite figured out which it was---I was only 12 or so." Immediately Doc's interest piqued, he straightened up---"No, I don't recall. Refresh my memory." "Okay. It was one year when a pow-wow was held here--- guest tribes arrived---of course, all were closely inspected by government officials who made certain we weren't going to go on a secretly planned war party, shoot arrows or scalp any white folks here in the 1900's." Hawk's chuckle had a tinge of bitterness---he then hugged his knees with his arms, clamping his hands tightly over each forearm. "One night after all the dancing, singing and chanting had ceased, the elders were in their smoke-tent tending the fire and puffing their pipes---I slipped in the back, hid myself in a cozy nook and rolled up in a blanket. Much later, listening to the droning of their tales, I think I dozed off to sleep." At this point Hawk grew silent---Doc was afraid he wouldn't speak further and thought---"I gotta prod him--a little."---so he queried aloud---"And?"

"And. I dreamed---or had the 'vision'. In the 'vision', I obviously was an adult because I could see over the heads of my people, some of whom were gathered around me. They were all looking at me—as tho I was---well, maybe somehow 'different' from them. I couldn't identify the dream's location but it was a nighttime setting. Up above, I clearly saw bright stars with occasional white cloud puffs against a midnight blue sky. Some sort of light mist was all around me---but not the others. I could hear wind sighing softly thru the trees while off in the distance a small waterfall made a slight roaring sound. It was then, off in the shadows, that I noticed someone slowly approaching me. The mist surrounding me opened-up, making a path for this person. At last I saw it was a white woman. Her hair was reddish-blond---eyes the color of ocean water---she was so very beautiful." Hawk's voice kept dropping lower---Doc strained his ears to keep up.

"She carried something in her hands, clasping it close against her bosom. When only a few feet away from me, she stopped, smiled and held out the object to me, offering it as a gift---it was a smallish rectangular box. I was hypnotized not only by her great beauty but also by the loving spirit I recognized inside her---and like a magnet that spirit was drawing me to her! I'd begun moving toward her when I woke. By then, the older men had mostly dozed off, so I lay quietly while going over and over that dream. I wanted to ask some of the elders what it meant---but I was afraid they'd be angry that I'd slipped in to hear their stories. So soon as I could, I wrote it all down. For over two decades, several times each year---I'd go over the dream---so as not to forget any detail. Even as a youth, I seemed to realize it's importance---it's message to be remembered and cherished---tho I never really knew exactly what the 'message' was! But the strange thing is, Doc, I hadn't thought about that dream for sometime now---not until this afternoon."

Hawk fell silent---the sun was lower---by now the valley below lay in shadows but there where Doc and Joseph sat, the golden mist still hovered. Without a sound, it had wafted thru the air, sifting over trees, gently invading their resting place---turning it almost mystical---thereby connecting with Hawk's tale! Doc thought he knew what was coming next but he couldn't take the chance that the man would stop speaking at this point! If Hawk spoke no more---then he, Doc, would never really know the truth--- but could only suspect it! He must be certain because IF he was correct in his assumption, then Captain Joseph Winterhawk would be in need of a good friend! And to Doc, it seemed that 'need' just may arrive sooner than later.

Doc cleared his throat and plunged into it---"Joseph, how big was the box?" "Oh..."---Hawk measured with his hands---"..8x10 inches maybe." Doc then asked---"What did th' box look like?" The retired Army Ranger turned to stare---"Pardon?!" "Th' box!!"---Doc almost hollered--- "Th' box in your 'vision'---th' one she was handing you--- what did it look like---what COLOR was it?! Do you remember?" Hawk thought Doc surely was over reacting to the wrong part of the 'vision'---he'd been certain Doc would pounce on the 'white-woman/red-haired/ blue-green eyes' part---especially since visiting with Mrs. McDougal! The handsome Omaha/Sioux looked thoughtful---then pursed his lips and stared at the ground. "Well?!"---Doc seemed ready to leap upon him so Hawk answered---"I think it was---a light colored background with---something, uh, some sort of image on it." Joseph Winterhawk concentrated his lips apart, eyes seeing the past.

Then suddenly staring at Doc and holding up a finger, he breathed---"Wait! Now I do recall---it had a picture of a tree on it! Yeah! There was a tree painted on the top---with writing above the tree! Doc, why're you so 'jazzed' about this box cover?"

Doc sighed as he painfully stood then slowly moved his body parts about---he'd grown somewhat stiff during their 'rest'. "Get up, m'boy."---he grunted---"You're going home with me an' spend th' night. There's a few things we gotta talk about an' I'm not gonna sit here till this tempting warm mist suddenly turns cold gray--an' all my joints stove-up on me! C'mon---let's go."

Chapter Three

"I'm feeling a definite need for confession and penance!"---Hawk laughed---"I've put away too much delicious food for one day! My penance shall be that tomorrow I dig out a new flower bed for you, Mrs. Doc! That is if you have need of." Doc and his wife, Ida, laughed good-naturedly---very pleased to have one of their all-time favorite 'sons' eat supper and spend a night with them! "Not necessary, Joseph, Doctor would DIE if I put in another flower bed for him to help me weed!"---Ida laughed and stood. "And I hate to leave good company but I do have a church meeting in a half hour, so I'm going to rush off---now, you gentlemen help yourselves to coffee and cake. Doctor?"---she looked down at her husband---"You know where everything is---including the brandy,"—she arched an eyebrow at him---"...without doubt, I know you'll be having some!" He laughed and kissed her cheek as she leaned over to say 'Good-bye'. "Drive careful."---Hawk lifted a hand toward her---"And thanks for a wonderful meal!"

After the car drove away, Joseph stood and stretched---"I'm going to bus the table, wash dishes and straighten up the kitchen---that is, if you'll take out the garbage—and feed your critters! We'll surprise the good-wife---deal?" "Of course! I think I got the best end of that offer, tho!" Doc stood and assisted clearing the table. After completing his two assigned outside chores, he returned and picking up a dish towel began drying dishes---"Soon be Indian-summer, Hawk---won't be too much longer now before snow'll be blowin' in outta Canada. On cool, still nights I can almost smell it in th' air." Silently Hawk nodded, continuing the clean-up without another word.

When Hawk was happy with the way Ida's kitchen looked, he nodded with satisfaction, hung up the towel and said--- "Done and done, Doc. Now, let's get to that statement you made as we drove up to the McDougals' place—that 'more to the story' bit about them---as well as those mystifying words back there on the mountain! I want to hear what we're to 'talk about later'--- it's 'later', so let's have at it!" Doc walked ahead of him to Ida's cozy living room softly lit with ecru shaded antique lamps---pointing Hawk to an over-stuffed swivel rocker, he replied calmly---"Just hold your horses until I get us some brandy." Soon he handed Hawk a glass then went to his usual shawl-covered rocker, sat down and began turning the glass between his hands, warming the liquid.

"About th' dream or vision---whichever it was. Hawk, if I didn't know everything about all this that I know right at this moment---why I'd say twas nothing but th' dream of a little boy who'd danced himself half t'exhaustion, who then crawled into a nice warm place, breathed in some 'grass' smoke then simply went t'sleep. An' that th' best thing for you t'do would be---'just forget it'. But th' problem is---I know better! However, the unnerving thing about all this is that until we went by th' McDougals today---I wasn't even AWARE of 'what' I knew!"

"Not t'mention,"—Doc went on---"..even a blind soul could've felt the---magnetic pull between Mrs. McDougal and you!! I thought---'Drat it, Doc, you've got competition for her attentions!! An' with a younger, handsome, stronger man—not t'mention one that you, yourself, dragged right in thru her door!' That attraction, Captain,..."---Doc paused to emphasize---"...it was more than 'usual'. Don't care if you admit it or not, it was a hit-to-th'-head or more likely---to-th'-heart! I figured afterwards, I'd have a little 'fatherly' talk with you---not that you needed it, you saw that varmint she's married to. I know you're not th' kind t'get involved with a married woman---I give you more credit than that." Doc exhaled then continued---"But, y'see I'm old enough t'know that things just 'happen' sometimes---as tho they were---oh hell, I hate th' term---but as tho they were 'destined to be'---an' if they are, nothing on this God's earth can change any of it!"

Hawk remained silent so Doc said on---"But it wasn't until after you told me about that dream-vision up there on th' mountain today that I realized there was a whole lot more t'this thing! Your introduction t'Mrs. McDougal, our afternoon 'talk'---PLUS what I'm about t'tell you now---well, it kinda brings us t'that something 'bigger' I'm referrin' to. My fear now is that it's 'bigger' than us four mere humans involved in th' events of this strange afternoon." He paused, sipping at his brandy and gazed at Joseph.

At this particular point, Hawk knew that he couldn't just 'outright' tell Doc that Mrs. McDougal WAS the woman in his dream. Already Doc was disturbed, if he knew she WAS the woman, without any doubt---it would end up troubling him too much, so Joseph quickly hit upon an evasive maneuver. "I understand why the dream is eating at you, even tho it happened long ago. But I don't want you to worry about this---this 'thing'---whatever it is, I'll handle it. I admit that Mrs. McDougal is---much more than 'ordinary', fact is she's extraordinary!! And you were right, she knocked me for a loop, I stood there speechless until you practically pinched my poor elbow to a nub! But, as you so kindly reminded me, she's 'married'--and with a capital 'M'! That man would just as soon shoot me as to look at me---I only had to be in the room five minutes to know THAT! God knows, maybe he felt this 'thing' between her and me.."---Hawk turned and looked into Doc's eyes--- "...you think so?" "No, Hawk, no---,"---Doc soothed--- "..he was just being his usual vile self. He isn't sensitive enough t'feel anything except what might have t'do with his own piggish self. I have t'tell you, I've never liked th' scoundrel---something with him don't ring true."

"Now, this is between you and me. During my countless trips out there t'check on his health and well-bein'? I've seen some 'white supremacy' literature halfway under th' pillow next to him also some peeking out from beneath his bed. I admit takin' my boot-toe an' edgin' out what was under th' bed---just t'see if it was th' same junk beside his pillow. I know th' Klan is big in a certain surrounding states---but I just never ran into them before. Wonder if he's---maybe in a spot of trouble somewhere else? I never did ask Mrs. McDougal exactly the reason they chose t'move here---but sure as shootin', she's not a part of THAT!" Realizing he was wandering from the matter at hand, Doc returned to their earlier subject. "Son,"---Doc became more personal---"...back there when you two were in th' kitchen, did she happen t' tell you she's a writer?" Hawk's jaw dropped---"A WRITER??!" O'Barr nodded---"That's how they bought th' land, remodeled that house an' bought those cattle, etc. Only a few days ago, she made a decision t'sell th' cattle soon---th' poor woman is already 'run ragged' without them critters added on! Like I said this afternoon, what she needs is some real help! A good couple---now that would fill th' bill! Carin' for McDougal is a 22 hour a day job---an' he makes it very difficult. Why, you wouldn't believe some of th' abusive things he lies there an' thinks up. With me now, it's his 'medications'— he thinks he's takin' me f'a fool but I know he's dosin' himself. An' you wanta know somethin' else? I don't really give a damn!" Doc paused then mumbled---"Maybe one of these days, he'll take too much!"

Hawk didn't comment on the drugs but finally spoke of the conversation with Mrs. McDougal. "In the kitchen, she and I talked about Georgia being her birthplace, then we talked about Atlanta and finally the book, 'Gone With The Wind', as well as the subsequent movie. That was when she got this odd 'look' on her face and asked if I ever had time to read novels! That's about the gist of our conversation. She seemed very sad that the author of GWTW had been killed." Hawk paused then mused aloud---"Now that I think about it, maybe she did want to say more---but chose not to! Tell me, Doc, do you know what she meant?! This is beginning to sound 'stranger and stranger'!" Doc closed his eyes---"Yeah. 'Stranger and stranger' is exactly m'point!! I think it's what your people used t'call 'mystical'---or that pre-arranged 'destiny' thing. And need I say THAT stuff didn't always have a happy endin'!"

Setting his empty brandy glass on a side table, he ambled off to the bookcase and searched about. Soon he returned with a paperback book in his hand and silently handed it down to Joseph who reached for it. He held it, examining it closely---the book had a slick pale cover and there on the cover was---oh, God! A tree! He swallowed at the lump beginning to form in his throat---adrenaline prickled at his entire body. The book was entitled *"The Postoak Tree"*---authored by 'Josie'. "Josie!?"---he thought---"Who is 'Josie'??" A sudden but short-lived relief began rising up inside him---the adrenaline needles retreating---whoever wrote the book, it wasn't anyone named 'McDougal'! 'Josie' wasn't even a surname---so it couldn't be her maiden name! Taking a few deep breaths, utilizing his military stone-face, Hawk calmly looked at Doc and shrugged---"So, who's this 'Josie' authoress? And what's *'The Postoak Tree'* about?" "You do-do bird!"---Doc exhaled a snort---"This 'Josie' is Mrs. McDougal's pen-name! SHE wrote the book! SHE designed the cover! Look inside the back cover---on the last page!"

The 'prickling' which had somewhat subsided began again---along with a trembling deep inside him. It was located in the same place he'd felt strange rumblings this afternoon when their eyes first met---the same place inside him when almost 30 years ago, he'd felt drawn to her loving-spirit in the dream!! It couldn't be! After 20 years of military, this was one hell of a piece of trouble to come home to!! Lord, being an army Ranger was beginning to look like simple war-games compared to everything that'd happened since the moment several hours ago when Doc picked him up in his truck! How could so much blow wide open in a few hours! This wasn't even a clandestine skirmish on foreign soil! There was no 'Def-Con' number in Montana or the Pentagon pressing him to the limits! There was just a 'Mr. and Mrs. McDougal' whom this time yesterday he never even knew existed---and this book called *'The Postoak Tree'* with an authoress named 'Josie'---plus his 'vision' on

the Indian Reservation that occurred all those years ago!!
And lest he forget, there was poor Doc, his beloved 'father-
mentor' who'd inadvertently been drawn into this 'mystical
happening'!

Gingerly Hawk lifted up the back cover---sure enough,
there with a mysterious little smile playing across her lips
was---not 'Josie'---but Mrs. McDougal! His beautiful long
ago loving dream-spirit---his true love. He'd recognized
her today and he thought she'd recognized him. But he
didn't know WHY she seemed to recognize him---surely,
she'd not dreamed of HIM! But whatever her reason no
words could pass between them! A wall of silence must be
kept because Hawk knew if either he or she ever spoke
aloud of it---what was now only dreams or visions would
turn into reality, there'd be no turning back! And surely
there'd be hell to pay---McDougal was unstable and with
his mindset---only God knew what he'd do to his wife! She
was HIS own love and he must protect her at all cost---tho it
probably meant they'd never meet again!

Desperate to vacate the room, Hawk gathered together the
last of his waning strength, pushed himself up from the
chair---"Doc, I'm bushed---it's been a long time since I had
sleep---the plane, the long bus ride, the hike, the great
supper, your brandy." Apologetic, Doc stood---"I'm sorry!
Look, go on up t'your old room---th' wife has it all ready
f'you. Clean towels an' everything in th' bathroom---you
take a good hot shower then fall into bed. Sleep late 'cause
I may be in th' office or out on a call when you get up!"

Hawk gave the shorter man a hug with a pat on the
shoulder---"Goodnight, Pops O'Barr." He'd started toward
the stairs leading up to his old attic room and picked up his
duffel bag when Doc called out---"Here! Take this book
with you." Catching up with Hawk, he handed over Mrs.

McDougal's book---"Read it, and finish blowing your mind off it's hinges. She autographed it for me, s'make sure an' take good care of it. T'morrow, after lunch I'll drive you out t'your Mother's house."

Watching the tall handsome man disappearing up the stairway, Doc thought—"Reckon th' time will surely come when I'll have t'tell him about old McDougal's fall that afternoon---but t'night just ain't that time!! I think Joseph's had enough 'mystical experiences' for one day. And if things aren't clear t'him just yet, reading that book will clarify any doubts he could ever have!"

Suddenly from the darkness at the top of the stairs, Hawk paused and called back down to O'Barr---"Hey, what's her 'given' name, Doc?" "Lizbeth."---he called back. Shaking his bowed head, Doc wondered why that afternoon, after picking Hawk up on the road---what reckless quirk of fate had made him stop the truck, turn around and head straight to the McDougals---when he could've taken Hawk directly home, THEN gone there!! That spur of the moment decision had most assurredly opened up an unexpected 'can of worms'!! Wondering what the coming days and weeks would bring, Doc sighed then turned out the living room lamps and went into the kitchen to await his Ida.

Chapter Four

After the two 'guests' had left the McDougal house that 'eventful' afternoon, Lizbeth began collecting the coffee cups, saucers, napkins---stacking all on the tray. Dark with rage, Mac's eyes silently followed her every move---before leaving, she paused at the door---"Can Ah get you anythin' befoah goin' t'the kitchen?" Mac continued his silent glaring for a moment---then bellowed---"Turn around and look at me when you talk to me!!" She turned back slightly and stared into his eyes---"Yes? Ah'm lookin' at you." His voice lowered---"That fool doctor obviously has a crush on you, God alone knows WHY---but he takes every opportunity he can find to just 'drop in' so he can lay eyes on you! BUT NOW!"---he yelled---"THIS TIME HE'S GONE TOO FAR! JUST WHO in the HELL does he think he is---by God! Bringing a damned redskin into MY house!! And YOU!!"---his voice dropped omniously--- "Making like he was real 'quality' folk---serving him like a nigger maid! 'Captain Wintahhawk, suh, may Ah poah you moah coffee?'---he mimicked her! "Army officer or no, my Daddy woulda hanged the Indian---and burnt a cross in your boyfriend O'Barr's yard!!" McDougal began yelling again- --"Don't you EVER come dragging something like that into my room!! NEVER---are you EVER---to allow him INTO this house again!! DO YOU HEAR ME??!!"

She stood motionless, her jaw set---waiting for him to throw something, break something or continue screaming insults at her. "With th' windows still open, Ah believe th' whole territory might've heard you. For some unclear reason, Mac, Ah've not been clevah enough t'know that yoah hatred for black people included th' Indian people as well. They lived heah first, remembah? So if yoah certain theah's nothing Ah can do---Ah'll be on m'way." She walked down the little corridor toward the kitchen, his string of oaths followed---then an object hit his bedroom wall--- probably one of his KKK textbooks.

How long had she known that Mac's father and most of his father's family were Klansmen? In the kitchen, she considered that question while standing at the sink washing up the china. Scenes of her life after graduating twelfth grade began running thru her mind. She'd met Mac fresh out of high school. A school chum of hers, who'd met Mac

at a local hang-out, had begged her to go on a blind date
with 'the stranger'. She'd been hesitant but finally gave in
to Joe's pleadings because his own girlfriend's father
wouldn't let her go out except on double dates---and after
all, Joe had been her school friend for 12 ½ years! It wasn't
easy to say 'no' to his pleas! Upon meeting her 'blind-
date', she was pleasantly surprised---he was actually nice-
looking and seemed a decent sort of Scotsman. When he
asked her out again, she'd accepted---afterward, their dating
each other became a habit.

All through high school, "beaus" had come and gone but
Lizbeth had an unusual but very real feeling that
somewhere---she had no idea 'where'---there was some
very special man waiting for her---and her alone! In her
mind and in her life, she was a 'realist'---but one whose
heart, soul and spirit was that of a 'dreamer'. This
'paradox' had always been a part of her and was simply 'her
way'---fortunately, early in life, she'd learned to accept
herself for who and what she was.

Thus when Mac appeared on the scene, she was still young
and immature. No one had ever advised her about career
opportunities 'out in the world', a world that was far away
from her hometown located near the foothills of the Smoky
Mountains. It was only when the summer after graduation
finally ended, that it hit her---her schooldays were over.!
She really missed her friends---and plainly put, she was
lonely! Mac was never overly attentive, but he WAS
'company' for her. So for the both of them---and for a
time---they simply filled a void in each other's life.

Almost two years later, his work, which had brought him to
her hometown, had been completed and he would be
leaving. Out of the blue, he'd asked her to marry him. By
then she was going on twenty---and he was twenty-five.

Her family approved, so she reasoned that it must be God's plan for her to say 'yes'. Besides what else WAS there except—'to marry'!? Her parents would never allow her to go to Bell Telephone Company in Atlanta---all alone?! Why it was out of the question! No proper young lady did such a thing! Ten more years, she'd wondered, would she still have a part-time job and work the rest of her time in Papa's field? So in the end, after considering her limited experience in life---and with the world in general---she accepted Mac's proposal.

Soon his job would be taking him to Ohio, their first home would be there. With a stab in her heart, she knew she'd miss her family. But they'd lived there all their lives surrounded by relatives and friends, and her sister Bess would probably have them a grandchild one day. Many times Lizbeth had her second thoughts about leaving yet in the end allowed herself to be comforted by the thought Mac was a 'good boy'. She'd be a 'good wife' and he'd take 'good care' of her---just as her parents had always done.

The wedding, a small affair, was held at the church that her paternal grandparents had helped to 'found' and build. But none of Mac's family came. He told her that his mother wasn't in good health and the distance had been too far for her to travel---he assured her that his family would 'love her' as he did. After the wedding, they left for Ohio---but stopped off in the mountains for a short honeymoon.

Lizbeth stood rinsing suds down the sink---all the dishes from the afternoon 'coffee' had been washed, rinsed and were draining in the rack---all except the Captain's cup. For some reason, she'd carefully kept it separate from the rest. Before washing it, she closed her eyes, raised it gently to her mouth and rested it there for a long moment allowing the place where he'd drank to rest against her lips.

Deciding against washing it, she set it aside to take to her room---she'd never wash it! It was her 'touchstone' with him---it was all she had left of his visit. And tho his 'presence' still lingered somewhat in the kitchen with her, chances were she'd never see him again! Her heart ached with a deep sense of loss---just as it had when he walked out the front door with Doc. She'd pulled back one of the sheers beside the door and watched as the two of them climbed into the truck and drove away. She'd seen Captain Winterhawk turn and look back at the house. Had he hoped for one last glimpse of her? "Stop it, you silly ignorant child!"—she scolded herself---"This was an 'event'. One of those things that happen only once in a lifetime---he came an' now he's gone from yoah life. Probably forevah."

Raising her eyes and looking silently out the window over her sink, she noticed the trees up on the higher rim---the cool nights up there had already begun turning the leaves to what would later become radiant hues of autumn. "How lovely..."---she thought, "...it reminds me of th' north Georgia mountains when we used t'drive up on a Sunday aftahnoon when th' apples were ripe and ready t'sell. Daddy would buy a burlap bag each of potatoes, cabbage an' apples---how delicious one of those apples always tasted aftah comin' home from school in the aftahnoon!"

Overcome by the wave of sudden homesickness, the years of Mac's continual railing at her and the unexpected afternoon 'visitor' with Dr. O'Barr---she grabbed her work jacket off a chair, hurried outside and sat down beneath a tree near the back porch. She needed to calm herself while 'drinking in' some peace and fresh air. By leaving the back door open, she could hear if Mac yelled for her.

Since her visitors left, the sun had already begun to drop. Looking down the little white dirt driveway, she watched

purplish shadows from the mountains grow longer as they
crept across their huge, wide pastured valley. Try as she
might, she couldn't shake the feeling that 'he' was still there
with her and both of them were sitting silently side by side,
watching the hot afternoon pass into the cool of the evening.

"Where was Ah?"---she thought absently---"Oh, yes. Th'
'Honeymoon'! What a disaster THAT was! Poah Mac, he
wasn't much of a lovah an' Ah---well, Ah knew absolutely
NOTHIN' about weddin' nights! It was a subject 'not
discussed' in owah home, at school---not even between us
girls! We giggled about 'it' sometimes---but we were dumb
as a post about sex!" As the weeks had passed between the
newlyweds, she recalled how she and Mac came to a
working solution about it. Sex was an act used to
perpetuate the human race---but not often for pleasure or
enjoyment then after meeting his family, she understood
somewhat more as to 'why' he was 'the way he was'.

They'd lived in Ohio that first year then he decided to
change jobs and move closer to his family. She'd not been
happy about the job change but after trying to discuss it
with him a couple of times, she found she only incurred his
anger---so she never brought it up again. That was the first
time she'd been the object of his anger---she'd been
shocked speechless when he verbally attacked her---saying
the wildest things! References to people and ideas that
made no sense to her!

"How many more times did THAT happen?"—she asked
herself as the sun sank lower, lengthening the shadows even
more. The answer, of course, was 'countless times' which
began overlapping each other until it became chronic---a
common everyday occurrence.

In the beginning neither of them spoke of having children---
then as time passed and Mac 'changed', she knew she never
wanted any little ones. Not for him to use for his misplaced
anger---and heaven forbid---to become as 'cowed' as she
herself! She had no idea what'd happened to make him
begin 'acting like another person'---someone that she, in her
innocence, didn't know how to cope with. It was years later
before she realized he'd always been that 'other person'---
having simply put on an act for her, her family and friends.
This unpleasant revelation had been long in coming because
before meeting him, she'd always taken people at face-
value, believing the best of them. By the time she came to
see the person Mac truly was, she didn't know how to get
out of the marriage in one piece---having never personally
experienced violence before, she was afraid of him.

It'd been after they 'moved closer to his folks' that Mac
had taken to going out nights---weeknights, weekend
nights---it didn't matter, he'd simply say---"I'm going out
for awhile---Dad and the guys have some things to take care
of and I'm going with them. Don't wait up." She'd hear
his car start then drive away---sometimes gone for hours.

They'd been married for six years the day she went to the
garage to search for some seasonal clothing packed away.
Picking up a box---then looking at it, she knew it wasn't one
of theirs. Loosening the lid, she pulled it up and peered
inside---what lay there looked like a sheet, all white---but
after picking it up, she saw it was some sort of costume!
There was a white pointed hood to match---with cut outs for
eyes. It was then that she saw the patch emblem sewn on
the shoulder of the robe---letting out a loud gasp, she felt
her heart lurch as she frantically searched beneath the cloth!
There were some books, pamphlets, keys and other items.
By that time her hands were trembling because she knew

she wasn't supposed to see this---nor have any knowledge of it! Mac was a 'night-rider'---a Klansman!!

Back home in Georgia, everybody'd heard of the KKK but it was considered a very secretive group of unidentifed men---nobody questioned their racial mind bend because almost no black people lived in that county! Therefore practically no KKK racial activity was 'needed'---unless a 'visit' was paid to some 'low, white-trash, drunken wife-beater' who warranted their attention yet hadn't actually broken a law!

Suddenly some of the crazy things Mac would yell at her during his rages began to make sense!! Frightened by her discovery, she quickly folded the items and put them back exactly as she'd found them. Closing the box, she stacked everything as it'd been---then shut and locked the garage. Once inside the house, she wept uncontrollably for what had seemed like hours. That day 'home' and safety seemed so very far away.

She took two days to think the whole episode thru. Had he ever helped kill anyone? Or was he only guilty of cross-burnings, beatings and attending meetings where loud, raving men wearing hoods filled his head with racial hatred and wild, unlawful ideas? For some time, she'd been unhappy, wanting to leave him and go back home---but now, she was more afraid of him than ever! After six years of marriage, her head told her Mac would rather kill her in a fit of rage then give her a divorce. It'd been three years since she'd seen her folks and it seemed like forever---sometimes when she'd ask to go, he'd say 'I'll think about it'. At other times, he go on a rampage of yelling and threats. Maybe she'd try just once more---she'd ask if she could go home to visit her parents and Bess whose twins she'd never even seen! And if she left, she'd never come back! Surely this time he wouldn't begrudge her a family visit!!

But he did, she well remembered how 'much' he begrudged it! That was the first time he'd physically 'pushed her around'---without actually hitting her! Round and round the room they went----violently he flung her into the wall, the furniture, the doorframe---as he 'dared' her to 'go home for a visit'---threatening not only her but the lives of her family as well! At first opportunity, she'd fled the room and house---then hid behind their woodshed until he went to bed and she figured he'd gone to sleep.

Suddenly she was brought back to the present by loud oaths peppering the air around her! "$#%*&(#@)!!!# Woman! LIZBETH!!! DAMMIT!!! I'VE BEEN CALLING YOU FOR FIFTEEN MINUTES!!! LIZZZBETH!!" Standing up, she felt a sudden tremor run over her. Shivering, she went up the steps and in thru the open backdoor. Once in the kitchen, she heard his continued cursing and swearing as she closed out the wonderful cold, fresh air and turned to tend the angry man. She'd never been quite able to put her finger on exactly when she admitted to herself that he hated her---but it was after she secretly wrote her book.

Around 11:00 p.m. that night, Lizbeth finally left Mac drifting off in the drugged stupor that he insisted upon. "Poah Dr. O'Bahrr,"---she'd thought as she handed McDougal the latest bottle of sleeping pills so he could measure out the number as HE saw fit---not what was written on the label. While she and the captain were in the kitchen, Mac must've pressed the doctor into giving him something else by lying about how he 'couldn't sleep' and how much pain he suffered when he 'couldn't get his proper amount of rest'. When Mac's breathing became deep,

regular and interspersed with snores---she left and went to
her bathroom for a shower.

Her open bedroom window had brought in the deliciously
cool night air-----snuggling between her sheets with one of
her mother's homemade flannel-backed quilts over her, she
sighed and started her evening prayers. Afterward, instead
of feeling sleepy, she found herself unusually alert. Finally
alone for a few hours---thoughts of the day began to spin
round in her head---this day HAD certainly brought its own
unexpected surprise! Even until after lunch---almost
everything had gone along as it had since the day she was
doing the laundry and found that handwritten letter in Mac's
pocket. That was the day he fell off the barn-roof.

"How could Ah have known when gettin' up this morning
that m'eyes would soon be starin' right into th' REAL
human eyes of a fictional man Ah'd 'created' in m'mind!
Once Ah began writin' about him---Ah fell in love with him
m'self! Ah even knew exactly how he'd look as a real
person an' not a character in th' book! How can such a
bizzare thing happen t' a sane person?! Must've asked
m'self THAT question about a hundred times since th' book
was written!!" Her head resting on the pillow, she turned to
gaze out at the night---"...Had t' be mah silly day-dreamin'
mind that did it. Still doesn't explain it tho...""

Sleep continued to elude her, so she relived writing the parts
of her book that contained her Indian warrior who'd been
labeled as 'the first Lance'---an hour passed, Lizbeth felt a
bit drowsy. Her last lingering thoughts were---"Ah wondah
what Captain Wintahhawk is doin'? Is he asleep? Has he
even given me a second thought since driving off with
Doctah? Was Ah just imaginin' things when we first
looked at each othah? Honestly, Ah don' believe Ah evah
felt that way befoah! Kind of like havin' yoah insides

38

suddenly swooshed out---an' all that's left is a poundin' heart." Suddenly her mind jerked her wide awake again, her heart racing---"Is he married??! Oh, that nevah occurred t'me. Somehow Ah have t'get that answer out of Dr. O'Bahrr!! But Ah'll come up with a nice way t'ask----so he won't think a thing of it!"

Switching on her bedlamp, she reached over and picked up her book but before opening it, she had an even worse thought---"If Mac evah thought Ah cared th' least bit about th' Captain---he'd have th'Klan kill him." Tears filled her eyes as her heart sank thru the bed to the floor---"No one can evah know Ah even gave a second thought t'him."

Chapter Five

So it was that Captain Joseph Winterhawk became plain 'Joseph Winterhawk' and settled in with his mother, Mary. For a month he worked around the house, shaping shrubbery, cutting back bushes, hauling away trash and junk that had collected at the back of the property. One day, he decided the whole house was due a new roof before winter, so he bought the materials---the labor he'd do himself. It would keep him busy and his greatest need was to be busy! He found both the front and back steps needed repair, so he drove their old family truck to the closed-down quarries, selected nice flat stones, bought cement and made new steps---like Lizbeth's. For 3 years, he'd only had short leaves home and during that time, several window panes had cracked so he replaced them---then ended up weather-stripping all the windows and outer doors as well. Soon the yard and house looked neat and when spring arrived, it would look great.

Around the middle of September, his older sister---Salle--
and her husband, Bill, came to stay for awhile---or until Bill
could find work. Two months earlier, his factory job in
Laramie had come to an end and he'd not found anything
else---so they came home while Bill looked for work. This
latest couple added onto his mother, a widowed sister---
Dottie, with her two children and himself---Joseph began to
feel a little 'crowded'. After arriving, Bill assisted him in
finishing up the new roof while on the inside, the ladies
washed windows and curtains, even doing some repainting.

Although the old homeplace didn't seem as 'big' as it once
did when he was growing up---still Joseph felt he wasn't
quite ready 'to build'---not yet. Each time he looked at
affordable property and thought seriously about his own
home, he began to have mixed-feelings so---he simply
backed off---and waited. "What is to come, will come."---
he'd repeat to himself. Without military regimen, his days
and nights had unexpectedly turned into a state of limbo.
He felt unfamiliar with himself and what was going on in
his life—more specifically what was NOT going on. There
was a strange, unexplained emptiness inside him when he
considered the present—so for the first time in his life, he
dodged his future.

 Occasionally when in town picking up groceries or odds
and ends, he'd drop in to visit Doc. One September day
Hawk climbed the stairs to Doc's office and returned *The
Post Oak Tree*. As he lay Lizbeth's book on the desk, Doc
looked at him closely and asked---"So, you finished it
then?" Hawk nodded, quietly replying---"Indeed. I finished
it---several times over. Sorry I took so long getting it back
to you." Doc waited and when Hawk offered nothing
more, he cleared his throat---"Haarumph. Well? What did
you think---about it?" A kind of sigh escaped Hawk as he

shifted his eyes away---"Doc, I really don't---I don't want
to talk about that right now. Okay?" He sounded tired.

"Sure."---Doc answered quietly---"Perfectly okay. But IF
you ever DO want t'talk about it---I'll be available."
Switching subjects, Doc hurried on---"I hear your sister,
Salle and her Bill are home from Laramie---they goin'
t'stay awhile?" "His factory job went down the tube---
company went bankrupt, so affirmative..."---Hawk
exhaled---"...they'll be here awhile. Between beating the
bushes all around here for some work, he's been helping me
fix up Mama's house---all of us together got the place
looking right presentable! You need to ride out, take a
look---perhaps you and Mrs. Doc could come for supper.
I'll ask Mama, she can let you know a time that's good for
her." Hawk then managed a partial smile. Doc had been
noticing as time passed, the younger man didn't seem
anything like as cheerful as he'd been on the day he arrived
home from the army.

"Have you found any property yet?"---Doc questioned.
"Not yet. Each time I think I've found the right spot---."
Hawk stood up, walked to the window and looked one flight
down on the town's main-street. "Go on,"---Doc
encouraged---"...what happens? You can't make up your
mind or what?" Throwing up both his hands in a 'helpless'
gesture, Hawk turned and went back to his chair---"I don't
know 'what' happens. A feeling of 'this isn't right' or 'this
isn't the time' boils up inside me and I walk away from the
whole idea. Over and over this feeling comes. I don't
know what the hell to do. Maybe I should just return to
what I know best---re-enlist in the army, go back to killing
our enemies or something. Maybe I've just turned into a
'killer' and nothing less works."

Doc's shrewd experienced eyes took in the man across from him---his whole demeanor had changed. He sat slouched down in the chair, his long muscular legs straight out in front of him, arms crossed over his chest with chin almost touching the chest. Doc watched Hawk's expression, the troubled eyes shone with a deep weariness of heart---but the physician didn't know how to help him. All he knew was that Joseph had begun looking more 'Indian' each time he saw him. The thick, clean, shiny black hair continued growing longer but remained neat---all brushed back beneath the cowboy hat he'd begun wearing. The army issue clothing had been put away---blue jeans, western shirts, leather work gloves, a denim jacket and boots had replaced them.

Suddenly Doc had an idea---it may fall flat as a corn-cake with no 'rising' but---by gum, he was going to try anyway! Leaning forward over his desk, he addressed Hawk---"Hey! I think I might know just th' place f'Salle an' Bill! Th' salary might not be s'great, but they'd have free food with a nice place t'live!" Hawk's mind came back to the present as he raised his questioning dark eyes to Doc---"Where??" "Wellll..,"—Doc knew he had to say this exactly right— "...remember when I told you that what Mrs. McDougal needed was a good couple t'help her out? Well, don'cha think this would be an ideal situation where both parties would benefit!? Salle an' Bill would have a place t'themselves---an' Mrs. McDougal would have some much needed help! What do you think??" Holding his breath, he watched Hawk's expression quickly change from one of sudden hopefulness to disbelief then to something akin to despair.

Joseph pressed his lips together, at last he replied—"I appreciate that and everything, Doc, but I'm not at all sure it's such a good idea." "Why on earth NOT?!"---Doc fussed, knowing full well why Hawk became edgy about such a suggestion. "Number one,"---Hawk enumerated---"...McDougal hates Indians along with most everyone else, I think. Number two, I'll bet you haven't talked this over with---with 'her' yet and number three, well,---you know number three. It can't be done, Doc. This is MY sister we're talking about---remember me?"---Hawk tapped fingers on his chest---"...old 'Tonto'? If my sister came into his house, that fool white man would rise up out of his invalid bed and do away with the whole bunch---probably his wife and you included!"

"He's in no shape to 'rise up' an' do anything, Hawk. Really, she desperately needs th' help---maybe she could even keep that herd, IF she had a little male assistance." Hawk's eyes were closed, shaking his head he reminded Doc---"He might not be able to 'rise up', Doc, but he'd make HER life even more miserable!! And you, your own self, told me he could think up the worst things imaginable to aggravate her---what if he hurt her??!"

Doc sighed loudly then leaned back in his chair---"Maybe you'd be right, maybe you'd be wrong. Sounds worth a try t'me. However, you know best, so it's your choice. After all, it IS your kin plus Mrs. McDougal that we may be putting in harms' way, I guess." Doc tried a play on Hawk's emotions and commented---"But th' fact remains, Lizbeth needs someone, Hawk, an' without any doubt at all, I feel certain she'd welcome help! We don't have t'let McDougal know Salle is your sister---her last name isn't th'same as yours! Would you just LET me ask Lizbeth about it before you say 'no' absolutely??"

Hawk stood up, looked down for a long moment at Dr. O'Barr. "Okay."—his voice ominous---"...ask her. But--- I'll say this, just between you and me!" Hawk placed both his hands flat on Doc's desk then leaned menacingly on his powerful arms and hissed---"If McDougal ever hurts either Salle or---or her, I'll take him apart and nobody will EVER find even the tiniest piece of him. Doctor-man, do we understand each other?" The older man nodded, replying quietly---" I understand---between you and me, it is."

Doc watched the frustrated Indian straighten up, turn and walk purposefully out, closing the door quietly behind him. Outside the wall, on the outer stairs, Doc could hear the boots descending in measured steps. Swiveling his chair toward the wall, Doc muttered to himself---"Well, old man, he sure put th' ball in your court---but good! Oh LORD! An' I clean forgot t'tell him how Lizbeth weaseled it outta me that he wasn't married! Maybe it's time I tell Hawk 'how it is' between the McDougal's. Possibly he might not be s'hard on himself about these feelings he has for Lizbeth---not when he knows th' honest truth about that so-called 'marriage'." Standing and walking to his window, Doc looked down and watched Hawk get into his new 4-wheel drive---"There's no doubt about it, he has deep feelins' and they're killin' him! I'm afraid he's in love with her---just as she's in love with him. I've always heard of love at first sight but this is my first contact with it."

Chapter Six

Next afternoon, Doc was smiling to himself as he drove down the lane, away from the McDougal house. When he'd arrived, Mac had been asleep so he talked to Lizbeth out near the barn where she'd been re-stacking their old firewood left over from the late spring. After his and Lizbeth's private conversation, Doc had gone inside to check on his patient. From then on, it was up to her. He had a bond of true friendship with Lizbeth, she needed help and he felt happy to assist.

Soon after Doc drove away, Lizbeth finished her chore and returned to the kitchen where she removed her gloves then washed her hands. Smoothing on lotion, she went to check on Mac. Standing in the bedroom doorway, she looked at him. He was awake, the television blasting away while he perused the ever-present KKK literature. "Well?!"---he snapped at her---"What're you staring at! I need some fresh water---I don't know how you expect me to drink stale water!" Taking the half filled pitcher, pouring it down the bathroom drain, she refilled it and called---"Doc says you're lookin' exceptionally well."

"What does that old quack know about 'looking exceptionally well!!? It's not HIM who's lying here without use of his legs---it's ME! No one else but ME!" She watched as he sent a fist flying into each of his legs then continued his tirade---"And to set things straight---I do NOT feel well! My legs are killing me---not to mention my back! Even my miserable skin hurts! Fill up this glass so I can take my painkillers---I need two! NOW, DAMMIT--- not in my next life!" His glare followed her every move--- "Sure as hell took you long enough to move that wood--- lolly-gagging around out there, taking your time! All the while, I lay here suffering---alone, helpless! Will you hurry up?!"

She'd do her best to coax him into 'the plan', so obediently she poured the water, handed it to him as he popped two pills. "Y'know, Mac, while Ah was out makin' th' shed ready foah new firewood---Ah was jus' watchin' Maggie herdin' th' cows---all by herself!" "Yeah,"---Mac snapped—"—and you gonna sell her and them! MY HERD AND MY HORSE!! If I could only get outta this bed, I'd

take care of your bossiness!! You'd never sell-off anything
with the excuse you 'don't have time t'do all th' work'!"

"Well,"—she replied meekly---"Ah've mentioned befoah
IF I had some help---but---you always have such a fit!" "I
don't want strangers mucking about on my land!"—he
snapped. Lizbeth took another approach---"Ah've been
thinkin' an' yoah quite right, it is bettah t'keep th' cattle---
bein' they're paid foah—an' Maggie. But we need a good,
hard-working couple t'move into th' apartment---without
much salary, of course! We could offer them free rent an'
meals. In turn they could do a lot of work---both inside an'
outside. Ah KNOW how you hate Indians—but heah me
out. Some don't read or write,"---she elaborated---"..so
what harm could they possibly do? They couldn't pry into
yoah business, b'sides they don't care about th' lives of
white people—they'd simply be hired hands. You know---
like 'niggahs' in th' old south?"

Mac's eyes glittered then turned thoughtful---"You never
used that term before, Lizbeth. Thought you were always
FOR the underdog, the downtrodden, the weary and the
freeloaders---what I call the shiftless, lazy, no account and
the dispensable!" "But even with ouah differences,"---she
began---"...we need help t'keep this place goin' an'---well,
Ah thought perhaps you wouldn't mind havin' a couple of
'colored slaves'. Money from th' book won't go on forevah-
-unless we get into a fourth printin'. Until then, an Indian
couple might be useful an' we could keep th' cattle an'
Maggie---plus havin' things look nice again."

Deciding she'd said enough, lest she sound too interested,
she turned to leave and prepare supper. He volunteered---
"I'll think about it. Not promising nothing, you understand,
but I will consider it in the light of the way you just put it."

Quietly, she twirled into the kitchen! If she let him 'think' having some low-paid help was his idea and would be somewhat like owning slaves---she knew he couldn't turn it down! Though exhausted from moving wood all afternoon, she suddenly felt like music, dancing, laughing---but she must contain herself. Mac must never find out she and Doc manipulated him not only into hiring help---but hiring Captain Winterhawk's own sister and husband---why he'd just have a spell! But thank goodness the last name was different! Doc had promised both he and the Captain would warn the couple never to divulge they even knew the Winterhawks---nor even speak that name in Mac's presence!

Since her book had been published, Lizbeth had known that at any time, she could've 'taken-over' the ranch---finances, decisions---all would've been infinitely easier if she could live her own life---in peace. Only an hour before his accident, Mac threatened her---haughtily telling her if she divorced him, he'd take everything they'd bought with the money from her book and leave her flat. And with his KKK 'legal' connections, she felt he could do just that. She'd given Mac a lot of her youth, her innocence and over a decade of her life. But she'd chosen to endure whatever she had to because there was no way she'd give over to him the rewards of her heart---her soul---her day-dream---nor the income from "*The Post Oak Tree*"!! That was and would always be 'her baby'. With God's help, she'd conceived it in her mind, she'd carried it inside her heart then in writing it out---in a sense, she'd 'given birth' to it! No, '*The Post Oak Tree*' would always be her very own. She didn't know what the future held but she'd not leave it all just to get away from him! One day things would be better. She believed that in spite of the fact that for 12 years, nothing had changed---except for the worse. Lately though, for some odd reason, she'd begun to feel more confident about 'better days' somewhere ahead in her future!

That night when she was ready for bed, she pulled the bedroom window down farther than usual---the night air was now cooler than it had been only two weeks ago. The trees on the high rim were more colorful as well---how she longed to climb up there! There'd been a pathway which she'd taken many times before Mac had hurt himself---but since then she'd barely left the place long enough for anything except to buy groceries and stop by the bank.

Each night, after her prayers since meeting Captain Winterhawk, she lay awake thinking of him. It had been during her hours of nighttime considerations that she'd come upon a line of questioning concerning the captain's marital status. When Doc had stopped by to see Mac--- before he left, she was playing some of his favorite songs on the piano. Taking a lengthy pause and busying herself with some old sheet music, she casually mentioned that the Captain's family 'must've been very happy t'see him'. He'd replied---"Oh yes, Hawk's mother an' widowed sister were overjoyed when they saw him get out of m'truck!" She'd waited a decent interval, her heart racing, then asked almost disinterested---"His daddy passed on then?" "Hmm." ---Doc had nodded---"A good long time ago--- Hawk was around 10 years old, I think. Oh, Lizbeth, could you play 'The Waltz You Saved For Me?" She smiled at him---"That's yoah favorite, isn't it?"

As she played his request 'by ear', Doc had continued to 'talk all around' Hawk's family and people yet never directly answered the question burning in her heart. Finally she commented---"So, y'say Captain lives with his mothah?" "Oh yes, he was there until he joined th' army--- he's helped them financially--- bein's he never got married-

--Mary, his siblings and their children are th' only family he has." At last! Doc had volunteered what she needed to hear---oh joy!! Her heart was so light that for days afterward, it floated all about inside her body bouncing off her ribs like a rubber ball!

She hardly remembered Doc continuing his conversation that same day telling her how she'd already met Hawk's mother, Mary! And indeed saw her each time they delivered food to the Catholic Church kitchen there on the reservation. Those little side-trips were something Lizbeth occasionally did while going into town to buy her own groceries. Doc, Ida and herself would buy, then use Doc's truck to deliver.

Doc had already driven away when she realized she'd not even asked which of the ladies was 'Mary'---Joseph's mother! Tho she'd struggled to keep composed and quiet during the rest of their conversation that day, Doc must've SURELY taken notice of how flushed and excited she became! But being the gentleman, he ignored any sign he might've seen. Inside herself, she felt that Dr. O'Barr knew a lot more about all this than he let on---God bless him, she thought, for many years now, she'd needed a good, trustworthy and loyal friend! On that thought, Lizbeth dozed and spent a restful night.

***

After breakfast, Mac told her he'd thought it over and agreed a couple could move-in to help out---"...for awhile! But only for a short time!" She'd politely told him that it'd be for the good of 'his' place---in case he ever wanted to sell it, things would be in good shape and he'd get more money.

49

Later on, after demanding his painkillers and Lizbeth was sure he was 'out' in a deep sleep, she called Doc to give him the 'go ahead'. After hanging up the phone, once again she checked, making sure Mac was still asleep. Over and over, before putting the phone extention beside Mac's bed---she'd debated with herself about it---but then, he WAS an invalid, so she acquiesced thereby limiting herself to no phone privacy. And after the installation, she knew the few calls to her parents and Bess had been 'monitored'.

Chapter Seven

Early next morning Hawk saw the dust cloud before he made out Doc's old truck and sensed the sight most likely had something to do with that job at the McDougals. "Here he comes..,"---Hawk swore to himself---"...rattling down the road at a trotting pace!" Since he and Doc had that talk involving Salle and Bill moving out to help Lizbeth, what little peace he managed to find earlier, had been reduced even further! Although the couple needed the work while 'his' Lizbeth needed help---and it would be great to have more room there at Mary's house once again---still it disturbed him that each day his own sister would be in the house with a racist—an Indian-hater!

With windows rolled down as usual, the old truck belched to a stop, Doc hailed Joseph---"Morning, m'boy! Gonna be a great day! Just breathe that cool air---look at th' sunshine an' blue sky!" Hawk approached the truck and almost snapped---"I don't feel like praising nature today---I feel like I'm about to be guillotined---but do get out, Doc, and come in for some coffee." "Thanks, I believe I will--- b'sides, I wanta take a good look at th' work you and Bill did on th' house!"---he circled around the front part of the house---"...By George, next time I need some fixin' up

done,I'm gonna call you! Positively professional work---I
know Mary's tickled pink, eh? Women folk love t'fix up
th' nest!"

Silently, Hawk ignored him and opened the screen door,
Doc entered in at a brisk pace---and walked on thru to the
kitchen---Mary looked up and exclaimed, "Morning,
Doktar! I told Hawk to invite you and Miss Ida for supper
tomorrow night! Is okay? You have nothing planned
then?" "Mary!"---Doc exhuded---"Of course we have
nothing planned! Certainly we'll be here!" Mary poured
his coffee as he babbled on---"You doin' all right these
days? Don't see you much at th' office...,"---Doc grinned--
-"...you wouldn't be takin' your own herbal brews, now
would you?" Hawk's mother giggled, put her fingers up to
her mouth---"Now, Doktar, ha-ha-ha, if I was sick, I'd be
right away to see you!" "Yeah, right."---he smiled down
into his cup then at her---"Then what are those bunches of
stuff I see hangin' from th' ceilin' t'dry---all hidden away in
that pantry room you usually keep locked??" Mary
continued to giggle, her light brown skin flushed burgundy
as she rushed to close the pantry door---"Hush now!! No
cause Mary trouble! Good herbal remedy never hurt no
one!" Doc nodded---"Okay, no trouble! I can be bought off
with coffee plus that supper tomorrow night! You shoulda
been a man, Mary, woulda made a good 'shaman'!" By
then Mary was so pleased that she bowed her head and
turned away.

Looking at Hawk, Doc asked---"Where's Salle an' Bill?"
"Gone to the store, Doc", Hawk replied testily.--"Why?
Could it be you wanta parley with them?" "Yep, sure do! I
think I've found a situation for them! Y'see th' folks livin'
up at th' Sanderson place---they need a couple t'help out!
The wife can't run th' place by herself---she was about t'sell
their herd th' other day! I'd talked t' Hawk only that

51

morning about Bill's need for a job---and well, I thought this might be just th' thing!" Doc rattled gaily on---"You could say this is just what th' doctor ordered'! So, I spoke to th' lady---she talked it over with her husband, this mornin' she called sayin' they'd love some help." Hawk stared at Doc with the same expression on his face---"And would you like to just run on off toward the store to scout-up 'the couple'?" "Good idea!"---Doc replied heartily as he set his empty cup down and slapped the table! "Think I'll do just that! Good suggestion, Hawk!"

Standing, he chortled---"Thanks for th' coffee, Mary---good t'see you lookin' so well---an' this house!! You hire some architect with landscape folks t'come in here an' fix this place up? I didn't know you had THAT kinda money!" Mary went into gales of giggling---"No!! No, money for that! Son Hawk and Bill fix up place! Nice, yes? Now all ready for winter, Doc!" "Fine, Mary, that's real fine." Doc nodded to her, headed toward the front door then called back---"See you tomorrow night for that supper!"

"You happy with yourself now?"---Hawk glared at Doc as they walked to the truck. "If not exactly 'happy',---Doc replied quickly---"…maybe I, at least, got th' ball rollin' toward a distant goal of 'happiness' for somebody! Th' worst can happen is that Salle an' Bill have a pretty sweet deal for awhile! Don't you think?" "Oh hell, just get in the truck and carry on!"---Hawk smacked the side of Doc's truck---"Go find them and spread the good news of 'the gospel according to Dr. Jerold O'Barr'!"

Doc climbed into the truck, slammed the door and grinned heartily---"Bye, Hawk! You have a nice day, now, y'hear!" With that he ground the engine to life, scraped into reverse, roared in a half circle then leaving a cloud of dust to settle behind him, he blasted off ---in the general direction of the store. Hawk coughed, turned his head, fanned at the dust with his hand, exhaled loudly in frustration---then swore as he kicked at a pile of dirt, sending it flying in all directions!

Chapter Eight

Several days after moving into the McDougal apartment, Salle drove down to visit a bit with her mother. Hawk was out back putting up a fence around the back yard because he'd thought he might get the kids a puppy for Christmas. Not finding Mary in the house, Salle went thru to the back yard where she discovered her brother hammering away, stretching and stapling chicken wire onto his already set posts. Hands on hips, she stared at the wire then announced---"You surely not fixin' to put chickens out in Mama's back yard!" Her brother paused, wiped his forehead and grinned---"Why not? We use a dozen eggs around here every two or three days." "Hawk, when did you last price a bag of chicken feed?! Costs more to feed those nasty, peckin' things than to buy eggs! Why're you puttin' up this fence anyhow?"

"If you can keep a secret, I just thought Dottie's kids would like a puppy for Christmas. What you think?" Salle made a slight grimace---"Puppies are hard to train, Hawk, besides they bark all the time---and they make 'stuff' to step in same as the chickens!" "It's no wonder you don't have any kids! You're too worried about 'stepping in stuff'! Okay! I'll change the subject." He busied himself, looking away from her before finally asking---"And how's the new place? You---er, getting along with the McDougals?"

"Oh, sure---at least with her. Y'know, in many ways, she's kinda like a little girl---gentle, sweet and all feminine--- except she KNOWS what work is, sure not afraid to 'mess her hands' or 'break her nails'!" Salle laughed, crossing her arms---"I'm gettin' used to her accent, too. Crazy, man! But I've only met the mister once, Mrs. Mac keeps his room clean and straight. She told me not to go in 'cause people bother him---like make him nervous. Bill is happier bein' busy and while I enjoy her company---I'd hoped we'd find a job with better pay."

Hawk stopped for a moment, looked at his sister and commented---"I understand from Doc that the McDougals really can't afford to pay a lot---with him being laid up like that. Doesn't free rent and food help out enough to pick up the slack?" Salle sighed and stretched her arms above her head---"Guess you're right, older brother-san. I just have to get accustomed to the change. Oh, by the way, I came to get a crew of men on the Rez who're wood cutters---Mrs. McDougal's regular cutter's gone off to Montana for a good while and her firewood will be gone long before they're back. She's all 'stressed' about it and I guess Bill could start cuttin' but---what she really needs is a 'gang' with equipment who can get a lot done, like right quick. The new wood's goin' to have to dry out some before she can even use it---you know anybody who could help her?"

Hawk busied himself and let the question drop for a moment. "Hawk! You hard of hearin'?! I asked if you knew any wood-cutters?" "Sis, I've been gone a long time!"---he found himself almost shouting at her and checked himself, he didn't like the idea of Lizbeth being without wood---"You'll have to ask Mama---she's doing something for Father O'Hara---why don't you trot on up there and find out! Or go and ask Doc, I'm sure he'll be able to help!"

Salle stared at Hawk for several minutes---"Could I ask a question without you gettin' all steamed?" "Sure."---Hawk straightened the wire and grunted at her---"I didn't realize I was 'steamed'." She came a couple of steps closer and pulled on the wire to assist him as he placed a staple then hammered it---"To me, you seem 'edgy'---somethin' I never noticed in you before. Is it the re-adjustin' to life---out here? Not excitin' enough for you, maybe? You need a girl! Mama said you'd not even taken anyone out as far as she knew! You can't STILL be pinin' over Jacinta!! That's been YEARS ago! Though I hear she still gives you 'the look' whenever you cross her path!"

Hawk listened to Salle babble on and finally, he stopped working, sat down on a stump, stared at her and snorted---"Who told you such unmitigated crap? Salle, wherever you are, I swear it doesn't take two weeks before you know everything that goes on whether it's the truth or NOT! The bald fact is I've only 'crossed Jacinta's path' twice since I've been home and believe me that was NOT planned! Can't you remember how after I'd only been away for a couple of years, first thing I know she's broken off with me and married somebody else? Back then, in my youthful ignorance of women, I'd labored on under the impression that one day we'd get married because she said we would---but like I said 'things change'! Sure, I thought we were 'tight' but obviously she wasn't willing to wait for me to work up in rank---she wanted a man who'd be around at her beck and call---so things changed! And they've been changed a long time---I have no interest in her whatsoever. Besides---looking back on it? I count myself 'well-off' that she married somebody else---man, she can be a little crazy at times."

"Well,"---Salle hurried on---"I'll have to 'fix you up' with a pretty gal---men go all sour when there's no woman in their life. Now on the other hand,"---she offered her store of knowledge---"…a woman without a man doesn't get sour!

She just gets kinda dreamy and mellow---like Mama---and Mrs. Mac, too, I guess. Y'see, I hear that husband of hers yellin' at her a lot, sometimes even throwin' things at her---but she never yells back. Has more patience than I ever could! Bein' bedridden doesn't give anybody the right to be downright nasty to others---'specially when they're tryin' to be good to you! Why, I'd bop him one in the head and stop that nonsense! But she never complains about it."

Salle paused for a breath then quietly offered more---"My opinion is that she misses her family back in Georgia--and that she's real lonely! Y'know, Hawk, the problem isn't that his legs are paralyzed---that's not the source of her loneliness or her meloncholy---it goes beyond that! Why these two have nothin' at all in common---I've never seen the like! If they loved each other, his legs wouldn't make any difference. Y'know what I mean? It goes a lot deeper."

Hawk took the opportunity to get in a word---"Like I said awhile ago, in hardly a week, you've managed to totally educate yourself about the McDougals, their lives, their personality flaws, their deep-seated emotional and psychological needs! Salle, you shouldn't get yourself too involved with these people---it's not a good idea." Rolling her eyes, her voice raised—"It's just that I LIKE her, Hawk, and I feel sorry for her! She deserves better---she needs LOVE for cryin' out loud! For sure, HE doesn't love her---and that leaves nobody---at least not within 2,000 miles! Emotionally, she's so 'needy' and I've decided to be not only her 'help'---I'm gonna be her friend as well!" With that said and hands on hips, Salle snapped—"And you can just forget about me fixin' you up with a girl! You can get your own dates!" She turned away, flouncing off to find Mary.

In a flat, lifeless tone, Hawk said 'Bye' to the deserted back yard as his eyes followed his sister's shirttail swirling around the corner of the house. Before picking up his hammer, he murmured aloud---"Sis, you just don't know! You have no idea that located on your own Mama's property, within only a few miles of the McDougal's house, there lives a man who finds himself dying of love for this woman. A man who'd do anything for her!"

Work, work, work and more work---he knew it was the only thing that would give him even momentary relief from that first and only time he'd seen Lizbeth's face and heard the sound of her sweet voice.

Once again the sound of his hammer pounding nails rang thru the air---and in his ears, it seemed to carry with it an emptiness which echoed thru the hills that separated him from her. He wondered if one day, in the end, he'd simply 'lose it' and go mad?

Chapter Nine

That night at supper, Mary passed Hawk the potatoes. "Hawk quieter than usual."---she commented---"... Anything happen while I was at church?" Hawk concentrated on his plate---"No. Salle was by looking for you---that's all. And I finished the fence."

Grasping for anything to change the subject, he looked over at Mary---"You absolutely certain it won't be a bother if I buy the kids a puppy for Christmas? Salle informed me that puppies bark, make a lot of noise and mess---just thought I should ask you again before too much time passes." He took a bite of food then began 'blatherin'---"I want to read up on the breeds---we need a dog who likes youngsters---

but not overly protective. That can be a problem if the kids have company and all of them start running, playing and screaming---you see, if it's the wrong breed, the dog may bite the other child. We can't have that!" "No, couldn't have that."---Mary agreed---"But if uncle want to buy children a puppy-dog, is okay with Gramma. But!" She put up a finger---"Gramma expect everybody help keep yard looking decent! I like 'new look' my son gave to house! Want to keep nice!" Hawk played with his food--- "Don't worry, Mama, I'll extract promises all signed in blood from everyone around here."

"Salle says Mrs. Mac need wood cut." Hawk cringed---she was cutting to the chase---"Is right you should help, Son. This afternoon, I put names of other men on piece of paper for you---tomorrow you talk? Get men together and cut wood for Mrs. Mac?" Joseph swallowed a mouthful---the otherwise delicious food had suddenly turned to sawdust in his mouth. Inwardly he groaned but answered in a mild tone---"If you say so, Mama, I'll help along with the crew. Not to worry, the McDougals won't freeze to death this winter. While we're at it, we'll cut more for us as well. Never hurts to have plenty of seasoned firewood on hand."

Mary smiled---"Joseph Winterhawk is good son---and good neighbor. Make good husband too, yes?" He ignored that so she discarded the idea of 'wife'---"Eat now. Look thinner than when came home. Maybe just work too much 'round here?" Hawk shook his head---"Only your imagination working overtime, Mama. I'm fine and accustomed to lots of physical work, it sweats the poisons out of my body. It's probably just the change in climate,"--- then he mumbled---"Or something else in the vicinity that's making me lose weight." Mary cast concerned dark eyes at her son.

Early the next morning, Hawk went to the store and found
addresses of most of the men whose names were on Mary's
list. By lunchtime, everything was ready. All that was
necessary was to top off the fuel tanks. Hawk listened as
Henry instructed his men--- "After lunch, we'll drive up and
start cutting. You fellas go on, now, have a good lunch."
He turned to Hawk---"Want us to stop by your Mama's and
pick you up on our way out?" "Sure, I'll wait on the porch.
Thanks. Uh---look, Henry---don't add the cost of my labor
onto this job. I'm doing it for free—since my sister and Bill
work for the McDougals---and I'm sure Bill won't want to
charge for his labor either." Henry nodded---"I understand.
No problem. See you after lunch then."

After doing all he could in every way possible NOT to get
involved with the McDougals---people and circumstances
had---like a swollen, raging river---swept Joseph helplessly
in a circle and soon he'd be right back on the McDougal
property! Right back to the place where this whole crazy
thing flared up! Shortly the cutters would come and pick
him up on their big flat-bed wood truck. He wondered how
he'd feel riding up to that house again---then lumbering past
it---knowing Lizbeth was just a couple hundred feet away
inside those walls??

An hour later three trucks rounded a curve in the highway
and Hawk watched as the McDougal house came into view.
After staring at it until he was close enough to be
recognized, he put on his hard hat and safety glasses then
deliberately seated himself on the side of the truck opposite
the house. Slowly they wound their way up the white sandy
drive and rolled noisily past the house as Joseph stared
down at the ground. Soon the vehicles halted and one of the
men ran to open a gate---Hawk turned his head just enough
to glimpse the back of her house. He knew there wasn't any
way he could talk to her---or her to him. All he had to hold

59

onto was the moments exchanged between them when they shook hands then later in the kitchen as he ate---and two sections of her book. After reading the whole book, he now 'knew' why she 'recognized' him when she looked at him that day---she was seeing 'the first Lance' whom she'd written about in her book---while she'd suddenly become the novel's 'Gramma Parnell'. That inner 'knowing' was as certain for him as next week would begin the month of October.

Just when he was giving up hope of seeing her after they'd passed the house---she and Salle came out into the back yard and stood watching them. So until her figure blurred into the surroundings and he could no longer clearly see her outline---he simply stared back at the place where she stood until the woods cut off his view of the house.

Late that afternoon as the sun began to set behind the mountains, the wood trucks again rattled their way slowly back across the sloped pasture behind McDougal's barn. Soon they creaked to a stop and Bill jumped off, opened the cattle gate at the barn, waving the trucks on through---"See ya in th' morning, fellas!"---he called as he latched the gate.

Before leaving the woods Hawk had his hard-hat once more pulled low on his brow. But in spite of his best efforts, as they neared the house, he couldn't keep his eyes from wandering toward the tree. She wasn't there! A deep sigh of disappointment escaped him as he straightened back against the truck cab, facing toward the woods---and suddenly, there in the hall of the barn---he saw her! She stood talking to Bill while feeding grain to a horse. Hawk forced his eyes shut and waited for the next stop which would indicate they were ready to pull onto the highway. "Lord, help me through the next 48 hours,"---he prayed silently---"...by then the wood should be in their shed."

Soon, he felt the truck jerk to a stop, heard the shift grind
into first gear then slowly the vehicle whined onto the road
where it finally picked up some speed. And once again, he
was leaving her behind.

That night Mary cooked a hearty supper---vegetables,
mexicali-beef, corn bread and egg custard. Dottie, Rammah
and Jerri sat across from him---"Hey,"---Hawk balled up a
paper napkin and tossed it at Rammah---"I missed you guys
at supper last night! Did you and Mom enjoy the movie?"
"YEAH!"---Rammah exploded---"It was great! You gotta
go see the big chase scene!" The bright dark eyes shone
with interest as he popped a question---"And if you do---can
I go and see it again!?" Hawk laughed---"Sure, why not!
Who knows, maybe you'll grow up to be a professional race
car driver---when you want us to go?" "This weekend!"—
Rammah piped---"Saturday's the last night!" Hawk turned
his eyes toward little Jerri, Dottie's younger daughter---
"Baby, you want to go too?" Looking shyly across the table
at her uncle, who seemed so tall, protective and handsome--
-Jerri remained speechless. "C'mon now, Uncle Hawk
needs a pretty girl to sit beside him at the movies---how
about it?" In spite of embarrassment concerning her two
missing baby teeth right in front, Jerri smiled then
whispered—"Okay."

Hawk nodded and began to eat his food---for the first time
in ages, he found himself starved! Half a day of wood-
cutting had somewhat taken the edge off his longing for
Lizbeth, so he ate unusually hearty. Mary smiled
approvingly—"More like my boy! Good appetite mean
happy man, yes?" "Sure, Mama,"---Hawk managed a little
smile then repeated softly----"...a happy man."

Chapter Ten

On the last day the wood-cutters would be there, Salle rose
early to find Lizbeth already in the kitchen busily clanking
pots and pans while she stirred then tasted the contents of
each one! Almost every area of the kitchen was in disarray
while the aroma of spices and baking ham filled the air!
"Mrs. Mac!!"---Salle blustered as she cast her eyes from
one place to another---"What in this world you doin'??!
You got some unexpected big company comin' for lunch??"
Sniffing at the spicy odor that wafted about over the ham
and other assorted foods, she asked---"Is that sweet potatoes
I smell?" Lizbeth laughed at Salle's obvious confusion---
"Now, now, m'dear. Ah couldn' sleep so ovah in th'
mornin' hours, Ah had this perfect ideah! All this..,"---
Lizbeth gestured grandly---"..is foah those nice men cuttin'
wood---you know they'll be starved! An' if they bring a
lunch---why, they can keep it foah a mid-aftahnoon snack!
You an' Ah are taking th' jeep so they'll have good hot food
an' coffee! Won't they be surprised!!?"

Salle stared at Lizbeth then around the kitchen---"Yeah.
'Surprised' may not be exactly the word, Ma'am!" She
exhaled then offered---"Mrs. Mac...my people, especially
the men, aren't---well, they're not used to folks 'makin'
over them. You know, like if they're workin' for you?
They get paid and don't expect anything extra...,"---again
her eyes took in the surplus of food being prepared---"...not
like this anyhow." "Oh pshaw, Salle! They can't resist
once we begin liftin' lids off these pots an' they smell baked
ham!!" Salle then looked back at her employer asking,
"What're you goin' to feed---er, Mr. Mac? We both goin'
to leave him and drive this banquet into the woods??" She
lowered her voice to a whisper---"Won't he be mad as hell
at you?"

62

Lizbeth lifted her chin a mite---"Salle, don'cha worry none 'bout him. Ah'll feed him early, give him his 'medication'--he'll drift off t'sleep. B'sides,"---she tilted her head at Salle with a grin---"Ah tol' him already we were preparin' a little extra food foah them." "And he didn't 'go off' in a tailspin??" "No worse than usual."---Lizbeth replied---"By now, he thinks it was his own idea t'feed 'his darkies'." "Uh---to do 'what'??" "Nothin'---sweet Salle---nothin' a'tall. Could you just check those rolls risin' ovah theah? Then we'll clean up some of these utensils that Ah'm all finished usin'."

By 11:30 a.m., Mac was dozing into his usual drug-induced sleep while Lizbeth and Salle packed the carefully wrapped food into a big box. Cozy warmth surrounded them as the jeep soon lurched across the pasture up toward some hardwoods where sounds from saws filled the air. Actually the house was only 10 minutes away from the cutters, so their food would still be palatably warm and the coffee hot. Salle sat keeping an eye and subsequent 'hand' on the shifting box containing lunch and sighed to herself---"Man. I sure hope this little idea doesn't fall flat as one of them quarry rocks! I'd hate to see her embarrassed because the men act stand-offish with her! She's so good hearted--maybe too much for her own good. Sometimes I worry about this woman! And as yet,"---her eyes wandered toward the lady driving the jeep---"I still don't 'get it' about why Hawk, Doc and Mrs. Mac think it best that Bill and I don't mention we're kin to Hawk---now, THAT is bloody strange! Let's see—what exactly did Doc say?" Carefully, Salle searched her memory---"He said he and Hawk had been out drivin' around, stopped off here to see Mr. Mac and that Mr. Mac didn't like Hawk because he hated 'the military'? Does that make sense? Naw, besides, Hawk retired from the military! More to it than that---gotta be!"

As the jeep approached the work area, Hawk's back was turned---his saw ripping smaller limbs off a felled tree. He continued working until he realized he no longer heard the roar and whine of the other saws---turning around to look, his heart almost jumped into his throat. Parked in a clearing was the McDougal jeep while Salle and Lizbeth stood busily opening up a huge box and setting out food on two card-tables and the jeep's hood! Staring in surprise and shock, Hawk raised his safety goggles then tilted his hardhat backward a bit. All around the cutters stared as well---an unusual silence now loomed heavily in an atmosphere filled with the smell of freshly cut wood and sawdust.

Salle's eyes caught sight of him first and she began to call out to him, waving her arms about---"HEY! JOSEPH! We brought hot food for all of you! C'MON! Hurry before it gets too cool! BILL? Where are you?! Joseph, get over here!" When he seemed unable to 'hurry'---before he knew it, Salle was at his side jerking him along, tugging at his arm and whispering furiously---"Get these damned men to eat, Hawk! I got up this mornin' and there she was, had been up all night cookin' this stuff! Just get them to MOVE---or say something---ANYTHING just so she won't be totally humiliated over their ignorant refusal of this 'wonderful surprise' of hers!"

Thinking 'military' to get his body moving, Hawk removed his heavy gloves, 'grinned' then yelled at the silent motionless crew---"HEY GUYS! IT'S HERE!!! OUR SURPRISE FOR THE DAY! C'MON----GET THIS FOOD WHILE IT'S HOT!" Hurrying toward the jeep, he kept up a steady stream of 'chatter'---"Pour some water over your hands, men---get washed up! Salle, I was beginning to think we'd have no hot lunch! C'mon, Henry---you first! You're the boss! Everybody line up behind Henry---right here, Bill! All of you---pick up a plate and get served! Let's get a move on, now!" Hawk 'herded' the men toward the tables. "Henry?"---Hawk joked---"...if you don't step lively, you gonna have to fight me for first place!" Slowly, one by one, the men began to follow as Henry walked up to the tables---Hawk urged them forward then stood at the end of the line. In a daze, he watched Salle help Lizbeth serve, all he could think of was what should he say to her---what would SHE say to him? The sudden shock of turning around and seeing the jeep, the women PLUS the food had tied his gut into knots---how could he possibly eat? Why did people insist upon turning his deliberately chosen, tightly-controlled life upside down on a regular basis?!

Slowly but surely Hawk inched forward as the dozen men in front of him dwindled to only one. In ignorance of the dilemma surrounding Hawk and Lizbeth---Salle saved the day by stating---"Mrs. Mac, I understand from Dr. O'Barr that you've met my brother here---Joseph?" Salle squeezed her brother's arm---"...so I won't do introductions, and if it's okay with you, I'd like to fix myself a plate, go over and annoy Bill---give him indigestion!" "Wonderful ideah, Salle! "---Lizbeth agreed---"You go right ahead an' sit with yoah husband---but no indigestion allowed! Make him eat enough now! In fact, have everyone come back foah 'seconds'---theah's plenty!"

This unplanned, unforeseen moment arrived and now for the second time in his life, Joseph Winterhawk stood looking slightly down into the face of Lizbeth McDougal. As at the first meeting, their eyes met and locked---since Doc wasn't there to pinch his elbow, he stood speechless as did she. Was it possible she was even more lovely the second time he laid eyes upon her? Finally turning to serve his plate, she spoke softly---"Captain Wintahhawk. Ah can't tell you how glad Ah am t'see you again."

65

Hawk's odd 'alien' voice returned as he answered---"Hello again, Mrs. McDougal And I am---ah, I'm very glad to see you, too. First let me say 'thank you' from all of us for this big feed you've prepared! I mean, it looks like an army chow wagon stopped by! How'd you get so much done in so short a time?" "Oh,"---she replied quietly---"sometimes Ah don' sleep well. So aftah watching th' men drive past yesterday, I thought—why not cook them a nice hot lunch on their last day heah? You been helpin' all along?"

Nodding 'yes' to her question, he suddenly felt quite grungy in her presence. He brushed a hand over the somewhat sweaty, sawdust covered shirt and jeans then scraped at several sap-encrusted smudges---"The first time we met, I was covered with dust! Now, it's sawdust and sap! Sorry our second meeting had to be while I'm cutting wood! I hope you'll pardon the way I look." A soft smile lit up her face as she took one of his hands and set a heaped plate on his calloused palm---"Nothing a'tall wrong with a man doin' a man's work, Captain. Don't you be apologizin' foah a little saw-dust. Tell me, do you miss th' military life? Ah was really surprised when Doc finally told me you were back foah good---retired an' all."

He stood foolishly holding his plate---hoping he could keep up his end of a conversation that up until now he'd only dreamed might one day happen. "After twenty years, uh, I do miss it some. But retirement, uh, coming back home was something I'd always planned---however, I can truthfully say, it's been..,"---he paused---"...a lot more than I expected." "Well, come and sit down---we can sit on th' front seats of th' jeep. You must be ready t'sit a spell--- we'll pass th' time---you eatin' an' me talkin'!" Her laughter tinkled amidst the trees like a little crystal bell.

"How lucky can I be?" He thought to himself as he sat down in the passenger's seat beside her. He found his entire outlook suddenly changed---he was wildly happy, felt reckless while wondering---"Why have I hidden myself from her like a crazed hermit?!" The zippered weather shields gave the jeep an ambiance of their being alone, except for Bill and Salle plus a few men, all sitting close by on tree trunks but too far away to hear their words. Besides, now that they'd tasted the food, the men were too busy talking, laughing, scarfing up the lunch to pay much attention to anything else.

"Tell me, Captain, what exactly you meant about comin' home bein'--a lot moah than you expected? Is everythin' all right with yoah family?" "Oh sure! Fortunately, everyone's doing quite well. Temporarily, I live in our old family home---with Mama, my widowed sister, Dottie, and her two children---Rammah and Jerri." He looked at her, smiled a little and went on---"It became a bit crowded when Salle and Bill arrived but we're used to lots of family around. However I did want to thank you for offering them a job, room and board. You and Mr. McDougal are very kind."

Their small-talk conversation bounced back and forth. "Really."---she replied---"WE'RE th' fortunate ones, we desperately needed some help. Foah months, Ah tried t'keep things goin' but,"---she shrugged slightly---"...by 'n by, it became too much. Th' shrubbery grew tall with vines in it, a summer storm tore some tin loose on th' roof and needed work---plus th' yard looked just awful. Then, too, Mac's care an' runnin' th' house---it was time consumin'. Finally, Ah was ready t'let th' cattle an' Maggie go. With wintah comin' on---Ah didn't think Ah could look aftah them properly. But now---thanks to yoah sistah an' her husband, things are lookin' much bettah."

67

"Who's 'Maggie'?"---he queried, trying to chew and
swallow some of what had to be great tasting food. "Oh,"--
-she chuckled---"...she's the horse! A dear creature. Ah
don't ride but she's taken a likin' t'me---probably because
Ah'm th' one who feeds her!" "I can see why she'd take a
liking to you, Ma'am. She'd be a fool not to."---his face
flushed---the words had slipped out---he had not meant to
say that aloud!

Tilting her head somewhat, she asked---"Might I ask you a
favah?" "Anything."---he answered softly—"Whatever you
need from me---it's yours." He wanted to bite his suddenly
loosened tongue! Words flowed heedlessly out of him---
things he shouldn't be saying! On this most glorious of
days, his mouth would surely be his 'undoing'—where did
all these words come from? How'd he suddenly become
such a smooth-cookie---a sweet-talking, silver-tongued
man!!

She looked into his eyes---"Th' favah is---do you think you
could call me---'Lizbeth' instead of Mrs. McDougal---or
'Ma'am'? Mah friends just call me---'Lizbeth'."

He heard himself saying---"On one condition, of course."
Her eyes were pools of deep water---in his soul, he was
swimming around in them as she questioned----"An' that
is?" "That you call me 'Hawk'---or Joseph."---he felt
warm, wonderful as her soft voice sluiced over him like a
pitcher of that same water her eyes had him swimming
about in. "An' which do you prefer, sir?" To that question,
he replied--- "Hawk. Being a man and living so long as a
military Ranger, I guess I need to feel something about me
is still 'hawkish'---now that retirement has clipped my
wings!" Her enchanting soft laughter filled his ears---"Then

'Hawk' it is. Hawk---an' Lizbeth. Right?" He could only nod and look back at her---his food now cool and forgotten.

So until the men began to mill about tossing their paperplates, plastic forks, napkins and paper cups into a trashbag provided by Salle---the two of them, Lizbeth and Hawk, sat looking at each other. He worked at filling himself to the brim with her hair color, her beautiful facial features, the sound of her voice and laughter, the way her sea-eyes were returning his unending gaze---never flinching. These moments had to be enough to last him--- maybe for the rest of his life. He felt 'almost being alone' with her this day had been a gift from God---and he wondered if that gift would ever again be within his grasp. In less than an hour, his original 'reasonable' decision had crashed---he'd changed completely. He now knew if the chance to see her again should ever be offered, he'd reach out and take it---no matter the price he'd have to pay.

As well, she'd been memorizing each feature of the masculine face before her, a face now surrounded by a growing mane of shiny black hair. His smooth brown skin, stretching lightly over perfect cheekbones, seemed to glow softly in leaf-dappled sunlight reflecting all around them. His tilted almost-black eyes---so dark and fathomless had hypnotized her---his stare weakened her practically to a state of immobility. Each time he'd smiled, clean white teeth shown between lips that were almost an exact replica of Joan Crawford's look! Joan had to paint her 'look'--but his 'bow' lips were his own. How very unique for a man! "Such a gentle person, s'strong yet humble,"---she thought to herself---"...wonderful, totally masculine. He's far beyond handsome."---she concluded---"He IS truly beautiful---both inside and out. Like an ancient brown-skinned warrior-god who got caught in a time warp---then found his way to a recent vortex an' descended into this world---right into th' center of mah life! His comin' has brought me joy---the only time Ah'm alive is when he is present."

After the woods clearing had been 'policed' and cleaned up with all kitchen items loaded back into the box, Lizbeth cranked the jeep and honked the horn. Both women waved as the vehicle soon disappeared thru the trees.

"Now, don't you think we did the correct thing, Salle---I mean about takin' this food out to them?"---Lizbeth held onto the steering wheel as they bounced across the pasture and down the rise toward the barn. "Looks like!"---Salle replied---"I honestly think you made a hit with every man out there! 'Specially my brother." "Why, Salle,"---Lizbeth replied, ignoring the mention of Hawk---"Ah wasn't tryin' t'make a 'hit'---Ah wanted them t'have somethin' special! Men who work hard sometimes need t'be pampered a bit --- don'cha think?" "Yeah. I guess so."---Salle considered--- "Never thought much about it. Up until this generation, all Indian men were overly 'pampered'! Like they sat on their butt except when it was time to go out and 'war' for awhile! Women did all the work, scouted up most of the food, birthed kids plus everything else! I just never been the 'pamperin' kind!"---she put a hand on her bosom---"I want ME to be pampered!"

"Now all that isn't true! Ah see you makin' ovah Bill like he was a big ol' chief or somethin'! Now, don't you be denyin' it!"---Lizbeth looked over at Hawk's sister and grinned. "Aw, get outta here, Mrs. Mac! I don't 'make over' him!"---suddenly serious, she stared over at her employer and asked---"Do I??!" A silvery laughter began in Lizbeth's throat then turned into a roaring belly-laugh--- Salle stared at her---"You lost your mind?? I never heard you laugh like that before!" Then both of them began laughing until tears ran down their cheeks. Lizbeth hadn't felt so good, so carefree, so youthful in a very long time.

It was 1:00 p.m. when she and Salle drove into the back yard and began unloading the cook-ware plus a few remaining left-overs. The only blight on her joy was that tomorrow morning, the men would bring all the wood in, unload it into the woodshed and then---before lunch, they'd be gone. But today! Today had been such a fine day that she'd not allow herself to consider 'tomorrow'. Jesus said that 'tomorrow brought it's own sorrows and worries', so she submersed her mind in the present exhilerating joy. She'd done something for the men---a 'good deed' for the day--and for her, that was 'fulfillment'. But she knew the depth of this almost manic joy stemmed from the knowledge that her 'love' felt the same way about her as she did about him. No longer would she have to lie awake at night wondering if it was only a 'fancy' of her own making---her youthful imagination back at work here during her thirties! Their actual words had been limited---but now, she knew the truth, she had her answer---and she could live with that.

Chapter Eleven

It was sometime after Winterhawk and Doc's impromptu afternoon visit, that Mac became 'suspicious' of Lizbeth's somewhat 'changed' demeanor. For years now, he'd kept her 'cowed down' and it didn't suit that for no apparent reason, she suddenly appeared---well, almost silently 'blooming'! Upon entering his room at times, her eyes had a faraway look in them and he noted an invisible smile playing around her mouth while not actually manifesting itself---other times her eyes sparkled and her face looked slightly 'flushed'. Studying her, he wondered---"What

makes a woman change like this, out of the blue---there
HAS to be a reason---and a damned good one!"

Several possibilities swirled about in his mind. Finally he
narrowed them down to a few considerations. "Pregnancy--
-and I know she isn't pregnant---or she damn well better
NOT be! Or there's something she's accomplished and
feels smug about---as far as I know, nothing like that's
happened! I've never given her enough time to begin
writing again---so there's no book in the offing. Or---
inheriting money and since no one has died, that's not it."
The final possibility infuriated him the most as he
wondered---"Is it possible she's met a man?"

Then anger and jealousy would began rising inside him
until he stopped to calculate the long hours of each day and
night since his injury---"No, I've kept her leash too tight for
that! She hasn't had enough time away from the house to
meet another man—much less have an affair with him.
Besides I've never caught her talking on the phone to
anyone except O'Barr and her kin. Is it possible just having
these two Indians around changed her outlook THIS much?
That doesn't make sense." Then he smiled---the thought of
Indians took momentary presidence over Lizbeth's
'blooming'. It was quite satisfying having the two 'work
for him'---and with almost no salary!

But as time passed and he thought more on the subtle
change in Lizbeth---he came to the conclusion that 'being
abed' was not only keeping him from Klan meetings and
activities but it was gaining him no information as to
something going on under his own roof! That was the
actual moment Mac chose to check-out some twinging and
burning in his legs that had started sometime back---he
couldn't remember exactly when the sensations began
because instead of mentioning it to anyone, he'd simply

downed some extra painkillers or sleeping pills with whiskey. Being aware he'd become dependent on both the pills and the booze---at the time, he'd tossed that aside, he'd worry about it later!

But one day, he did make a decision---he determined to try and walk again! Thus began his 'secret' leg-massages---as many times as he could without getting caught---NOT getting caught was THE key! After each workout, he'd use his drugs and whiskey to temporarily ease the discomfort in 'bringing his legs back to life'---that is IF his efforts were successful and they DID come back to life!

Lizbeth, Doc, Salle and Bill were, of course, left in the dark about the sudden 'rehab' program. So instead of yelling for Lizbeth continually, instead of deliberately making messes by spilling food and water then cursing her when she appeared answering his screams---instead of 'dropping' things and calling her to come pick them up---Mac began using the time to work on his legs and back.

A superior smile twisted his lips each time he recalled it'd actually been that fool, Dr. O'Barr, who'd first put him 'on to' the remote possibility this might happen. Just after the accident, O'Barr had murmured something about future physical manifestations might mean the nerves had not been permanently damaged after all---and at some point could even start healing themselves! At the time, he'd let O'Barr go on---never commenting nor blinking an eye. Thus when Lizbeth seemed recently changed for the better---Mac never spoke a word but stopped medicating himself heavily and went to work! Once again he revived the plan he'd had before his injury---that of securing a 'new life' for himself. Actually he'd never changed his mind---and, if he was lucky, things had only been delayed a few months.

Of course now that Lizbeth had these two nigger-redskins on the place, he'd have to be extremely careful about his secret! He must never allow Lizbeth to go to bed at night without pulling his curtains---lest one of those damned 'natives' should be plundering about after bedtime, wander past his window and see him exercising.

After beginning his 'program', at times physical pain held him momentarily in it's grip. To see himself 'thru' it, he'd concentrate and imagine various scenarios---'stories' he could utilize when the time arrived to actually bring about 'his goal'! He 'endured' by reminding himself---"This is only temporary---I'm back on track from last spring! I've chosen the only course that can really change MY life---and after all, changing my life so I can enjoy a better one is all that counts---nothing else matters!" As the nights passed, the more intense pain initially encountered by moving his unused muscles and ligaments now grew more bearable. After two weeks, he added alternate leg-stretches. Before quitting for the night, he worked on the hamstring by gently pulling the toes on each foot in a backward motion.

His body responded with unusual speed and by the end of September---he was ready to get off the bed. This part of his plan would require all caution---he must make sure he was alone so as not to be 'caught' out of bed---thus he chose after midnight hours. By pretending to swallow his drugs and not drinking any whiskey, he asked Lizbeth to put the glass of whiskey beside his bed---'just in case he might need it during the night'. While she was pouring the liquor, he'd take the pills from his mouth, hiding them beneath his pillow for later---after completing his work-session.

The first night he'd chosen to leave the bed was a red-letter moment! When it was safe to begin, he began from a sitting position. Turning over on his stomach, he slid closer to the bed's edge and dangled his legs---getting the circulation going. Next, he carefully slid his body to the floor. At this point by straining his arms, elbows and entire upper body---he alternately rolled, pushed and pulled himself along on the floor---around the bed and back. After months of total inactivity, the first few trips were hellish but gritting his teeth, he struggled on. Back and forth, he pulled himself---as many times as he could tolerate---he used the pain to fuel his burning desire for meeting 'the goal'!

As the nights passed, he put his feet and legs into action, taking over some of the weight his upper body had been carrying. By resting on his elbows and hands, he'd begin a 'lunge' forward with his body---at the same time, he forced the lower legs and toes to follow suit and within only a week, he felt stronger! One day while lying in the bed, he looked around the room then carefully chose a target for that night---the large heavy recliner across the room! After he was certain Lizbeth would be asleep he lowered himself to the floor---slid along, making it to the chair in only minutes! Allowing himself a short breather, he pulled himself up by holding onto the heavy chair! His legs were shaky as a newborn colt but determined and dedicated, he willed himself to stand! Thus with his upper body and arms leaning across the chair's top, supporting much of his weight---he rested. And in spite of leg tremors, he kept standing as long as he could manage---within a few nights he was rewarded as stability slowly returned to his legs!

His nocturnal trips to the chair for 'standing' upright had turned into attempts to walk around the chair while holding on to it's tall back. The first time he actually felt himself 'walking' with feeble and unsure 'baby-steps'---he began to chuckle aloud! Later, falling into the chair to rest---he grabbed up a small pillow, crammed it against his mouth to muffle his victorious---and almost uncontrollable laughter.

One day soon, he'd send all three of them off someplace---
then he'd search the house! While they were away, he
figured that by going at it one hour at the time---he could
'take the place apart' in two or three weeks! Surely there'd
be some scrap of information, a bit of 'evidence'---
something that would tell him what or whom had made
Miss Lizbeth so---'pink and sparkly'---so 'different' during
the past weeks! Besides, he'd use the time alone to give
Rita another of his 'collect calls'---which he normally did
when Lizbeth went to do outside chores! But this time---
he'd have REAL news for her!

Chapter Twelve

Quietly Lizbeth carried her dust-caddy into Mac's bedroom,
walked toward the window and set it on the recliner. "Good
mornin', Mac."---she said in a low tone, turning to approach
his bed. "Odd,"—she thought---"...evah since he was hurt,
he'd be awake an' howlin' th' first thing every mornin'.
Lately, he's been dead t'the world when I come in! He
must be restin' much bettah with that last medication."

Mac groaned, turned slightly and squinted his eyes open,
staring at her---"Whaatsa matter?!" "Ah just said 'good
mornin'."---she repeated pleasantly while straightening his
covers---"You seem t'be sleepin' much bettah these nights."
"Whatever the hell gave you THAT fool notion?!"---he
coughed then snorted---"Get me some fresh water!! How
MANY times do I have to tell you---I can't tolerate stale
drinking water!" After emptying the pitcher and turning on
the tap, she heard his voice rising---"You didn't bring my
coffee? My God! Do I have to beg and plead for every
little courtesy around here? You got that redskin working

for you out there in the kitchen and you can't get a cup of coffee to me when I wake up?!"

Carrying the fresh water to his bedside table, Lizbeth poured him a glass---"You were asleep when Ah came in, Mac---b'sides, Ah only brought th' cleanin' things. T'day is th' day we dust, straighten yoah room an' change th' linens, remembah?" "Hell, no!"—he snapped even louder---"I don't 'remembah'—everyday is the same to me! I lie here all day every day and all night every night—so what's to tell ME when it's cleaning day!! For God's sake!! You think a red signal pops up inside my eyelids or something when it's 'cleaning day'? You're such a blinking idiot!"

Lizbeth started out the door—he snapped---"Where you going NOW? You just said you'd come to clean up!" "Mac,"---she looked patiently back at him---"Ah was only goin' t'get yoah coffee an' breakfast. Maybe you should take a couple of 'pain pills' befoah you eat---y'seem a mite cranky this mornin'."

In a few minutes, Lizbeth returned carrying his breakfast along with a carafe of steaming hot coffee. Setting the tray across a nearby chair, she assisted him to his usual sitting position so he could eat. "So I'm a 'mite cranky' this morning, huh?"---he swore in an ominous tone as she placed the tray across his lap. "Now, please ---let's not fuss. You need coffee an' breakfast---an' I need t'get started on th' room." Turning away and picking up the coffee carafe, she leaned toward the tray to pour him a cup---suddenly he grabbed her left arm---the jerking motion tilted the carafe in her right hand! "Listen, you lazy syrup-mouthed mountain-trash,"---he snarled---"..don't ever call me 'cranky'---or anything else!!" His voice rose---"YOU HEAR ME??!" "YES!! AH HEAH YOU!"---she screamed---"TURN ME LOOSE, MAC!!! YOU'RE

GOIN' T'MAKE ME SPILL THIS SCALDIN' COFFEE
ON YOU!!" Jerking her arm harder, his voice bellowed---
"YOU BURN ME AND I'LL BEAT THE HOLY HELL
OUTTA YOU!!"

He turned her loose so quickly she almost fell across the
breakfast tray---the hot liquid sloshed crazily about inside
the carafe! Taking her left hand, she righted the container
but in so doing, burned herself. "Oh!"---she gasped
instinctively. " DAMMIT!!"---he raved---"WHAT IN
HELL IS THE PROBLEM NOW??!" "NOTHING!"---she
shouted back then remembering Salle in the kitchen, she
lowered her voice---"Nothin's th' problem but if you want
coffee, Mac, then stop all this foolishness! Why're you
spoilin' foah a fight this mornin'? I thought you'd been
feelin' s'much bettah." She poured his coffee, set the carafe
on the bedside table then went to the bathroom to put cold
water on her burn.

Mac's mouth pressed together then turned up cruelly at one
corner as he struggled not to laugh in her face! The idiot!
She hadn't a clue that he could walk! And as yet, he'd not
come up with a good idea to get the three off to town---
therefore no opportunity to search the house---but it'd come
to him! Sooner or later, he'd think of a way to get their
asses out of the house---then he'd be able to confirm his
suspicions of Lizbeth's behavior! And when he did!!

At the lavatory, Lizbeth splashed cold water on her left
palm. Tears of pain and humiliation filled her eyes then ran
onto hot flushed cheeks---"Ah think somethin' moah than
cold watah ---maybe Ah have burn ointment in th' kitchen
cabinet!" Blotting off her tear-stained face, she hurried
back to the kitchen without looking at Mac.

Salle heard her walk into the kitchen but went on cleaning. Lizbeth rummaged about in a cabinet---finally Salle asked, "You lookin' for something, Miss Lizbeth? Maybe I can help." Coming to Lizbeth's side, she asked in a low tone--- "What's the matter? I heard him yellin' at you..," Salle stared at her employer's red cheeks with tears coursing down them---"...why, you're crying! Did HE hurt you?" "NO!"---Lizbeth over reacted to Salle's concern—"..I mean, 'no'---I just burned th' palm of mah hand. That's all."

Taking Lizbeth's left hand gently in her own hands, Salle stared at the burn---"And just how did 'we' do this number on 'our' hand, huh?!! Would you just LOOK at that---why, it's gonna blister up bad, Miss Lizbeth!" Her angry dark eyes scanned the shelf---"I don't see anything in here! I'm gonna take you to see Doc!" "No! Really, Salle, if we just get some ointment---it'll be fine." "Doc will be foamin' mad if you don't at least call him and tell him about this--- 'accident'!"---Salle's lips curled over the word 'accident'--- "B'sides, it's gonna hurt awful for a couple of days!" "Ah'll manage, Salle, go ahead with what you were doin'. Maybe this aftahnoon you can go to town." Salle then nodded and went back to her work.

Lizbeth went to her own room and washed her face, put drops in her reddened eyes then patted her face with a fresh, wet bathcloth. Pulling a clean white cotton glove over the burned hand, she waited to calm down a bit---determined not to let him see her tears nor her pain. Soon she marched right back to Mac's room for his breakfast things.

After returning the tray, Lizbeth began dusting. He was reading his 'literature', ignoring her presence as she did his. Picking up her dust cloth, Lizbeth's attention was momentarily diverted---she didn't remember moving the square cloth 'protector' atop the recliner---but it was gone. Glancing at the floor---it was nowhere in sight. She picked up the caddy but it wasn't underneath.

"What on earth could've happened t'it?"---she wondered to herself. "It can't have been gone since last week's cleaning." Shrugging, she began dusting. Later while running a dust-mop over the polished floor behind the recliner, her eyes caught sight of the cloth beneath the chair! Squatting down, she pulled it out---"How did this get heah anyway! It looks like someone knocked it off and just left it! But who? No one comes in this room but me!"

Chapter Thirteen

Noting how subdued Lizbeth had grown by lunch, observing the pain in her eyes and how she 'favored' the white-gloved hand as she attempted little chores---Salle advised, "Miss Lizbeth, looks to me like we need to call Dr. O'Barr. You know, before the day gets away and all. At least let me see if he's in---could be he's out makin' calls or fishin'. The office could radio him---maybe he'd drop by. You gonna need somethin' for the pain---take my word for it---my mama used to 'nurse' folks. She still makes up some of her own concoctions and may even have a burn mixture, but I'd rather Dr. O'Barr saw this." Exhaling, Lizbeth nodded---"You're right, Salle. It hurts like th' very dickens--an' Ah probably wouldn't sleep t'night. Go ahead."—she whispered—"Call him."

Around 4:00 p.m., Salle heard Doc's truck rumbling up the road. Hurrying to the front door, she opened it as he was coming up the steps. "What's th' problem, Salle? I got a radio call that Mrs. McDougal had an accident---what happened! She all right?" Salle's tight-lipped mouth

whispered---"We'll talk about that later. Come on in and
see about her hand---and while you're at it, take a real good
hard look at her! See if she seems 'all right' to you or not!"
"Where is she?"---Doc asked as he hurried thru the front
door. "Out on the back porch."—Salle pointed---"She's
been sittin' out there most of the afternoon---just starin' up
at the woods. God knows what she's thinkin'!" Then
quietly Salle snapped---"But I know what I'D be thinkin'---
and DOIN!!"

Salle closed off the hall door leading to McDougal's
bedroom then after Doc went out, she closed the back door
behind him and made certain the window over the sink was
also down. Satisfied, she sat in a kitchen chair with her
arms crossed---"I'll see to it that old buzzard, McDougal,
won't hear a word she says to the doctor---that is IF the
poor soul tells him anything that even borders on the truth!
But you can bet I'LL tell him!!"

"Lizbeth!"---Doc spoke to her from the back door---"I just
got a message from th' office sayin' you needed me!
What's goin' on?" He went down the back steps and
walked over in front of the woman sitting on the porch
floor---her head was bent low, her eyes on her feet. He set
his bag down beside her, tilted her chin up so he could see
her face, she'd been crying.

"Why, Lizbeth---what's th' trouble---what's made you cry,
m'dear? Are you sick?" Slowly she shook her head---"No,
Doctah O'Bahrr, Ah'm not sick---not in th' sense that you
mean. But Ah burned mah hand a bit this mornin'. Ah
don't think it's damaged much but it does hurt some---too
much t'sleep probably." Her voice, almost a whisper
sounded so sad---close to despair. He picked up the hand
she held out and gently began peeling back the glove---
"Well now, let's have a look." In a couple of minutes, he

commented---"Why, you DO have a right nice injury there--
-but don't you worry---I have some topical 'gel'---kills th'
pain right away. And I'll leave you a few capsules t'help
you sleep for a couple of nights---till th' worst is over."

After cleaning up his hands with some solution---he coated
her palm with the soothing gel and asked-- "How'd you do
this, may I ask?" She shrugged her shoulders---"A silly
accident. Ah was about t'spill a pot of hot coffee an' put
m'left hand up t'steady it---an' burned m'self." "Then why
is it I'm thinkin' this isn't th' whole truth?"---his voice was
quiet as he stooped, bandaging her hand with snowy white
gauze before lightly taping it. She never answered, he
looked over at her face and saw tears welling up in her eyes
again. "It's all right, m'dear."---he assured her---"You
don't have to talk about it right now." Then he added
softly---"But maybe another time you'll feel you can
discuss it---I'm always there. All right?" Gratefully,
Lizbeth nodded and attempted a smile.

"You're chilled, don't you think it's time t'go inside?"---his
hand patted the thin shirt covering her shoulder. Obediently
she stood while he held her arm as they walked up the steps.
"Just like a little girl,"---he thought--"A child somebody's
hurt real bad!"

Inside, he asked Salle to make some hot tea for Lizbeth.
"Now, m'lady, you go on back an' lie down awhile. Salle
will bring you th' tea---an' I'll put your pills in a little box--
-she can bring everything to you." "Thank you, Doctah."---
she replied then asked Salle to get her purse. He scolded
her quietly---"No such thing! Don't worry about that now--
-you can drop it off next time you're in town." A soft smile
touched her mouth---"Such a good friend---yoah concern
an' gallantry---so very rare. Thank you foah comin' by.
Oh---an' if you promise t'come again latah---we'll make

some fried fruit pies, okay?" "Wild horses couldn't keep me away, m'dear---off you go t'rest now."

She disappeared into her bedroom as Doc turned to Salle---"When you take the tea, put a blanket on her---she felt chilled." Busying himself counting out some medication, he then looked up at Hawk's sister and shoved the sleeping potion into her hand---"While th' water's heatin' up, c'mon--follow me out---I want t'know what happened t'her."

Outside, Doc slid his bag across the dusty truck seat, sat down and demanded—"All right. Let's hear th' short version for th' time bein'!" "Doc! I don't know what IF anything she told you but that man is mean as a rattler---and crazy t'boot! Sure as Custer, he's got somethin' bad wrong inside his head!"---she blustered quietly---"I've heard it since Bill and I have been here but this mornin'---from what I could tell---he grabbed her when she set his breakfast tray down! And he almost scalded himself by jerkin' her around, you shoulda heard him raisin' hell---and all the time, her tryin' to keep from hurtin' him! If I was married to that man---some night when he was asleep, I'd tie him up in a sheet---take a stick of firewood then beat him half to death!"

Doc nodded---"So you would, Salle, so you would. Okay. I'll write up a report that I doubt it was an accident. But one day---one day he'll 'get his'! Almost happened once, too bad it didn't work out." Doc was cranking the engine when an idea hit him---"Uh, you think you could sorta sleep in her room at night until those pills are used up? I, uh, wouldn't want her to wake up groggy an' go to th' bathroom or somethin'---maybe fall an' break a bone." "Sure. No problem, she has a big recliner in each bedroom--I'll sleep on the chair beside her bed."

Doc winked approvingly, nodded at Salle and drove away talking to himself---"Why do I think she needs somebody t'sit with her while she's takin' those pills? Hell, he can't walk---there's no way he can hurt her while he's flat down!"

Chapter Fourteen

The burn improved and three days later, Doc called asking Lizbeth to come by his office so he could take another look at her hand. Mac took advantage of this golden opportunity and gave Bill orders to drive the women into town using the flat-bed truck to bring horse food for Maggie and range pellets for the steers that would be sold in another week.

From his bedroom window, Mac stood watching as they drove away. Then he walked into the living room where he riffled unsuccessfully thru the piano bench as he waited to make certain none of them had fogotten anything and came back. For them to make an untimely return and discover him out of bed---or going thru whatever she kept hidden in her bedroom would more than ruin his plan---it would mean the rest of his life would be spent bitterly regretting that one small, imprudent move! There was plenty of time---he'd waited since spring---he could manage to wait until it was safe to move about.

It had been the day of his fall when she'd moved into the other bedroom, therefore he had no knowledge of what was kept hidden away from him there in her 'sanctuary'! As he lay in bed after seeing her 'change' for the better---the 'not knowing' drove him crazy and in the end had pushed him to 'walk' again. Throughout their marriage, as long as he could secretly plunder thru her personal papers and keepsakes, he held a certain 'power' over her! He read her mail, listened in on her telephone calls but above all else, his accumulated 'store of knowledge' had been carried out by stealth! That gave him a sense of 'being invisible'---made him high! And for years, HE'D been 'in control' until that fateful afternoon last spring!

Power over others, especially a wife, was a heady thing! During his years of covert 'snooping' he never failed to get a 'rush' from going thru the belongings of others---his heart pounded wildly in his ears, blood raced thru his veins, his hands trembled in excitement! In a sense it could be 'dangerous'---IF you were stupid enough to get caught, that is---but a smart snoop never gets caught! However, she'd kept that damned book a secret, successfully so---something for which he'd never forgiven her. Even tho it had brought him a financial wind-fall---still he was angry and hated her because she'd created something successful. It'd only been a few years after their marriage that he began to hate everything about her---her cursed southern drawl---her mousy 'ladylike' ways, her polite behavior---and what others called her 'beauty'! He hated her innate stupidity while others referred to her 'talent'---he hated her femininity and her women's weaknesses---he hated hearing her bang on that damned piano---most of all he hated her ability to talk to anyone on any level about any subject! She only had a high school education---why did people think she was so damned intelligent---so 'sensitive'---so 'lovely'? Thinking about it made him want to puke!

How many times since spring had he cursed himself for being dumb enough to forget that letter Rita had written! When Lizbeth had approached him about the letter---a huge brawl ensued---and as was his habit, he'd slapped her around several times! Then out-of-character, she'd turned on him! Before he realized what was happening, she'd grabbed a fire poker, cracked him across the shoulder and neck with it twice before he could take it away from her. As he chased her with the poker, she'd fled to the kitchen, picked up a butcher knife and threatened if he ever hit her again, that she'd cut his throat---then she'd screamed for him to get out of the house because she was divorcing him! Afterwards, she'd driven off in the jeep.

Watching her race out the driveway that day, he determined the time had come to carry out the plan he'd been 'hatching'---for well over a year! Taking advantage of her absence, he'd hurried out to the two-story, high roofed barn planning to retrieve one of several hidden, unmarked, unregistered Klan guns. After they'd moved into the house and the builders had updated the barn, making it secure— he'd had Lizbeth write them a check and dismiss them. Then on the pretext of some 'finishing out'---he sawed into the top side of several huge log rafters then painstakingly scooped out holes to fit each gun. Later, he cut some covers for the holes, whittling them to set perfectly into place. However that fateful spring day, when he'd gone to pick up the gun of his choice---his foot had slipped before he could get to the firearm---and he'd fallen.

Later on, she'd come home and found him when she came to the barn to feed Maggie, that's when he made up the story of falling off the roof to keep everyone out of the barn. After finding his legs were 'paralyzed'---he knew if she divorced him, he'd lose hold on her---and the money. That's when he threatened, and made her believe, that with his Klan connections---if she filed for a divorce, he could get their attorneys to make her out a slut leaving a 'crippled' man all alone! There would be 'witnesses' who'd swear she bought and took illegal drugs---had several lovers---she'd lose her reputation entirely---not to mention being left empty-handed while, being an invalid, he'd end up with most everything. He wasn't certain about the 'truth' of that threat but she knew little about KKK---and thus far, he'd successfully bluffed her out!

"But that was then and this is now! As Daddy always said, 'adversity is the mother of struggle for change'!"

Since he'd begun walking again--- he'd twice safely finagled a half-hour alone! Both times he'd concentrated on the desk where the ranch files and correspondence were kept. He'd analyzed her personal telephone directory, the telephone bills and read every scrap of paper he could find. He'd closely scrutinized all letters that were postmarked after his accident---and come up with nothing! Absolutely nothing! The bedroom! That HAD to be her 'hiding place'---all women had hiding places---they hid things from their husbands---once out of sight, women could never be trusted. No matter how many idiots believed that women could make men jump through hoops---saying it didn't make it true! Any man worth his salt could control any woman!

Females had been evil since Eve 'messed around' with Lucifer who'd taken on the form of a 'serpent'---and nobody really knew just what that particular creature looked like before God cursed it to crawl on it's belly in the dust! Just the shape of a snake should be suggestive as to what had REALLY happened in the 'garden'!! His father had told him THAT decades ago! And because of what 'mother Eve' did---it was a man's God-given right to USE all women---just as he chose! How disgustingly easy it was to twist the gullible creatures around his finger with sweet words, little 'kindnesses' and 'thoughtful' gestures. A smooth man could get anything he wanted from the 'fairer sex'! Life and sex were nothing more than a little game the genders played with one another. But the unwritten law for any man was very clear---he must only use women---he could never like, love nor trust any of them!

Today, merely opening her bedroom door was an adventure! After all these months, the very act of entering her private territory heightened his excitement almost to a nervous frenzy! It was like a smorgasbord---he didn't know where to begin! "Calm down, McDougal,"---he breathed while pacing the area rug around her bed---"Pretend it's just another room. Be methodical---be careful to leave everything just the way you find it! Remember everything you've been taught ---never make a mistake---even a small mistake has the possibility of bringing about some very unpleasant future repercussions!"

His hour of searching yielded exactly nothing! Nothing but an unwashed coffee-stained china cup, which sat forgotten on her dresser alongside a copy of that damned book---*The Post Oak Tree*!! A kind of frantic anger was building up inside his whole body---"WHERE in hell did she keep her 'secrets'??! It'd be just like that fool, O'Barr, to drive up and catch him out of bed—OH, DAMN that meddling old goat! Damn ALL of them! And most of all, damn her!"

His earlier frenzy of excitement had now turned to rage--- perspiration soaked his clothing as he stalked frantically about the room, clenching and unclenching his fists! Due to his fruitless searching, he felt a compulsion to tear the contents of her room apart and strew it all over! If he could but slash every piece of cloth---shatter the mirror---cut up her mattress and chair---then leave it for her! But he couldn't---the moment for such actions had to be put on hold for the time being. "I gotta have a drink!"---he spat then headed for his room.

Sitting on the side of his bed, he gulped the last of his whiskey then lay down, pulling the covers up to his waist. "This searching of the house is fruitless---next time I can get them out of here---I have to take the chance of being seen! I must go to the barn for my gun! I want her dead. Nothing about that has changed."

Chapter Fifteen

That night as Lizbeth got ready for bed, she reached for her pajamas and noted they were somewhat rumpled up beneath the pillow---not neatly folded as she always left them. Exhaling wearily, she sighed---"What's wrong with me!? Lord, it does seem like Ah'm losin' what's left of m'mind with things not bein' as Ah left them---like a couple of weeks ago when Ah put two receipts in th' desk drawer an' th' file cover was on th' wrong way! Last time Ah used it---Ah put th' top back on straight! Not t'mention all th' correspondence bein' askew when Ah paid ouah property-tax notice! Or..."---she whispered softly---"...maybe it's just that Salle knocked some things off on th' floah while she was cleanin'. A perfectly reasonable thing---but just th' same, Ah'm goin' t'ask her tomorrow mornin'!"

After her shower, she stroked the gel on her hand. By now, the burned area had thickened and had begun peeling at the edges of her palm. Thoughtfully, she walked to her dresser---"Doc suspects somethin' about this burn. He's nevah said much but it's pretty cleah he believes Mac had somethin' t'do with th' whole thing. Maybe Ah should jus' tell him th' truth. If Mac's behavior gets worse, it would be best if someone other than poor Salle, knows what's goin' on now---an' what's gone on foah a very long time. Had Mac not fallen---ouah lives would've gone in different directions an' been settled by now! We'd both be free, he could be with Rita an'...,"---her thoughts immediately turned to Joseph Winterhawk, who was never far from her mind.

"Oh, Hawk, how Ah miss you---Ah'm forlorn without you."
Picking up his coffee cup, she kissed it softly then placed it
carefully back down beside her book---and began brushing
her hair. It seemed so long since she'd seen him! From the
moment they'd sat together in the jeep, she'd known those
precious minutes and seconds would have to last a long
while---but as that 'long while' slowly passed---she'd not
known Mac would turn into the devil himself! "Guess Ah
could ask Salle about him,"---she thought as she gazed at
her image in the mirror---"...but somehow it doesn' seem
quite propah. No, it wouldn't be right t'involve her, much
as Ah'm dyin' t'heah news about him---Ah must wait an' be
patient."

Later Lizbeth had gone to sleep but suddenly, in the middle
of the night she was wakened by the sound of a loud crash
or bang---had something fallen at the front of the house---a
picture from the wall maybe? With pounding heart and
prickles stabbing at her body, she quickly jumped out of
bed, hurrying quietly to where she could look into the living
room. The moonlight sifted in thru the windows, she could
see nothing---no one was there---vainly her eyes searched
about—but nothing moved. Then tiptoeing to the front
door, she made certain it was locked---thinking to herself---
"Thank God, I DID lock it earlier! With th' way mah
mind's been lately, I had t'make suah!"

Back at the door of her bedroom, she stopped---a chill ran
over her. Recently, someone had been in her room---she
sensed it! Closing her door, she slid the big bolt into place
before returning to bed. "Wondah if Ah should go into
town an' buy a gun---all we have is Mac's old shotgun an' I
don't even know wheah that thing is! First trip t'town, Ah
must see what's available! No one's evah bothered us here,
Ah've always felt completely safe---so why are mah legs
shakin' now? Why am Ah scared?! It's possible Mac

90

could've thrown something but he's always dead t'the world at this hour---an' Ah didn't even check on him." Sighing, she thought---"What if he rolled off th' bed!" So getting up, she unbolted her door and tiptoed down the hall toward his room.

His door was closed! She stared---"Ah don' remembah closin' it!!" Then she thought a sudden strong breeze must've come thru his window blowing his door shut. Of course, that had to be what awakened her---so without disturbing him, she returned to her own room, re-locked her own door and lay back down. But still she felt something--- an invisible presence---'someone' had been in her room and not long ago---someone that shouldn't be there! Again, she shivered. Sleep came late for Lizbeth that night---and when it arrived---it was neither restful nor undisturbed. She thrashed about in her bed, turning from side to side while struggling to escape indistinct nightmarish images of dark threatening figures which, as they neared her, grew to frightening proportions!

Chapter Sixteen

While Lizbeth fought off encroaching dark dream images--- several miles away, on a reservation mountain-top---Hawk built his fire then prayed, chanted, drummed, played his flute and danced the moonlit night hours away. Around 3:00 a.m., he knelt for one last prayer then rolled up in his sleeping bag and lay gazing upon a few dying embers—all that was now left of his bonfire.

Upon returning home, he'd come to his mountain twice but after seeing Lizbeth the day she and Salle brought lunch to the woods---he'd been here at least once a week since. Deep inside, his heart's desire was that the wind would carry the sounds of his mountain-top visits to her spirit---that she could 'hear' him---then their spirits could communicate.

Just as he kept his weekly mountain-visits, so he kept regular confession to Father O'Hara on afternoons before Mass. He didn't talk to Father about his mountain-top retreats---he didn't know how the 'good man' would take it---he hadn't been around the reservation long enough. Father Murphy would've understood just as Doc understood. But several years back, Father Murphy, himself, had passed on to a good reward. So Hawk's 'confession' simply included his venial sins and always one mortal one---"O my God, I am heartily sorry for having offended you and I detest all my sins. I dread the loss of heaven and pains of hell. I confess I love a woman who is married. I have not committed sin with her physically nor in my mind. She is a fine woman whom I respect but whom I stay away from---because I must remain faithful to You. I am sorry for all my sins, offenses and I firmly resolve with the help of Your grace, to confess my sins, do penance and amend my life. Forgive me, Father. Amen."

The forty-five year old Father O'Hara would absolve him---give him some penance to do, then wonder if he should make an office appointment with Joseph so they could talk. In the confessional, each time Joseph confessed his 'great sin', Father also wondered if he should ask Joseph if the woman was aware of his feelings for her. Father thought highly of the Winterhawk family---Mary was a godsend to him, as well as a wonderful mother, member of the Church and the community. So instead of cornering Joseph about having that private 'chat'---he simply 'put it off'.

Lying there waiting for sleep, Hawk himself wasn't sure if
God heard when he spoke to Him about this thing between
Lizbeth and himself---her being married left him at a loss as
to how to converse with the Almighty. But he felt God
knew McDougal's heart better than any human! However,
no matter how black the man's heart may be---Hawk
guessed it cut no ice with God---married was married---
vows were vows, covenants were covenants. But surely all
of heaven must know that something evil lurked within the
heart of Lizbeth's husband! Oh, it wasn't just that he'd
been rude as hell to both Doc and himself that first day---
there was a 'feeling' of something ungodly in the whole
atmosphere of McDougal's room. The mixed
Ohmaha/Sioux blood in Hawk 'knew' these things---no
pole had ever had to hit him between the eyes to show him
truth!

From early on in his life, he'd had the gift of discerning
people, their spirits and certain situations. His Dad always
told him---out of Mary's hearing, of course---that he'd have
made a great warrior chief---even a shaman. And his
father's words had, in a sense, become prophetic, for he had
become a 'warrior' of sorts, though it had been among
'white warriors'. His uncanny way of reading people and
quickly accessing the correct status of most emergencies
had been rewarded by promotions in the military.

"Oh, Lord."---Hawk prayed---"If You still give dream-
visions---send me one. Tell me what to do. I've been
coming here for weeks now, yet You've remained silent.
Do my feelings for Lizbeth McDougal offend You? More
than others, You know I have not sinned. I believe more in
the spirit realm than I do in this physical one because it was
Your Spirit who sent me the dream I had many years ago.
And even as I thank you daily for the spiritual bond with
Lizbeth---because I am certain You meant it to be---yet I am

weary, my God, and I am lonely. Look down on your servant, Joseph Winterhawk, give me a dream to keep my spirit alive, for it is slowly withering away inside me. Like Jacob's son, Joseph, I am a 'dreamer' as well---both of us having and interpreting dreams. Stay with me thru this and when the time comes, help me do the right thing! Give me insight, Lord, help me see the 'truth' of matters that are not only hidden from me but which disturb me greatly. Don't remain silent and far away from me---O My Lord, do not leave me alone with so much confusion!"

Before long, dawn would break on the far horizon, east of his mountain---and unless a miracle happened---with it would come another lonely, empty day. Joseph Winterhawk closed his eyes, waiting for whatever sleep might come to him.

Then the wind lifted him! Light as a feather, he soared far above mountains, skimming effortlessly thru shreds of wind-torn clouds. Beneath he saw some higher points of the mountain range, their bedrock formations jutting thousands of feet skyward like stone fingers that reached up toward him. Farther down and below the sharp rock formations, scrubby bushes clung ferociously to bits of grainy soil making dark green shadows---here and there isolated clumps of wildflowers cast dollops of beautiful summer color over the gigantic landscape. Riding the wind currents, he drifted downward---soon the scrub turned to evergreens, the cool air carried their sharp piquant fragrance into his nostrils---onto his tongue then deep into his lungs!

What had happened to his eyesight? Everything had been magnified to an incredible range! Below him, he could see birds' nests cuddled between forks of tree branches--- branches that were covered with rich, green summer leaves! Here and there, small forest creatures darted back and forth!

The birds flew at him, squawking angrily---and each time he closed in for a better look, the creatures scurried out of sight as tho terrified of him! He opened his mouth to give them his usual whistle---but only a loud, piercing noise came out!

Before he could ponder on that---the wind changed---picked him up---soon he was being tossed wildly about the mountainside as though caught in a downdraft! Surely he would be flung mercilessly against the ground and crushed---or worse, become impaled upon the sharp trunk of some isolated and long dead pine tree! He struggled and fought---but in vain---he was whirling madly about---soon he would be dead! But then, just as suddenly as it had begun, the wind evened out and he was at ease, soaring peacefully once again.

Where was he now? He had no idea how much time had passed since he'd fought the fearsome wind currents---it seemed---a long time, perhaps. His concept of 'time' was no longer the same---he realized he'd changed in some way---but how and in what way, he couldn't be sure.

Now, his flight was carrying him lower---much closer to the ground---about tree-top level. With his new improved vision, he scoped out the territory below him---it had a familiar look. Wheeling to the left for awhile then to the right, he was soon able to make- out his mother's home and the church with the cross on top---and just below like a dirty brown ribbon was the gravely road winding out to the highway. He found himself following it and in a flash, the highway appeared just below him---he banked northward.

Soon, off to his left he viewed South Mountain---he felt drawn to the ballpark where he and Doc had parked then walked part-way up the mountain! That day, the leaves had

been green with a golden sunlight shimmering thru them---
but at this moment the area looked stark and strangely bare!
Most of the leaves were gone! But how could that be?
He'd just experienced summer greenery---hadn't he? But
he accepted what he saw and sensed that below him---
autumn had come, then gone and was well on it's way to
being only a memory. All that was left was a gold, brown
and burgundy leaf-covered earth with only the most
stubborn of leaves still clinging to their parent-trees in
sparse, scattered, brilliant clusters. He breathed in air that
now tasted vaguely of recent rain, dampness, clean earth
and dying leaves---it felt cool and clean in his lungs. It was
as tho the scent of autumn's death had somehow given a gift
of new life and vigor to him!

As he wheeled and circled in a strange kind of ecstasy, he
found he was once again climbing higher and higher---
suddenly, instinct directed him back to the highway. Right
turn then north he traveled---upon recognizing the
Sanderson place below, he felt a throbbing within his
breast!! Lizbeth! He was flying to her---wasn't he! Why
else would he be here? Would she be outside where he
could call to her? What would be his words when he saw
her? Deep inside his head, these questions all whirled in an
odd unfamiliar way---at the same time, they seemed to
belong both to him and some other entity!

Circling the general area and carefully scrutinizing the barn
roof, the housetop, the yard with it's bare tree limbs---he
questioned as to what he should do!? Perhaps he should
glide low and hide in that nearby evergreen tree, surely
sooner or later, she would come out where he could get her
attention. Then out in one of the barns, he heard a grinding
noise---a jeep engine turned over, so he drifted lightly down
into the evergreen to wait. Soon the jeep carrying Salle,
Bill---and Lizbeth drove past him! Within moments they

reached the highway and hastened away. His heart was crushed! He'd come so far and had only seen her at a distance---yet her eyes seemed as close as if they'd stood next to one another---he saw each silky strand of her red streaky hair---but now she was gone. Should he follow? Was he to wait for her return? Was he to leave?

All at once he found himself considering---who was with McDougal? Recently Salle said he'd begun staying alone for brief periods. He'd bark orders, insisting all three leave to pick up certain items in town. So, here he'd flown around mountains, across the reservation and over his mother's home---now, like a fool, he found himself sitting on a tree limb in Lizbeth's yard. Odd, he thought, all during this flight---he'd seen no human beings but Salle, Bill and Lizbeth.

Before he could make up his mind as to what he should do next---he heard the back door slam. Had someone gone into the house!? Experiencing a compulsion to be nearer the back of the house, he immediately found himself once more in the air---climbing higher, he increased the width of his circles just a bit so he wouldn't be too noticable. As he made his last circle---what his eyes saw astounded him!! He had to be mistaken! But---NO! IT WAS HIM! His new eye-vision made that very clear---there was no mistaking the man---it was McDougal---and he was WALKING!!

"Walking"!?---he clucked to himself---"McDougal CAN'T walk!!" Confusion filled his breast then he thought---"But he mustn't see me!" Quickly, he pulled higher into the sky and watched McDougal go toward and into the barn!! Incredible! At this point, there was no doubt, no question as to his own strange mission---he knew it was his job to see what McDougal was up to! So, landing near the gable, he

97

crept along sideways desperately searching for a small hole to peek thru. There was none! What would he do NOW? In a flash, it came to him---zooming off the roof, he settled gently on the ground just at the barn entrance! Slowly, he stealthed along, the soles of his feet felt distinctly foreign as he moved across the barn floor---once inside he must find a place to hide and see what the 'walker' was up to!! Did Lizbeth know? No one had said a word about this!! Why hadn't someone TOLD him?! Was he having some kind of wild nightmare??

That thought quickly disappeared as he hid behind some bags of cattle feed and watched McDougal climb to the second floor of the barn! Now he could no longer see the 'walker'! He, too, must go higher! Sailing quickly out the front barn door, he came to the rear where finally he spied the upper door opened a crack, affording a place to view the interior! His strange feet clung and hung on to the wood as he peeked inside---there McDougal was prying loose what looked like a piece of one of the log rafters! His heart raced---he blinked his eyes several times, focusing in on the rafter---then he saw part of the wood give way! There was a cutout in the log! McDougal thrust his hand inside the log, brought out a carefully wrapped item---he watched as the 'walker' removed the cloth---it was a handgun!! Why would a man hide a handgun? Unless he had something else to hide as well! And what was he going to do with a gun that had been put away in such a secret place? He continued to peer in as McDougal stuffed the .38 Special into the back of his belt, made his way toward the ladder then climbed down out of sight!

He had to follow him! But where was 'the walker' going? Worse yet, WHAT was he going to do when he got there?! His thoughts clicking swiftly, he let go his perch and swooped quickly over-head---he continued circling as 'the

Shelby Jean Roukoski Clark

walker' stepped up on the back porch of the house! The
man meant to harm someone---he was certain of it!

Abruptly an unnatural force rose up swiftly inside him,
taking him into a dive---he felt his mouth opening to
challenge McDougal! Once again he heard only a fierce,
high-pitched shrilling squall come out of his mouth! Oh
God! What was wrong---he couldn't talk! He could only
shriek! McDougal then turned---came forward, jumped off
the back porch and leveled the gun at him while shouting---
"SON-OF-A-BITCH THIEVING HAWK!!! I'LL KILL
YOUR ASS!!!" BLAAAAM!—he heard the ear-splitting
sound and felt something hot tear into his hand!

"I'M HIT! We're drawin' fire!!"---"Get down!"---"We'll
all be dead---the 'Cong' have set booby-traps!!! HIT THE
DIRT!!!" ---"Cap! CAP!!! They're all over us!! They're
cuttin' us to pieces!!" ---"STAY DOWN!! Hueys comin'
in!!!"--"Captain!"---"LISTEN UP!! There they are!!
RESCUE AT 3:00---just over the trees---hang on!!
LOOK!! Our gunners are dustin' their ass!!! THERE GO
OUR ROCKETS!!! GET READY T'RUN FOR IT!!"---
frantically he stood motioning his men toward the rescue
gunships hovering at treetop level---"C'MON!! GO---GO--
-GO!! IF THEY CAN'T DO GROUND HOVER---GRAB
TH' RAPPEL DESCENDER!"

With a start, Joseph jerked straight up, a sick dizziness
almost overwhelmed him! Dazed, he looked around---
where was he?? His breath was ragged, uneven---his heart
raced unnaturally! It was too cool to be Nam, tho for a split
second he'd 'been' there!! It was daylight---overhead was a
clear, brilliant blue sky---the early morning sun hurt his
eyes and sent his purplish shadow far past dead, black
embers of last night's bonfire! He could hear several crows
in a scream-fest with a lone hawk and recognizing the

99

location, he groaned while placing two shaky hands over his sweat-covered face. Then he recalled bits of a dream---a vision? OR was it something more? Why did he feel--- numb, sick, nauseous as though he'd been torn in half--- with part of him here and part of him someplace else!! In flight, the earth had appeared as when viewed from a chopper---he'd soared as though he'd been born with wings! Pressing his open trembling palms against his eyes to keep out the brilliant sunlight---he set about to recall the whole thing! This 'before dawn' experience was what he'd been waiting for----he couldn't afford to forget any of it!!

Later, after putting the dream-vision together, he became aware that the fingers of his left hand had been constantly throbbing, stinging and burning---removing the hand from his face, he rubbed his fingers together---then stared numbly at the raw flesh and smeared blood stains!

Chapter Seventeen

Around 11:30 a.m., a red-eyed, unsettled Joseph wearing dusty wrinkled clothing practically burst into Dr. O'Barr's office! The nurse's face momentarily registered surprise--- "Why, Captain Winterhawk! I almost didn't recognize you- --are you all right?" Joseph looked at her strangely as though he'd expected no one to be there and she'd just materialized out of nothing! "Fine."---he replied in a distracted tone---"I'm okay! Where's Doc??!" "He's home having lunch---it's almost noon, you know!" The Sioux's abrupt entrance had unnerved her---as well as his uncharacteristic disheveled appearance! "He'll be back soon!"---she assured him---"You may wait if you like, I-- I'm sure we can work you in!" Joseph stared for a moment then replied---"No, this can't wait!" With that, he rushed out.

Pressing a hand over her collarbone, she exhaled a sigh of relief and whispered aloud---"What on earth?! I've never seen him look like that since I came here!" Hurrying to the window, she watched as Joseph almost ran up the path to the O'Barr house.

Banging on the back door, he leaned against the wall momentarily still trying to gather himself together! Only in that second did he realize Ida was probably in the kitchen having lunch with Doc---he mustn't frighten her! Gazing down at the gauze wrapped around his left hand, it came to him what to say if she answered his knock.

The doorknob rattled and sure enough, it was Ida. Her smile welcomed him—"Why, Joseph! We're having lunch, please come in…"---she pointed toward a chair---"…sit down at the table and I'll get you a plate---you can eat with us." Doc looked up from his food---"Wouldn't you just know he'd turn up near th' stroke of noon! Well, don't stand about there blockin' my doorway, come in an' close th' door---grab a chair! Ida's outdone herself with this beef stew! Best I ever ate!" He shoveled another spoonful into his mouth.

Slowly walking toward the table, Joseph asked---"Could I please have a glass of water, Mrs. Doc?" In giving him the water, she finally noticed his appearance then the gauze-wrapped left hand! "Dear me!"---she exclaimed in concern, taking his bandaged hand in hers! Laying aside his spoon, Doc questioned---"You've hurt yourself! Why didn't you say somethin' instead of standin' there like a tree-trunk?! Unwrap his hand, Ida, let's have a look at it!" "No, no."---Hawk replied quietly and reached out his right hand to stop her---"It's just a scratch---I mean, I mashed it with the hammer! It can wait. Please finish your lunch first, Doc."

101

Ida set a bowl of beef stew before Hawk---there was nothing to do but try and eat it. "I didn't mean to invite myself to your meal,"---he tried to smile---"...but with the kind offer, I might as well take advantage of your great cooking." His mind now alert, Doc kept staring at Hawk who ignored the glances and kept busy forcing his food down. Looking up from his bowl, the Indian finally commented---"You're mighty quiet today, Doc. Somebody upset your apple-cart?" With a canny gleam in his eyes, O'Barr replied---"Not yet but---'somebody' might do exactly that---probably right soon."

Joseph ate most of his stew, noting when Doc took up his napkin and wiped his mouth. "Now, let's have a look at that smashed hand. C'mon, we'll use my home office!" Hawk stood quickly, nodding his head toward Ida---"Thank you, Mrs. Doc, the stew was wonderful. I feel better already—guess I honestly forgot it was lunch time." "I'm glad you liked it."---she patted his arm---"Now, you run along and let Doc fix your wound!"

Doc's home 'emergency' was one of their spare bedrooms just off the front hall. As Hawk followed O'Barr past the area, he remembered how cozy the living room had been that night they'd had brandy, re-opened 'his vision' then discussed Lizbeth's book. Breaking into his thoughts, Doc pushed Hawk toward the examining table---"Here, sit down and let's have a look-see." After expertly removing the hastily applied bandage, Doc took one close look then stared up into Hawk's face---"That's not from a hammer! You think I don't know powder-burns when I see 'em??! What th' hell happened?" Quickly closing the door, he demanded---"Now---let's hear it, Winterhawk!"

Before Joseph got 1/3 thru his story---Doc had already sat down, his mouth hanging open---a look of total disbelief continued as he listened until the end! Hawk exhaled then commented softly to the speechless older man---"You look pale beneath that tan." "Pale?"---Doc rasped---"You come in here with gun-powder burns on your raw, bloodied fingers an' tell me a sci-fi story like this? How do you EXPECT me t'look? This is like seein' Elijah flyin' off in a whirlwind!" The older man rubbed a palm over his forehead---"Gimme a minute, will you? This is more than an old white man can digest all at once."

Hawk waited as long as he could then demanded—"You're the physician on this case! What do you think? CAN McDougal walk!?" Shaking his head, Doc exhaled, the stunned expression still on his face---"I dunno. It's possible, I guess. Dear God,"---his tone low--"..as bad as it's been for Lizbeth, caring for him all these months---I'd hate t'know th' scoundrel was able t'walk again! Hawk?" He scrutinized Joseph's face and his eyes---"You sure you didn't---er, take---'anything' out there on th' mountain, no mushrooms or anything?" "You mean 'hallucinogens'?! ME?"---Hawk pointed to his chest—"You KNOW better than that---if I didn't take drugs in 'Nam---why in God's name would I start now?! Life hasn't rendered me quite THAT desperate yet!"

Beginning to understand how he must've appeared to all who'd come in contact with him since leaving the mountain, he added---"Guess I look like hell---but I didn't even smoke a cigarette much less anything else---and I didn't swallow anything, inject it or snort it! Doctor-man, you're the only one I could come to! You're the only person who knows all about this craziness between Lizbeth and myself---and you know me, personally, better than anyone except God and Mama---and I sure couldn't tell HER!"

Doc sat silent, still numbed by everything Hawk had told him. "Doc?"---Hawk went on---"Say if he CAN walk and has kept it to himself---why would a person go to that much trouble hiding the fact he's not paralyzed anymore? Not to mention camaflouging a firearm in his barn! Why not keep it inside the house where it's handy if needed?"

"You got me---I don't know! BUT,"—Doc held up a finger---"… seein' him on a fairly regular basis for months now, I never liked him, nor trusted him! Plus, I think,"—his face began to look even more troubled. "Think what??" ---Hawk prodded. A deep sigh escaped the physician before he continued---"All right, kiddo. Let's get this hand fixed up. Looks like th' time has finally arrived when I gotta fill you in on th' true story, th' one Lizbeth told me th' very afternoon old Mac fell off their barn."

Joseph leaned forward and watched as Doc pulled on latex gloves then plunged the powder-burned hand into a sterile basin filled with antibacterial solution. It began stinging but Hawk never flinched---"Say on, Doc. As you said earlier--- 'let's have it'! I just hope whatever you have to tell me isn't---maybe too long overdue!" Carefully rubbing at the submerged hand to throroughly cleanse it, Doc replied---"I trust it isn't overdue, Hawk, like th' Good Book says--- there's a time an' a season for everything. I guess right now's th' time for you t'hear about our McDougal 'couple'."

"Y'see,"---he began---"I knew th' Sanderson place had sold way last year---an' each time I was out that way, I made sure t'take note if any renovation process had begun. Later on, Mr. Donnelly at the café told me there was this strange red-haired woman 'who talked funny' who was out scourin' th' country side lookin' t'buy old barn logs an' quarry rock.

By then, I must admit my curiosity was gettin' th' better of
me so I decided th' very first time I saw somebody around
th' place, why I'd just stop by---say 'hello', introduce
myself, be neighborly---an' offer my professional services if
ever needed."

"A few weeks later, I was passin' by when I saw a big
dump-truck out there puttin' down a load of rocks---I
decided that was th' day t'stop! Sure enough, standin' there
ready t'sign for th' delivery was a red-haired lady, so after
she finished up with th' driver---we began walkin' toward
each other. I tipped m'hat then gave that introductory
speech---th' moment she spoke, I knew f'sure Mr. Donnelly
had been right! Her accent was so thick you needed t'cut it
with a cross-cut saw! Cute as a kitten she was, Hawk,
wearin' her dusty coveralls an' sneakers, her workgloves
hangin' out of both pockets. An' I remember there was this
smudge of dirt across one cheek as though she'd felt a tickle
or something then reached up an' rubbed it. That reddish-
blonde hair was all piled up on top of her head with some
little loose strands blowing around in the breeze."

"We became friends from th' first moment, I guess. Later
Ida invited them over one night t'have dinner---she
captivated Ida just as she had me." Hawk interjected ---
"And McDougal?" "Well."---Doc went on---"He didn't
hide th' fact that he had no use for anybody in town. He
complained about th' price of those stones she'd bought, th'
logs, renovatin' th' house---plus th' cost of electric an'
phone deposits---then he really embarrassed her when he
went on about her repairin' what he called ---'a damn barn
that should be burnt down'! He couldn't understand why
she'd want t'live in a place that needed s'much work ---
hang history, sentiment an' all that. On an' on --- by
evenin's end, he'd let us know people in this town were
unfriendly, clannish --- just out t'skin you for a buck. I

felt like tellin' him if he hated it all so much, why didn't he just pack up, leave---go back where-ever th' hell he'd come from! But, for her sake, I endured th' nasty warthog---an' went right on endurin' him---'cause t'me, she was worth it!" Doc lifted Hawk's hand out of the solution and began patting it dry with sterile gauze squares, talking as he worked.

"Sometimes she came into town f'groceries, goin' by th' bank an' such---she'd stop in t'see Ida an' me---just for a minute though. He wouldn't let her out of sight long---not without him---an' those were th' moments we got t'know her better. Once she spoke a bit about her folks an' growin' up back in Georgia. After awhile any person with half a mind could tell that beneath her smile an' pleasantries---she veiled a deep sadness---lonely for like-minded companionship, I guess. Now that I think back on it, she must've been scared too. But unfortunately we really didn't know just how deep th' fear ran inside her---OR why! When it was time f'deliverin' food t'your mother's church out at th' Rez, Ida'd think up something t'tell McDougal so she could be away from th' ranch longer than usual. She took great pleasure in doin' what little good she could."

"Then came th' day of his accident. Earlier that very afternoon, she showed up at th' office, askin' for me. When she walked in, I could tell she was upset---an' angry too. So I offered her a chair then sat down just across from her askin' what was troublin' her. Her face was tear-stained, flushed---eyes big as a doe-deer caught in headlights---then with a burst of new tears, she told me she'd been doin' laundry when she found a letter from some woman in Mac's pocket. When he came in, she confronted him about it---a literal fight ensued---he hit her a few times but she grabbed a fire poker an' whacked him with it. After he'd taken the poker away from her then attempted usin' it t' beat her---she ran in th' kitchen an' took a butcher knife to him---she told him t'leave, get out of th' house---that she wanted a divorce! Then she drove t'my office---poor thing, she was afraid an' had no safe place TO go!!"

"At that point, I encouraged her t'get that divorce---maybe it was sheer selfishness on my part---but I wanted her free of him. It was my opinion she couldn't see th' last of him too soon! She informed me whichever attorney she chose would have t'be ready f'a fight because Mac had promised with help from KKK attorneys utilizin' false witnesses, he'd do everything possible t'ruin her reputation then take as much from her as he could. So, I gave her my recommendation for a divorce action."

"After we talked for a couple of hours, she said she felt calm enough t'go back home. I insisted she stay with Ida an' me---at least over night---but she said it might only make things worse an' she wouldn't hear of involvin' us. So I let her leave on one condition---that she let one of Logan's deputies follow her home an' inform McDougal if he didn't want t'end up in jail, there'd be no more physical violence. Don't know if she honestly felt safer but she sorta brightened up when I said that. M'biggest regret is stupidity, plain blindness---Hawk, at that time, I had no idea that fool was practically off his rocker!" Doc sighed then went on---"Anyway when I saw th' deputy arrive outside, I walked her to th' jeep, urging her every step of th' way t'start proceedings th' following morning. By then, th' afternoon was already gettin' on so I told her I'd call th' attorney m'self an' give him th' story---that way he'd be ready t'see her first thing next day."

"They'd had enough time t'get out t'the ranch when I had a call from her---she told me there'd been an accident out at th' barn so I ordered an ambulance then Logan and I headed straight out there."

Having finished drying Hawk's hand, Doc rummaged about in a cabinet, brought out a couple of medications and began applying them over the raw areas. After taping up the hand, O'Barr asked---"Ready for th' needle? A little something t'keep down any possible infection...,"---Doc arched an eyebrow at Joseph---"...no telling what all you dragged your poor wing thru or whacked it up against on th' way back t'your nest up there on th' mountain top!"

Hawk sighed---"I'm just relieved you don't think I've lost my mind!" "Well, at least not enough t'do this t'yourself!"---Doc commented dryly. Waiting a moment he then decided he may as well 'go one more' and began--- "Another thing, while she was here that afternoon? After questioning her closely, she reluctantly admitted she'd suffered all sorts of abuse from McDougal---f'years! THAT'S why she was angry with him---it wasn't the 'other woman' thing---it was his treatment of her, usin' her money then betrayin' her when all he had t'do was ask for a divorce! I think she'd have run all the way to th' courthouse just t'give it to him too! Problem was, Hawk, he must've KNOWN that all along an' didn't want t'lose his 'gravy-train'! When I asked her why she'd never told anyone about his abuse, she replied it wasn't only what he might order done t'her—but her family if she ran home. Remember how I told you McDougal kept that supply of KKK literature? Well, not only is HE a Klansman, old buddy, but most of his family are as well." He could see Joseph's jaw clenching and unclenching.

"One last thing, don't know if she told you or not but last month, Salle called an' said Lizbeth had 'burned her hand' with some hot coffee---so, I went out t'check on her. When

I got there, Salle was in a temper---she pointed me t'Lizbeth sitting on th' back porch floor, ---out there in th' cold without a jacket. Been a long time since I saw anybody lookin' so---'despaired'. Later I asked Salle what really took place, she said when Lizbeth took his breakfast tray in t'him that morning, she heard Mac yellin' an' swearin'. It's your sister's opinion he began jerkin' Liz around, th' coffee started t'spill on him---then t'keep him from being scalded, she grabbed th' carafe with her bare hand!"

Doc paused, shrugged then added---"Th' rest, you pretty much already know. So now you have th' whole truth of their relationship. Joseph, at th' beginnin' of this thing, I felt it best you didn't have t'deal with all I've just told you---because t'be honest, I didn't know one single thing you could actually DO about her situation! If you'd tried t'help her---you could've gotten in God knows what kinda trouble---an' with him bein' a member of them rogues---why, not only you but your whole family could've been in harms' way! Native Americans are th' same as Negroes t'him an' his ilk."

Hawk sat very still, for the past 20 minutes Doc had watched the man's expression run the range from needing answers to 'visions' and hidden guns---to one of seething rage! When Joseph spoke his voice cut like a scapel---"You should've told me!" "Joseph! I couldn't have you carryin' this load around inside you---not when I know you're in love with her! Hell, man---it doesn't take a PhD to figure that one out! I've known you since you were a child---you can't hide that much emotion from me! Please believe me when I say---from th' day you arrived back here, I've spent a lotta sleepless nights tryin' t'figure out what I should an' what I shouldn't tell you!" Then he muttered----"Much less wonderin' why I turned my truck around that day an' took you right t'her front door!"

By then both Hawk and Doc were standing facing each other. Hawk oozing with desire to wreck havoc on an enemy---O'Barr wondering why he'd been chosen to pass on information that, on top of such a 'vision'---only fueled the Indian's intense fiery nature! But what else COULD he have done back at the beginning!!? He'd kept all this from Joseph for 'his own protection'. He had to tell him the truth, he couldn't have a fine man like Winterhawk eaten up with guilt for innocently loving a 'married woman'---he deserved to know. And with what Hawk had just told him about McDougal---Doc worried he'd already stayed 'quiet' too long! WAS IT---could it really be true?! There seemed too much 'evidence' to ignore Hawk's story---he wasn't a 'flake' nor a 'mental case'---and he didn't go around telling crazy stories!

Doc watched the flashing black eyes and angry scowl for several moments then gently took hold of Hawk's strong muscular arm---"Now, don't you go native on me, Joseph! Sit down in this chair for just a minute! We gotta use our heads! We're both fully aware we can't go to th' sheriff so you can tell a story that'd go something like this---'Look, guys, I had this vision wherein I was a hawk an' while out flyin' around th' county, I saw this man! One whom I think is up t'no good---he took a gun outta his barn, where he'd kept it hidden in a log! Then he took a shot at me, burned off a coupla feathers from my wing-tip an' I think he may have plans t'do th' same with someone else.' It's like you said t'me not long ago---it's 'you and me'—'babe'! We're th' ones who have t'take care of this BUT we gotta do it in th' right way! By that I mean so that neither you nor Lizbeth get in any hot-water! For twenty years now, you've lived a life of 'taking care of' seemingly hopeless situations---so THINK! Think, man, think! Come up with a way we can find out if Lizbeth's in danger from her old man or not---an' do it a.s.a.p.!!" Doc sighed---"Guess you must've had this wild vision in order t'help her---so you can add me in---I don't want that devil hurtin' her either!"

Doc left the room briefly then returned with a bit of brandy---"I'm going over an' see this afternoon's patients. I'll tell Ida that you need t'rest awhile, so you go up t'your room an' drink this---then for heavens's sake, lie down an' take a rest! After all, you've been flyin' all night! If you can't sleep---soon as your blood stops boilin', use your mind t'dig back into your training. Come t'my office later an' we'll make a decision. Okay?"

Joseph nodded then as Doc turned to leave, he said—"Call her, Doc, make sure she's----still all right. You can think of some excuse for the call, say anything. But listen---be extremely careful of your words! Small talk only---like in 'the walls have ears'??" Doc nodded and left.

Chapter Eighteen

Quickly downing the brandy, Hawk stretched out on the attic-bed while sorting thru certain 'past assignments' in his career. He concluded---"Right now, I can't allow myself to think of Lizbeth as someone I love. She's nothing more than the 'subject' of a mission---someone I've heard of but never met---a political prisoner we have to rescue or she'll be executed soon. Her life depends upon us being one step ahead of the enemy, finding out his plan and all the while keep our involvement top secret." Realizing that possibly Bill and Salle might come to harm as well as Lizbeth, he sat up on the bedside---"Doc! Dammit! I tried to TELL you not to get Salle and Bill mixed up in this! Now look at the mess! Suppose McDougal really isn't going to use the gun for anything---just clean it up after storing it in the barn for awhile?" Then he swore---"'Stored' my hind leg!! That 'piece' was hidden and hidden very well! Besides WHY didn't he tell anyone he could walk? That alone raises my suspicions to a high alert!! He's slick---and cunning---mean as hell and won't be taken down easy! We got our work cut out for us---but I'm up to it, I know I can be tougher than a year of 'hard-time'---and I can beat him at his game--- whatever it is!"

His temper somewhat calmed by his experience and confidence, Hawk's trained mind now began to take over, coolly calculating the situation---viewing it from a distance. What he needed was proof. Some kind of proof that McDougal meant harm to Lizbeth. What did they have at this point? Her single testimony about years of abuse, a case of adultery, then more recently---his sister, an Indian, as a witness who 'thought' she knew what happened in another room---plus a man keeping a gun in his barn then taking it into his own house?! Hawk realized that none of this had a vague ring of real 'evidence' or 'proof'---there wasn't even an actual THREAT! Even if they proved McDougal could walk AND that he'd kept it from everyone else---so what? It'd take a hell of a lot more info---more than any of them had at this moment---worse yet it was information they had no way of acquiring!

"Oh God." Joseph stood and began to pace---"Am I out of line? No! I'm not out of line, the man is probably dangerous---like a time-bomb waiting to go off! I can 'feel' it in my bones---I 'know' it in my spirit. Lord, help me! You gave me 'the experience' I had last night---now please help me to do what You know will bring an acceptable end to this dark situation---and with no harm to Lizbeth, my family---or to Doc. The old meddler!"

112

Thoughts, ideas, pieces of past experiences---none of it seemed to fit his need. He was no longer a Ranger---he was a civilian living under civil law! But fortunately, he DID still have a few connections to comrades from 'other' days! Finally he came up with what he thought might be their best bet. With that fixed in his mind---he slipped down the stairs and over to Doc's office. By then the nurse and receptionist had gone home.

Doc motioned him to sit---"Did you come up with anything?" Hawk asked---"Did you call out there yet?" The older man nodded—"Yep. Seems everything's 'as usual'. I spoke both t'Lizbeth an' Salle---talked about th' weather, th' upcomin' holiday season---all kinds of 'sweet nothings'." "All right,"---Hawk replied---"I'm tossing this in as a possible beginning. When dark comes tonight, you and I will be in the woods behind McDougal's barn, we'll gain entrance thru the backdoor---that is IF the jeep and trucks are there, meaning everybody is home---AND McDougal won't be on the move! We'll check out not only the 'hiding place' that I saw---but we're going to search the other logs for places just like that one. It'll take a little time but could prove worth the effort. Besides, if we find that empty space hewn out with a cover on it---then we'll both know I'm not crazy! And if we find other guns---well, we'll go from there."

O'Barr rubbed his chin thoughtfully, asking---"What's th' 'from there'?" Hawk exhaled---"Then I'll do something I can't talk about---you just be my wheels and don't ask questions. Not that I don't trust you, understand---it's simply that you don't need to know if you're ever questioned about it! I'm almost certain, without a doubt, that no one will ever know---but, just in case." Hawk could see Doc's face take on an expression of apprehension--- "Joseph, you're not going to do anything you could go to

jail for---are you?" The Omaha/Sioux looked straight into
the eyes of the older man---"Right now, I don't know the
answer to that---but I CAN say I'm not going to hurt, maim
or kill anyone! Satisfied?" Taking off his glasses and
rubbing his eyelids, Doc nodded--- "Guess I have to be,
seein' I'm as deep into this as anybody else in this room!"
"Oh,"—Hawk stood to leave---"..and one last thing before I
head out to pick up some things---make certain the gas tank
on your truck is full. I don't want us giving out of fuel
tonight. Now, I'll be back before sundown and park close
to your back yard. Tell Mrs. Doc we're going to ride
around in the wilderness and listen to the wolves howl.
Don't mention any particular place or give any person's
name---you have to be vague, just in case!"

With that, Joseph Winterhawk exited the office. Doc could
hear him going downstairs with those measured, determined
steps---laying his head back on his chair, he whispered to
himself---"I think I'm way yonder too old for what this is
turning into!"

Chapter Nineteen

Parking the truck in some brush on the backside of a hill
facing McDougal's barn, Doc and Joseph exited, quietly
closing the doors. Joseph began changing clothes and
tossed a bag to the older man---"Here, get into these." They
dressed in dark pants and pullovers that looked something
like sweat clothes, finally adding insult to injury---Hawk
then pulled a dark knit cap down over Doc's white hair!
Chuckling at his reaction, Hawk stated—"Just be glad I
haven't painted your 'white-eyes-face' in camouflage
colors!"

After stashing their regular clothing inside the truck, Hawk handed Doc something else---"What's this?" "Just carry it---doesn't weigh much---it's a special light! While I'm certain McDougal can't see the barn from his front bedroom---I'd sure hate for Lizbeth, my own sister or Bill to see regular flash-lights in the barn and call in about intruders! Now, when we get in the barn, hold the light while I do the searching,"---he looked at Doc---"...you sure you're okay with this? If you're not—now's the time to be telling me!" "Oh yeah,"---Doc breathed with a bravado he didn't feel—"If you're ready---I'm ready---let's do it!"

Joseph put his hand on his mentor's shoulder and stopped him—"Listen carefully to what I'm about to tell you. Once we start across the meadow---we can't talk anymore. If you think you should tell me something---put your hand on me and I'll halt whatever I'm doing. If you see something, hear something---just touch me then point at the 'trouble-spot'. Got it?" "Yeah---I got it. Like I said---let's get this over with!" "One last thing.."---Hawk instructed---"...keep those gloves on, Doc! I don't want to have to stop and pull splinters out of your hands---besides---we can't afford to leave our prints or ruin any prints that were left on other possible guns!"

Traveling toward the target, they were hidden by the early dark---and except from a few feet away, not much could be seen. Joseph used no kind of light as he moved swiftly across the way! Doc hurried close behind and with each step, his back complained bitterly about the slightly bent position! Within ten minutes, they'd silently opened the back hall door to the barn and were inside. Hawk stood for several moments listening, waiting for his eyes to adjust. In a few minutes, he began moving along the wall, his fingers searching for the ladder---it was just where it'd been in his 'vision'! Guiding Doc up on the first rungs, he followed---that way just in case the older man made a mis-step, he could prevent him from falling---while he'd be useless if Doc was behind him!

But O'Barr was still pretty sure-footed, soon they were in the loft, both sliding around on stacks of baled hay. Doc held the odd light close on Hawk's hands as he searched and felt around for the log where he'd seen McDougal remove the gun. After some methodical searching, Hawk felt something---he put a hand on Doc and pointed to the spot! Both peered at the topside of the log and sure enough, Doc watched as Hawk slid a piece of wood---then his eyes almost literally bulged out of their sockets!! It was an empty hole! "Damnation!"---Doc expostulated in a whisper---"You were right, after all!" "Shhh!"—Hawk warned! It was at this point of discovery---proving Hawk's wild Indian adventure---that Doc began to lighten up a bit---maybe this covert-stuff wasn't so bad after all! Why he suddenly felt younger and more reckless than he had in years!

When Hawk finished searching each rafter, it was around nine p.m. and he'd found six cut-outs in all! Five of them held firearms, three of which were military issue semi-automatics---but obviously, McDougal still had the .38 in his possession.

Hawk descended the ladder first then assisted Doc on the last three rungs. In moments, the barn door was closed and they were traveling back toward the trees. Once back at the truck, Doc unlocked while conversing about their 'find' and Indian 'folklore' concerning 'skin-walkers' and 'shape-shifters'---however Hawk stopped him by speaking in a low voice---"All right. Now, I'm going back---there's something else I have to do." "How about me?"---Doc asked. Hawk put his hands on both Doc's shoulders---

"Listen up, I want you to go back to town---find the nearest
pay phone and in exactly one hour and fifteen minutes, call
Lizbeth's number. Let it ring several times or until she
answers it---or him, whoever. Don't say a word! Just hold
the line open---when they hang up, you hang up, drive back
here and park in this spot---I'll meet you when I'm
finished." Doc sputtered---"But...but.." "No buts,"---
Hawk cut in---"Just do it, Doctor-man! Then maybe we'll
know where we are!"

"What're you gonna do?"---Doc sounded worried---"You
promised you'd not---er, hurt anybody, remember?" Hawk
assured---"This won't physically hurt anybody AND if I
luck up---by the end of another day or two, we may have
proof of 'something'. I'm not exactly sure of 'what'---just
'something'." Joseph picked up the heavy items that filled
his full sized back-pack and promised---"I'll tell you about
it after it's over." Watching him disappear all alone, off
into the night---Doc whispered, "Be careful!"

Chapter Twenty

Reaching a clump of vines growing on a trellis located
beneath a window beside Salle and Bills' apartment, Hawk
laid the bag down to rest his shoulders---he sat for a
moment then gave a rare, specific bird-call. He could only
hope Salle remembered it! For fifteen minutes, he 'called'
with no results---all the while thinking---"Thank God
there're no dogs on the place or they'd be raising havoc by
now!" Just as he was giving up hope---he saw a curtain
move at one of the windows---he gave the call again---Salle
pushed the window up a little. He got to his knees, raised
his hands, moving them back and forth! "Salle!"---he did
his best to throw an almost inaudible voice at her! Then he
grabbed the vine and rattled what few dry leaves were left

on it and projected again---"Salle!" "Hawk? That you?!"---
she hissed. He repeated---"Let me in!" "What?"---she
snapped! "I said, let me in!"---he was losing patience, time
was wasting!

The window closed, he grabbed up his heavy bag, crouched,
then ran up the stairs taking two at a time! He could make
out Salle holding the door open for him---hurrying inside,
he saw Bill switch on the bedroom light! Pressing against
the wall, he looked to make sure her curtains facing the
house were closed.

"Good Lord, Hawk! What on earth are you DOIN'?!!
Why're you here? You got HAY all over you! What's in
that bag---a dead body?" Shaking his head---"Do be quiet,
Salle! Must you talk so loud---and so much?? I need a
great favor!" "Favor? You kill somebody---the law after
you?"---she demanded! "Dammit, Salle, I haven't killed
anybody and no, 'the law' isn't after me! Do you think you
can stop talking for a minute and listen to me?" "All right,
all right!"---her voice sounded exasperated---"But you
better TELL me what you're doin' here in the middle of the
night---settin' out there whistlin' like a stupid bird!!"
Hawk said quietly---"Kill the light, will you, Bill? I'm just
glad you remembered the bird-call, Sis,---and to coin an
over-used but recent personal phrase---'I'd been up a tree
without it'!"

He'd had Doc remove the bandage from his wound then
simply pulled a thick white cotton glove over it so the
injured hand would fit into another glove---now he was
grateful Salle couldn't see his injury and start asking MORE
questions! As he looked at her, he thought 'what a curious
cat' she'd always been! And like a member of the cat
family---if she had any idea what'd been going on with him

since the day he arrived home---she'd go ballistic and
they'd have to tranquilize her for certain!

Without telling her about his 'flying experience'---he
explained he'd 'come upon information' from a reliable
source that possibly guns were hidden in McDougal's barn--
-also that Mac was a Klansman 'whose past activities were
in question'. Expressing mild concern, he vaguely spoke
about 'being instructed' to tap the phone. "A tap on the
PHONE---what for! Why? Are WE in danger?!"---Salle
gulped---"Is Mrs. Mac in danger too!?"

"I can't answer your questions, Salle. Believe it or not,
sometimes it's better NOT to know too much! I need to set
up here then wind this little wire around your outside
power/phone post---going from in here to the pole where
I'll connect it to McDougal's phone line. Think you can
'act normal' and keep quiet about this for a few days---until
some important information gets on tape? The authorities
will be grateful---even though the 'info' may not be used in
court---it could lead to other things that CAN be!" Salle
looked at Bill---"What do you think, Bill?" Before he could
answer, she turned back to Hawk---"What if---if somebody
finds out---somebody like McDougal!?" "Now how can he
find out!"---Hawk chided---"He can't walk up your stairs,
can he? You seen him walking about lately?" Looking
sharply at Hawk, she snapped---"Well, don't be silly---
certainly I haven't seen him walkin'!"

"Wouldn't you like to see this creep in some hot water---
even doing some time, if he has ties to---er, maybe some
unsolved crimes?" "You're scaring me, Joseph! How can
Bill and I be sure McDougal won't find out about this---this
contraption you're wantin' to hook up on his phone? Don't
those things make beeping noises or something?" "Not this
one, Sis! It's a smaller version of what 'intelligence'

sources use---it's quiet as a cat watching a mouse---you can
depend on it." Looking up at both of them, he continued---
"Look, Bill---Salle. All you have to do is look the other
way---I'll hide the recording equipment in your closet---you
don't have to touch it---in fact, you must NOT touch it!
And since you never have visitors, no one could possibly
know it's here! Right?"

Bill agreed---"You're right, Hawk, nobody's visited us
since we moved in here. B'sides, Salle's been telling me all
along that McDougal's---well, he's a few sticks short a cord
of wood! You go ahead, do whatever you have to! I've got
a brand new lock, I'll put it on our door first thing in the
morning---then nobody can come in." "Thanks, Bill."---
Hawk nodded gratefully---"Salle, I promise I'll have this
'contraption' out of here as soon as the right information
comes in!" "And how'll you know, brother of mine?"
"Because I'm coming over each night after dark, pick up
that day's reel of tape---and set another in. The device
comes on automatically whenever there's any in-coming or
out-going calls---so don't worry---that's a very long tape---
it won't run out."

Hawk set to work and soon the inside system was ready
then taking a length of wire, he fed it outside beneath a
window. Now for the dangerous part. Earlier, he'd put
every tool needed onto a lineman's belt that he now quickly
fastened around him. Then slinging a pair of lineman
spikes over his shoulder and carrying a roll of wire plus one
roll of clear utility tape, he eased out into the night.

Salle watched thru a crack in the curtain as the shadowy
figure of her brother fastened on his spikes, picked up the
loose wire from the apartment window---then deftly
climbed the power pole. Nearing the top, he pulled gently
on the loose wire until it was taut enough, giving it the

appearance of 'one of the apartment electric wires' leading out to the power pole. Taking great caution not to touch the power wires, he set about splicing into the telephone wire that ran to McDougal's house.

"How can he see out there as dark as it is, Bill?"---Salle pondered as he stood watching over her shoulder. "If I were you, Hon, I wouldn't worry about that---your brother is part human and part something else---that 'something else' sees at night! A true Indian! But just in case, I think I should go out on the landing and watch the house---I'm sure everyone's in bed but I'd feel better if I kept a watch out for Hawk." Salle held his hand for a moment then nodded at him---and whispered---"Go! Go!"

Joseph's right hand worked quickly and expertly while his left hand sort of 'held things in place'---before long, he had everything completed. It should work---"God,"—he whispered softly---"I'm depending on You! You and all of heaven, 'Pray for me, O Holy Mother of God, that I may be worthy of the promises of Christ.' Right now, I need time--please send Your best warrior, 'Big Michael', to be on MY side!"

Back down the pole, he took off the spikes and joined Bill on the porch---quickly they entered the apartment. Looking at the two, Hawk sensed that Salle seemed more upset and tried to assure her---"Don't worry, Sis. It would've been simpler had there been an extension phone here in your apartment, but it's done now---and it may save Li---er, Mrs. McDougal's life. There're things I can't go into right now---I just don't have time---but one day, I promise, I'll tell you the whole story."

Looking at his watch, he said---"In a little while, someone is going to make a call to the house over there---I don't know

if anyone will wake up and answer or not---but if you'll
watch over my shoulder---you can see how this works!"
Joseph sat down next to the recorder and waited---Salle and
Bill hovered close by, their eyes peeled on the machine.

Ten minutes later, the machine clicked on and began to
record. Forty-five seconds later, it stopped. Joseph put on a
head set, rewound the tape and listened---smiling, he
removed the earpieces, placed them over Salle's ears and
replayed it for her. "Crazy Horse!"---she whispered
loudly—"I can hear the phone ringing, Hawk! Bill! It
works!!"---she could barely keep her voice down!
"Shhhh!"---Hawk cautioned---"...keep listening!" Salle
heard McDougal pick up the phone and say---"Hello."---no
one answered---he repeated "HELLO!"---still no answer.
After a moment, McDougal shouted---"GO TO HELL,
YOU $#%^&**@!S.O.B.!" and slammed the receiver
down! Salle stifled her laughter---"You may be my brother,
but you're smarter'n Solomon! I never believed it'd do
what you said!" Hawk grinned at her---"When you gonna
learn to trust big brother? Huh?"

Moving a good-sized stack of woven rugs and blankets in
front of the recorder, Hawk started for the front door---
suddenly Salle stepped over and put her arms around her
brother---"Take care of yourself, you big Indian!" He
stepped away, squeezed her arms then crept off into the
night---and he hoped---with no one the wiser!

Driving back into town, Doc decided to ask the million
dollar question---"You don't think McDougal will---uh,
bother Lizbeth t'night, do you?" Thru the windshield,
Hawk watched the highway rush beneath the truck lights---
"I can't allow myself to think about that, Doc. Dear
God...,"---he sighed---"...I never thought I'd be hunting the
enemy in our own community! This is different---and

judicially, it's another ballgame altogether." He turned to Doc---"All I know is, with this 'enemy'---we have to figure out his battle-plan ahead of time and before he moves, we gotta be there waiting!"

Chapter Twenty One

The next morning Salle was already in the kitchen when Lizbeth came in for coffee. "Good morning, Salle! Ah see you already got those curtains down!"---she smiled---"You pass a good night?" "Oh, yes."—Salle entoned, remembering Hawk's disturbing nocturnal visit---"Nothin' like a good uninterrupted night's sleep! And yourself?" "Ah got a few hours worth. But you know,"---Lizbeth's tired, drawn face had a puzzled look---"Foah weeks now, Ah've had th' feeling that---well, either Ah'm losin' mah mind or---somethin's strange is goin' on---an' Ah don't undahstand any of it, a'tall!"

"What you mean, Ma'am? What kinda 'strange'?" Her employer shrugged slightly---"Little things---small stuff---items bein' out of place---not as Ah left them. An' you remembah me askin' if you dropped anything while cleanin' th' desk!" Salle nodded but said nothing. "Seems I keep hearin' noises Ah didn't use t'hear." "Noises?! When, Ma'am?"---nervously Salle occupied herself by pouring Lizbeth some coffee then topped off her own cup.

"Mostly at night. But th' first time Ah really felt uneasy was th' night when Ah thought something came crashin' down on th' floah then when Ah looked around---theah was nothing. Only Mac's door was closed---an' it was open when Ah went t'bed---so th' noise must've been th' wind blowin' it shut! Then theah are moments when Ah feel

someone's either IN mah room or BEEN in it. You evah
feel that way, Salle?"

Relieved, Salle nodded then replied---"You could say I have
my 'nervous' moments." And knowing the purpose of
Hawk's visit, she wondered if something bad REALLY was
going on here in this house or around the place! Salle
wanted to ask Lizbeth if the things just mentioned were the
reason she'd taken to bolting her bedroom door at night.
Twice during the past few weeks, Lizbeth had slept a few
minutes late in the morning and Salle had gone back to call
her---instead of the door being open as usual---it'd been
bolted!

Lizbeth sipped her coffee while putting together
McDougal's breakfast tray. "You think Ah'm goin' crazy,
Salle?" "My lord, Miss Lizbeth---NO!" "Since all these
silly things began, Ah've given serious thought t'buyin'
m'self a gun. But when Ah mentioned m'idea t'Mac---well,
you'd thought Ah'd asked t'burn down th' house! Says he
doesn't want a gun in th' house, can you beat that!? Hasn't
been THAT long ago when he used t'talk about guns a lot---
an' thought everybody needed at least two or three---an'
why he's changed his mind about that, Ah'll nevah know!"
Lizbeth shrugged then glanced at Salle---"You an' Bill keep
a gun foah protection?" Salle shook her head---"No,
Ma'am." "Well, Ah plan t'find that shotgun---an' buy some
bird-shot! May not kill anybody---but th' sound of it would
certainly scare an intrudah away!"

Immediately, Salle's mind pounced on what Hawk said
about guns hidden here on McDougal's place----guns that'd
possibly been used in crimes. Silently, Salle asked herself--
-"Wonder why old Mac is suddenly against havin' a gun in
the house---'specially one for his wife!? Maybe when
Hawk comes around tonight, I'll just tell him everything

she's just told me---and about 'white-eyes's sudden
aversion to guns. You never know when a little piece of
information can make a world of difference---especially
with that stuff Hawk told us last night! I wish I could tell
Miss Lizbeth---guess I better not though. Hawk'd kill me!"

Completing Mac's tray, Lizbeth paused before carrying it to
him---a thoughtful expression came over her face as she
looked at Salle, murmuring—"Addin' on to night-time
mysteries, Salle, last night Ah heard th' strangest bird-call.
Least Ah figured it was a bird---Ah've nevah heard anythin'
like it befoah!" "Did it scare you, Miss Lizbeth?"---Salle
looked closely at her. Confidently shaking her head,
Lizbeth's face took on that mellow, 'glazed-over'
appearance ---"Oh no, oddly enough, it didn't. Poah thing
sounded lonely---like it'd lost it's mate an' was callin',
tryin' t'find it. Anyway, a little while aftah that, I dozed
off." With that Lizbeth exited the room.

Salle caught her breath---"That brother of mine! Hasn't
even been 12 hours yet---and already him and his 'covert
activities' are bein' talked about! What if she'd decided
t'come out LOOKIN' for that 'poah lonely bird'---and
found HIM up the electric pole tappin' this bloomin'
phone?! Would WE be in a bottomless pit of trouble!"
With anger tingeing her anxiety, she snorted—"I'm gonna
KILL him! When he shows up, I'm gonna kill him!"

In Mac's bedroom, Lizbeth placed the breakfast tray over
his lap, poured his coffee then asked---"You have a good
night?" "No different than usual,"---he snapped---"..why do
you ask? You hearing things again?" "No, just inquirin' as
t' yoah well-bein', that's all." She bent and began picking
up his deliberately scattered handwritten notes and books
that lay all about.

125

Carefully watching for her reaction, he asked---"Did you
hear the phone ringing last night?" Her arms filled with his
'literature', she replied in a disinterested tone---"No. Who
was it? No bad news from home, I hope." Angered
because her face exhibited no emotion, he blazed---"Some
idiot with a wrong number---or one of those 'heavy
breathers'! Nobody said anything but I knew the line was
open and somebody WAS there!" Then with a sneer, he
went on---"Was it your boyfriend, Lizzie? Did he expect
you to answer but I surprised him instead?" Wearily,
Lizbeth exhaled, finally replying---"What a truly asinine
thing t'say, Mac. If Ah HAD a boyfriend, would he be
callin' HEAH! An' you with an extension at hand! B'sides
just when would Ah have time t'take up with another man?"

"Now, Lizzie!" He was enjoying his verbal taunting---just
daring her to mention Rita---"There's always time to 'take
up with' another man! A woman can always find a few
stolen minutes away from her poor husband. Hell, for all I
know, you might be sneaking out of your bedroom window
to meet some piece of buzzard-puke right here on my own
land!" "Ah'll be back foah th' tray soon, Mac." "You
forgot again, Lizbeth! My fresh water?"---his voice rose---
"Would you kindly drag-ass in there and get me a pitcher of
decent water? Every morning, noon and night I have to
remind you---DAMMIT!"

She brought fresh water and had almost made an escape
when he called her---"I got something I need you and that
redskin to do for me this morning!" Slowly turning toward
the 'invalid', Lizbeth clenched her fists behind her back
then answered---"Mac. We've already planned a whole
day's work! It might rain tomorrow." Abruptly, he moved-
--almost toppling his tray onto the bed---"I don't give a
considerable 'damn' whether it rains tomorrow or not!
Didn't you HEAR me, woman? I SAID I need things from

town---and you two are gonna take your useless rear-ends there to GET them! Clear enough?"

Knowing it'd become futile to communicate normally with him as of late, Lizbeth said---"Whatever y'need, just make a list. Ah'll be back when we get th' kitchen cleaned up from breakfast---th' stores should be open by then." "Now, ain't that my good girl!"---his harsh laugh grated---"You see how well we get along when you're agreeable?"

Upon Lizbeth's return to the kitchen, Salle took one look at her employer's expression then stated---"On it again, I hear." Lizbeth nodded and replied---"Salle, he's foamin' at th' mouth foah you an' me t'go into town with his list of things. Ah know you already got th' curtains down but just forget them,"—wearily, she waved a hand---"...an' forget th' windows. We'll do all this anothah time---or nevah do it." She exhaled then continued---"Y'know, Salle, things were a lot quietah when he drugged himself into a stupor an' slept between fits of rage. Now-a-day, it appeahs he stays awake just thinkin' of ways t'make trouble." An odd look came over her face, she looked at Salle---"Y'know, he acts almost th' same as he did befoah he had this accident--- th' very same way. His system must've adjusted t'all those drugs he insists upon havin'---now he needs somethin' stronger." Her stare intensified---"Odd thing is he doesn't complain about pain th'way he used to, it's as tho he doesn't HAVE pain anymoah! You think that's unusual!?" "I never knew him before his accident, Ma'am---and I've only been in his room a few times with you when we do special cleanin'. Don't think he even wants me in his sight." Holding Lizbeth's gaze, she suddenly asked---"...do you know why he hates 'Indians'?"

Lizbeth sighed and touched Salle's arm---"Oh, m'dear. It's not just you---or Bill---or 'Indians'---maybe one day we can

127

discuss it. Y'know, human beings can carry around just 'so much' inside themselves---then we have t'dump some of it or go nuts! An' I feel mah 'dumping-time' is near. One day soon---you an' I will have a long talk---about a lot of things."

Considering the curtains lying in a heap waiting to be laundered, Lizbeth snapped---"Let's just finish th' breakfast things, get his precious list then---go t'town!" Taking a deep breath, she gave her friend and helper a little smile--- "Sorry. Didn't mean t'go off th' deep end there. Look, hon, if you want t'change into somethin' else or pretty-up a bit, just go an' do it. Also if you an' Bill need anythin'--- make yourself a list---oh, an' write down some 12 guage bird-shot! Meanwhile, Ah'll finish up heah." She turned away, began wiping down the counter while muttering--- "It's been a long while since Ah cared very much about HOW Ah look---heah, in town or anyplace else."

Chapter Twenty Two

After the women drove away with his list, Mac once again kept vigil at his bedroom window where he could see the end of the driveway. As he waited---he rehearsed the game plan. Everything depended on him---he held power over her life---how long it would last and when it would end! It'd been a long time since last spring and now after secretly becoming 'mobile' again---his whole being strained, lusting for freedom that awaited him! Why, he'd be totally unencumbered! Single again---but THIS time he'd be a man of means---owning a house, ranch, cattle with enough money to get by for quite awhile---counting the life insurance policy he had on her! Initially, he'd wanted half a million but after more careful consideration, had decided against it. He musn't be greedy---such a sum might possibly arouse future suspicion---after his poor wife became a 'fatal stastistic'. "Even in today's world,"—he muttered---"I must admit $250,000 is nothing to sneeze at!"

He thought, ducks are in a row---things look pretty safe and this crap of sneaking around is getting the best of me! And do I ever need to be out into the world again! "Boy?"---he grinned at himself in his bathroom mirror while leisurely combing his hair, turning his head this way and that---"You got yourself some living to do!!"

Pleased at last with his grooming, he went to check out the latest mail from the past two days. It had been that long since he'd had a chance to roam about the house freely. The male redskin was still here but he never came near the house except at mealtime---and when the women were away, he wouldn't even come into the yard. No one would see him wandering freely about the house---besides, he was quite agile now and could move fast if he had to!

Again he searched the desk, the mail---even going into Lizbeth's bedroom again---still nothing! There HAD to be another hiding place! As yet, he'd not been able to check out the barn---he'd only hurriedly taken that one chance of being seen---the day he picked up the .38! Laughing aloud, he recalled the fool hawk that had tried to sail into him--- how the feathers flew when his shot found it's mark on the dumb-ass bird! Mac stopped for a moment, his expression had a questioning look to it as he considered---"But the bastard never did fall! I should've put two more pieces of lead into him---but then there was the possibility somebody might drive up while I was on the porch!"

Meandering into the kitchen, his eyes glided about for anything that 'appeared' interesting! "What I'd REALLY like to do is go into that apartment!" Then he remembered--

-"But that ranch-hand is around here someplace, he might see! So at first opportunity---I'll send all three of them off---then go up there and have myself a nice leisurely look-see---might find some fascinating info! Not to mention, I can see first hand what these people keep lying around in their houses!"

Looking down at his watch, he saw it was time for Rita's break---pulling a chair over near the wall, he sat down and began dialing on the kitchen wall phone. This time he was going to tell her he'd be seeing her, real soon---and when he did---'things' would be changed considerably, no more Mrs. McDougal! He'd feed her just enough to further rouse her already fired-up curiosity! Afterwards he'd call his father---he needed to touch base and find out all the Klan news since they'd last spoken. Going out to the barn for the gun had reminded him of some unanswered questions he still had about that business back in Omaha two years ago.

***

When Salle and Lizbeth left for town, instead of going to repair the catch-pen where one of the larger steers had loosened some boards, Bill began changing the lock on their apartment door. "Old son,"---he said to himself, "...try to be quiet as possible---don't want the white-eyes lying down there in his bed thinking I'm not 'working'---God forbid!" A shudder passed over him as he worked---"We'd leave tomorrow if I had a job elsewhere! Dam' straight about that! 'Course it'd probably be hell prying Salle away from Mrs. Mac---she's determined to 'look after' the woman!"

Looking around his small work area, Bill sighed with aggravation. Before beginning his job of installing the new lock this morning, he'd sat on the sofa checking all hardware included in the lock-packet---and now realized

130

he'd left two screws lying on a lamp table near the window. Standing to his feet, he stalked across the room to pick them up.

He never knew why he glanced down at the house and toward that kitchen window---maybe because from early on he'd formed a habit of sometimes waving at Salle when she'd be working at the sink. She'd grin back at him then make a face. But now it wasn't Salle that he saw! Salle was in town with Lizbeth---he'd seen them drive off in the jeep! His heart raced---someone was moving around in the kitchen---his breath caught in his throat! "Oh God!"---his first thought---"Don't let it be Hawk with his 'secret-agent-man' stuff! Hell!" Then he considered---"Hawk's not THAT stupid---he KNOWS better than to go in McDougal's house!" Flattening himself against the wall, Bill then stole another look but this time, he peered between the curtain and the wall! His next immediate thought was--- "Maybe it's Dr. O'Barr!" Weak with relief, he took another look to survey the drive and the yard---but there was no sign of O'Barr's old truck! Bill's heart beat even harder!

It was during his third 'look-see' out the apartment window before he realized the kitchen curtains over at the house had been taken down---and from his vantage point he could see across the kitchen! Suddenly, Bill's stomach dropped to the soles of his boots---there was McDougal---sitting in a kitchen chair talking on the phone! His eyes glued upon the incredible sight, Bill watched transfixed as McDougal got up from the chair, walked toward the naked window, stood looking out for a couple of minutes then turned his back and leaned against the sink! All the while talking on the phone and dragging it's long cord with him!

A slight nausea briefly rose up inside Bill---then sweat broke out over his body as he realized that Hawk may be

131

right! "Dear GOD! Who and what kind of man IS this?"
In that moment he remembered the recording device here in
their bedroom closet!! Wiping a shaky hand across his
damp brow, Bill realized McDougal could come up here---
at any time! The lock---he had to finish it immediately!
The very thought of that man climbing the apartment stairs,
coming in and finding Hawk's phone tap made Bill's hands
tremble so that he could barely get the wood screws started
in his newly tapped holes!

Finally his slippery, shaking hands finished the lock but
now he was afraid to leave the apartment. What should he
do!?? Even with a new lock, he couldn't leave---not taking
a chance that while he was working out of sight McDougal
might try to get in! One good strong kick would break the
door in half---it wasn't solid and it wasn't metal! Fear rose
up inside him as he realized no regular door could keep out
a man like McDougal---not if he made up his mind he
wanted to come in! Then he'd discover 'the machine'!!

One thing for sure, he had to stay in the apartment---at least
until the women returned! While waiting, he tried to think
calmly about what he'd seen. It was obvious no one knew
McDougal could walk!! Why Mrs. Mac would've surely
shared such an event with Salle! Not to mention O'Barr
would've been out here---then 'talked' when he got back to
town---people would know! Hawk would know! It'd be all
over the community!

The phone tap!! "Oh, man! Whoever he's been talking
with---it's all on that tape!" Looking furtively around, Bill
tried to think---"And I have absolutely no way of getting a
message to Hawk!! I can't use McDougal's phones---Salle
told me he has an extension beside his bed! And before I
can use the truck or jeep---I have to ask his permission---
plus have a damn good reason for asking!" Going back to

the window, Bill peered cautiously toward the house---but McDougal was out of sight, no longer visible.

He'd have to tell Salle---maybe together they'd come up with an excuse to drive into town! She'd know what to do because she knew the McDougals' better than he! Hawk couldn't come to retrieve his tape until dark---but soon as he arrived, he'd be told the truth about the 'invalid'! And Mrs. Mac needed to know as well!! "How in hell do you tell a woman her husband's been woo-hooing her, for Lord-knows-how-long, about being unable to leave his bed!!? How'll she take it?" He knew how Salle would take it, she'd pick up a shotgun and make a bloody pile of hamburger out of him---a woman like his mother-in-law would be hurt but she'd accept it---but a lady like Mrs. Mac? He just didn't know how she'd react---but Salle would know! "Yeah."---he thought attempting to comfort himself---"Salle will know exactly what's to be done!"

Thoroughly shaken, Bill went to lie down on the bed, then just as quickly realized he should be watching the house--- what if McDougal thought he, Bill, was in the woods or off repairing fences and decided to 'come and visit'!! Should he go over, bang on 'white-eyes' window---call out saying he felt sick and needed to call the doctor?? No, not good enough. He had no idea how long this 'walking' business had been going on and the only reason he had to sweat it out at this time was because of the phone tap! That 'secret' in their bedroom closet meant he must remain in the apartment and pray McDougal never took it into his perverted white-supremacist brain to come up the stairs before the women returned! "If he does,"---Bill determined—"I swear to God I'll hide behind the front door, knock him out, drag him downstairs and out to the back yard---then just leave him there for somebody else to find!"

Chapter Twenty Three

When the two women drove up, Bill called out to Salle from the apartment landing. Looking up at him with her arms full of grocery bags, she responded---"What you doin' home, Billy-Bob?! You got nothin' better to do than bother me?" "Salle, honey, I'm not feeling s'good--,"—he complained---"..maybe I ate something for breakfast that disagreed with me. Can you come up and fix me one of your mother's brews? Maybe it'll settle my stomach." Salle sighed to Lizbeth---"Lord. He's never sick! I hope he's not comin' down with a flu-bug or worse!! Let me help you carry these bags inside then I'd better go see about him!" "No, no, Ah'll carry them in, you go see 'bout him!"---Lizbeth reached, taking the bags from Salle---"An' if you think he's really feelin' bad---we'll call Doc t'come check him. Take your time, no rush. Ah can start lunch!"

Several minutes into Bill's story, Salle simply collapsed onto the sofa and for the first time during their marriage, was rendered speechless! He looked at his now silent wife ---"Hon? You okay?" Beneath her bronze skin, she looked positively ashen. Taking her hands in his and rubbing the limp wrists, he tried again---"Salle, baby---say something! Anything! Never saw you without words---not since I met you!"

Finally she blinked a couple of times and whispered--- "William Redwolf!! You better NOT be foolin' with me! Please tell me you're jokin'!" Swallowing at the tightness in his throat, he said---"I just wish it WAS a damned joke, Salle! I swear to you I saw him---big as life---talking on the kitchen telephone, just strolling around all over the place--- leaning at the sink, sitting on that chair! It shocked me so bad I almost got sick! When I finally realized I wasn't seeing things, the very first thing I remembered was that phone tap and---it scared me witless! We gotta TELL somebody, girl! We can't just let this go---it may be the undoing of all of us, including Mrs Mac!"

Salle bit at her upper lip--- "You've had longer to think about it than me!!" Quietly, he sighed, telling her the only thing he could come up with was to make up some story to get him off the place—then go find Hawk. After a few moments, she replied---"Gettin' away---that's it! Help me think up some 'fabrication'---I hate to do it but---." "Hon,"---he broke in to assure her—"...it may be a 'lie' but I think at this present time, a VERY 'needful' lie."

Suddenly, her face brightened---" I know what to do! After an early lunch you say you have to repair a broken fence across the road---you leave, follow the fence out of sight then keep going to Fargo's place! McDougal hates Fargo and he'd never call over there in a million years! When you get there, just tell him the truck needs a 'part' and the jeep's in use! Ask if you can borrow one of their trucks to go in town! Drive straight to Mama's---if you can't find Joseph---go to the store and call Doc! Tell him he absolutely MUST send my brother out here—or come himself! While I'm workin' this afternoon, I'll watch the driveway and when one of them arrives, I'll amble out to say 'hello'---and relay what you just told me!" Nodding, Bill listened carefully then spoke---"All right. No holes in that story big enough to fall into---I'll do it the minute I eat!" He looked at her--- "You gonna tell Mrs. Mac?"

Still in a quandary, Salle slowly shook her head back and forth. "She's not been herself for sometime now, Bill, gets worse by the day---no tellin' what such news might do to her. Uh, maybe....I got it! If Doc shows, I'll get him to take her out for a walk---HE can tell her! That way if she has a spell of some sort, he can take care of her! How does that sound?" Bill nodded---"For the moment, about the best we can do, I guess." He gave her a quick kiss---"Hurry on back and get lunch ready, call me from the back porch when it's ready. I'll lock up with the new key then slip it to you later."

Through the window Bill watched as Salle hurried to McDougal's back porch and disappeared into the kitchen. After pulling on hiking boots, he lay a jacket across his knees, put on his hat and sat waiting. On the floor beside him set the canvas shoulder bag filled with nails, staples and a hammer---he was ready to go for help!

After assuring Lizbeth he felt 'fine', he ate a bit of lunch then slipped the new key to Salle as he said 'good-bye'--- finally he was off to 'repair broken wires around the west-pasture'. Hiking quickly across the meadow toward the hills, he prayed fervently that the tape on the recorder would reveal everything Hawk needed to know and that the dratted machine could be removed as soon as possible! Bill knew he'd not draw another peaceful breath until that thing was long gone!

Once out of sight, Bill hid the canvas bag behind some rocks and hurried on---in a few minutes he spied Fargo standing beside his equipment shed. Bill hailed him from the woods' path then after a few words of greeting, Bill proceeded to spin his tale of needing a truck part. "Well, jes' feel free t'take any truck y'like, William!" "The old pick-up'll do fine, Fargo---I just need to get there and back soon as I can. To tell the truth, I hated to run over here, bothering you---knowing how McDougal treats you---but I'm in a sorta bind! And the less I have to say to that man, the better I like it."

Fargo spat tobacco juice, laughed and replied---"Don't
worry none 'bout old Mac, he hates everybody 'round
chere! Tain't jest me! Strange bird, don'cha think so?"---
Fargo scratched his unshaven jaw as he continued---"I was
real surpised t'hear you an' Salle had moved in over there!"
"Well,"---Bill shrugged---"...having no paycheck gets you
hungry real fast! Besides, I try to stay out of McDougal's
way. Do me a favor?"---he looked at Fargo---"Don't ever
tell him I came over here to borrow anything! I'd get fired
for sure." Successfully aiming another stream of tobacco
juice at a cow-patty, Fargo laughed and tossed Bill a set of
keys---"Yer secret's safe with me, boy!" "Thanks! See you
later!"---Bill grinned then headed toward the older truck and
grinding her to life, he was soon bouncing and clanking off
down the road toward the highway.

***

Braking to a stop in Mary's yard, the dust cloud caught up
with him as he slammed the truck door and hurried toward
the house. He didn't see Hawk's 4-wheel drive but
fervently prayed it was parked out back! After several
knocks on the door and receiving no reply, Bill ran toward
the back of the house---but no one was home! Soon he was
back in the truck, heading toward the store.

Only a few men were standing about when Bill fed a coin
into the outside pay phone and got Doc's receptionist.
"Ma'am, this is Bill---Captain Winterhawk's brother-in-
law. By chance, would he be visiting with Doc?" "Why,
no. The doctor's out on afternoon calls then said he might
do a bit of fishing. Can I be of help?" "Hope so, is there
any way you can get up with him?" "I can use the radio.
You folks have an emergency?" "Well. Not exactly but if
you could just get on the radio and tell Dr. O'Barr to stop by
the McDougal home as soon as he can!" "And you say

137

there's NO emergency??"---she harped. "Doc's services are needed---I'm only a ranch hand, don't know much about it---but I believe he's expecting a call! Tell him to come soon!" "All right. But if you'd just tell me the trouble, I could pass it along to the doctor!" "Ma'am, I don't know the boss's business, just doing what I was told!" "Oh, very well. I'll see if I can find him!" "Yes, Ma'am." Bill hung up the phone. "Now, WHAT! Reckon I should go back and leave a note for Hawk at Mary's house---just in case Doc can't be raised on his radio!"

By the time Fargo's old truck neared Mary's house, Bill could see her unlocking her front door. "But, what'll I say?!"---Bill wondered while driving on past her house---"I can't upset her! There's nothing she can do anything about any of this and if I told her—she might come all undone! Sure as hades can't tell her Hawk put a tap on the McDougal phone---just knowing her son had done something like that to a white man's telephone would give her a running-fit!" Then it came to him---reaching into his shirt pocket, he took out the small notebook he kept for noting the dates that each cow was bred---and if she 'took' or not. He borrowed a stubby, dirty pencil lying there in the truck and wrote---"Hawk. The bird from last night must sing again tonight! PRONTO! Bill." Tearing out the note, he folded it, replaced the pencil then pocketed his cow-record book and started to Mary's door.

Lastly, after buying enough gas to replace the amount he'd used, Bill drove back to Fargo's and parked near the corn silo. After thanking him for the vehicle and telling him that the part had to be ordered, Bill hurried back down the woods path toward McDougal land and the fence. "Now,"—he thought---"I guess we wait. Please, Doc! Be there!!! And answer your radio!"

Chapter Twenty Four

Around 4:00 p.m., Doc's truck turned into McDougal's driveway---then speeded up the drive. Finally spying the truck, Salle snapped to herself---"High time, I must say!!" Turning off the stove, she went out the back door and around to the side of the house. Doc stopped close by, Salle glanced back toward the house then hurried toward the truck. As usual, even in the cool air, his window was down---looking at her, he asked---"What's up, Salle? My nurse radio'd me sayin' Bill left a message that I should come over here this afternoon. Uhh,"---he looked at her sideways---"...nothing bad wrong, I hope." Salle's face wore an anxious expression as she replied in a low voice---"Doc. I don't know any way to tell you this but to spill it right out. So get yourself out of the truck while I start rollin' this wheelbarrow---you and I are goin' out to the wood shed. We'll talk on the way---and you'll never believe what I'm about to tell you!"

As he walked along beside her, Doc prodded---"Well!?? What is it I'm 'never gonna believe'? You savin' it till Christmas or somethin'?" Looking at him in exasperation, she hissed---"I have to be far enough away from the house---I can't go tellin' you somethin' like this 'til I'm certain nobody can hear but you!" Several feet further, she said---"Doc. McDougal can walk!" He stopped dead in his tracks---hearing it from Hawk was one thing---but hearing it from Salle was another! He gasped---"What!!?" Salle kept walking pushing the wheelbarrow forward---he hurried to fall back in step with her! "WHAT'd you just say t'me!!" Salle never hesitated---"I SAID, McDougal is walking!! Bill saw him this morning!" By then they'd reached the shed, Salle pushed the wheelbarrow inside then straightened up, hands on hips! Doc stood frozen in the doorway gaping at her! "Whatsa matter?"---she asked---"After all these years, the cat finally got your tongue?"

At last, Doc sputtered. "Woman! When and where did Bill SEE this---this miracle?" "From our apartment window---after old 'white-eyes' had sent Mrs. Mac and me off to town on another of his wild-goose chases! Y'see, sometime back, several times a week he started this wild-hair-idea of wantin' stuff from town---maybe even sendin' all three of us off. Now, I think I know why!" Still staring at her like she'd lost her mind, Doc sputtered---"Why? I mean, do you think he sends everybody away so he can walk in secret?!" Making an impatient gesture, she snorted—"Exactly! Walk around---AND rifle the house!" "Rifle the house?"---Doc repeated. "Yes, you know,"—she stared at the older man "...like 'plunder' the premises?" Doc stammered--- "I---I guess I don't understand why he'd---'rifle' the house---you think he's lookin' for somethin'?"

"I have NO idea WHAT, Dr. O'Barr---but he IS lookin' for something! Miss Lizbeth began noticin' things bein'..." she shrugged---"...misplaced, out of order, shuffled about. She'd ask me if I'd moved certain things when I was cleanin'---or if I'd dropped 'em. I'd say 'no' and ask 'why'---then she'd comment that she'd left 'thus and so' in a certain way and it wasn't 'that way' no more! One time she told me she'd heard a crash that woke her up in th' middle of th' night---she got out of bed, found nothin' broken, the front door locked---and nobody robbin' them. BUT his door, which was left open when she went to bed, was closed! She added that 'it must've been th' wind'! Then she said she'd lain awake wonderin' about buyin' herself a gun! In town this morning, she bought some kinda 'bird-shot' for a shot-gun her husband had misplaced---which she finally found this afternoon! Doc?"---Salle looked at him, her eyes wary—"...she's taken to boltin' her

bedroom door at night---the woman's SCARED! Now
HE'S walkin'!"

By this time Doc had begun filling the wheelbarrow with
wood---"Well, one thing for sure---she can't hurt him much
with bird-shot!! Salle,"---he looked over at her---"...have
you told her that he can walk?" With a sharp sigh, she sat
down on a large piece of unsplit wood---"No! And I'm sure
she'd have told me if she knew! Miss Lizbeth wouldn't
keep nothin' like that from me!" Salle shook her head---
"What is he up to? I thought---'what harm can he do her
from his bed?'. Now he's on his feet, Doc!! I have no idea
how long he's been 'walking'---and if he cursed her,
carryin' on such a way when he was crippled, why---what'll
he do to her now?"

The wheelbarrow was full. Dr. O'Barr could do nothing but
think about Joseph's 'flying experience' and last night's
visit out here to the barn where they'd found all those guns-
--less the missing one---the one Joseph 'saw' McDougal
take then use to shoot at 'the hawk'! Salle's voice broke
into his thoughts---"Doc? Could you take her for a walk on
some pretext or other---and tell her? Somebody has to and
I'd rather it be you! You know it wouldn't be right to keep
this from her---not with things bein' the way they are
between her and that fool man!! That's why Bill slipped up
to Fargo's, borrowed a truck and went into town---we knew
we had to tell you or Hawk!" She went toward the
wheelbarrow---"And Hawk wasn't around, so Bill called
you. He also left a note with Mama for my brother---Doc,
please go find him for me! Tell him that I said to get out
here tonight---on the double!! It's a matter---of importance.
Maybe life or death."

Pushing the load of wood, Salle said—"I'll get supper
goin'. This man won't get out of bed while I'm in the

house, so why don't you go inside and t'make things 'look right', you pay him a regular visit THEN take her for a walk. You can pretend you want to see Maggie---that silly horse---then tell her the news out at the barn! If she faints or something---she'll be out of sight and you can help her!" He nodded---"You're right, she has t'know! I'll tell her." Stepping toward his truck, he took out his medical bag.

A few feet from the back steps---Doc paused, whispering--- "Salle, there're things you may or may not know about McDougal. And th' way it looks, things around here are quickly comin' to a head.! Hawk and I are counting on you and Bill t'keep a close watch on Lizbeth! If you notice anything—no matter how small---you call me! Even if you have t'send Lizbeth into his room t'keep him from picking up th' extension---you call an' let me know! After I talk t'her this afternoon, she'll be onto his 'little secret'---and I'm certain she'll go along with us!" He looked at the Indian woman---"It's possible all hell could break loose before long---you ready for that?" Thinking of the wire-tap Salle wondered if Doc knew just HOW much hell could break loose, then she nodded and went inside.

Lizbeth was glad to see Doc but her appearance was far from what it should be. Her normally shiny hair now looked unkempt, slightly tangled---her complexion paler than usual but those dull, hollow eyes bothered him most. Looking carefully at her, he asked quietly---"That burn about well?" She held her hand out for him to see---her smile and nod appeared 'forced'---at least for Lizbeth. "An' how's your 'mister' these days?"---he asked---"I haven't been by in awhile---things been all right with him?" "Reckon he's 'bout th' same, Doc."---she replied without emotion then slid down into a chair and slumped---as though too weary to sit properly. He decided she definitely wasn't herself.

"Tell you what,"---he said---"I'll go back an' have a short visit with him---you stay in here with Salle. Afterward, I want t'have a look at your filly----th' other day, I ran into a fellow up in th' next county who was lookin' for one like her to breed with his stallion. Thought if you ever wanted a foal from her, this would be a good bloodline t'get into."
Lizbeth nodded---"Course, Doc. She looks real good. Behavin' bettah too, since Bill's taken t'ridin' her---Ah guess horses are like people---need a little attention."
"True, m'dear, a little attention works wonders for th' heart an' soul---whether it's man or beast!"

***

If Lizbeth looked pale, wan and weary---McDougal looked fit as an Irishman's polished fiddle! Clenching his jaw as he walked thru the door, Doc thought---"Sitting there in his bed like a king on a throne."

"So,"---Mac began---"...I see the good doctor has decided to favor us with one of his little visits! Thought maybe you and your fair-haired Lizbeth had a falling out?" Doc set his bag on the bed, took out the stethoscope then stared at McDougal's face---"Been busy lately---strange things happenin' around here these days." "Like what?"---Mac demanded---"The 'flu'---more dumb-ass cold weather viruses?" Doc listened to the man's heart and thought---"Surely I must be mistaken---his heart sounds like he's been practicing for a marathon! Strong as th' proverbial ox!!" Sweeping the stethoscope several times over Mac's wiry chest and back, he listened longer---but there was no mistake! The heartbeat was definitely stronger while the upper torso appeared well toned---as compared to earlier exams!

"You still taking th' prescriptions for pain an' sleep, Mac?"
Doc busied himself taking out the blood-pressure cuff and
wrapping it around the long muscular arm. Seemed the
arms had miraculously become as 'fit' as everything else
he'd examined thus far! "I'm trying to cut back." Doc cast
a bland gaze at the arm in front of him---"Your pain's
decreased then? An' you're sleepin' better?" "Oh hell, no"
Mac snapped, "The pain's still there and a good night's
sleep is something of the past---but I do all right, you could
say---I get by." "Hmm."---Doc murmured as he placed the
stethoscope back in place and began pumping up the b/p
cuff----he listened carefully for the 'bump'---the reading
was an unbelievable 120/70! Doc repeated with the same
result.

"Your b/p an' heart rate are better than most ranch hands,
Mac, improved muscle tone---you wouldn't be liftin' any
hand weights, now, would you?" "Me? Lift hand
weights?"---Mac sniffed---"Don't be stupid, O'Barr---that's
for sissies!! Why if I could, I'd be outside right now---
swinging an axe-handle, splitting wood!" "Then how'd you
get so fit?"---Doc asked suddenly as he folded the b/p cuff,
lowering it gently inside his bag along with the scope. Mac
was silent. Completing his 'dumb' routine, Doc glanced at
the face beside him---"You didn't answer my question."
"What question?"---did Mac look a mite pale? "Oh, about
how you got yourself s'fit here all of a sudden! Share your
secret---I seem t'be fallin' apart while you're a perfect
cardiac specimen!"

"Well---uh, my books! I read--a lot. And---the books are---
really heavy. Maybe just stretching and moving them
around while in bed all day and half the night has finally
had a positive effect! Exercising both my brain and my
body, you could say!"---he laughed aloud as tho he'd made
the joke of the year. "Yeah, right. That must be it."---Doc

murmured---"Well, whatever---keep it up, I must say, it's doin' you a world of good."

Making as if to leave, Doc suddenly stopped near the foot of the bed and before McDougal could twitch, he'd lifted the covers off his patient's legs and feet! "You know,"---Doc sat his bag down on the bed---"..I just can't believe I've been so negligent of you! Why, I haven't checked your legs in---what? Months?!"---Doc stared at Mac whose face had suddenly turned chalky white---"Lord, man, you could've had a toe rot off here an' never felt it---you should've reminded me of m'duty. Here, let's just have a short look--- you don't mind, do you?" By then O'Barr was already pressing the feet, examining the toes, running expert hands over the lower legs.

It was all Mac could do not to jerk his feet and legs away from O'Barr then kick him in the face---feeling threatened, he exploded---"You don't have to do that! Hell! Nothing's different down there---and COVER ME UP! Cool air makes me get those odd pains in my legs---and feet! If you keep messing about, I'll have to increase my pain medication again! DAMMIT! Cover my legs up and GET THE HELL OUTTA HERE!" Realizing suddenly that this wasn't Lizbeth he now found himself screaming at, he lowered his voice and snapped---"I'm fine, I tell you! As well as I'll ever be! Just leave me alone!"

"All right, Mac, all right! Calm down! I didn't mean t'upset you! Just thought how nice it'd be if maybe we could see improvement in those legs, get back some muscle tone---y'know, like you've got now in your upper body? Uh, you want me t'send that physical therapist back out here?" Mac was livid---grinding his teeth together, he swore---"NO THERAPIST!" "Sorry, Mac."---Doc lifted his palm out toward his patient---"I'm leavin'---I won't trouble you anymore t'day---good evening t'you."

Chapter Twenty-Five

Before taking Lizbeth out to 'have a look at Maggie', Doc slid a couple of valium tablets into his pocket. Once at the barn, he attempted to explain how this very morning Bill had seen---first hand---a 'miraculous' recovery that had at some point, secretly taken place in her own house! For several minutes she stood staring blankly at him while his words sunk merciless into her brain---but how could such a thing be true without her knowing about it? She'd caught the phrases---'Mac could walk'---'had kept it a secret'--- 'Bill had seen him'---suddenly clarity departed, Doc's words became jumbled, meaningless! His voice became a soft buzz which echoed round and round inside her head--- she could feel herself detaching from the scene.

Doc took hold of her shoulders, shook her slightly and called her name---"Lizbeth?! Lizbeth!!" Momentarily, she came back---wondering why was he shaking her? She tried to ask but couldn't find the words. The soft buzzing in her ears became louder---putting her hands up over her ears, she tried to call out but there was only a weak choking sound. Surely someone had jerked out all her bones---she could barely stand---then Doc's face faded---without her bones, she knew she'd collapse!

Lizbeth's legs went limp but Doc was ready—he caught her and helped her over to some bales of hay covered with canvas. A shudder went thru her half-reclined body while Doc took her pulse, it was weak and rapid---he removed his jacket and put it over her. Never having seen Lizbeth this way---he felt strangely inept! Months ago when she'd come in to talk to him about getting the divorce, she'd been angry, hurt, crying---but 'the fight' was still there inside her! Now she was a rag-doll! It was clear to him---and the few who knew her---that she'd been thru too much---for too long. His experience had been that seeing people express anger when anger was appropiate was better than what he'd seen in Lizbeth this afternoon! That barbarian in the house had almost turned this lovely woman into a zombie! At this point, Doc was ready to help Hawk do whatever was necessary to put McDougal away!

"Lizbeth! Here,"---he broke a capsule of inhalant beneath her nose! Immediately, she began to choke, cough and struggle! "It's only me,"---Doc rubbed her forehead and took one of her hands in his---"...you're back, Lizbeth, we're at th' barn. You've had a nasty shock an' I'm goin' t'give you something to help ---it's important you try an' relax. "He kept talking to her for a few moments then asked---"How do you feel---still dizzy---weak?" Shaking her head slowly back and forth, she whispered---"Ah--- think Ah'm all right, Doc. Just had a--a weak spell, Ah reckon." He felt her pulse---it was a little stronger, more regular than before.

Soon she began to cry, then sob---and he knew she'd be all right. So taking one valium, he cracked it in four pieces then placed it into her half-open mouth---"Try to get this down! Sorry I don't have any water, m'dear!" Unscrewing the top of a flask he sometimes carried, he gave her brandy to follow up the fractured pill. She swallowed then began gasping from the alcohol---"Don't gag, Lizbeth! Hold it down! You're goin' t'be all right! But from now on, our key t'victory is that YOU remain very 'cool, calm an' collected' around your husband! Mac must NEVER suspect that you or any of us know his 'secret'---not yet---I know I'm askin' a lot, but carry-on exactly th' same toward him

as you've been doin' so he won't become suspicious! At
this point, not arousing his suspicion is vital. Do you
understand?"

She nodded, her sobbing turned to occasional quiet
whimpers---Doc waited, then said---"Soon as I leave here,
I'll find Hawk, we'll come up with a plan an' be in touch
with you or Salle. Until then, just be your usual self with
Mac! Th' scoundrel thinks he has you under his heel
permanently---but hopefully, all that will soon be past
tense! For right now, listen t' me---I want you t'understand
you're no longer alone in this! Salle, Bill, myself---Hawk,
all of us together are going t'get you outta this hell-hole---
which I suspect has been th' state of affairs for a long time,
far too long." He shook his head---"I wish you'd have told
me---or Ida."

The moment he'd mentioned Hawk's name, she lifted her
face up toward his. Doc continued---"Old Mac isn't quite
th' smart laddie he thinks! Lizbeth, you should see th'
improvement in his whole body! Th' minute I began
lookin' at him, I could tell he'd been out of bed an' movin'
around quite a bit but he sure as hell didn't want ME t'know
that!" Doc snorted then went on---"The very idea of tellin'
me---a physician---that he'd improved his upper body
simply by movin' his 'books' around all day. Why---he as
much as threw me out when I surprised him by lifting th'
blanket off his legs!" He heard Lizbeth's quick intake of
breath---"Oh, don't worry, m'dear! I covered myself by
lookin' an' actin' dumb---then I proceeded t'babble-on
about therapists, more exercise, etc." Nodding, he went on
confidently---"He doesn't know I'm on t'him! But Salle
an' Bill are uneasy about why Mac doesn't want anyone
t'know he can walk---I'm of th' same opinion. An' as for
Salle's brother---he's been in many a military fracas---a

good man t'have on your side--- an' more than you know, Lizbeth, he IS on your side. "

Her eyes searched his, she asked softly---"Joseph knows we have a dreadful marriage? You told him?" "Let's just say that he's a man who doesn't have t'be 'told' things, he discerns them. An' he---uh, only wants you t'be safe." The tinest flicker of a light came on in her eyes---"How does he 'discern' these things?" "It's a gift, m'dear,---Doc murmured---"...a gift from th' Almighty." "It seems a lifetime ago since Salle an' I took food up to th' wood cutters! Ah didn' know Hawk would be among them but...,"---her voice shook---"Ah'd hoped so---honestly, Ah had hoped! Was that wrong, Doctah?" Patting her hands, he assured her it was not wrong and it would be absurd for her to assume 'guilt' over experiencing what was only 'natural human emotions'.

Twenty more minutes passed as Dr. O'Barr continued to talk with Lizbeth, by then it was his opinion she was able to return to the house—and act natural. As they walked back, he observed her carefully---it appeared she'd overcome her 'weak spell' as she'd called it. Suddenly, he realized there was a much more pressing problem! The upcoming night hours! Would Lizbeth be safe tonight---tomorrow night---the night after? Salle HAD mentioned about Lizbeth forming the habit of bolting her bedroom door when she went to bed---but would that mean she'd be safe if McDougal took it into his head to harm her? Her 'birdshot' wouldn't stop him, that was for sure! And should he attack her, would Salle and Bill hear the disturbance? Certainly, he didn't want to frighten Lizbeth unnecessarily---besides, neither he nor Hawk knew for certain if Mac even planned to use the .38 on Lizbeth! That was only yesterday's theory---but considering Mac's behavior toward her, his intolerance of everyone around him---added on to this unusual secrecy about 'walking'---Doc now knew McDougal truly was dangerous!

Somehow, they'd have to come up with an idea that'd force Mac into action---otherwise, he'd continue having 'the upper hand'. Unfortunately Doc knew personalities well enough to know Lizbeth's husband would not only 'have to be stopped'---but stopped permanently. Otherwise he'd just come after her again and again---until one of them was dead. "Is there a way Hawk could 'force' Mac's hand---say---tonight?"---Doc tried to assure himself by thinking positive---"He'll know---he'll have an answer! But I must get hold of him quick!"

Lizbeth and Doc entered the kitchen as Salle was setting the table. Turning toward her, he winked and stated, "Your brother an' I had plans so, I'll take my leave. Lizbeth?" He nodded toward her as he started for the back door, "See you ladies again soon. It's been---interestin'!"

As the truck left the driveway, bouncing onto the paved road, Doc swore aloud ---"Damnation! I can't believe it's been less than twenty-four hours since Hawk an' I were out here searchin' this place!! An' ever since, I've wondered what he did after sending me t'make that phone call! Today we find out f'certain that Mac really IS a 'walker'--- as Hawk referred t'him! M'Lord Almighty! Did Joseph really turn into a hawk --- what actually happened night before last? If it was a vision—why th' powder burns!?"

Not understanding his own unusual sense of urgency, Doc drove the old truck hard --- pressing the accelerator to the floor while rushing toward the turn-off leading to Mary's home! "I've always been one for 'thinking things out'!! Now I'm practially foamin' at th' mouth for us to DO

SOMETHING! Last night, I never dreamed we'd be 'in' this far over our heads---not quite so soon!" The temperature was dropping yet Doc's hands felt slippery on the steering wheel---he looked only to discover his palms were sweating!

Chapter Twenty-Six

By the time Doc located Hawk, there was only about a half-hour of daylight left! They stood on the roadside near his pick-up with Hawk's 4-wheel drive parked opposite them--- each vehicle headed in an opposite direction!

"Why didn't you just wait f'me at home!?"---Doc was in a bit of a temper---"Salle said you'd probably wait there because of Bill's note---so I stopped---but oh, no! You weren't there! Mary said th' minute she handed you Bill's note, you took off like a scalded piglet---then SHE wanted t'know what was wrong---so I had t'take time, makin' up th' best story I could manage! Finally, I got near enough th' door to practically run from her an' roared off straight t'town, I get there only t'find you weren't anyplace t'be seen! So I looked all up an' down th' street ---but did I see any sign of you?! Oh hell no!" By then O'Barr was gesturing, his hands fanning about---"So, I turn around an' start back t'Mary's house---then suddenly, in th'middle of th' bloomin' road, I meet you drivin' like some fighter jet off on a straffing mission! I am tellin' you, Winterhawk, I'm too damned old for such craziness---this whole 'happening' is LUNACY from the very day I picked you up on this very road."

"Doctor-man, my friend! Take it easy! Everything's going to be okay!"---Hawk tried to soothe the old guy! "Take it easy, my hinny!"—Doc roared and gesticulated all the more then jabbing a finger at Hawk's chest, he fumed---"YOU started all this! We spent 2/3 of last night acting like two cat-burglars in th' Louve---now Mary, Bill an' Salle---not to mention Lizbeth---are all wrought up! What th' HELL did you DO last night when you sent me off t'make that asinine phone call?!"

Hawk put a hand on Doc's arm---"Why do you think that has anything to do with today, Doc. Just please tell me what's going on! Bill's note was nothing less than a 'call for help' and if he was desperate enough to slip off McDougal's place---he had a pretty good reason! So, tell me---what started shaking today that I don't know about! Spill it, my man, then we can BOTH worry! Good enough?"

By the time Doc finished 'the news'---Hawk stood leaning up against the pickup with arms crossed, his western hat pulled low over his forehead as he watched several vehicles pass. Silently, he considered their status at this point. "Well?"---Doc asked as he hung over the truck's back-gate. Exhaling, Joseph turned toward O'Barr---put up one finger and replied---"Tell me again precisely what 'the walker' said to you when you entered his room this afternoon---his exact words!"

"Well, let's see, he went on about my "finally decidin' t'come by"----Doc paused then shrugged---"Oh, an' that business of Lizbeth 'bein' my fair haired lady an' did we have a fallin' out'?! It was later when he threw his little tantrum! Does what he said have anything t'do with where we are now?"

"Doc,"—Hawk began—"Did it ever occur to you that maybe he's actually jealous of you and Lizbeth?" Doc did a 'double-take' expression of disbelief! "I'm serious."---

Joseph stared down at the ground, making circles with the toe of his boot---"And if he is, we could take advantage of it and---who knows---maybe force his hand!" Looking straight at Doc, he continued—"If he gets mad enough---no matter who's around, he'll come out of that bed! I promise you, he'll fly around the house like a crazed hornet!" "You ARE one addle-pated Indian!"---O'Barr gasped---"I've never heard such a fool thing in my life! B'sides, what'd happen to Lizbeth if we, say, do get him mad enough, out of his bed an' he's busy---'flyin' around the house'!? What about HER?"

Hawk looked around at the dusky shadows---"Soon there'll be enough dark. We will go back to our parking place--- then I'll see. You game?" Blinking his eyes, Doc finally asked---"Knowin' this dimwit can walk---you suggestin' we go visit th' McDougals t'have coffee or something!?" In the dimming light, Doc could barely make out what Hawk's eyes were saying---but he knew the body language well enough to know they'd definitely be on their way back to the hill---probably within the next ten minutes. Groaning, Doc asked if they could have supper first---in answer, Hawk reached in his coat pocket, took out something sealed in foil then tossed it at Doc---"Eat this while you follow me out to Mama's, there's a couple of things I need to pick up!" Feeling like he'd 'been had' again, Doc murmured---"An' will I be needin' another full tank?" "No. Not this time, m'friend." ---Hawk grinned, Doc could just make out the flashing white teeth in the dimming light---"We'll take my 'fighter jet' here and zoom right out there! But first, we go by the house---then stop to fill MY tank. Oh---and before I forget it---I need you to make another phone call!"

Nagging anxiety continued building up inside Doc as he fairly stumbled into his truck while Hawk make the cleanest U-Turn in the smallest space he'd ever seen---soon the tail-

153

lights were fading off in the distance. "Ohhh me."---O'Barr sighed—"And t'think, last night after we got started, I felt a temporary elation over this 'mission'! A few faint lingering testerone rushes in an old man, I guess." But now, just knowing what had transpired during 24 hours---he had no words left and besides, there was no one to say them to--- unless he directed them toward God! And considering the whole picture---maybe THAT might not be such a bad idea! Buzzing the engine to life, he pulled onto the road, then began tearing the foil wrapper off his 'supper'---wondering exactly what he'd be biting into!

Doc pulled up, his headlights picked up Joseph as he was locking his storage building---in his hand, he carried something resembling a thick briefcase. "Now what?" Doc mumbled to himself as he locked his truck and approached Hawk's 4-wheel drive---barely managing to climb in before Joseph had it moving again!

At the store, Hawk filled the tank and went inside to pay. Doc slumped slightly in his seat, choking down the last of what tasted like a bar of toasted horse grain with unidentifiable nuts and dried fruits sprinkled thru it. Fervently, he hoped Joseph had forgotten about that 'other call' he'd just mentioned because due to their earlier conversation, he felt it might have something to do with Lizbeth. And the very idea that Mac would even 'suspect' him of having a 'thing' for Lizbeth---why he loved her like the child he never had. In the midst of Doc's delving into deep profundities, Hawk returned with a good-sized paper cup of water and handed it to him.

"What in hades is THAT for?"---Doc peered down into the cup---"You gonna drown something?" "Nope. You drink at least half of it."---Hawk replied, moving the vehicle toward the darkened side area of the store where he stopped.

Doc saw he hadn't 'forgotten'---"Why do I have t'drink water? I'm not thirsty!" "Because it'll 'expand' the food you just ate. In short, you won't be hungry anymore!" Doc snapped---"I may not be alive anymore either! Let's get ON with it, man! Who do you want me t'call and what bald-faced lies shall I tell them? So what is my dastardly deed---I wanta do it and end this madness!"

Hawk talked as Doc's expression grew horrified---"I absolutely WILL NOT call Lizbeth and say that t'her! NEVER!" Joseph looked at him---"Not even if it might jump-start ol' McDougal's engine a little prematurely---thereby giving us the edge on him?" "NO!"---Doc bleated! Hawk sighed and rubbed his forehead---"Oh, all right! It was just an idea. We're wasting time arguing---let's get out there and park. We'll shelve the phone call for right now but I still can't see why you couldn't begin a conversation with Lizbeth, give McDougal a chance to pick up then say something like---'Lizbeth, I just had to let you know---well, that I'd stayed away so long because---because I'd come to understand that I look forward to seeing you---far too much. I wanted to come by, believe me---but for everybody's sake, I knew I shouldn't. Don't feel hurt, m'dear---I couldn't stand it if you were!'" Blithely Hawk looked at the older man---"Doesn't sound so bad to me! After that talk you and she had this afternoon, she's bound to know you want her to verbally 'play along'! Man, you'd make a poor 'go-between' for any two lovers! Capt. John Smith and Pocahontas would've NEVER got together if you'd been their messenger!" Relieved that he didn't have to call---at least not yet---Doc agreed he definitely would be the worst of 'go-betweens'---then with a huge sigh of relief, he downed the whole cup of water. Soon the two roared off for their evening rendevous.

Chapter Twenty-Seven

Upon parking behind their brush shield there in the woods,
Hawk removed his boots and put on running shoes---"Doc,
you should lock up and catch a nap! This could be another
long night. I'm going to run the distance and pick up
something that I hope will tell us what we need to know---
and there's nothing you can do right now except wait! My
hope is that I've trapped something concrete. After you told
me what Bill said about watching McDougal this morning--
-that revved up my hopes! Doc, I gotta confess---I've
involved you to the gills---which was nasty of me---but who
else could I trust? Like you said, all this started with you
and me the day I came home---can't change destiny,
m'man, it's all written up there," ---Hawk pointed upwards-
--"...in the stars." Removing his coat and hat, he handed
them to Doc then wriggled into a hooded, heavy dark
sweatshirt then he was off again---silently running thru the
darkness to what Doc fervently hoped was 'something
concrete'!

Both Bill and Salle were waiting for Joseph when he paused
outside their darkened apartment to give his bird-call---she
waved at him from the open window. Soon he was in their
living room where Salle started on him---"Joseph
Winterhawk!! This has been THE very worst day of my
life! You and your----your 'machine' could've caused Bill
and me ruination! Especially after---,". Suddenly
changing subject mid-stream, she asked---"You seen Doc?!!
You talked to him?!" "Yes, dear, I both saw and talked to
him!"---Hawk apologized---"I'm awfully sorry, you two! I
had no idea what would come down this morning---reckon
it was a big shock to everybody around here, huh?" "Shock
doesn't begin to describe this day!"—she whispered—
"Knowin' how Miss Lizbeth's things have been riffled thru,

why Bill's sick with worry that 'white-eyes' over there might come sneakin' up here and find this 'set-up' of yours! What you plannin' to do now, Joseph?" Her brother squatted beside the recorder, removed one reel and put on a new one---"First thing I'm going to do is change out the tape and see what we have. When Doc told me Bill saw Mac talking on the phone---I thought 'Bingo!!'---maybe we got him! Of course, he could've been talking to the corner grocery, who knows---but I doubt that!" "Yeah, me too!"---Salle knelt beside her brother---" C'mon! I'm anxious to know what's on that tape! Hawk? Why is it you don't even seem surprised that old 'white-eyes' can walk?!" Ignoring her, Hawk sat on the floor and slid on the headset.

For the next hour, he sat listening to McDougal talk to his girlfriend, Rita---then with his father. When he was sure there was nothing more that was taped while Lizbeth and Salle were away from the house, he carefully removed the reel, zipped it into the front 'kangaroo-pocket' of his jacket then stood.

"Well!?" Salle demanded as she stood beside Hawk---"I wanta hear too, Joseph!" "Honey, I don't have time to let you listen right now---that'd take another hour! And from what I just heard---well, we don't have even an hour to waste! Mrs. Mac shouldn't be alone with him any longer." "Then you mean he DID say something---er, about---Miss Lizbeth?" ---Salle whispered in alarm! For a few moments, Joseph didn't answer. Salle reached over and touched his arm---"What'd he SAY about her??!"

"Sis,"---Joseph's voice took on a slight military tone as he gently put his hands on her shoulders—"Please go over to the house---get her alone, tell her that I want you to stay there for awhile---then both of you do---say, some kind of special work,like planning next week's Thanksgiving meal." Sally replied, "To be truthful, I don't think Miss Lizbeth feels much like doing seasonal celebrations." Hawk exclaimed, "I don't care what you do but STAY with her for awhile. And Salle?" He walked directly in front of her and stared into her eyes---"Whenever you come back over here? Tell her from now on, Doc and I want their back door left unlocked each night---that's very important. She'll agree because I think she suspects she could be in danger. Hurry on now, before it gets too late for this visit to 'look right'---should McDougal question it. At least the two of you will have a great excuse for staying up late."

Recognizing the wisdom of her brother's words, Salle simply nodded, put on her coat then went out the front door. Bill put a hand on his brother-in-law's arm---"Look, Hawk. I know you think you're doing what you believe is best— but how can you be sure McDougal won't---well, take it into his head to hurt both of them? Can't you at least tell me what he said on the tape that made you decide Mrs. Mac can't be left alone with him tonight?" Joseph sank onto a chair---"He plans to kill her, Bill. Exactly when, he didn't say---but he inferred that 'the next time he saw Rita'---the 'old' girlfriend?---'things' would be different---that he'd be a 'free man---with money, land,' etc. He wants this to look either like a break-in or---maybe an accident, therefore, he won't do anything tonight if others are in the house." Hawk looked up as Bill stood near him---"Now, I'm going to ask you for a big favor, too---will you go over and just sorta 'help out'---by shelling some of those southern pecans for Thanksgiving?!"

Suddenly, out of nowhere, Bill remembered the 'lunch' scene in the woods that day---a 'light-bulb' went on! "Good Lord, Winterhawk!!"—he whispered---"You're stuck on this woman, aren't you!?" Shaking his head back and forth several times, he walked around his brother-in-

158

law's chair---then squatted in front of Hawk and stared---
"Why, you are IN over your head! Man, how could I have
been so blind!" "I can't talk about it, Bill. Here, take
this,"---Joseph stood, Bill followed suit as Hawk handed
him a snub-nose revolver---"Just in case. I have to leave for
a short while, but I'll be back just as soon as I can and
believe me, I'll be here until this thing is settled! That is, if
you let me hide out in your apartment during the daytime---
until it's over?" Slowly Bill nodded---"Sure, hide out as
long as necessary. In fact, I'll feel a whole LOT better if
you ARE here! After this morning and what you just got on
that tape, I really do understand why somebody has to do
something. So, take off---slip on out. After you're gone,
I'll go and---'shell pecans', for crying out loud." Bill went
to the dresser---"Here. These are our spare keys---one for
each lock---you take them until, as you say, 'this is over'.
Salle and I can make do with one set."

Joseph Winterhawk stood, took the keys and zipped them in
with the tape. Taking Bill's hand in his, he said---"I owe
you, Bill. Sure as I'm living, I'd never send you and Salle
over there tonight for a couple of hours unless I thought it
was safe enough. Killing your wife and trying to make sure
it looks like an accident is one thing but killing off three
people is quite another! When I return,"---he looked at his
watch---"...two hours 'max', I'll come near the kitchen,
make the bird-call---then you and Salle tell her to leave the
back door unlocked---TELL HER I'm going inside her
house. And I'll BE inside each night until this thing is over
---one way or another. Also during the time I'm here with
you---the two of us will talk---Indian-talk. I have things to
tell you---hopefully then you can understand why I have to
be here!" Bill nodded as Joseph crept out the front door and
off into the night.

159

Approaching the truck later, he found O'Barr napping. "Good,"---he thought---"Poor man, I've caused him and my family a lot of trouble!" Doc roused as Hawk unlocked the door---"Sorry to wake you, but my re-con turned up big news, Doctor-man! Just listen to this as we drive back to Mama's! I gotta pick up a few MORE things." He opened the 'brief-case' revealing a reel-to-reel tape recorder/player ---taking the tape from his jacket, he wound it into place then turned it on. Driving back onto the highway, Hawk watched Doc's face in the glow from dashboard lights. As the miles passed, his expression changed from one of curious interest to shocked disbelief then horror as the sound of McDougal's own voice revealed the unbelieveable inner blackness of his soul.

The tape wasn't finished when Hawk drove into Mary's yard---"I'll turn the volume down, Doc, you can listen while I'm inside." "What you pickin' up, Hawk?"---Doc looked at him. "Oh, a toothbrush, hair brush, clean underwear, loin-cloth, feathers, warpaint---you know, stuff like that."--- by then Hawk was turning to leave the vehicle. Doc sighed, returning to the frightening taped conversation. So far, Hawk had been right, Doc figured he couldn't afford not to trust the man's instincts---especially now! Or Lizbeth would surely die at the hands of this madman.

 A little while later, in Doc's driveway, they finished listening to the tape. "Well,"-- Joseph stated---"I'm gonna depart, Doc---I'm not sure when we'll see each other again- --so, for heaven's sake---stay NEAR a phone---or close to your truck radio! And when you're out in the truck---to make matters less curious for your receptionist---just tell her that Mr. McDougal is experiencing some 'emotional difficulties' at the present time and the household must have immediate access to you." Doc nodded as Joseph added— "My vehicle will be parked in our hidden spot, it'll be

locked---but,"---he moved a hand toward Doc, between his
fingers was a key---"..here's my spare key---that is, should
it be needed for any unexpected---emergency."

Reluctantly, Doc opened the door, got out and stood looking
in at his young friend---"Joseph, I gotta say somethin'
t'you! First, I hate lettin' you go off like this---all by y'self.
Second, I feel I started this whole damned thing by gettin'
Salle an' Bill a job out there! So, I'm apologizin'---in
m'wildest dreams, I never thought nothin' like this would
ever take place. Look, you rarely speak about Lizbeth—but
I owe you this---she loves you. This afternoon, when we
were at the barn an' I was tellin' her about Mac? I
mentioned that Bill, Salle, myself---an' you—were on her
side, that we were there for her---at th' mere mention of
your name, her poor face just lit up like an angel. I'm truly
sorry---I never meant t'put Salle an' Bill in harms way."

Hawk had sat quietly listening to Doc's humble apology,
his face staring out the windshield---after several moments
he turned toward Doc. Love for the older man jabbed at
him like a knife---then he replied firmly---"Hey, Doctor!
Had it not been for you, why I'd never have met my red-
haired dream-girl---the love of my life since I was around
12 years old! What can I say? You asking me to hold you
responsible for the way things are turning out? So if I gotta
say it---okay, here goes---'I forgive you'---for whatever you
think you've done wrong! Haven't you figured out by now
that you're not 'in charge' of capricious, fickle fate? What
will be, will be and all that? Didn't I go out on that
mountain-top for weeks---begging God to help me---and got
no response? But when the time was exactly right---what a
revelation! This 'ranger' never had a trip like that before---
even jumping out of a plane in the dark can't measure up!
All I have to say is---in more ways than I can count, you
were around for me after Daddy died! You honestly think

161

I'm gonna throw all that away? Not so, I love you, man!
You've never done anything except what you thought was
good—or right! Besides, you got me between a rock and a
hard place---you know I can't finish this without your
help!" With that, he buzzed the engine to life---looking
back at Doc, he barked---"Now, don't forget, 'Kemosobe',--
-stay near the bloomin' phones!"

Doc exhaled, relief washing over him---"You got it, Tonto!
Be careful now and don't be flyin' too low!" White teeth
flashed in the dark face---"Get on inside to your bed or Mrs.
Doc will be after both of us! I've been taking too much
'night-time togetherness' away from the two of you! And if
it were me,"---Hawk arched an eyebrow at Doc---"I just
might resent that!"

Watching as Joseph drove away into the night, O'Barr felt
something deep inside his soul. He wasn't sure it was fear--
-maybe only disquiet or a rumble of foreboding. All around
him---for months now things had been changing---
considerably so! And after the past two days, he honestly
no longer knew 'WHAT' to expect!

Chapter Twenty-Eight

After Salle explained that Hawk wanted the three of them
to 'work' in the kitchen until he could 'make
arrangements'---Lizbeth readily agreed and for almost two
hours, the three cracked and shelled pecans. The women
pored over cookbooks for holiday recipes, planning out a
tentative menu---each person strained to make 'small talk'.
Salle spoke of past 'Thanksgivings' that her family had
enjoyed while Bill kept casting uneasy glances in the
direction of McDougal's bedroom---the revolver Hawk had
given him hung heavy inside his jacket pocket. For the

third time he asked---"Mrs. Mac, you sure we're not
disturbing your 'mister'?" Lizbeth looked at him---"No,
Bill, 'course not. Ah went in just aftah Salle arrived an'
told him th' three of us would be makin' some Thanksgivin'
preparations. He's restin' or watchin' television, Ah expect.
Don't you be worryin', Bill, if we were annoyin' him---he'd
surely have let us know by now."

When the pecans were all shelled, Lizbeth placed them in
an air-tight container and dumped the shells into the trash.
Salle had just begun sweeping as Lizbeth wiped down the
table---suddenly Lizbeth heard it again---it was her 'bird'!
He'd come back! "That's it!"---she whispered excitedly
and ceased her wiping---"Listen! Salle, that's th' bird Ah
was tellin' you about!! Did you heah him?" Bill stared at
his wife, both recognized her brother's signal---a thoughtful
expression came over Salle's face---"Why, I sure did hear
'him', Miss Lizbeth! And 'he' DOES sound lonely---my
goodness, imagine that, Bill! A single lonesome bird
singin' at night." Bill stood, urging Salle---"If you girls are
finished---Salle, you and I should run along, Mrs. Mac?
Could you walk us outside?"

"Yes!"—Lizbeth agreed hastily---"Ah'll go out with you---
-an' maybe that sweet, strange bird will whistle foah me
again." Following the couple out the back door, she closed
it behind her. "Bill?"---she spoke in a low tone---"Explain
t'me about leavin' th' doah unlocked!" "Uh---Salle's
brother and Doc---well, it's their idea!"---he bit his lip and
looked nervously over his employer's shoulder making
certain no one was near---"Ma'am---if you should---uh,
maybe 'hear' something during the night---please don't get
up to see about it! Okay? I think you'd be safer in your
bed---or UNDER it!"

"Hush up, Bill! You're scaring her t'death with your silly talk! Miss Lizbeth…"---Salle stepped close to Lizbeth. Bill followed, speaking in a low tone---"All right, here's the word---Joseph is planning to stay IN your house tonight to protect you! He's already here, on your property!" Lizbeth turned this way and that! "NO!"---Salle warned, grabbing Lizbeth's arms---"Don't be lookin' all around like that---you act normal! Most likely you won't even hear my brother when he comes inside, but be assured he's there and---don't you be afraid of him! He'll only be protectin' you from any---any unfortunate 'accident'---okay? Like Bill says---'stay IN your bed'---unless Joseph comes into your room and tells you otherwise. Miss Lizbeth, the three of us standin' here know what went on this mornin'---now both Doc and Hawk know it as well! And a minute ago, when that 'sweet little night bird' called out---something just told me that maybe---this time tomorrow---God willing, we'll all be thru with dangerous 'secrets'!"

Trembling with fear and the cold night air, Lizbeth reached up and grasped Salle's hands in her own—"Th' Captain will be in this house?! Did he say so!?" Bill leaned closer to her---"Yes, exactly. That's why you must leave the door unlocked---so he can come inside! Miss Lizbeth, you gotta understand, both Doc and Hawk are convinced your husband is up to no good---and they're trying to get hard evidence of that! In order to do so, Joseph has to be hidden in your house---to protect you if necessary. He'll never let anybody hurt you---I can promise!"

"But what about th' sheriff?"---Lizbeth stammered---"Shouldn't they be th' ones heah---Ah don't want th' Captain hurt! This isn't his problem!" "Ma'am,"---Bill went on---"… there's no reason for them to be here---not at this time! Seems their job begins AFTER a crime has been commited---unfortunately." His words alarmed Lizbeth leaving her speechless---loosing her hands from Lizbeth's iron grip, Salle whispered---"A lot can happen BEFORE the law arrives to do anything about a 'possible situation'! Now, you go back inside before that man gets suspicious! Miss Lizbeth---you 'just believe' things will be all right. Remember Hawk will take care of you!" Bill literally pulled Salle away and across the yard toward their apartment as a thoroughly frightened Lizbeth turned, forcing herself to walk back into the kitchen---careful to leave the back door unlocked.

"Maybe Ah should just let Mac know Ah'm going t'bed---that way he'll know Salle an' Bill are gone. Then we wait---all of us. We wait on this wretched man whom Ah married t'make some kind of---of 'perceived' move against me! They think he's plannin' t'kill me! Nobody used those words but seems t'me that's what they all afraid of---oh, God! What if they're right?!" Upon reaching Mac's door, her legs were so weak and trembling that she leaned against the wall, struggling to sound 'normal'---"Mac? We're all finished in th' kitchen---Ah know it's late---but can Ah get you anything?"

"W—what? I didn't hear you."---he pretended she'd awakened him from a light sleep. Her heart raced, she knew her voice sounded weak---"Ah a-asked if you needed anything befoah I retiah?" "Nooo, "---he said easily---"...I do believe I have everything I need. Come in for a minute?" Lizbeth choked at the lump of fear in her throat---then stepped forward, stood in the doorway and looked at his reclining figure---"Yes?"

"So."---his head propped on one arm, he tested her---"There you are! You hiding out in the hall, Lizbeth?" "No, Mac."---she replied quietly---"Ah just want t'go t'bed. It's been a long tirin' day an' we still have curtains an' windows t'do

165

in th' mornin'---since we didn't get it done t'day." Without
waiting for his reply, likely another invitation to fight, she
turned to walk away.

"JUST a minute, lady! You're not excused yet! Get your
ass BACK in here!" Silently Lizbeth pleaded---"Oh, God.
Why'd you let me take th' bait AGAIN? Ah'm tired an'
Ah'm scared---why couldn't You just let me ignore him---
especially t'night?!" Tracing her steps backward, she once
again stood just inside his door---she faced the hall that
seemed to frantically beckon her from his room---"What is
it, Mac? You want fresh water?" Without waiting for a
reply, she whirled around, picked up his pitcher and headed
for the bathroom where she dumped what she'd put in 3
hours ago---soon, she returned and placed the pitcher of
fresh water on his bedside table.

"What else?"---she asked quietly and looked down at him.
"Well now,"---he suggested 'amiably' as his cold eyes
bored into hers---"I thought perhaps we could---maybe,
spend a little---say, 'quality time' together?" Staring
speechlessly down at him---she swallowed, found her voice
and feigned ignorance of what she suspected he meant---
especially now that he could walk! "Quality time?
Whatevah is THAT!?" "You never can tell, Lizbeth---
'quality time' means different things to different folks. But
then...,"---he excused her with a wave of the hand and
picked up a magazine from his bed---"...we'll put it off---
until later! Besides,"---his voice took another tone---
"...you don't seem to be quite yourself tonight---exhausted
from a 'difficult' day and too much holiday preparations, I
expect. So, run along to bed where the sandman awaits
you!" Before she could remove herself from the spot, he
turned toward her again and suggested---"You should sleep
late tomorrow morning---who knows, maybe all you really
need is a good sound sleep---a nice, long one."

"Goodnight, Mac." Lizbeth managed to control herself but as soon as she was far enough away---she literally 'flew' to the kitchen---commanding herself to squelch the powerful desire to run right out the back door! Mac's last words were uncharacteristic---coming from anyone else they might express concern---instead at this point in time they only sounded---sinister!! Was her fanciful imagination again working overtime because of what her friends were thinking and the little they spoke---or was her panic because their few words had only clarified what she'd already sensed in her heart but had refused to admit as 'truth'?? So upset was she that the scene with Mac momentarily erased Hawk from her mind---then she remembered! "Dearest Hawk---oh, thank God yoah already heah so Ah'm not alone! Ah'm NOT alone!"

She didn't know where Hawk was at this time---and she couldn't go wandering all over the house searching for him---Mac would HEAR---and now Mac could WALK!! Hawk had made his plans, already he was carrying them out---she trusted his ability completely---and there was nothing left to do except be as brave as he! If, because of his love for her, he'd put himself in harm's way---then she must do her part! So it was Hawk's bravery and willingness to protect her the only way he knew that braced Lizbeth as she hurried to her room for a shower.

Not trusting her frazzled mind up to this point---she paused, retraced her steps making certain the back door was unlocked then ran to her bedroom! After closing her window, she hurried to the bathroom. Hot water from the shower ran over her neck and body---it felt so soothing, inviting her to linger---but heat couldn't wash away terror so several minutes later, she was dressed for bed. Turning off the last light in the house, she crawled beneath the covers---and there she waited.

Chapter Twenty-Nine

Unable to calm down, she felt little more than one huge mass of tangled nerves. Mac's last words echoed in her ears as she lay in the dark 'waiting' ---as someone once said 'waiting …for what might come'. A huge dose of fear and dread of the unknown sent spasms coursing thru her body rendering her weak, trembling! Inside her chest, a fearful heart bumped unevenly while the dark quiet of her room filled her ears with her silent terror. Only the knowledge that Hawk was someplace in the house kept her from losing the battle for control and not to go screaming into the darkness outside! Today's revelation of Mac's secret ability to walk AND the possibility he wanted to kill her--- together, it'd become too much---she knew she was balancing on the edge, the breaking point---but she couldn't fail Joseph---nor herself! She must hold on---for everyone's sake---'waiting' was HER part in allowing evil to run it's course!

There were moments she felt her tremors shook the whole bed! She strove to reign in the wild thoughts clamoring inside her head---running the gamut of frightening possibilities! Her ears picked up each usual nighttime 'creaking' from the old house as it settled down for the evening---tonight, however, they seemed magnified seven times over!

Outside there was no moon, only a hint of unearthly star-light sifting over everything, softening the shadows in her room---what her mother used to call 'light nights'! "Oh, Mama!"---she prayed—"God, GRANT I should live long enough to see you---just once more! Please God, let me see Mama again---it's been so long."

Time passed and the living room clock struck twelve---twelve-fifteen---twelve-thirty---Lizbeth had just fallen into a fitful doze when the clock struck one! Her vigilant overworked consciousness 'exploded' back to life---her body broke out in a cold sweat! "When will he DO something!?"---she muttered to herself turning over for the hundredth time---"Will it happen t'night? Please, Lord, calm me---lest Ah lost all control an' run from this room, howlin' like a banshee---spoilin' everythin'!!"

***

Wearing thin gloves, dark clothing and a black military face-mask over his head, Joseph had entered the house while Lizbeth was in the shower---he could hear the water running as he slipped down the hall toward her room. The floor plan Salle had drawn was clear in his mind---he'd memorized each nook and cranny that might afford a hiding place. Taking advantage of Lizbeth's absence from the bedroom, he hurriedly placed a small voice-activated tape recorder beneath her bedside table, making sure it was well hidden. Retracing his steps, he slid into a hall coat closet across from the half-bath and arranged a crack in the door so he could watch the entrance to her room! Soon, he saw her cross the room dressed in pajamas---then the light went off---and he assumed she'd gone to bed.

Time passed as he, too, heard the clock striking. He couldn't see Lizbeth's bed but he knew she wasn't asleep! "Not possible..."---he thought—".. not with a thing like this hanging over her poor head!" He was so sleepy---"I can't remember the last time I had more than an hour's sleep---had to be two nights and two days ago---the 'vision', I

169

guess." He smiled ruefully to himself---"Wouldn't exactly call that 'restful' sleep, what with getting 'shot' there at the end! The rest of the time I've spent running across the meadow around here---or on the road gathering up electronics from 'people I know'!"

The clock had just struck 3:30 a.m.---even Joseph was about to give up on 'it' happening that night when suddenly he heard a light scrapping noise! Where was it coming from--- which direction?! He felt muddled---a lack of sleep plus warmth and darkness in the closet had dulled his perception! "Wake up, man!"---he chided himself then deliberately bit into his lip---sharp pain with the taste of blood immediately rendered him wide awake! Then the scrapping came again! Easing silently from the closet, Joseph stood listening---30 seconds passed---the sound stopped! "What the hell was it---and WHERE?!"---his breath was shallow as he strained to hear.

Suddenly there was one longer, louder scrape then a loud thump---Lizbeth screamed---he knew no one had come via the hallway---no one had been near her door!! Had Mac come in thru the window? That had to be it!! The window---Hawk's eyes saw movement---then a voice spoke there in the room---"Lizbeth, darling-wife! Hello! Musn't scream! It's only me, your 'romeo'---just looking for his 'Juliet'! I forgot to call from beneath your window---but then, we don't have a balcony, do we? Surprised, m'love??"

"You had to gloat and identify yourself, didn't you, Mac! Thanks be to God!"---Hawk thought to himself as he carefully manuevered across the threshold and into a shadowed area behind the intruder whose only present interest was terrorizing his prey! Joseph's 'walker' now hovered close to Lizbeth! And though she knew about Mac's 'walking', when she heard him speak and made out

170

his features standing there in the star-lit room---true surprise
belied the fact she'd been pre-warned---thus he assumed his
'surprise' to be a complete success! Finally she whispered--
"Mac!! Y—Yoah---standin'!! Mac! How can this be? Ah
jus' saw you awhile ago---an' now---you can WALK!!
Why, it's a miracle!! Ah can't-----b-believe this!"

Crawling onto the bed opposite her, Mac rested on his knees
and growled---"Oh yeah! I've been working on this
'miracle' a long time, baby! Been practicing all over the
house when I could get you three bums off the place long
enough! You and those two 'Indians' are a pain in the ass,
you know that!?" Lowering his face over hers, he hissed---
"Been all over your room here, too! Been thru everything
in this house with a fine-tooth comb! Where you hiding
them—WHERE!??" As usual, he began interspersing his
insults with yells--"I know you're hiding them--WHERE
ARE THEY??!" "WHEAH'S WHAT?!"---a terrified
Lizbeth screamed!!! "ALL OF THEM!"---he cursed---
"THE $#%*(&^%@! LETTERS FROM HIM!" "FROM
WHO—WHO!?"---she cried---"WHAT ARE YOU
TALKIN' ABOUT---WHOSE LETTAHS?!" Only a second
before, Lizbeth saw something behind Mac---she attempted
to further enrage him so he'd lose control and finally 'do'
whatever it was he'd planned! So desperate was she to find
peace of mind that she now 'welcomed' this encounter---
however it ended, she was ready!

In the shadows, Hawk gritted his teeth as he listened! Like
a building dust-storm, anger swirled about inside him as he
was forced to stand motionless and listen to this sick mind
give birth to loud, jealous, insane accusations ! If he
revealed his presence before McDougal made his move to
kill Lizbeth, the whole thing would blow up---but what if
the idiot had rape on his twisted mind!? At the horror of
this thought---Hawk's emotions and his military training

began fighting with each other! Psychology told him that rape wasn't a crime of 'passion' or 'lust' even---it was a matter of 'control'---a 'power-thing'! And there was no way he'd ever allow the act to happen---yet legally, she was still McDougal's wife---and what if he didn't threaten her life?! Instantly, Hawk made up his mind---if the man made any overt sexual move---he'd take him out with a 'pressure-point' hold---THEN think of something! At this point, it didn't matter what he had to do to stop him from such a thing. So, with the possibility of sexual assault now growing in his mind, Hawk knew this could turn into more than he'd bargained for! His thoughts raced as McDougal continued to badger, insult and threaten Lizbeth!

"You're going to TALK to me, Missy!! Tell me WHO your lover is!!"--- visceral hatred continued to roll out of his mouth---"If you DON'T tell me, I'm going to beat you within an inch of your miserable, useless life!! All these little 'slapping-around' events we've had thru the years? Why, honey, they're nothing---you gotta know what I REALLY wanted was---to get you OUT of my life!!" "HOW did you come t'hate me so!! WHY?"---she distracted to further incense him. "WHY? MY GOD! YOU RUINED MY LIFE, YOU LITTLE FOOL!"---he stared down at her---"I can't believe you didn't know YOU were the reason I was never made 'Grand Dragon'---after my Daddy! HELL! It was---YOU!!"---she turned away as his spittle sprayed across her face—"YOU AND YOUR DAMNED BLACK SYMPATHIZING!!! NOW IT'S FREAKIN' INDIANS!! YOU ARE A WHORE!! NO DECENT WHITE WOMAN GIVES A 'GOOD' DAMN ABOUT ANY BODY WHO DON"T HAVE WHITE SKIN!!! YOU JUST NEVER COULD LEARN THAT--- COULD YOU??! Well--,"—suddenly quiet, he hissed— "...now, it's MY TURN, 'precious'! I'm gonna pay you back for every miserable HOUR I've had to lay in that bed

172

and think about the low level on the totem-pole that all your nigger-loving attitudes brought me to! Every honor you stole from me!! You got ANY idea what it's like to just lie there listening to you---my own personal albatross---going on and on blathering, babbling and whining in that damn-ass accent of yours----'charming' the drawers off everybody---except me??! GOD!"—he yelled!

In one quick move, Mac straddled Lizbeth, grabbed her by the hair and began to shake her upper body like a rag-doll! "Bitch!"---he rasped as his fingers dug mercilessly into her scalp—"So unbelievably stupid, you had no idea I could walk, now, did you?? I had you completely fooled---which wasn't difficult!!" More violent shaking—the voice low and menacing---he twisted one of her wrists, exerting pressure as he bent it behind her---"But your 'deah doctah O'Barr' almost had me going there this afternoon! Thought for sure when he snatched the covers off my legs he suspected a little something---but the old bastard---he's just as empty-headed as you are! A couple of moss-covered relics---the both of you---you belong in a museum---you live in another world---another time! Him, the 'kind' country doctor and you---the 'genteel' southern bitch-lady sipping mint juleps together out on your veranda---eating those miserable 'fried pies'---banging that damned piano---I can picture it now!! Neither one of you realize at this moment, this whole country---is crumbling into nigger-hands! RIGHT BEFORE OUR EYES!!---AND SOMEBODY'S GOTTA STOP IT!!"

Lizbeth now remained quiet except for an occasional gasp or groan as he took another jerk at her head or twisted her arm further! Suddenly he paused, reached behind him for something beneath his shirt! "See this?!"---he crowed breathlessly---"Look at it good, babe---it's gonna be the last

173

thing you ever see in this life!" In his hand, he held a shiny chrome-plated handgun then pushed it hard against Lizbeth's face---Hawk recognized it immediately and forced himself to stand perfectly still as Mac raved on--- "This is MY gun, sweets!" Lizbeth managed to ask---"Mac, oft' times Ah've wondahed---have you evah---killed anyone---." Before she could speak further, he bragged— "Have I ever KILLED anyone? You twit---you boring hi-toned lump!" He began to chuckle---"I've personally killed four people with this very gun, kiddo! In your general stupidity, you never figured how serious we were! Dad sent the guns, they're hidden in the barn---guns that have killed more than you can count on ten fingers!!"

At this Lizbeth became silent---now she knew! All the years when that unasked question had hung over her mind now suddenly vanished! The question had been answered and the truth made her almost violently ill! Her husband was no longer sane!

Mac's unstable laughter filled the room as he went on--- "And YOU, Miss 'Georgia Peach', are gonna be number FIVE for my chrome 'special' here!!" The excited voice quavered with an edge of lunacy---Hawk watched as madness began spiraling out of control! The .38 remained jammed against the side of her jaw---"Let me tell you how this little adventure is gonna be reported to the law! I want you to know the whole plan before I splatter your brains all over this wall! After all we've been thru together---I wouldn't wanta cheat you out of that! You see, dearest little piss-ant, some sick 'intruder' came thru your bedroom window tonight---he beat you and murdered you! And me, the 'poah' husband! Why, I was forced to listen to the entire ghastly episode---how could a crippled, paralyzed man come to the aid of his dying wife!!! And wouldn't you know---some careless person left the kitchen phone off the hook---so I couldn't even call for help!! Oh,.."---he chuckled softly---".. I'll suddenly regain my ability to walk!! Naturally, once you're in the ground, I'll inherit everything including any remaining money from your 'precious' book---another bit of trash from your liberal brain! Then one day---after a 'decent' interval of time has passed---I'll sell out and move---getting away from all the 'bad memories', you know! But the truth is---I'll be---as you white hill-billy trash say---'walkin in high cotton!' Nice, huh? I've given up too much already and nobody's gonna take anything else from me---YOU HEAR?? NOBODY! This time----I'm gonna get what's termed 'rightfully mine'---my 'just desserts'!"

Lizbeth gasped---"But Ah changed th' will, Mac---AH CHANGED TH' WILL! You won't get ANYTHING!! Already it's in 'trust' foah a charity!! You may kill me, Mac, but th' last laugh's on you!" She began to giggle---softly at first then louder as the volume and tone graduated into general hysteria amidst theatrical HA-HA-HA's! Behind McDougal's back, Hawk stood almost paralyzed by her behavior! Dear God! Either her 'madness' was superb acting---or a temporary condition brought on by everything she'd been thru---either way, she was damned convincing!

After her sentence about changing the will---Mac became utterly silent! Hawk knew the chances were he'd shoot her without another word---or suddenly begin to viciously pistol-whip her! The proof was on tape—it was zero hour---he took a step forward to grab Mac and disarm him!

Joseph never expected what happened next---one second he was readying himself to pounce upon the man who was about to murder Lizbeth---going forward on one foot, he shifted his weight---a loud creak sounded from the aged wood floor! Mac whirled around, swinging the gun away from Lizbeth and toward him---then it happened again---the sharp gun report! Hawk had heard, seen and felt it all before---the day Mac shot him in the left hand!! Hot searing pain followed as this time, the bullet tore thru his side---then he was falling toward the bed but before he passed out, his hands reached out, hoping to wrestle the gun from the killer---or turn it back on him and pull the trigger! But he was going down---falling far short of the 'walker'! Lizbeth's screams filled the air around him as he faded away, slipping into blackness.

Chapter Thirty

Joseph groaned---all was dark---his whole left side was one white-hot burning pain---he was lying flat on the floor---someone was holding his head and wiping his face with a cold, wet cloth! Pushing the hand away and ignoring the pain, he forced himself up on his right elbow---blinking his eyes several times, he could make out the foot of a bed. He began to remember---this was Lizbeth's room---Mac--- Lizbeth!! How long had he been out? Where was she---and why wasn't HE, himself, dead!!? He'd been shot point-blank at close range with a .38!! "LIZBETH!!"---he tried to yell! But the sound was hardly more than a ragged rasp in his dry throat---again he tried---"LIZBETH??!"

As his vision cleared more, he saw Salle moving toward him---she seemed nothing more than a greyish pre-dawn ghost somehow attached to this living nightmare! He could feel Bill there beside him---kneeling on the floor supporting his shoulders. "JOSEPH!"---his sister cried as she sat on the floor and smoothed his face with her hands---"Thank th' LORD you're back!" Weakly brushing her hands aside, he reached, took hold of the bedpost and struggled to pull himself to his knees---he took a couple of deep breaths as

Bill hurriedly stood, helping him to his feet---he felt dizzy, almost falling onto the bed! Pain in his side tore at him as he drove his left fist into it---someone had bound the wound tight---"LIZBETH!!?"---at least he could hear his voice now! No one answered him, it was ghastly silent in the room! Slowly inching toward the head of the bed, he could see her lying there---"O-OH NO! Oh, God---n-no!! Please d-don't let her be---dead!" Salle threw a towel over the bed as he leaned over it, forcing himself to look! "Oh, Lizbeth, m-my poor love!"---he whispered. His right hand touched her arms, hands, her face---"Lizbeth, please---answer m-me!" Clearly, she'd been beaten about the head---other cuts, bruises and whelts covered what he could see of her body! Her flesh was cool to his touch---he felt her neck for a pulse---if it was there, it was much too faint!

"Bill?---Salle? Is--s-she's not---dead, is she---I mean, she feels cool but—she just can't be--! I was supposed to---P-PROTECT HER!! She counted---on me a-and I---I let her down!! LOOK---AT THE B-BEATING SHE'S TAKEN!!"—now on one knee beside the bed, he found it hard to ask his last question, afraid of the answer but the words came at last---"D-did he---shoot her?" It was Bill who now took charge---"Hawk, sit back down before you fall down!" He and Salle helped the wounded man back to the area rug where he'd been---"Just lie back! Doc is on his way! He knows the situation and will have everything he needs to fix you both! Thanks to his phone instructions, Salle's already slowed your bleeding---and Mrs. Mac--- well, I think she'll be all right, too."

"You didn't—a-answer my--question."---Hawk kept demanding as pain and perhaps some 'shock' threatened to take him out again---"I-I have to know---a b-beating---is one thing---but a b-bullet---in the--w-wrong place is q-quite--another! I know---I've h-had my—own share." Bill

177

knew his brother-in-law wouldn't let it rest until he gave him some sort of answer---"Go easy, we didn't hear a second shot! Salle said she didn't think there was a bullet wound on her." Hawk now lay flat, his strength expended, his breath shallow---he reached to touch the clean towel pressed around the exit wound where a strip of sheet held it tight---then asked--- "How m-much blood?" Bill replied--- "Not too much! You and I got the same type---if you need some, Doc can transfuse directly! I'm sure he'll take care of the two of you right here at the ranch---it definitely would not be a good idea for both you and Mrs. Mac to show up at a hospital at the same time! And somebody has to find old 'white-eyes'---God knows where HE got off to after the fracas!" Hawk's eyes were half-closed but he whispered---"Did you---see him? T-tell m-me what happened---what--did you hear and—w-what did you see when you got---over h-here? Tell me n-now---before Doc gets here! Let's h-have it. This damned---thing isn't o-over with---yet."

"If you'll promise to hush-up and save your breath---I'll fill you in! Not that you'll remember any of it when Doc gets thru with you---but I know how you are. So, here's the story. Salle and I never undressed for bed---we just lay under the cover with our clothes on and left the window up about an inch so we could hear better. I was about to go to sleep when we heard a shot! As we ran out, I told Salle to lock our door behind us while I ran ahead to get here fast as I could! I'm telling you, man, I didn't know WHAT we'd find when we came thru that back door! It was dark---I had the revolver---."

Salle squatted beside Bill, breaking in---"Hawk, just as we came thru the back door and slammed it shut---we heard somebody stumblin' around back here in her room---Bill shouted and ran down the hall with me right behind him!

When Bill put the flashlight on him, old 'white-eyes' was
bent over you---we both saw his face then he turned,
jumped out and ran away toward the highway!" She put a
hand on her chest---"I took one look at you lyin' on the
floor lookin' deader than roadkill---and poor Miss Lizbeth
there on the bed---I felt sick to my stomach! I was near
throwin' up when I said to myself---'You just stop this
nonsense, Salle! They need you---an' here you're actin'
like a three year old at first hog-killin'!' While Bill was
lookin' after you, I leaned over Miss Lizbeth, feelin' for a
pulse---and it WAS there!" Hawk exhaled, nodded slightly
as Salle took her brother's hand and continued babbling---"I
went over her real careful---honest, brother-san, I couldn't
find a gun-shot! Meantime, Bill finished checkin' you and
called Doc---! Joseph!!" Salle lept ahead to another
subject---"Old 'white-eyes' still doesn't know who you are-
--he hadn't managed to get that stockin' off when he heard
us and hauled-tail out of here!! So here's your stockin'---
I'm tuckin' it in your pocket. Hawk, somebody has to get
that man otherwise the three of us won't ever be safe again,
we're witnesses! He may even try a hit on Doc---he sure
hates him enough!"

"What happened, man?!"---Bill gazed closly at Hawk who
was practically unaware of the two of them---"How'd he
ever get the drop on you like that?" Joseph grunted but
never answered. "Salle!"---Bill whispered as he realized
what the room would look like to a lawman—"His blood is
all over this rug where he fell! Listen, we need to carry
your brother on up to the apartment! I don't think the blood
has gone thru to the floor yet but I need to have a good look
at the wood beneath Hawk and the rug---it's pretty thick!
We'll get Joseph out of here and tucked away then drag it
out back, later Doc can haul it off the ranch! Okay?" Salle
nodded as Bill continued---"He'll have to file a report on
Lizbeth and McDougal---so in a few hours, the law could be

179

crawling all over this place! But before they do, we need to do a little house-work and 'clean things up'---you catch my drift?" Salle looked into his eyes, replying---"You better believe I catch it---we're Indians, aren't we? I'll put an oil-cloth over our bed, fold a couple of old blankets over that and we'll lay Hawk on top! Then after Doc finishes takin' care of him, he can help us get rid of everything that has Hawk's blood on it!" Reaching over and grasping her husband's hand, she whispered---"Thanks, Bill."

He glanced at his wife---"Actually, since nobody but 'us chickens' know that Hawk was here---the sheriff most likely won't be taking any blood samples. He'll figure as she obviously wasn't able to get off the bed, there's no need to do that---but just in case, let's be prepared! I'm almost certain 'white-eyes' didn't suffer an injury---unfortunately. You check that closet for me, the one where Hawk hid out! If we start now, we should be thru by the time Doc gets here! And one last thing, Salle, just before the law arrives on the scene---you and I must change our bloody clothes. Later we'll take them to your mother's place to launder them!

By the time Dr. O'Barr hurried on the scene, a pink/gold dawn was spreading over the sky. Hawk lay on Bill and Salle's bed---drifting in and out of consciousness---while all traces of both his presence and his blood had been removed from the McDougal house.

Chapter Thirty-One

"Sorry I'm late---th' faster I drove---seemed th' truck got slower, th' road got longer! I parked out in back---so's not t'arouse neighborhood suspicion by bein' here this early! How they doing? That towel-pressure bandage stop th'

blood on Hawk's wound?"---Doc's eyes looked straight
ahead as he trotted to Lizbeth's bedside with both Bill and
Salle in tow. "Don't think he's bleedin' much now, Doc!"--
-Salle answered---"But he goes and comes---we just got
back from takin' him to the apartment---we thought it best
to get him out of here!" "Good thinkin'! Fill me in while I
give Lizbeth a quick going-over, just t'make sure she'll be
all right for awhile---then I'm goin' straight up t'Hawk!"
"Well, at least her old man didn't finish her off!"---Bill
stated---"Besides we didn't hear but one shot and Hawk
took it---at close range! How can we help?" "Don't know
about here...,"—Doc grunted---"...but I'll need your help
with Joseph!"

Briefly, Redwolf detailed the past 12 hours to Doc who
nodded and continued examining the woman on the bed.
When Bill heard Doc tell Salle to remove Lizbeth's pajama-
top, he knew it was time to vacate the premises—"I'll, uh,
just go and stay with Hawk now that you're here, Doc!
When you're finished, come on up---I'll let you in!" He
then beat a hasty retreat to watch over his brother-in-law.

"Salle!"---Doc whispered as she finished wiping away all
signs of a carpet on the bare floor beneath Lizbeth's bed---
"Anybody know Mac's whereabouts? I mean, he can't
sneak back into th' house---can he?" "Lord, I hope not!"---
she flustered---"Bill said he ran away toward the highway---
but he might decide to come back! I'm finished with the
floor, if you don't need me this minute---I better go and
make certain every window and door in this whole house is
locked tight!" "Good! Do any of you have a gun?"---Doc
looked up at her, suddenly her eyes lit up---"Yes! Hawk
gave Bill one---a handgun!" "Well, we really need two!
One here in case old Mac comes back t'finish what he
started when you an' Bill interrupted---I'll tell Bill t'keep
th' one he has over at your place! I always carry a shotgun

181

in my truck so when I'm finished here, follow me outside
an' I'll give it t'you for this room. You know how t'shoot?"
"Yep."---she nodded---"Hawk taught me! And don't you
think I wouldn't turn old McDougal into a pile of sausage if
he sticks his head back in here while you and Bill are takin'
care of my brother!!"

Doc conversed as he took care of Lizbeth---her breath came
in short, painful gasps punctuated with slight moans---
"Even tho Mac doesn't know 'who' he shot---we don't want
anyone t'get nosey! The minute I'm finished cleanin' up
your brother's wound an' I'm sure he's all right, I'll call an'
report this! By then, Lizbeth'll be better able t'identity Mac
as her assailant---then Bill can verify her story by sayin'
how he saw Mac walkin' in th' kitchen yesterday mornin'.
Shouldn't be a problem there---no one will want t'go into
your apartment for anything. Unless---,"---Doc looked
warily at Salle, her voice quavered---"Unless, W-WHAT?!"
Doc shrugged---"Unless Logan wants t'look out that same
apartment window! You know---t'see if Bill's tellin' th'
truth about seein' Mac. But should they wanta go up there,
I'll suggest that Bill stay over here an' walk around in th'
kitchen, imitating Mac---meanwhile I'll go over with them
an' unlock, makin' a great fuss about how fortunate that Bill
kept two locks on th' door! I'll tell him there's only one
key---that way they won't suspect that Mac could've
slipped back an' hid in th' apartment an' wanta search it!
Once they're satisfied Bill could see th' kitchen, should they
get interested in th' bedroom---I'll side-track Logan with
'huntin' talk! Don't worry, Salle!" He looked at the
expression of dread settling over her features—"I've known
him for years---I know how t' get his attention away from
that back bedroom!"

 Doc seemed so deep in thought that she figured he was
taken up with worry over all the happenings---so she

182

checked the hall closet where Hawk had waited for Mac's arrival then was off to the kitchen where she began making coffee and cooking breakfast.

Meanwhile Doc had a plan---"Th' slug that went thru Hawk! It should be somewhere behind where he was standin'!" With Salle out of the room, he took a small flashlight from his bag and began searching the wall. It didn't take long to find what he was looking for, there in the old board wall, he saw the slug and concluded that after hitting Hawk, it lost momentum then stopped halfway into the wood! Pulling on clean latex gloves, he gently lifted the bullet out without disturbing the wood. Standing back, he studied the wall---then backed away even further and looked again. Among natural knotholes in the old boards, the man-made indention was barely visible but if a trained eye searched, they could locate it by the fresh wood-color made by the slug. Laying the bullet on a chair near his bag---he turned about the room, his eyes taking in it's decor---spotting an antique chest of drawers with a good sized framed print of Sallman's 'Head of Christ' hanging over it, he determined it was just right!!

He pushed the tall chest until it was setting squarely over the bullet hole, then took the picture down. Turning the screw-hook, he hastily removed it then put it into the wall above the chest. "Sorry, Lord...,"---Doc murmured--- "...but sometimes, we gotta do what we gotta do---in spite of th' law. Right?" Once again he cast his eyes about the room---then proceeded to pick up a large family Bible and placed it atop the chest---just beneath the Sallman print. "There---just perfect."---he murmured.

Opening his bag, he rummaged about, brought out a bottle filled with liquid and headed for the half-bath in the hall. Plugging the lavatory, O'Barr poured out half the liquid then added water, dropped in the slug and let it set for three minutes. He could hear Salle out in the kitchen as he watched the liquid meticuliously kill off every microscopic hint of blood on the metal, without disturbing the somewhat 'oily' gunpowder residue. Any minute amount of blood still clinging to the slug would be so contaminated by the solution that no lab could even say it was 'blood'---much less what type. At last, he lifted his treasure out of it's 'bath', held it up between two gloved fingers and blew it dry with his breath while rinsing the lavatory with his other hand. After wiping down the lavatory with a hand towel, he carried everything back to the bedroom.

Smells of bacon and coffee began drifting back as Doc replaced items back in his bag and set his brain in motion once again. "Okay. Now, if Mac was on his knees holdin' Lizbeth down---he's about 6 ft.---so, on his knees, that would put him--uuhhh—about up t'here---an' with his arms down a little, one hand holdin' th' gun toward Lizbeth's head." Doc measured with his arms and hands as his brain spun out a new version of last night's scenario. "Let's say they were strugglin', she saw him about t'pull th' trigger--- but rolled her head aside at th' last split second---th' shot would take this direction---so…"---with his eyes, he pinpointed what he considered a believable spot. Opening his pocketknife, he leaned over Lizbeth who'd dozed after he'd adminstered her a drug. Re-sighting his original point between the iron rods making up the head of the bed, he began to bore then chunk out a smallish hole---taking the slug, he pushed it in as far as it would go. Pocketing his knife, he lay down on the floor, scooted beneath the high old-fashioned wrought-iron bed and wiped up every bit of wood shaving scraped from the wall---with the area carpet now gone from under the bed---he had no trouble spotting each tiny speck.

"Now, Logan can 'discover' th' bullet an' dig it out. And if I play my cards exactly right, one day soon, he'll decide t'compare this slug with a few suspected Klan crimes during th' past decade. When they catch McDougal, he'll naturally come up with a cock-n-bull story about a masked intruder beatin' Lizbeth---but this way, she can squash his story---flat as a cucumber slice! It's not as tho Mac is as pure as th' driven snow---he planned t'kill her an' but for Hawk, would've done it! So for all involved, th' direction of that shot has t'be changed!"

Doc made his way to the kitchen, ready to go and care for Hawk's wound. Looking at Salle, he asked---"Th' doors an' windows taken care of?" She nodded as he went on--- "Lizbeth is restin'. I gave her a shot, poor thing. Later, we'll rouse her with some ammonia an' give her a cup of coffee---because th' three of you---Bill, Lizbeth an' yourself---have t'rehearse last night's events a little different than they happened---an' do it before Logan gets here."

Salle looked closely at Doc---"Don't we have a problem with---er, Hawk's 'equipment' over in our closet?" "What?"---he stared at her---"What 'equipment' you talkin' about, Salle?" Quickly, she looked away---"Oh---nothin'. Don't worry about it." All the while she assured herself--- "Surely, Doc knows about that phone tap---he has to know! Hawk must've either played the tape for him---or told him! In all this excitement, he's just forgotten all about it---I'll remind him after he takes care of Hawk!"

Salle followed Doc outside, took the shotgun he handed her along with a box of shells then returned and lay everything on the kitchen table.

She loaded the shotgun then took it and the shells to Lizbeth's room where she safely leaned it near the big old-fashioned bed. Salle could see Doc had cleaned and treated Lizbeth's facial wounds then put in some required stitched ---bandages covered the worst and by now other bruises were quite swollen, turning an angry dark, purplish-blue-bloody red color. The flesh on her hands, arms, chest and neck was severely abraised, blood-shot and raw in places--- Salle knew it must've hurt like the dickens while he was beatin' her! Pulling up a straight chair near the bedside, she kept watch over her employer, her friend.

After awhile Lizbeth's eyelids began fluttering---Salle leaned toward her---"Ma'am! It's me, Salle! You okay?" Soon the puffed eyelids over her blue-green eyes opened---closed---then opened again, she moaned—"Hmm----oooOH!" Her gaze shifted around the room and back---"Salle?" "Yes Ma'am---it's me, I'm here!" Lizbeth groaned---"Ah---uh, hurt soo--bad." Painfully raising one hand and arm slightly, she gasped---her face blanching at the sight of her bruises. Salle sat down on the bed---"He tried t'kill you, Miss Lizbeth---remember?"

"Salle! W-whose gun?"---she whispered when her eyes caught sight of the firearm. "It's Doc's---he's lendin' it t'us---in case we need it before he gets back! He's takin' care of my brother!"---Salle assured the woman in bed---"Don't you worry none, Miss Lizbeth---I can use this thing! Hawk taught me how t'shoot the eyes off a gnat at 30 paces--you're in good hands!" Lizbeth couldn't take a deep breath---the pain from her bruised ribs was too intense, her head ached horribly as did her jaw, face and neck---"Mac was---sittin' on top of me---shakin' m-mah head--yellin' nonsense---t-theah w-was a noise---then a gunshot. Ah kinda w-went--into h-hysterics. T-then he began---beatin' me---Ah can't---remembah, Salle. Please t-tell me---tell me

what else h-happened! Ah--need t'know---about---him."
Salle leaned closer---"Who, ma'am?" "Y-yoah brothah!
He was in th' room..."---Lizbeth whispered---"...Ah s-saw
him---theah was a—a noise o-of some sort---then th' gun
went off—! Salle---wheah's Hawk?"

As Salle related the story, Lizbeth wept profusely---"Ah
nevah---w-wanted him t'be hurt! He--he's a warrior, Salle--
-how did this h-happen?" "Miss Lizbeth, I don't honestly
know---there was so much confusion in here when Bill and
I burst thru the back door! But even you couldn't have kept
Joseph away---not when he---er, thought something might
happen to you. Try not to worry---Doc will have him goin'
again in no time. One bullet can't stop my brother, he's
tougher than a bulldozer tread---count on it!"

Refusing to be comforted by Salle's attempted
encouragement, Lizbeth continued to weep quietly. After
hearing about Hawk---her heart now felt just as bruised and
battered as her body. Th' captain had tried to protect her
from her own husband---and received a bullet for his
trouble! Salle decided perhaps she could get Lizbeth's
mind off Hawk and onto her account of last night's events--
-which she needed to rehearse.

"Miss Lizbeth---Doc says, when the sheriff arrives, you
gotta change your story and all of us must tell the same!
When he's finished with Hawk, he'll fill us in on changes
about the shootin'! But basically--you, Bill and I can talk
about the three of us shellin' pecans until a certain time last
night then he and I went home and you went to bed. But
you must never mention my brother bein' here!" Salle
looked away then spoke in a low voice---"While it's true,
my brother 'dotes' on you, Ma'am, he's still an 'Indian'---
so if you would, please do keep his name out of this."

187

Lizbeth held out a hand to Salle, whispering---"My sweet Salle, y-you know Ah'd nevah, not---in a m-million yeahs---implicate Hawk---in a-anythin'. Ah'm simply too grateful--too t-thankful that h-he cared e-enough---t'get involv--ed. Most folks wouldn't---they'd jus' say it---w-was 'a family mattah'. Had it n-not been---foah him—y'know Ah'd be dead at this minute. So you might s-say, Ah 'dote'---on h-him too. Y'sure y-you didn't---g-guess?" A small painful smile crossed the swollen, bruised face as Salle took Lizbeth's hand between hers---"You both did a pretty good job of stayin' away from each other---I give you that! Seriously---no, Ma'am---I never guessed. After retirin' from the army, he mostly stayed to himself---like a sad, ailin' old hermit---an' I thought he 'needed a girl friend'!" Salle laughed self-consciously---"Never had any notion he was smitten and that was what was really eatin' away at him!" Lizbeth whispered---"We---you and I---are goin' t'stop--all this 'Miss Lizbeth' an' 'Ma'am' stuff---we're 'Lizbeth' and 'Salle'---a-agreed?" Salle smiled at her then nodded---"Agreed, now I'm goin' to bring you some coffee, you don't exhaust yourself by anymore talkin'."

Chapter Thirty-Two

"You sure know how t'get your fool-self half-killed! It's a lucky 'Injun' that you are---bullet went right thru you!"---Dr. O'Barr snorted as he examined the wound and prepared to clean it out! Hawk was half-conscious, murmuring something to Bill---"Y-you gotta get it! N-now---go r-right now---." "Get what, Hawk?"---Bill leaned close to catch the words. "Th—the recorder---L-Lizbeth's room." "Where in Lizbeth's room?" "Under---th' table---bedside---table. Get it---outta---there---b-before the l-law---comes. Hurry!" "All right, Hawk! It's as good as done!"---Bill looked at Doc---"Sorry! You'll have to wait on me, Doc---

he's right. I had no idea he put it in there---but we gotta
bring it over here before the sheriff arrives! If it's still
running, the tape will implicate a third person when all this
happened, plus all we've been up to since McDougal
vacated the premises! Hawk'll have to 'doctor' it before
anyone listens---other than us!" O'Barr nodded---"First get
me several clean sheets then go---get it! But put a move on-
--I've wasted enough time---this wound must be cared for!"

Bill ran down the steps as Doc turned to Joseph, taped the
IV line and injected some anti-biotics then asked---"How'd
you let yourself get shot up like this, Winterhawk? That's
what I'd like t'know!" Hawk's voice mumbled---the
morphine was beginning to work---"...I waited an'--waited
for t-the fool t--to m-make his move---then he came in—
t'thru th' window---wasn't expectin' that! He—he got on
the bed---an' began v-verbally tormentin' an' threatenin'
her---forcin'---his face---right d-down into hers! I--I
wanted t'jerk his g-guts--out---on th' spot. Then—he started—pullin' her—hair---but I must—wait---an' get verbal
proof---proof that'd--s-stand up in --court---she'd n-need it
a-as I couldn' testify f-for her. Hell, oh---hell. Then--he
started bangin' her head a-aroun---finally, he s-said what we
need--ed t'hear. I was---r-ready t'take him. B-but th'
floor---board creaked---h-he whirled toward m-me---an'
fired. Doc, I mss-miscalcu—lated m'distance from---him---
I shoulda---j-just killed the s.o.b.---when he f-first--put h-
hand---on her----an' been done with it---been d-done---with
th' whole th-thing. Now---n-now, he'll---only c-come back
to—finish th' job. He's--not human---but a 'devil'---'d-
diablo'---y'know?" Doc agreed quietly---"I know what he
is, Joseph. But you'll be fine---just gonna take some time."
"H-how much--time? This isn' fi--finished....I---didn't do-
--my job. Gotta—d-do it right..." His slightly accented
deep voice trailed off into mumbles of ---"never quit, never-
--give up, ne-ever quit...th' best—of th' best...."

189

"I'll be puttin' you out soon."---Doc leaned over him---
"Joseph? You listen t'me, you keep th' faith—I'm right
here an' I'm taking good care of you—an' Lizbeth—think
on that. An' this mess? Don't worry 'cause I got it figured
out—I'll tell you about it later. Let's say a 'Rosary'---I
think I remember---okay? Let's go--'Hail Mary, fulla
grace--th' Lord is with thee--blessed art thou amongst
women an' bless'd is th' Fruit of thy womb, Jesus. Holy
Mary--Mother of God--pray f'us sinners now—an' at
th'hour of our death.' C'mon Joseph, help me talk !" On
the next decade---Joseph quietly began murmuring the
words with Doc---they continued until Bill returned.

Staring at them---a reluctant Bill then crept closer,
whispering--"Something happen while I was gone? Doc?
He okay??!" Doc nodded, giving Bill a pat then tied on his
scrub gown, by that time Joseph was under anesthesia.
"He's OK---just getting his mind in th' right mode---he's
out now. Go to th' bathroom, scrub your hands with that
brown betadine then rinse with th' solution in that white
bottle next to it---dry off with the sterile blue towel I laid
out---tie on th' gown, pull on those gloves---let's begin! All
you gotta do is listen carefully, do exactly what I tell you---
everything we need is laid out over there.."---he pointed to
another blue towel with sterile instruments lying across it.
"What time is it?"---Doc glanced at Bill as he washed down
Joseph's entire mid-section with alcohol then poured
betadine over both front and back until the wounded man
lay in a brown puddle. "Seven o'clock in the morning,
Doc."---William Redwolf swallowed, took a deep breath,
blinked then nodded---"Ready when you are!"

By eight a.m., Doc had finished and was taping special
absorbent bandages especially around the bullet's exit
wound---"Bill, let's get things 'in order' over here before I

call Logan. Earlier when you two brought Joseph up here
then 'cleaned' over at th' house---where'd you put your
'throw-aways'?" "Everything we took from the house is in
garbage bags, Doc, I put all of it in my work truck---then I
cut that area rug into four pieces, rolled up each one and
stuffed each in a separate plastic bag—it was pretty bloody.
You think we could carry the house stuff plus these surgery
things off someplace in the hills then burn them
completely?" Doc nodded---"Absolutely. I'll hide th'
entirety of it at my house for a couple of days, then you and
I can get rid of it! Right down to ashes which we'll stir into
the earth---or strew off some cliff into th' wind!"

"Now, you're th'one who lives here, how does it look---like
normal?" Doc glanced carefully about the room where
Hawk lay between clean bedsheets, still hooked up to the IV
and sleeping peacefully beneath warm covers. Bill turned
all about---"When we carry out these bloody things—it'll be
fine. Long as you keep 'the lawmen' outta here! Did Hawk
tell you he had---er, 'something' hidden in that clothes
closet over there?"

Exhaling, Doc didn't know where or how Hawk had set up
the phone tap---so THAT must be what both Salle and Bill
meant. "He wouldn't tell me anything until he—uh, played-
--a reel of tape for me."---Doc stared at Bill---"You connect
with that?" Bill nodded---"The 'thing' that made that tape
is in our closet---hidden behind a stack of blankets and rugs.
It's hooked up outside the window---oh, dear GOD!!"---
Bill's face blanched---"If they come up to the living room
and look out that window to check out my story---for sure,
they'll notice the wire Hawk used! Oh HELL! DOC?!
That wire has to go!!" Doc's face had paled like unto new
fallen snow---"You talkin' th' window where you stood
when you saw McDougal in th' kitchen!!?" Bill nodded,

swallowing at the lump that steadily grew larger in his throat!

Dr. O'Barr rubbed a hand over his mouth---"All right. Let's not panic. First off, we'll make certain about in here---th' bedroom pass inspection?" Bill was so addled that his glance was extremely brief---but he'd just finished saying it was 'clean'---so he nodded.

"Then let's get th' damned wire loose! We gotta make haste here!"—Doc snorted---"While you take care of that, I'll check on Lizbeth an' call Logan---we can't let too much time elapse before speakin' to th' authorities! You got a ladder?" Again Bill nodded. "Then go get it---climb up th' pole out there an' take Hawk's wire loose from th' phone company's wire! And for God's sake, man---BE CAREFUL!! Don't electrocute yourself---that's ALL we'd need t'complete this day! Remove every clamp, any tape or piece of wire---get absolutely everything he used and toss to th' ground. When you get thru---we'll pick it up an' bag it like we've done all the rest! Then th' ladder's gotta go back where it was---an' while you take it back, I'll pull th' wire back inside. We'll put th' recorder from Lizbeth's room plus all that phone equipment in some brown paper grocery bags, haul 'em downstairs t'my truck, I'll take it home with me an' hide it. Later on, Hawk can take care of it!"

Doc looked at Bill---"Comprende? Got th' list in your head? Can you do it?!!" Poor Bill nodded once more as Doc slapped the surgery 'trash' into his hands---"C'mon now, Mr. Redwolf, th' worst is behind us! Trust me! Let's get this stuff down t'my truck an' transfer what's in your truck t'mine---then you can start on that wire! Thank th' Good Lord for camper tops! I'm gonna be loaded down with paper sacks an' garbage bags!!"

About the time Bill thought he had everything straight---
Doc stopped him---"By th' way, Bill---when we get
everything ship-shape 'round here? Don't go runnin' off---I
gotta talk   with you, Salle an' Lizbeth---and BEFORE
Logan gets here! After Hawk hears that recordin' from
Lizbeth's room---then maybe 'doctors it' a bit, it'll lower
th' boom on McDougal---that is IF it's even needed. But
we got another trump card! In a manner of speaking,
Lizbeth must do a good job of---well, tellin' a half-truth
about a whole truth! She has t'say that McDougal fired th'
shot at HER!" Bill's mouth hung open, he went two shades
whiter! "Not t'worry!"---Doc soothed---"I took care of
everything, you're finished with 'underhanded chores'!
Actually even Lizbeth won't have t'change her story either-
-except th' part about Hawk an' th' gunshot. All you an'
Salle must do is tell th' truth---up to th' point of seein'
Hawk lyin' on th' floor! Tell Logan how you two heard a
shot before day, let's say around 5:00 a.m.---that'll explain
away th' hour I used t'patch up Hawk---tell him you an'
Salle rushed over, let yourselves in with your key an' heard
someone bumblin' around in her bedroom. You then ran
down th' hall with your flashlight---leaving off th' part
about carryin' th' revolver Hawk gave you---after seein' th'
intruder, you flashed th' light in his face---thereby
identifying him---that's when he went out th' window,
makin' a getaway. At that point, Salle tried t'do what she
could for Lizbeth then called me---that's it! You, Salle,
Lizbeth an' Mac have t'be th' only people in that room this
morning---now don't be afraid---Logan'll expect everyone
t'be nervous---I'll be right there with you. Mostly tho it'll
be Lizbeth's story that'll carry th' most weight---after all, he
WAS tryin' t'kill her! I'm certain she can handle this---
she's endured enough---and she doesn't need Mac runnin'
around loose just waitin' t'kill her off at some future
opportune moment that suits him! You know as well as I, if
Hawk hadn't been there, Lizbeth would be dead right now!

193

She's ready t'end all this---an' believe me, this should do exactly that!"

Bill finally grumbled in an uncertain tone---"Man. I sure will be glad when this day ends---I'm going back to the reservation! This is NO kinda life for me! Makes me wonder if all white people live such exciting lives as you and the McDougals!!" Doc laughed, slapped Bill's back as they temporarily separated paths.

Chapter Thirty-Three

From his vantage point there in the hills cross the highway and just north-west from the front porch---Mac decided there wasn't much going on. He'd seen the 'famous' O'Barr truck go tearing into the driveway just before sunrise! For a doctor, he'd sure as hell taken his time about getting out there---probably didn't want to leave his warm bed for a 'domestic' dispute---however---it WAS his beloved 'Lizbeth'! And now with her 'injured', Mac thought, the old fool would likely camp out at the house for the next week---along with those damned 'Indians'! He wondered how he'd ever finish her off with all this interference!?

"RED-SKIN NIGGERS! Before they came storming in---I had her!! DAMN! Why didn't I shoot her the first thing! The minute she told me she'd changed her will---that's when I shoulda finished her off---then beat her beyond recognition!! But what she said took the wind clean out of my sails for a few seconds---then that floor creaked behind me and I had to defend myself! Mistake number one---I shoulda kept my head, held off the beating until I'd put a bullet in her! Still it was only one shot that woke the 'Indians' and the sound brought them running! Never thought that he'd come flying down the hall at me like that---figured if they heard the shot, both of them would cower in that apartment 'till doomsday! Mistake number two, never underestimate a nigger or an 'Indian'." He coughed, trying to spit but his mouth had dried-up hours ago---"This is exactly why I never wanted anybody hanging around there! How can a person carry out private matters with people milling in and out like ants on a damned ant-hill?"

"But her 'lover' being there---now THAT threw me off completely!" Amazement covered Mac's face as he shook his head---"A man in her room, the bitch!! She sure had me foxed---walking around day and night looking like warmed over death! Who'd even take a second look at her---except her 'deah Doctah O'Bahr'---and obviously he was home in his own warm bed! This bastard in her room was there when I opened the window. What I can't figure out is why he didn't just leave by the back-door and run like a bee-stung dog?! No---'whoever' he is, he's not the type to run---he's some brave, arrogant 'mother's son', I gotta say---standing behind me like that! He heard everything I said---and was coming after me too---that creaking board saved my ass, I guess! Left alone with him another 10 seconds, I'd have had that stocking off his face---but once again, thanks to those wretched Indians, I have no idea who he was! Bastard!! I hope he's DEAD by now---one less witness to worry about!!"

Looking down at the ground, he absently dug into the leaves with a stick---"You're getting slovenly and careless, McDougal, not as sharp as you were this time last year. While you were learning to walk again and honing up last spring's plan---it seems you didn't give your mealy-mouthed little wife enough credit!" He'd used the past few hours to think it all over---and over again. "Who in blazes WAS the man?! I searched the place from top to bottom and found no sign of 'another man'---no letters, no notes, no scraps of paper with words or phone numbers or time written on them! No suspicious long distance calls! Hell, she never wore any new jewelry---or clothes---she'd stopped even wearing 'make-up'---and rarely combed that ugly, ratty hair! WHO? And who'd be there at 3:30 in the morning EXCEPT a 'lover'!! Wish I knew if he's still alive! And IF he is---where is he---did the 'Indians' see him? They HAD to have seen him!!" Suddenly a light clicked on---"THEY KNOW!! THEY KNOW ALL ABOUT HER AND HIM!! AND THEY'VE HELPED COVER HER ADULTEROUS TRACKS! AND THAT DOCTOR AS WELL!! FOR HOW LONG!!? HOW LONG HAVE THEY ALL BEEN IN CA-HOOTS AND WHO IN HELL IS HE?!?"

At the mere thought of being deceived by anyone, much less by THIS bunch, Mac's anger boiled over for the umpteenth time since he'd been on the run---"THE BITCH!! HE WAS THERE IN THE HOUSE---ALL THE TIME---RIGHT UNDER MY OWN ROOF!!! DAMN THEM ALL!!" Cumulative hours of frustrated ambition, fear, jealousy and rage were too much, suddenly he stood and began kicking at leaves and bits of dead wood. Then grabbing up a sizeable fallen limb, he flailed away at a tall pine tree until he grew breathless and some of his bottled up emotions were spent! Finally he swore in disgust and throwing down the limb, sat once more---the important question at this point was 'what should he do now'!!?

Rubbing his aching head, he wished for a warm coat, some hot coffee and wondered how he could call Rita. Even if Lizbeth was unconscious and couldn't talk---since he wasn't home in his bed, the 'Indians' would definitely report they'd seen him running away! He was 'fingered'--- unless---his mind began to spin! Unless he could make up a

196

story to convince the law that the man in her room had dragged HIM from an invalid-bed, taken him outside to a waiting vehicle---then went back and assaulted his wife! In that case, he could now choose a place where he was certain to be found then claim he'd been lying there since the intruder had dumped him after leaving the house! "That would fly! Sure---why not?! With only Lizbeth and two 'Indians' as witnesses, the Klan attornies can beat them by saying Lizbeth had a lover---and the four of them planned to get rid of me but had a falling-out---then one of them killed my 'poor wife'!!"

Mac's face brightened as he stood and leaned against the sunny side of some rocks---"What jury would take the word of two 'Indians' against the word of an invalid! But HER testimony---what about that!?" He reasoned---"Now, that COULD cost me jail-time---unless Daddy can 'get me off'---or better yet, his people could see that she and/or the 'Indians' meet an untimely demise!" Mac began to chuckle---"A little action for the guys to polish up their skills---keep 'em from getting too rusty!"

So for the first time since his plan had unexpectedly 'gone bad', Mac felt better. "Maybe things can be 'fixed' yet! A little 'forethought'---remembering the details of last night and repeating the same story over and over! Then with some clever future planning---plus a little help from Daddy, the Klan and Rita---it could be done."

Mac's 'grin' was short-lived, in the distance came the sound of sirens approaching! Peering toward the highway, he saw two 'county-mounties' skid into the driveway then speed to the house! "Dammit! I guess O'Barr couldn't WAIT to sic the law on me---or maybe the 'lover' IS dead! So, make up your mind, McDougal, what you gonna do? You can't stay here---it's time to 'get in motion'!"

Chapter Thirty-Four

Later as the two county cars drove away, Doc and Bill stood in the back yard watching them head toward the highway. "How do you think it went, Doc?"---Bill asked, his eyes never leaving the cruisers with their blaring radios. Doc pursed his lips, exhaled and finally replied---"Fairly well--- good, in fact. Lizbeth's face an' body would convince anybody---but Salle's idea of leavin' those blood-smeared sheets on th' bed and Lizbeth wearing th' same torn, bloody pajamas---that was outstandin'! It roused even more sympathy, not t'mention those photographs they took! All that aside, before five minutes had passed, I could see Lizbeth had both Logan an' his deputy just about in her pocket!" Doc couldn't help chuckling---"Even in her condition, she's still quite a charmer, huh!" "She's a nice lady,"---Bill shrugged---"..if that's what you mean. And she told the story well, hope they believed her---especially about McDougal shooting AT HER---otherwise, we're all knee-deep in digested cattle food that's been 'dropped'!"

"Why!"---Doc looked at him--"They got the slug out of the wall behind her, didn't they? They not only believed her, they believed all of us!" Bill wasn't quite convinced--- "Yeah, but---there's a difference. Salle and I aren't 'like you'---or her, Doc. Lucky for us, you're not only respectable and 'been here forever'---but you're 'anglo'. Not to mention that for years, you've been 'doctoring' everybody within 50 miles--with all this going for you, your word carries a lot of weight in these parts." Doc's soft 'hoot' was tinged with guilt thinking not only of the 'liar' he'd recently become---but now, he'd tampered with evidence in an attempted murder investigation and dragged others into it as well! Looking away, he muttered---

"Appreciate your confidence, Bill, but don't go overboard with your summation of my 'good character' nor abilities!"

Both headed upstairs to check on Joseph who'd slept thru the whole thing. "How's he doing?"---Bill leaned over Doc for a gander at his brother-in-law. Doc sat on the bed, taking vital signs---"Not bad considerin' a bullet passed thru him then had his wound fixed in a make-shift 'surgery'--- and remained 'out' f'two hours! It's high time I brought him 'round. I don't mind tellin' you I held m' breath when I brought Logan AND his deputy up here so's they could peer thru that window while you imitated Mac walkin' around in th' kitchen!" Laughing he went on---"All I could think of was Joseph wakin' up in an untimely fashion an' those two hearin' all these moans, coughin' or vomitin' sounds echoin' from th' bedroom!! I think I would've strangled Joseph!! I couldn't WAIT t'get those two out that door an' outside!" An uneasy Bill shook his head--- "Remind me about all this sometime next month---maybe it'll sound a lot funnier then than it does now!" Still peering over Doc's shoulder, he repeated---"Y'sure he's okay!?"

"Bleedin' is under control---things look good, now if he doesn't get an infection an' if he behaves himself until his insides heal---I don't foresee any problems. His vitals are almost normal---blood-pressure needs t'bump up a notch or two but that'll happen as anesthesia continues wearin' off. Better hand me that little pan over there---just in case he starts t'get sick on his way back from 'lah-lah-land'. 'Course I really don't expect him t'puke---after all, it'd be unmilitary t'show such a sign of weakness!"

Doc began the waking process---at first, Hawk was weakly combative and for several minutes, it took both Doc and Bill to hold him so he wouldn't re-injure himself. As Hawk settled down, he seemed to slip from Viet Nam--to training maneuvers--to the reservation---and finally some 'nonsense' about flying like a bird! That's when Bill hooted with laughter---"Have you ever heard such stuff in your whole life, Doc? Does EVERYBODY carry on like this after they've been put to sleep for surgery?" Bill wiped at his cheeks and went on---"Because if they do, you can train me to assist---this is the most fun I've had in ages! Salle is gonna love it!" Chuckling, Doc cautioned kindly---"Not professional, William Redwolf!! Bein' a doctor or nurse is like bein' a priest---you can't talk about what you hear--- professional medical ethics an' all that! Oh, sometimes it's almost too good NOT t'pass around when things are dull in th' barber shop---but certain things must be 'sacred'! AND as professionals who see th' human body naked an' helpless while th' brain is under the influence of drugs---'discretion' is definitely required!" Doc grinned up at Bill--- "Remember, one day---it could be YOU lyin' here!"

"Oh, GOD FORBID!"---Bill laughed again---"God forbid! Tell me, is it a fact that everything people say under anesthesia is 'the truth'?" "Naww. Sometimes they go back over past events in their lives but they can be hallucinatin' from th' drug---plain an' simple 'seeing things'!" "Hmm."---Bill reconsidered---"You're right then! I better not mention this, I wouldn't want to get on Hawk's bad side---that's for sure!" "Neither would I."---Doc agreed---"He's gonna be mad enough when he remembers all his efforts t'help Lizbeth went down th' drain in one moment---worse still, McDougal's on th' loose! We'll have one sweet time keepin' him down until he's well enough t'have another 'go' at it!" Bill looked at O'Barr ---"Where do you think 'white-eyes' took off to?" "Dunno,"---he pondered---"Could be t'his father, his girlfriend---or th' Klan. Th' bad thing now is he has advantage of returnin' in his own time---on his own terms. Meanin' a new plan t'murder Lizbeth---an' whoever was in her bedroom IF he

can find out who!" Exhaling and turning to Bill, he added--
-"Even you an' Salle---because you're witnesses. Not
t'mention me, however for old Mac---that'd be just for the
hell of it! But with Lizbeth's 'statement' awhile ago,
hopefully none of us will have to worry about it for too
long. Just until the heavy arm of th' law lays hold on him!"

***

Lizbeth pleaded---"Ah must go an' see Joseph---Salle,
please help me out of bed an' dressed?" Salle was adamant-
--"Why, you can't go walkin' over there---you can't even
stand! You'd fall on your face if you tried to get up right
now! Doc gave you some medicine to quiet you---now, you
lie down and allow it to work! No, absolutely not---you're
too 'woozy' for bein' up and about!" Salle smoothed the
covers, tucking them about Lizbeth who grunted and fretted
about in the bed---"But he's---he put himself in—danger
foah me! Th' least Ah can do---is go see 'bout him!"

"But, he'll not be feelin' well for several hours, Miss
Lizbeth---after the surgery and all! Now,"---she appealed to
Lizbeth's sense of decorum--- "…you know a man doesn't
want a lady to see him---sick, puny---or vomitin'! You not
bein' married to him and him throwin' up in front of you---
why just the embarrassment'd kill him right off!" Lizbeth
sighed---"Oh me, such silly pride. Reckon yo'ah right, Ah
wouldn't want t'embarrass him---but---when do you think
Ah can go see him?" "When Doc comes over---you can
ask. Here..,"---Salle helped Lizbeth to lie back in bed---
"…you rest and I'm goin' to make some nice fresh coffee---
I'm dyin' for a cup---aren't you?" Lizbeth sighed, nodded
and began thinking on the 'story' she'd given Logan. While
the Sheriff had questioned her, Doc stood right beside him,
assuring both Logan and his deputy that she'd been given a
sedative and might sound 'a bit muddled'.

***

Thus things on the ranch continued to be 'quiet' with no more violence that day. The moment Hawk was conscious, he listened as Bill repeated the morning's activities plus the latest on Lizbeth's well-being. He then insisted Bill go immediately to the reservation and bring back men to 'help'. Puzzled, Bill thought his brother-in-law was still 'loopy' from morphine and reminded him that he'd done the chores for months now and didn't need any help! Hawk looked up at him from the pillow and raised a palm---"It isn't the work, William---it's for our safety as well as finding McDougal! You see, if we cover this place with 'Indians' plus 'trackers' spread out among them--- McDougal isn't going to take a chance on slipping back here! He may hate us, 'bro', but he's afraid of us--- especially when he's outnumbered to the hilt! When you divide the men up into groups---make certain the trackers go in first---the rest following several feet behind so they don't spoil any trail! Put them to work on both sides of the highway---all over these hills! The aim is for them to find any 'signs' of McDougal---I don't know where the bastard is hanging-out---but until I get on my feet---he ain't gonna be hanging-out HERE around the house or out-buildings! I won't give him another chance to kill Lizbeth---or you and Salle. I screwed this up royally last night by waiting for what's loosely termed 'admissable evidence' to come from a murderer' mouth---and I won't be making THAT mistake again!"

Bill interrupted---"But Joseph, you heard Doc---he wants to get you out of here--- he plans on driving you to his house tomorrow night---and keep you there till you're well!" Hawk shook his head—"You know as well as I that McDougal 'has it in' for you and Salle, now more than ever.

Doc says the newspaper plans a story about how you two
probably saved Mrs. McDougal's life when her husband
was beating her! So be ready for an interview. And what
about Lizbeth? Is everyone just going to waltz off and
leave her here? With Doc back there in town taking care of
business and me---why, you'd be the only man near the
house and apartment! That's not a 'wash', Bill---there has
to be a better way!"

Bill's eyes took in his stubborn brother-in-law and snorted--
-"Look at you. Barely awake after being scoured out, sewn
up and doped into unconsciousness yet already you're 'into
it'---full throttle! I hate to disagree with you, man, but
you'll be disabled for almost two full weeks! Didn't you
hear Doc? You tear something loose and you may bleed to
death! Don't be making that kind of trouble! Think of your
mother, your family---yourself! And her---your Mrs. Mac!!
Let the law handle him---with her story about him firing
that gun at her head and with the bullet in their hands---
they're after him for attempted murder as well as assault
with intent!"

Joseph gave a half-nod but insisted---"..let's think about it.
For now, go bring the men---I'll pay them the 'going-rate'
for trackers and hands. But I want them here, camping out
tonight for an early start at dawn's early light, tomorrow
morning!" Bill sighed---"Oh, all right, whatever you say---
but Hawk? When this is over? I want you to know that
Salle and I are gonna be 'history' around this place! We
can't live here any longer than necessary---there's a curse
on this damn land and I can't wait to drive away---leaving it
behind, like permanently---I never want to see it again!"

Chapter Thirty-Five

At sundown, Doc returned---saw to Lizbeth then went to
check on Hawk. Bill let him in---"How's our patient?
Good, I hope!" "Oh sure! He's just fine---lying in there
making like General Patton---so I hope you brought some
animal tranquilizers! Already he's propped up on pillows
making all this noise about how to keep everybody 'safe'
and then 'search and destroy' the enemy! I'm glad you're
here, maybe YOU can talk some sense to him---I can't do a
thing with him! He's gotta be THE most determined man I
ever run into! Keeps mumbling 'Never Quit'---over and
over! Right now, he's got the hills and woods around here
full of reservation 'trackers' and men---all camping out
ready to 'work' at first light tomorrow morning---but mostly
to find old McDougal!"

Once in the bedroom, Doc stared at Joseph---"Well, I see
you're alive an' back t'your usual ornery self! I expect
that's good in a way---but Winterhawk, I am TELLIN' you-
--IF you mess yourself up, you'll only be helpin' McDougal
out---doin' him a favor! It's true th' bullet burroughed
clean---but there's STILL a fair-sized messy hole goin' thru
and out your back! You're damn lucky you didn't get it in
th' gut, th' heart, a lung---or a kidney! Don't carry on so
over details---Bill an' I have done a fair job of cleanin'
things up around here! Your 'equipment' from the closet
and all that wiring from the pole outside---it's all in my
storage-building, locked up tight in an old trunk---you don't
have t'think about anybody findin' it! Tomorrow or after
sundown, we're takin' the rest off an' burn it. Salle's
lookin' after Lizbeth an' you're goin' home with me 'til you
recover! So what else IS there that can be done right now?"

Hawk lay back on the pillow with a grimace on his face---
"I'm tired, Doc. Don't you start on me, too! If you'll just

listen, I'll tell you 'problem'---it's 'security'! We can't
secure this area---unless all of us stay at the house---or all
stay up here! We don't have enough people who haven't
been either shot or beaten---it isn't a safe environment---not
unless we discover McDougal's whereabouts! Suppose the
fool gathers the Klan and brings a gang back here---they
could do anything---kill everybody present---or burn down
the house and buildings---with us IN them! Can't you
understand this? We're NOT safe! None of us."

Doc sat down and motioned Bill to do the same. "All right-
--all right. I can see th' sense of what you're sayin'---guess
my plan DID stretch it a mite too thin. So instead of all this
useless roilin' an' foamin'---let's put our heads together an'
change th' plan. Now, you're correct, we do have a
security-breach---so we'll just do something different."

Looking back at Joseph, Doc asked---"Did you take th'
liquids I told Salle t' bring over this afternoon?" Annoyed
with unimportant matters, Hawk exhaled---"Yes. Yes, I
'took' the liquids." "An' did you happen t'vomit anything
up?" "NO!"---Hawk snapped. "All right."---Doc retorted--
-"Don't get nasty! I reckon you could have some soup,
crackers and tea for supper. Now, let's get you clean an'
pretty---Miss Lizbeth wants t'come an' see you. Can you
stand some company?"

Joseph looked odd—"Lizbeth? NO! No, don't let her come
up here! I mean---she's not in any condition to be out in the
cold---or climbing the stairs." Doc folded his arms and
nodded---"That's what I told her but---she's a lot like you---
she doesn't listen very well. So, you want her t' come or
not come!" Hawk stared over at the corner---"You seem to
be the doctor!" "No!"---Doc corrected---"I'm just this boob
hoverin' about on th' side-lines---while everybody ignores
my best advice!"

Joseph exploded---"Dammit, Doc! I---of course, I want to see her! I've wanted to come back here and 'see her' ever since the first time I laid eyes on her! But---take a look at me---what do you see? Some old buffalo who's been strung up by his heels and partially gutted! My plan was to--to overcome 'white-eyes' last night---leave him for the law to scrape up while I'd be Lizbeth's secret hero---her white knight or maybe her 'brown' one. Boy! Was that ever a laugh! I let that reptile practically torment her to death while I stood there like a statue in the shadows waiting for him to 'attempt murder'---when I finally had what I needed on tape and moved---he shot me down! And there I lay--- sinking into a humiliating black hole while her screams joined the ringing in my ears! Then while he beat her senseless, obviously, I remained cold as a sack of potatoes in January! HOW can I look at her? I failed to take care of her---I love her more than my own life yet I failed her! I-- CAN'T--SEE--HER!!"

Doc sighed---"That's your ego talkin'---not your heart! Joseph, all she wants is t'assure herself that you're all right!! You really should see her, m'lad. It's an extraordinary woman who'd let th' man she loves look at her face after th' beatin' she took." "And just how do you think I can LOOK at her knowing both her pain and her appearance are MY fault?? The answer is still 'NO'---I cannot see her---not yet." Joseph turned toward the wall refusing any further communication.

Before long, Salle came in with the light supper---"Joseph? Hon, it's me. I brought you a bite---," He cut her off without looking at her---"I'm not hungry, Sis. Please---take it away." Suddenly, he lifted his head slightly and snapped- --"WHO'S WITH LIZBETH?? All of you haven't left her ALONE in that house—have you??!" "Ease back down, brother-san!"---Salle put a hand on his shoulder---"...Bill's with her---they're talkin'. And there's a shotgun right next to her bed---so it's okay. Be calm. I locked every door and window in the house, every curtain is drawn---nobody but nobody can see in! She's not alone---but she's sure been beggin' to see you since early this mornin'! Doc says you're 'all clean and groomed'--now, you gonna eat so I can go back and tell her she can come up?"

Joseph shook his head---"No---on both counts. I'm not hungry---and I just---I'm not well enough for company--- not tonight. Tell her---oh, make up something you think is- -'suitable'. But for God's sake, Salle,--"---he pleaded--- "...make it sound 'kind'---don't hurt her even more by sawing into her with your usual blunt honesty---you can be like a nicked knife blade, y'know!" Salle leaned and kissed his forehead---"Don't worry, Hon, I'll say somethin' nice--- especially now I know how much she 'dotes' on you!" Joseph stared warily at his sister who ignored his expression---"I'll tell her you've had a bad afternoon and that you're sleepin' the pain off! How's that?" Joseph closed his eyes in dismay and whispered---"For you, Sis? That's good---'nice'---'well-put'---such a statement should do away with all her worries!"

After Salle left, Bill returned and Doc took him back to the bedroom. "Now, listen up. Earlier this afternoon, Logan called me at th' office an' told me they had an APB out on McDougal then asked if anybody here had seen or heard anything of him---I told him so far as I knew, nobody had. Then he offered t'send a car with a deputy out here for th' night---I told him I'd planned t'stop by an' see Lizbeth later an' would ask. You want him here, Joseph? Shall I call Logan t'send out some help?" Hawk nodded with relief--- "That's great, Doc---it'll buy nighttime protection plus some hours to figure out what's best. I'm hoping the trackers will turn up something in the morning. We'll all feel better if a deputy is with Salle and Lizbeth while Bill's here with me." Doc nodded---"Good. Then it's settled--- I'll call. A deputy should be here within th' hour---I'll hang around till he arrives an' meanwhile we must come up with something more permanent---until McDougal is caught."

Before leaving for the night, Doc checked Joseph's vital signs one last time and gave him a sedative plus some pain medication then after cautioning him about lying still and resting---he bade him a 'goodnight'. Doc showed Bill three bottles of pills with printed directions, minus the name--- "Bill, make sure he doesn't go too long between doses of this one,"—he held up the brown bottle---"…it's for pain, give him two every four hours. This blue bottle is anti-biotics, 500 mg. X four a day---an' th' white one is a sedative---as needed. And should he get into difficulty of any sort---bleedin', breathin' or excessive pain---you call me, I'll come right away." Bill looked at a loss---Doc patted his shoulder and suggested---"Just stumble over at th' house an' tell that deputy you have 'chronic' kidney colic an' I always give you a shot for it---try an' look like your back an' lower belly are killin' you!"

"One last thing,"---O'Barr looked at Bill---"…what did Hawk tell Mary about his bein' away---I hope he said he'd be gone awhile!" Bill replied---"He told her he had some military business---might take a few days or long as two weeks---said he wouldn't call until next week." Doc picked up his bag and went to call for the deputy.

Once the lawman arrived, Doc said 'goodnight' and started home. On the way back to town, he thought perhaps he'd finally come up with a plan for their safety dilemma as well as getting Hawk off the ranch. It was somewhat 'involved', required some shuffling around---but at least the whole crew would be safe! First thing in the morning, he'd go out to see Lizbeth and tell Salle to pack some bags for the three of them---then have her veil Lizbeth's face and hair. Soon as the deputy cleared out, he'd examine Hawk. When the coast was clear, he and Bill would get Hawk into his truck, take him over to the hidden 4-wheel drive and stash the patient. Then while Hawk and Bill waited there, he'd drive back to the house in his truck, pick up Lizbeth and Salle. Bill would then drive Hawk's vehicle, following them to town. Once there, he and Bill would put Hawk on a roll away bed in his downstairs junk-room where Ida could help care for him---then Bill, Salle and Lizbeth would get into Hawk's vehicle and drive to Mary's house---they'd be safe there. Hawk and Bill could communicate with the trackers thru radios. They could tell Mary about Lizbeth's story--- all except the part Hawk played in it---as far as his mother was concerned, he was still 'away on military business'. The whole plan meant nobody would be left at the ranch--- in case McDougal came back---either alone or with some thugs!

Sighing aloud, Doc thought---"At least with this plan--- maybe all of us can finally get some sleep---that is, until Joseph goes into action again! But I'll drug th' stubborn ass just as long as I have to!" And with that thought---Doc arrived at his driveway, shut off the truck engine and went inside to get some much needed sleep.

Chapter Thirty-Six

After giving it more thought, Mac decided against the plan of 'placing' himself near the roadside where he could be found. Too many people might say they'd traveled the road early that morning and hadn't seen him. He had to 'disappear'! At least until he found out what had transpired

when 'the law' came to Lizbeth's rescue---as well, he had to
know what verbal damage that goat's belly, Dr. O'Barr, had
done to him!

So, crossing over the wooded hill where he'd been hiding,
he trekked north-west until he came to a small valley---the
upper end of 'his' ranch---where it joined Fargo's place. He
couldn't go to Fargo's house and use the phone---the
moment last night's events passed from one neighborhood
wag to another and finally made it's way to him, that
tobacco-chewing, loose-lipped relic from the old west
would be calling the law! Around mid-morning Mac found
a hunting trail leading far to the north of their area---he
followed it.

Around lunch, he drank from a stream of water then sat to
rest and assess his location. Noting a high point on the next
hill, he thought---"Maybe from there I can spot something
close by that has a phone---I'll call Rita 'collect'---and she
can pick me up at the highway. Hopefully Lizbeth won't
make too much news today---and if I REALLY luck up, this
whole thing will be treated as just another of a hundred
other 'domestics'! After all, there's not a man alive who
hasn't beat his old lady---at some point! I need to find my
safe place before this 'story' gets out!"

Once on the high point, Mac could make out what appeared
to be one of those places that rich folks build to 'get away
from it all'---after they've made a fortune! As best he could
tell, it was a fancy 'A' frame thing setting on a hillside
about half a mile away. Beneath the roofline, glass
windows covered the whole south section and flashed
brilliantly in the morning sun. He set out and before too
long, neared the house. Pausing, he dusted at his clothing,
ran his fingers thru his hair several times then approached
the front door.

And just as he'd thought, a tall aesthetic-looking, middle-aged man with long neatly combed greying hair and matching trimmed beard answered his knock---they stared at each other. "Hello!"---Mac grinned, offering a dirt-stained hand---"My name's Leo Marshall, I'm in the area on vacation---flew in here for a little hunting, you know! After being out for awhile earlier this morning---I went back to the rented truck---and it wouldn't crank! I just wondered if you might have a telephone I could use to call a friend over in the next town? Uh, if it's long distance---I'll pay you for the call now."

Ignoring the proffered hand, the homeowner continued to look warily at the odd, straggly male wearing dirt-stained clothing with bits of dead leaves and grass clinging to him---he didn't look like a 'hunter'! And certainly wasn't dressed for hunting in these parts!! "Hunting, you say?"---the homeowner snapped---"What were you hunting---dressed like this? Surprised you didn't freeze to death wearing such an atrocious, not to mention inadequate get-up!" Mac laughed self-consciously---"Well, would you believe when I was ready to head back in---I was stupid enough to take off my outer warm clothes, put them plus my gun IN the truck then found it wouldn't start. So I opened the hood and started fooling around with the battery, starter, etc.---in all the getting in and out, I got a bit aggravated..."---he shrugged innocently—"...I locked myself out! Dumb, huh."

"Yes---exceedingly so." The 'recluse' wasn't exactly thrilled to have someone show up at his door—he'd come out here to escape all that---and more. He didn't need either strangers or local yokels bumbling around---trying to be 'sociable' or looking for help. Exhaling noticeably, he snapped---"I have a phone---but do remove those shoes

211

before you come in. Where is it you wish to call? What
town?" Hurriedly, Mac slipped off his dirty, wet shoes and
said---"Blalock. You familiar with Blalock?" His back to
the intrusive 'hunter', the 'recluse' rolled his eyes and
replied dryly---"Not really. But for the price of the call, you
can do me the favor of NOT describing it to me." He
pointed to a phone---then stood staring at Mac, an
unfriendly expression on his bearded face. "Ah, yes!"---
Mac exclaimed---"Er, do I dial---or call 'Operator'?? I'm
not exactly familiar with your system." "Hand me the damn
thing!"---the 'recluse' snatched the phone from Mac's hand
and snarled—"Come, come---the number?" Mac gave him
Rita's home number---not certain if she'd left for work yet
or not---he'd forgotten his watch.

"Obviously there's no one home---m'dear man. And plan
'B'?" ---the 'recluse' arched his trimmed, combed
eyebrows. "Uh---oh, the work number. Yes, try that---I'd
appreciate it."---Mac regretted stumbling onto this bad-
tempered jerk who might, at a later time, remember placing
these calls---but it seemed he had no other choice, so he
gave Rita's work number. A couple of moments later, with
an exaggerated flourish, the homeowner handed over the
phone---"Sir! Your call!" Mac stood foolishly looking at
the man---was he going to stand there and listen to the
conversation---it seemed so as the suspicious host never
moved an inch nor took his eyes off him. Swallowing, Mac
stammered---"Hello. I---uh, could I speak to Rita, please?"
He felt intimidated by the presence of this pompous ass---he
was unaccustomed to being humbled by any 'overlord'! In
a momentary flush of rage, he wondered how the prig
would like to see his fancy 'A' frame crumble into a heap of
coals and ash! Who'd be the 'overlord' then??!

"Oh, Rita---Hello! Glad I got you---er, I---uh, need you to
come and pick me up."----"Pick you UP!? Where ARE

you, Mac? I don't understand what you're saying---you're NOT home, are you? You KNOW I couldn't come THERE!!"----"Of course not, Dear. I---uh, told you about 'walking', remember? I was out---hunting---and when I got ready to leave---uh, the truck wouldn't crank!"----"The truck! You DRIVING, TOO???"----"Actually that isn't important. Now, listen carefully, here's what I want you to do---can you leave work, drive down the highway toward---er, the one that passes by the ranch? I'm about 8 miles north of there---but I'll meet you at the highway! Keep an eye out for me, I'll be to your left---when I see you, I'll hurry out and wave you down. Okay?" ----"I guess so, you know Roger takes a dim view of folks leaving work for anything other than dire emergencies!"----"Well, honey, you just tell him this IS a dire 'family' emergency! I can expect you then?" She sighed---"Sure. I'll be there soon." "Don't come TOO soon!--- I---have a little way to walk. I'd say, uh, about 1 ½ hrs."---- "Okay, then I'll work awhile longer---maybe that'll appease Roger."----"Rita, dear, now this IS a matter of---of expediency!" He hung up the phone, turning to his 'reluctant host' who still stood staring rudely at him.

"How much do I owe you, Sir?"---Mac reached as if to pay him knowing he had no wallet with him. "Five dollars."---came the reply. "Oh MY god!"---Mac patted his clothing and managed to look torn with embarrassment---"My wallet is locked up in the truck!! Could I drop by later to pay you---after Rita and I get a tow truck?" The eyebrows went up two inches then drew down into a frightful scowl while a sarcastic expression edged over the bearded face! "I knew it."---he rasped---"You're nothing but a scoundrel---you have no truck that 'won't crank'---somebody kicked you out of a car before daylight this morning!! AFTER a night of good-old-boy bar-hopping, carousing or whatever else!"

Mac swallowed---being 'talked-down' to in this outrageous manner was not 'his thing'---suddenly the man pointed to the door and shouted---"GET OUT OF HERE!! DON'T BOTHER TO COME BACK AND PAY! In fact---,"---his thundering voice lowered two octaves—"...don't ever let me see your face around here again! Or I'll feed you to the wolves! OUT!"---he screeched---"OFF MY PROPERTY, YOU UNDERBELLY ---INTRUSIVE LIAR!"

Hurrying from the house, black fury raged inside Mac---yet he could do nothing but 'take it', stuff it and go on his way---then he remembered the gun! He'd go back and kill the SOB!! Reaching into his pocket, he realized the .38 was gone!!! GONE? @$%#^&**!!! He'd LOST it! So, once again at present, he had no choice---he couldn't go back to the door and shoot the 'overlord' right now! But there'd be another time---he whispered, "Contrary to your dismissal, sir, we'll meet again! You over-educated, arrogant, ivy-league, liberal, bearded bastard! Over-the-hill yuppified piece of dog-dook! When I get thru with you---YOU may be the one the wolves feed on!"

By the time Mac reached the highway, he was exhausted from his pre-dawn flight, long hours of hiding out in the cold, a lengthy trek to use a phone---and the final straw, taking insults from that prig then discovering he'd lost the damned pistol! Selecting a place near the road where he could see the sparse on-coming traffic in the direction Rita would be driving, he sat on the ground behind some evergreen bushes and young saplings. Resting to catch his breath, he tried forgetting the lost firearm plus the 'treatment' he'd just received by salving his wounded ego thru fantacized threats--- "Oh yes---you'll get yours---you'll regret talking that way to a McDougal!" Soon Rita would appear in the distance, she'd pick him up and come dark---he'd be showered, fed, warm, cozy and safe. Already he

felt safe---Lizbeth knew OF Rita---but she didn't know
WHERE Rita lived!

Chapter Thirty-Seven

Thanksgiving was now almost upon the community. Time
had passed since Doc settled Joseph in the O'Barr
'junkroom' and Lizbeth privately settled-in at the
Winterhawk family home. The latter eased Joseph's mind
considerably, which was part of Doc's strategy---'less
fretting' always meant a speedier recovery for any patient.
Besides, not being exactly a young man himself, the past
weeks had pretty much worn O'Barr to a frazzle---plus what
it'd done to Lizbeth and Joseph. Even Salle and Bill were
due some peace of mind and rest. In his darkened state of
mind, McDougal had touched and changed all their lives---
some more than others. Each of them still had a 'way' to go
before their world could return to some sense of 'normalcy'.

Two afternoons after the 'shooting', Logan dropped by
Doc's office for more info on the McDougals. He wanted
to know where they grew up, what kind of work McDougal
did, how long they'd been married, if they had any local
friends, what he knew about them personally and if he knew
why they'd come to live in this area. Despite the initial first
day television and radio news coverage on the case plus the
newspaper story picturing McDougal, there'd been no leads
on his disappearance. In the 'wanted' posters issued to
surounding lawmen, he'd been described as 'armed and
dangerous', but it seemed no one had noticed a man
resembling or fitting Mac's description.

Being very careful to say the 'proper' thing as a physician
and 'passing acquaintance' of the McDougals---O'Barr
didn't offer too much personally one way or another---yet

he did his best pointing to Lizbeth as 'an innocent victim'. He realized he couldn't over-do it---not at this point! There were other things he had to consider---it wasn't quite the time to become known as Lizbeth's confidant.

With Lizbeth and Hawk safely stashed away in separate locations, Doc began keeping up on the case by 'coincidentally' running into Sheriff Logan at various watering holes around town. On the fourth day after the attack, Doc found himself driving past the courthouse--- suddenly a parking place practically appeared right in front of him! "Wonder if they've had any informants by now! Think I'll drop by and see!" After parking, he meandered into the sheriff's office for any progress-report on McDougal's whereabouts. After a bit of their usual banter-- -Doc allowed Logan to 'extract' more information from him concerning McDougal's treatment of his wife during the time period he'd treated the man after his accident.

Logan had begun by stating he'd hoped to discover why a man would want to keep his wife, the 'help'---and especially his physician from knowing he'd overcome paralysis of the legs and could walk again! Doc shrugged, described his last revealing 'patient visit' with McDougal on the afternoon just before he attacked Lizbeth that same night, strengthening Bill's earlier testimony about Mac's ability to walk. Doc knew the more witnesses---the better!

By the time O'Barr paused, he sensed Logan's interest begin to smolder, so he fanned the coals by relating the 'burned hand' incident and how over the years, McDougal had psychologically brow-beat this lovely charming woman to the point of becoming an unkempt, lethargic shadow full of despair and hopelessness. (He made a mental note to warn Salle he'd told Logan about Lizbeth's burn, so she could back up the truth of his story---as well as McDougal's

continual verbal abuse which Salle heard many times.)
Blowing one last puff of wind on 'the fire'---Doc
'confidentially' brought up 'the other woman'---a so-called
'Rita' in another town, whose letter to Mac had started the
fray out at the McDougals earlier in the year. "That was
this past spring---the same day we went out there after his
accident?"---Logan queried. Doc nodded---"Yeah. After
seein' him through his 'invalid-state'---gettin' t'know him
th' way I did---I've often wondered what he was doin' at th'
barn after such an argument---instead of takin' off t'follow
his wife an' see where she was headed?! Why th' way that
man controlled her life with an iron-fist?! In my opinion,
that's exactly what he would've done—instead of watchin'
her drive off t'some unknown destination --- an' her just
tellin' him she wanted a divorce?! Not a chance!"
The sheriff mused ---"While you were out there that day,
waiting for an ambulance to take him to the clinic --- did
you ask him what he was doin' when he fell? To tell the
truth, I forgot what the report said --- but I thought you told
me once that barn was refinished completely by a
contractor---and not long before he fell!" Doc nodded.
Logan wondered aloud---"Why would he be up 'on the
roof'--- the damned thing is nigh 100 ft. off the ground!??
Think he was plannin' to jump?" Doc snorted out a
surprised spurt of laughter --- "Good Lord, Logan! A man
like McDougal?? This person loved himself far too much
t'consider EVER killin' himself! Somebody else---yes!
But suicide? Th' answer t'that question is emphatically
'NO'---period. Durin' th' past summer, I found he had too
many 'ear-marks' of a socio-path personality --- an' as of
late, obviously th' psychopath as well! You woofin' up th'
wrong tree there!"

By now Doc hopefully had Logan interested in the barn---so
he added, "I do remember askin' him what he was doin'

when he fell but he made very little of 'why' he was out there---like it was a big mystery or something. Th' only fact I know is when his wife got back home, she found him an' called straight away." Doc shrugged and planted more doubt pointing to the barn---"That time of year, there was no feedin' t'do---grass was lush an' green with plenty of water in all their waterin' holes---wasn't time t'fertilize or plant grazin'. B'sides, Mac didn't do much of that sorta work---he never bought a tractor or equipment---he always hired somebody. At th' time, his wife had plenty---or I should say, had 'enough'---money t'make-do. She wrote a 'best-seller' book, you know." Logan made a 'you-don't-say' expression as Doc went on---"Don't think he was much of a 'farm' person---grew up in some town---back in Illinois."

"So you said earlier. You know---I'd like to find out a little more about his background---think Mrs. McDougal is up to my paying her a little visit? Surely she's well enough to give me background information on him---especially if it might help us find him!" "Uh-oh!"---Doc thought---"I gotta think fast!" Clearing his throat, he rolled his eyes and replied---"Lord, it completely slipped m'mind, Logan---but she's off somewhere stayin' with acquaintances! She asked an' I told her after three days it'd be okay if she promised t'see a doctor should she have any problems. T'be truthful, sheriff, she didn't talk about exactly 'where' she was going---I think she wanted t'keep it quiet---y'know, afraid Mac might overhear someone talkin'! Back last spring, when she came t'me askin' about a divorce---she told me th' only reason she'd not left him before, she was afraid he might possibly go after her parents---th' family back in Georgia, so she wouldn't go there. She's deathly afraid of him, Logan, especially since he tried t'kill her! I tell you what, let me go t'my office---I might've jotted something down in her chart---some little note I've forgotten. That way she

could give you a call an' fill you in!" Logan nodded---
"Fine. I'd appreciate that. Thanks for your help!
McDougal thinks he's slick but sooner or later, we'll get a
lead---he couldn't have just disappeared into thin air! There
has to be a person, somewhere around---who might've
given him a ride or at least seen him."

After Doc left, believing he'd primed 'confidential'
information from the man---Logan sat mulling the facts.
He'd known O'Barr for ages---even before he became
Sheriff---back when O'Barr was a reservation physician.
He was known to be shrewd, tough and at times a no-
nonsense doctor—he was also a good, loyal friend, a
servant of the people, a credit to the town, Logan was
positive he could believe everything O'Barr had told him.

Another day, Logan questioned Doc about the Redwolf
couple. "Them?"---Doc put up a hand---"Fine folks! Why,
I've known th' families since I first came here! They're
good, clean-livin' intelligent people---they're honest,
dependable---we need more folks like them. Maybe I
should tell you..,"---Doc pointed to his own chest---"... I
was th' one who asked Mrs. McDougal if she could use
some help out there. Back before th' Redwolf's came back
from Laramie---that whole place was beginning t'look
pretty ragged, I can tell you! There was no way she could
do everything by herself---not an' nurse him constantly.
Mac was a very difficult man even when he was up an'
about---but after th' accident---well, t'say he was
'impossible' would be puttin' it mildly! Sometimes I think
he rather enjoyed his role as a demanding, nasty invalid.
Oh well,"—O'Barr gestured---"... back to th' present.
Logan, every time I think th' Redwolf couple might not've
been around th' other night an' heard that shot? Why, I
thank th' good Lord I had a hand in gettin' them out there or
Mrs. McDougal would be dead an' in her grave, at this very

moment! No doubt about it a'tall!" Doc paused to let that fact sink in---then asked---"Oh, before I forget---you, uh, hear from ballistics on that bullet yet?"

"No, but I expect it anyday though!" Rubbing his chin Logan rocked, swiveled about in his chair behind the desk then requested---"I want you to think back. Are there any other bits of information that you might've seen or heard at some time---and just forgot, believing it was unimportant or---maybe none of your business? I need everything I can get on McDougal because if we find him---I'll see to it the D.A. throws the book at 'em!"

Suddenly, Doc remembered Mac's 'text books'!! He felt sure the deputies had found them and taken them in as evidence---should he mention anything about it? He knew the books would tie in with 'the barn'---AND the secrets hidden there in the rafters! He also knew Logan---but still, nobody really knew exactly WHO might be a Klansman--- even in law enforcement---maybe one or more of Logan's deputies! Deciding that for one day---discretion was the better part of valor---Doc put it away for later on. Maybe another day as he and Logan talked, he'd sneak in the subject of the KKK---then at that point, he'd observe Logan very closely.

His chance came sooner than he'd thought! Two days later, the morning paper brought a story of one KKK rally in a neighboring state that caused a riot! So, watching for the opportunity to catch Logan at the café for his morning doughnut and cup of coffee---Doc waited for the right time then drove past the café where he saw the county car parked close by. Parking across the street, Doc wandered inside though Ida's more than ample cooking already filled his stomach! Giving his order at the counter, he glanced around---spying Logan at a table, he nodded at him---Logan

motioned him over. Doc said to himself---"All right,
O'Barr, now's your chance t'feel out this KKK situation!
Watch your step---an' your mouth!"

"Morning, High-Sheriff! How's th'crime rate t'day?"---
Doc slid in Logan's corner booth opposite him. The Sheriff
yawned---"Bout the same, O'Barr. How's the 'ailing'
rate?" Doc chuckled---"No new babies an' it seems we've
missed th' flu so far! Haven't seen a case yet---may God so
bless us till spring. Saw on the news that it's spreadin' this
way---some blasted thing from th' orient, I think."

Logan lay the newspaper down as the waitress brought his
doughnut and freshened his coffee---Doc picked up the
paper---breathed in loudly---"Say! Look at that!" "Look at
what?"---Logan mumbled busy with his doughnut. "Looks
like KKK is on th' move again!"---Doc replied gazing at the
paper with interest. "Yeah!"---Logan swallowed---"Mean,
cowardly sons-of-bitches---always stirrin' up trouble! Why
the hell these 'separatist groups' can't leave well enough
alone, I'll never know! These days, you get one fire put out
and before you can take a deep breath, another group is
bellowin' about their rights---raging, burnin' flags and draft
cards---gettin' hauled off to jails that can't hold all of them!
Now these white-hooded idiots are burnin' crosses and
rallyin' again---no end of it." Logan paused his tirade to stir
sugar into his coffee, then went on---"Thank God we don't
have any around here!" "Uh, you WOULD know if there
WAS a cell of them---wouldn't you?"---Doc murmured still
perusing the paper---"I mean---of all people, YOU have
'private' information sources---you'd certainly be aware if
they were in this neck of the woods, correct?"---Doc looked
down at his toast which had been just set before him---
smiling and nodding his 'thanks' at the waitress.

"Hell yeah, I'd know!"---Logan snorted---"There's no way they could be in here without my department being made aware of it! We DO have our sources---I can't tell you WHO they are, of course, but let's just say it's 'high up'!" "Logan! You got connections with 'the feds'?"---Doc replied in 'wonderment', adding polish to the apple! Logan grinned---"How many times I told you I can't talk about things like that---though we've been fishin' buddies for 30 years---there's some things that are 'QT', y'know! Wouldn't do for it to get out!" "Hmmm."---Doc agreed--- "Oh, absolutely correct! I understand your position---only those with a proper level of security can be privy t'such information---such as yourself, maybe a judge or two. Guess your men feel th' same about th' KKK as you?"

Logan stared at Doc who was feigning innocence by 'shoveling' in his food---then he huffed---"Well, naturally! Why I personally.."---he tapped his chest---"...do a background check on every man who's ever filed an application with my department! Ain't having no damned klansman or draft-card dodger in my department!" "Oh, by th'way an' speakin' of---'background checks'?"---Doc mumbled thru a mouthful of toast---"...I got hold of Mrs. McDougal for you! She's gonna call you around ten this mornin'---so don't wander too far off th' premises! You can quiz her on old McDougal! No new information overnight?" Logan washed down the last bite of doughnut with his coffee, wiped his mouth, tossed down the napkin and rose---placing his hat on his balding head, he looked down at Doc---"Nope---nary a word. But don't worry!"--- he tossed his head---"These things take time. This case is bound to pick up---who knows, maybe today---after she calls! Be seein' you---take care and have a good day."

"Same t'you, Logan!"---Doc nodded and watched as the sheriff readjusted his gun-belt and holster---complete with baton, flashlight, big new .357 Magnum and it's high count of ammo. Then straightening his shoulders, he sashayed toward the cash register. "Damnation!"---Doc thought to himself---"Carryin' that load, it's a wonder he doesn't have herniated discs or hip-displacement! Give me a doctor's bag any day!"

Chapter Thirty-Eight

A despondent Joseph sat in a chair beside his bed. Thus far, he'd managed to chafe thru the days and nights that'd passed since what he considered 'the humiliating debacle' in Lizbeth's bedroom. He couldn't stop chastising himself for not keeping her safe and each time he remembered, he died a thousand deaths knowing McDougal could've killed her just as easily as he'd beaten her! And all the while he--- Captain Joseph Winterhawk, the great army ranger---lay helpless on the floor, out cold as a piece of dead meat! One consolation alone kept him from slipping away during the long night hours to find McDougal---and that was his Lizbeth was safe with his own family. Hard as it was for him to admit, maybe Doc had been right. Perhaps it was better for him to mend in this quiet, safe haven---a familiar house with so many pleasant memories.

And although McDougal's trail grew colder and colder as days then weeks passed---Joseph waited---biding his time, trying to regain his strength. Already he knew where Rita lived---already he was making plans by telephone to pick up his chase! He knew he'd find the man! Even if he had to dig to hades and back---and when that moment finally came---there'd be no 'Queensbury' rules---there'd be only Sioux rules! Joseph no longer cared about 'lawful' or 'unlawful'---he only cared about absolute right and wrong, light and dark, good and evil! Truth plus the 'heart' of a man---those were two things he'd always looked for in people! Attempting to put his recent failure behind him--- Joseph counted down to 'zero' hour and waited. What was that quotation---'good things or all things come to him who waits'---he wasn't sure about the exact words---he just knew it was his turn to wait. Later the good things would come. And if he asked for only ONE 'good thing' out of all this---would God hear? Could he dream, hope, pray for that one gift?? If granted his one request----Lizbeth would be more than enough---she was all he desired---and like Jacob of old, he'd 'work' fourteen years to get her---and longer if required.

Still, he'd been on edge since Doc told him about the 'planted bullet' and Lizbeth's 'cooked-up' story. What if something went wrong and Lizbeth had to be questioned again? However, Doc assured him the statement she'd given about McDougal shooting at HER---how at the last moment, after tussling with him, she'd dodged the bullet as he beat her unconscious---all had been accepted without suspicion on anyone's part. The bedroom scene fit her story plus the authorities never doubted that Salle and Bill's arrival, and that alone, had kept McDougal from fatally wounding his wife. His running away only added 'credence' to Lizbeth's story! Salle, Bill and Doc's statements---added to the evidence, gave further credibility to her statement. "And,"---Hawk clenched his jaw--- "...while all this went on---ME, the 'hero'---remained under anesthesia---quietly hidden away."

He'd never forget standing there in the dark bedroom, listening to McDougal rave about the people he'd killed with his .38! Sooner or later---IF Doc hadn't 'contaminated' the bullet---Hawk knew it would check out as coming from a murder weapon used in the past. IF the authorities had done their investigations and lab work

correctly back then! McDougal was a 'wanted' man----
deadly assault and attempted murder of his wife---that
added onto what ballistics would reveal would cook his
goose. Now the law would 'dog him' until they found him-
--no matter how long---finally there'd be a trial. Still that
knowledge never satisfied Joseph, the Hawk,---he wanted a
piece of McDougal before the law got their hands on him!
But, for the time being, he vowed to show a more grateful
face to Doc and Ida for their generosity---past and present.

Ida came in to put fresh sheets on the roll-away bed---he
looked at her---"You sure I can't at least come out to the
kitchen and do something, Mrs. Doc? I could wash dishes
or stir your cook pots. Body and soul, I'm withering away
in this room---NOT that I'm ungrateful, mind you!" Hawk
hastened to add, remembering his vow to be 'nice'! "Don't
get me wrong---I realize I'm starting to sound like an old
wart-hog. You and Doc have fussed over me, cooked for
me, cleaned up after me, given me medical treatment! So
far all I've done is grumble and act discontented---I'm
sorry. The army hospital should've just kept me with
them."

Ida finished making the bed, straightened up and smiled at
Hawk---"Now, now Joseph. You know you were better off
here with us than in an army hospital where---well, where
an enemy might've been able to get at you again! Doc told
me how you were sent in by medivac and he picked you up!
Of course, he wouldn't tell me 'where'---too hush-hush.
My goodness, you've led such an interesting life---although
much too dangerous in my opinion! But you're retired
now—you should tell the military to find someone else to
take your place!"

"Besides---'recovery' is just harder on men than it is on
women, my dear. You're not ungrateful---and you aren't

grumbling---you're just tired of this junk room!" Laughing she went on---"And I don't see any reason why you can't come out to the kitchen while I bake a cake for Thanksgiving---I'm certain there're no 'snipers' around to get you in their crosshairs! Come along, we'll put you in a comfortable chair and we can chat while I mix the batter." Joseph forced a smile and nodded---baking and chatting when what he truly wanted was to be 'warring' with his enemy! Hunting him down like the mad-dog he was--- slugging it out----flesh pounding flesh---blood flowing--- retribution! Hawk sighed, stood and followed Ida to the kitchen---to bake a cake.

The cake was in the oven and Joseph had journeyed back to the junkroom when Doc came home. He found his patient drawing more make-shift maps---"What are you plannin' NOW, may I ask?" Hawk exhaled---"Nothing much. The trackers lost 'white-eyes' trail here at the highway, remember?"---he pointed to a spot on the map---"I dismissed the men when they lost his trail and couldn't pick it up again. He could've gone north---I'm almost certain he's with that 'Rita' person." Doc looked at him---"How about that house they tracked him to---the one in the hills a few miles north---what about that?" Hawk shrugged--- "Last account, no one was about the place---the guys said someone had been living there all right but it was deserted---at least for now. Maybe they're on vacation---and I'm wondering if Mac might've gone inside---helped himself to the phone and called somebody to pick him up. Could be the phone company might help. What you think, Doc?"

"A possiblity. If Logan knew what the trackers found---he has the authority to go up and look around that house---or keep an eye on it and if anyone does turn up, he can question them. Plus he can look at the phone records." Joseph looked sideways at him--- "And how would I explain being so interested in this 'case' as to hire trackers who led us to that house? Besides the place is in another county---outside Logan's jurisdiction." "You're right, Hawk. Forgot about both of those facts."---Doc scratched his head then brightened---"But I do have a bit of news for you---the ballistics report is back!"

Hawk's throat tightened, his heart pounded---though he knew civilian lab work wasn't technically 'pure' as the government intelligence labs---still there may be a chance that some eager-beaver assistant might've found what could be blood OR some odd microscopic mark Doc could've made on the bullet.

"Well?"---Joseph's nervous black eyes bored into Doc's face---"You plan to keep it to yourself or share it with me? What does it say?" "My own abbreviated version---and I almost quote---'matches up with several unsolved killings in Ohio, Kentucky and Nebraska." Relief washed over and thru Joseph---"You sure there's no---uh, unusual scars or 'material' on the bullet?" "Nope, narry a problem! Logan's tickled t'death---says he can really go t'work now. Gotta find th' gun though---nobody's seen it as yet!" Hawk laughed so loud that pain shot through his side---Doc fixed his eyes on him---"You havin' a delayed break-down? I haven't heard you laugh like that in so long, I'd forgotten what it sounded like! What's so funny?"

"Apropos the gun---the trackers found it, Doctor-man. Bill has it---for safe keeping! Don't you know you can trust an Indian to be extremely thorough?" Doc's eyes bulged-- "They DIDN'T screw up th' finger-prints on it, for God's sake!" "Now, now, don't get all jazzed up, Kemosobe! It's just like it was when McDougal dropped it down near the highway---in that tall grass just outside their front yard? I'm certain he didn't even know he'd lost it! Therefore he didn't take time to wipe the weapon down---I'd almost bet! So,"---Hawk grinned at Doc---"…if you'll let me use your phone, I'll call Bill and tell him when it's time to feed the cows later today---that the time has arrived when maybe 'something shining in the late afternoon sun' should catch his eye! He'll trot over to 'investigate'--and by jove! Whadda ya know—a chrome-plated .38 Special!"

Doc laughed, began shaking his head and sat down on Hawk's bed----he put one arm across his mid-section and placed the other hand over his mouth. "By DAMN! I thought I was a clever chip of th' Conemara Marble---all us Irish lads are born canny---but you people have got us beat by a country mile!" Hawk gestured palms up, grinned and replied---"What can I say, Doctor-man? We are what we are---don't blame me if your parents didn't have 'Red-man' blood!" Hawk began laughing again---"You had red hair instead, didn't you!?" O'Barr stared up at the ceiling and ignored the Omaha/Sioux who'd suddenly become more like his old self----laughing yet!

Later after Hawk called Bill and supper was over, Doc removed Hawk's bandages. "How's it looking today, m'man?"---Hawk inquired---"Am I well yet?" "Other than lookin' like you've spent th' better part of your life in gun an' knife fights," ---Doc reached into an open storage box, bringing out the broken half of a dresser mirror---"…guess it's time you took a look for yourself." Hawk observed his newest scar---front and back---and commented, "The exit-wound looks like hell, Doc! Uh, you think I'm good to go?" The older man sighed patiently---"NOT for any row or fight! Absolutely no, but IF you behave yourself---an' since tomorrow's Thanksgiving, Ida and I have a surprise---we're takin' you home! B'sides, I think it's time you saw Mrs. McDougal an' she sees you. So,"—Doc shrugged—"..when you get up in th' morning, put on th' best duds you 'took on your military trip'. We'll tell Mary you just got into town. But PLEASE---for God's sake, don't drive for another few days! If you muck around in that vehicle of yours, drivin' every rough trail from here t'there an' back--- well, let's just say, not enough time has passed that you should attempt basic trainin' all over again! I'm demandin' a promise you'll continue wearing this light weight brace-bandage ---AND!"—Doc held up a finger---"That you do NOT drive for at least three more days! Otherwise I damn-well won't take you out there. Now, do I have that promise or not!?"

"SIR! It's as good as done, Sir!"---Joseph saluted with enthusiasm---"Honest Injun, Doc. I'll behave myself. Home for Thanksgiving with my beautiful Lizbeth there--- whatever more could I want!" Doc questioned---"So, you're settled that it's time t'see her?" Hawk nodded--- "I'm ready---at least I think so. If I'm very fortunate, she won't hate me." The joy in his voice diminished, worry filled the dark eyes---"Doc, what'll I do if she---if she feels—,"—he gave a small unhappy shrug---"..well, if she feels 'different'---toward me?" Noting anguish in the handsome face, the older man replied---"Well, I can promise this much---she doesn't blame you, Joseph, no worry on that account! But she won't be staying at your mother's for long either, so th' two of you best go for a long hike t'talk this thing out---just as soon as th' holiday meal is over!"

For a moment Joseph looked puzzled---then Doc explained---"With Bill an' Salle still there---your mother's house simply isn't big enough for another adult! So Ida an' I plan t'bring Lizbeth back here for a spell. I'll tell Logan she returned an' wants t'stay here with us where she'll be safe." Hawk pressed his lips together, arched his eyebrows at Doc then asked---"Couldn't she just stay at Mama's---I could bunk with her!?"

Rolling his eyes, Doc muttered---"Why do I suddenly get this feelin' you're definitely on th' mend! Get your butt over here so I can put this thing around you." Hawk complied, raising his arms. Doc fastened the light brace over his patient's fresh bandages while commenting dryly---"B'sides, don't you think SHE might have something t'say about who she lets 'bunk with her'! ANYWAY, what WOULD your sainted mother say!?" Hawk grimaced---"I don't even want to THINK about that!" Then lifting his eyes to the ceiling above the junk-room, he quipped---"I can just see Lizbeth upstairs here in this very house tomorrow night---sleeping in MY upstairs room while I'll probably be sharing a set of saggy springs with my niece and nephew!" "Aww---poor boy. If you behave yourself an' are 'real good', Mary might let you sleep on her sofa...,"---Doc winked at him---"...beats sleeping with two kids!" Joseph mumbled---"Taking Lizbeth away the moment I walk into the house! Don't think I'm not 'on-to' what you're doing, you Irish brigand---you're getting me back about the 'Conemara Marble' thing---aren't you!"

Chapter Thirty-Nine

It had been two weeks since he'd called for Rita's assistance---and Mac was bored with hiding out, even though it meant he was with Rita whenever she wasn't at work. Still, she was only a woman. After being 'closed up with her' for near fourteen days, he'd come to the conclusion that NO woman was the best choice of regular 'companionship'! When a man hung around a female too long or paid too much attention to her---she became possessive, demanding---and Rita was beginning to act like a 'female'.

Thus far, all previous calls to his father hadn't brought forth the immediate rescue he'd expected. After first giving his son a thorough tongue-lashing about 'leaving behind such a mess'---his failure to close Lisbeth's mouth permanently, the elder McDougal's advice to his troublesome son had been to 'sit tight' and not be seen---lest a fate worse than 'being bored' should befall him! But on the day before Thanksgiving, Dad McDougal seemed to be having second thoughts.

Mac received an unexpected call telling him a car was already on the way to pick him up---it'd been decided he should stay with the family for awhile. Not having been included, Rita pouted as Mac grew even more impatient with her. Ready to 'be rid' of her for awhile, but remembering his father's strongly worded orders, Mac assured her it was 'really best that he leave the area--- because sooner or later, someone would see him report it--- then she would be involved! Why, she might even be implicated as a possible accomplice in his crime'! Given the present situation then mulling over Mac's words, Rita's sense of self-preservation gave short life to her sulk. Naturally, she was unaware that the family's real reason for 'protecting her' was just in case Mac should be forced into hiding again—the family could then move Rita to another state and Mac would have a safe house! That is IF they parted on 'good terms'!

Before the 'invitation-call' had ended, the old man insisted Mac must leave a 'bond' with Rita by proposing marriage to her—'when things settled down', of course! Should the authorities uncover Mac's relationship with her and come to call, such an offer would surely keep her mouth closed! In order to save her 'future husband' from prison, she'd relate whatever information his family fed her---hopefully 'saving' her fiance from that fate. Forced into a corner by his father, Mac sullenly agreed to propose---silently assuring himself that later on, he'd 'figure something out'! All he wanted at the moment was to be free of the woman--- her very presence had begun to annoy him, he'd stoop to the necessary level to flee the scene! And though Mac was going into 'hiding' using a false name and ID---Rita was elated by 'his sudden proposal'---and accepted by throwing her arms about him, almost hysterical with 'tears of happiness'!

When the car arrived to pick him up, Rita invited the driver inside. The blonde, heavy-set, fortish man handed Mac a wallet---complete with fake SSI, driver's license and other info. While Mac perused his new ID papers, the driver handed Rita a camels-hair top-coat, black suit---complete with accessories. After reading that he'd become 'Reverend William Black', he was highly amused and asked---'who in hell was William Black!?' His stoic driver replied the 'reverend' had died two years ago and was selected because the description fit---plus a minister wouldn't be regarded as a suspicious individual. If, for any reason, the law 'stopped' them during the trip---the story was that he was being driven to visit 'a close family friend' who was very ill and not expected to live. The driver then exited the house to await his passenger.

A weeping, wailing Rita now held on to him, trying to extract a promise that he'd call her to join him as soon as possible---so they could 'be married'! On and on she went about being 'ready to give up everything' for him---finally to stop the incessant rattling of her mouth, he kissed her while extricating himself from her embrace then escaped to the waiting car!

So adding a false mustache and a pair of clear-lensed dark rimmed glasses to his new ID---Mac made his departure--- one that would take him miles away from the area---and from Rita! "Women."---he thought in disgust while staring out through the car window---"How they drain men of their God-given life-force---like leeches they suck you dry with their endless female whinings, weaknesses, demands, complainings---clinging like a parasitic vine. A man wakes up to see there's nothing left of him but a shell because some female has devoured his insides! He opens up his eyes to find himself chained to some bitch of a woman while each freedom, each potential or dream he took for granted as a young man has been completely erased! Then resenting---no, HATING, the invisible prison she's built around him---he plans a 'break-out'! He does whatever he must in order to break the shackles of wedding rings, marriage certificates, 'husbandly' responsibilities and such trash---and most of all financial support! Alimony alone leaves a man without any choice in his life ---she lives high with other men, never having a job while he merely exists, scraping along! In order for a man to become one of those 'ancient-men-of-renown'---men who gave no thought to women except when the physical occasion demanded it---he must leave this modern drivel behind, broaden his horizons, search out new places with new possitilities!"

The Buick rode like a dream and his driver was alert as well as careful but he listened to piano music on the radio---it reminded Mac of his stupid wife and the fact he'd bungled her murder! He shouted toward the driver---"Turn that damned thing off---I don't want to hear it!" "Yessir, young Mr. McDougal!"---immediately the radio clicked off.

Mac relaxed in the comfortable back seat while behind them, an escort pick-up truck rode 'shotgun'. Since neither

Mac nor the 'driver' were exactly fountains of information
or a barrel of laughs---even any polite conversation that
might've been---fell by the wayside. But that was of no
consequence to Mac! After a decade, he'd just been
respectfully called 'young Mr. McDougal' again---
identifying him with his father's rank! Smirking in the
darkness, Mac once again reveled in 'being somebody'---
never again would he endure Lizbeth's company, her dumb-
ass 'social' occasions nor those hated introductions to her
friends! She'd soon be out of the picture as well as out of
his life then everything would be his way! And with his
attempt on her life, hopefully he'd be forgiven for her
radical ideas of 'racial equality'---possibly even restored to
his rightful position in the organization! Oh, he'd be asked
to go back and 'finish the job' on her, all right---but he'd
worry about that later! At this moment, he was 'young Mr.
McDougal' again! And as such, he didn't have to
communicate---not with the driver---nor with anyone else!
Unless, of course, it was of his own choosing!

After passing thru several small towns, Mac noted the two
Harley KKK riders who pulled out from a small service
station and rode a short way out in front of them. There
were two women passengers riding with the cyclists, Mac
sat forward and watched for a moment, recalling earlier
times---the days before he'd been sent to Lizbeth's
hometown for a 'cooling-off' period! He'd owned a Harley
then and rode with a group of klansmen who, for their
'work', preferred two wheels instead of five.

"Maggie." Closing his eyes, he 'recalled' her. How many
miles had the two of them covered back then? "Hell. I feel
old!"---he silently complained as his thoughts meandered
back---"Wonder whatever happened to her? Damn, I hope
she didn't end up marrying that fool Ledford Baker! Man!
What a fight the two of us had over her!" The smile that'd

come across his face faded as his normal state of mind returned---"So young and stupid back then---no woman born is worth a fight! One is as good or as bad as another---they're all the same. No matter what the outside of the can looks like---inside they all contain the same 'Mother-Eve' spoiled, rotted goods."

As the Buick hummed quietly Mac listened to the Harley engines out front as they geared up and down---their pipes echoing on mountainous turns. But it was when they hit a straight-away and increased their speed that they really 'sounded-off'---how he longed to be out there with them instead of riding in the car. Maybe another time---but right now, perhaps he should just let the Harleys lull him off for a rest---he needed to be on his toes when he saw the old man!

Thus, in the back seat of the car sent for him, young Mr. McDougal---or Rev. William Black---dozed. The night hours sped away, putting hundreds of miles between him and Rita---and 'the mess' he'd left behind.

Chapter Forty

Mary received a call from Hawk early Thanksgiving morning, eagerly she announced to all in the house that he 'was back', would hitch a ride with the O'Barrs and be joining them for lunch. For fifteen minutes, Mary talked of nothing but her Joseph, meanwhile Lizbeth became 'all thumbs'---dropping things, not hearing when spoken to. As the three prepared the meal, Salle was the only one who took note of Lizbeth's sudden 'condition', so each time Mary left the room, Salle tried to reassure her friend.

Finally Mary went to dress for Mass. Salle whispered---"He'll be every bit as jumpy as you! I'll bet by now, he's chewed every fingernail he's got down to a nub---probably didn't sleep a wink all night long! This was Doc's surprise for him---lettin' him come home today! For two weeks now, our hawk-man has probably worn the shine off Doc's floor by pacin' up and down---and Miss Ida's ready to get rid of him!"

"But Ah want t'look nice foah Joseph!"---Lizbeth put her fingers against her cheek, touched the skin then moved on to her hair---"Ah must look a fright! Tho Hawk and Ah ended up in th' same room that awful night---we didn't even see each othah! He has no idea Ah've turned into---such an ugly, unattractive 'thing'!" "I beg to differ, he did look at you once!"---Salle announced---"Soon as Bill and I got to your room that night, my brother was still unconscious---but when Bill brought him 'round, all he cared about was seein' if you were all right! Not bein' satisfied with what we told him, he started pullin' himself up by the bedpost---then Bill helped him so he could see for himself that you were all right! He touched your face, felt your neck for a pulse and---maybe I shouldn't tell you this but...,"---Salle put a hand on her hip, tossing her hair---"...I'm gonna say it anyway, that was when he called you 'Lizbeth---my love'!" Catching her breath, Lizbeth flushed then looked down at her hands---"An' he didn't say how Ah'd let m'appearance 'go'---or anything like that?" "The way YOUR face looked after that fool got finished with you?!"---Salle flashed a look at her---"I should say NOT!! He was overwhelmed that you were alive---all the time he was lyin' on the floor---he kept askin' if you still had a pulse! My brother would feel the same about you if all your hair fell out and you lost all your teeth!" Lizbeth couldn't help smiling at Joseph's saucy sister who'd lifted her spirits since the first day they'd met---and valiantly tried to keep them up.

"But Salle, it was because of me that he's been through so much! It's up t'me t'make certain he doesn' blame himself foah what happened, Hawk did all he could! When he came in there t'help me that night---he already had so many strikes against him---all he had were disadvantages! Yoah brothah did everything by th' book, as they say—an' just look what he got foah his trouble!"---Lizbeth turned and grasped Salle's hands in hers---"You don't think something's been---destroyed between us---do you?! Oh, Ah shoulda called him, Salle!" Dropping Salle's hands like a hot potato, Lizbeth paced the kitchen---"We nevah shoulda let all this time go by an' not spoken t'each othah!" Salle put out a hand to Lizbeth---"But you couldn't take a chance! Bill never stopped impressin' on me how important it was that no contact be made between the two of you! Even when Bill and Hawk used the phone, they spoke only 'in code'! And those garbled radios---why, I never understand a word they say!"

Salle sighed, gave each pot a good stir and put everything on 'low' heat, then taking Lizbeth by the arm, she commanded---"C'mon! We gotta talk---AGAIN!" Dragging the fretful women to a side bedroom, she closed the door as Lizbeth plopped on the bed. Then Salle plopped right beside her---"Now, I've told you a hundred times his reason for not seein' you before we left the ranch was---he was all 'undone' about the way he blacked out on you there in your bedroom! His only problem was a humongous 'male ego'! My usually confident brother was afraid you'd think he'd failed you and that you'd no longer see him as 'the big shot' army ranger protector! Once you two see each other---all these uncertain feelin's will disappear---just like fog when the wind blows into it! Trust me!"

Lizbeth's eyes dimmed with tears---"Ah still think he's mah 'protector', Salle! Just because he was shot---would Ah think anything less of him?! How could he prevent a bullet goin' into him?!! T'me---he's STILL th' fine man he's always been---an' always will be! You're his sistah, you know him bettah than me---so how can Ah tell him all this without embarrassin' him---an' makin' a big fool of m'self in th' process?!"

Salle sighed, looked at her watch---"Look, it's almost 9:00—let's get the rest of lunch in order---most of it's done already. When we finish up in the kitchen, if we can keep the kids outta the bathroom long enough---you can take a nice bath to get the onion and sage smell off you! I'll help you fix your hair up real pretty! We'll make you totally irresistible to him!"---Salle struck a dramatic pose--- "...He'll be struck dumb when he lays eyes on you!" Twisting her hands and casting worried glances out the pristine window pane, Lizbeth whispered---"All Ah want is foah him t'look at me th' same way he did th' only two times in th' whole world Ah evah really saw him. Ah'd settle foah that alone."

"Then he will. Come on, times a wastin'! The sooner we finish in that kitchen---the sooner you can start your primpin' process! Look at you!"---Salle turned Lizbeth's face this way and that---"The stitches are out, most of the bruises have faded, the swellin' is practically gone---an' what's left, we'll cover up! All a body's gotta do to see the improvement is remember those pictures Sheriff Logan took of you! Why, you'll be---simply stunnin'---the very sight of you will ravish his eyeballs!"

Salle took Lizbeth's reluctant hand and pulled her toward the closed door---suddenly Lizbeth halted---"Salle! Yoah Mothah! She doesn't know---about Hawk an' me---what'll we do? Ah mean---how shall Ah act when he walks in? Oh LORD." Lizbeth stood motionless, her mouth slightly

238

gaped---"She must NEVAH think her son had 'eyes' foah me---a married woman! Oh Salle!! How could she possibly come t'terms with th' things Ah've told you--- about what Ah wrote in that book---an' how when Joseph came with Doc---we felt we already knew each othah!?" Turning away, Lizbeth held up one hand, stating solidly--- "It would be too much---she'd always have doubts about me! B'sides---,"---she almost wailed---"Ah'm WHITE!!" Sitting heavily back down on the bed, Lizbeth hugged herself and began rocking back and forth in misery, tears rolling down her cheeks.

"Dear Lord,"---Salle muttered in exasperation---"White southern women! Please God, tell me why I'm GLAD nobody told us before this morning that he'd be coming out here today! All this 'excessive drama' is exactly WHY!" Storming to the bedside, she quietly stamped one foot and admonished---"Lizbeth McDougal---though I hate to use that last name--we gotta do somethin' about THAT--- anyway, I've TOLD you that Mom only thinks of you as: Number One:---The generous, beautiful 'white lady with red hair' who comes with Doc and Miss Ida to bring food to the reservation church kitchen. And Number Two:---The kind woman who gave Bill and me a job when we needed it---and Number Three:---The poor thing whose bastard-husband beat then tried to murder her! Now that's ALL she knows! But t'be honest, I don't think she's going to be 'shocked' that her fine son--who's way yonder past the bloom of his youth---might find you 'attractive' when he 'meets' you! Tell me, what's not to like? Mom thinks you're 'quality'---I've told her so and she believes me!" Salle preened---"Doc, too---he's always singin' your praises! Now, just stop all this southern nonsense--- whatever it is!"

Pulling Lizbeth back to her feet, Salle took a clean paper towel from her apron pocket and wiped the pale face in front of her---"We'll have no more of your 'vapors' around here! We haven't the time for it today---b'sides, we got no smellin' salts 'foah Miz Scarlett'!!" Lizbeth began to giggle thru her tears---soon both were cackling like two youngish hens over their eggs.

Later when the O'Barr truck arrived amidst it's usual cloud of dust---Lizbeth heard the metal doors slamming, followed by greetings at the front door! She remained 'hidden' in the kitchen 'tending the food'---she didn't really know where she should be---not when Joseph made an appearance! So the kitchen seemed her safest bet!

Mary Winterhawk was elated to see her son at last! After greeting Ida and Doc at the door---she opened her arms toward Hawk---"Your trip, son! It went well, yes?" He held her for a moment until inadvertently she squeezed him! Over her shoulder, he grimaced briefly---then putting on a smile, he pulled slightly away. Putting his hands on her shoulders, he looked into her eyes and replied---"It went well, Mama, and it is good to be back here on this special day." Mary looked around the room before replying--- "Whole family cannot be here—too far away but—in spirit, we will remember them at table! Salle?"---Mary turned to her daughter---"Remind me to set out plates for absent children." Salle nodded patiently.

Dottie's two raced in to greet the guests---then after a couple of noisy 'rounds' in the living room, they hurried back to the kitchen to keep Lizbeth, whom they'd grown to love, from 'being alone'! "Uncle Hawk is back, Miss Lizbeth!"---Jerri clamored excitedly! "Yes, Honey. Ah heard---you glad to see him, huh?" The little girl shyly tilted her chin to her shoulder and nodded. Her smile, still

missing some front teeth, grew larger. Rammah sniffed---
"She thinks he's 'Crazy Horse'!" Then in a superior tone,
he announced to Jerri---"He's NOT a 'chief', kid-sister, he's
a WHITE warrior! There's a difference, you know!"
"NOT TRUE!"---Jerri yelled back---"He's an INDIAN
WARRIOR! HE'S 'CRAZY HORSE'!" Rammah rushed
past Jerri giving her a little whack on the shoulder,
screeching---"WHITE WARRIOR!"---he then bounded
away! "GRAMMA!"---Jerri hollered, heading for the living
room!

"WHOA! What's all this commotion! I haven't been home
five whole minutes and already there's yowlings and
discontent?! Rammah still giving my girl problems?"
Lizbeth heard his voice---and promptly dropped a stirring
spoon onto the floor. Bending down to pick it up, she heard
Jerri voicing her 'complaints' about white and Indian
warriors! Then came Hawk's answer---"Well, sweetheart,
you just never mind---because I'm BOTH! I'm a 'white
warrior' and an 'Indian warrior'! Even Crazy Horse
couldn't say THAT, now, could he? Hmm?" Lizbeth
rinsed the spoon---and out of the corner of her eye, she
could see Hawk's hand smoothing the little girl's shiny
black hair. "No, he couldn't!"---the child's voice was filled
with amazement at the mention of such a fact---"I never
thought about that, Uncle Hawk! WOW!" The echo of her
galloping feet faded as she cut toward the living room to
inform her brother of the latest truths on 'warriors and
chiefs'---both white and Indian!

"Lizbeth…"---at the sound of his voice softly speaking her
name, she grew even more trembly and weak---but
presently after taking a deep breath or two, she turned
toward him. Oh! How glorious to see him---to know, at
last, that he really was all right! "Hawk…"---she choked
but could get no further, the rinsed spoon fell from her open

hand, clattering to the counter top. Their eyes met---and melded together---he began walking toward her and had almost reached her when Mary returned to make certain the last preparations had been seen to.

Putting a hand on Lizbeth's back, she smiled at her guest then at her son---"Hawk? My son---you introduce yourself to Mrs. McDougal? She has been with us since---a day or two after you left." Joseph continued looking at Lizbeth--- "Mrs. McDougal,"---he saved the day---"I thought it was you! I'm most pleased to see you---again." Mary eyes widened---"So. You have met before?" Joseph nodded--- "Yes, Mama. I was with Doc one day when we dropped by the McDougal place---also, I helped cut wood for them---at your suggestion, I might add. Remember?" Her brow furrowed slightly---"Getting old---forgot. Yes, now I remember." Mary's generous smile returned---"Mrs. McDougal is good guest---she work all day---all night if I not stop her. We have come to think of her as—'family'." Mary's gentle voice was like balm to his heart---"You, too, will come to think of her as such---my son." Hawk nodded to his mother, returned his gaze to Lizbeth, then replied quietly---"I am certain I shall, Mama."

Mary bestowed another proud smile upon her son--- "Here..,"---she pushed Hawk past Lizbeth---"...you help Mrs. McDougal put food into bowls---set on table." Hawk bowed slightly and went to work. To keep her trembling hands from dropping anything more---Lizbeth filled the bowls then allowed Hawk to pick them up off the counter. All the while her heartbeat drummed so loudly in her ears that she could barely hear the conversation around her—she could only pray his fingers wouldn't touch hers in the passing of pans and bowls! She knew her flushed, hot face certainly must be the color of Mary's scarlet chili-pepper ristras which hung beside the pantry door!

Later after lunch with the food properly stored and dishes all put away, everyone sat in the living room. Doc stared at Joseph, arched his eyebrows and gave a slight jerk of the head. As yet, Hawk hadn't come up with a way to get Lizbeth alone for their 'talk'! Each idea that came to mind over the past 12 hours had met with incongruity---then like frost when the sun rose, it melted away! What would 'make sense' and not seem 'out-of-the-ordinary' to his mother or Dottie?! He didn't have any idea how much---IF anything---his mother or Dottie knew!

Salle's 'antenna' sensed a call for 'assistance', so she stood, stretched and stated---"As usual, I ate too much! Mom's feasts do me in---if I don't take a walk, I'm goin' to sleep in my chair. Who's for a walk??! C'mon, everybody, it's a beautiful day---we should take advantage..."---she peered out the window---"...weather report says early winter rains are already on the way. It'll be too late to enjoy the sun then! Bill?" He picked up her 'look' which strongly suggested he comply!

Temporarily, a blank expression covered his face but he 'went along'. "Sure! Why not?"---he replied heartily. "Dottie, maybe you and the kids would like to join us---let's get out and do something---a game maybe?" Dottie sighed, barely dragging her eyes from the television screen---"Uh, no thanks. Helping take care of crying babies at the church nursery all morning wore me out---I'd rather sit right here and watch the ballgame---'walks' just aren't my thing. But the kids can go if they want." Rammah promptly announced---"I'm gonna watch the game with Mama! Jerri can go---!" With that, he plopped down on a bean-bag chair, gluing his eyes to---'3rd down with five yards to go'.

243

Doc jumped up, offered a hand to Ida then pulled her unceremoniously from the comfortable chair---"I'll just grab our coats an'---we'll be on our way! Jerri?"---he whispered---"Get your coat an' cap, I have somethin' in my truck just for you!" The child jumped up from her coloring book and crayons and took Doc's hand. Soon everyone was bundled up, going out the door.

The 'walk party' soon disappeared leaving behind Joseph, Lizbeth, the two football fans and Mary who seemed about to doze in her chair---suddenly she looked over at Joseph--- "Son? Why you not take Mrs. McDougal on small tour--- show her your favorite spots? Fresh cool air do her much good. Maybe you walk her to church---show her 'Our Lady' and 'Our Lord'---also stained glass windows donated by wealthy Indian actor!?"

In silent relief, Hawk exhaled, restraining his inner joy--- "Good idea, Mama. I'd be delighted to escort our guest." Lizbeth flushed bright pink as he asked---"That is if you'd care to accompany me." Her hands clamped tightly together in her lap, Lizbeth answered---"Ah think some fresh air might---be nice, Captain. Let me get mah coat an' scarf." He stood as she hurried from the room---his eyes following her.

Since he'd arrived, Mary's discerning spirit noted her son's eyes following Lizbeth about. She murmured to him--- "Pretty, gentle lady but very sad---possesses loving spirit, Joseph. Maybe even 'old soul', sometimes seems 'old'--- strange, mystical things in eyes. Your company be good for her---help her get well, I think." He picked up his jacket and hat then sat briefly on the arm of Mary's chair, touching her hair, he replied softly—"I'll give it my best try, Mama."

Chapter Forty-One

Since leaving Mary's house, they'd walked in slience, sharing and treasuring a quiet that was much too precious to be broken by mere words. Wearing a plaid woolen coat, her red hair hidden beneath a heavy bandana, Lizbeth reveled in the brisk cold wind---and in the company of her companion. Clearly, she was not certain if the occasional shiver she experienced was because of the weather---or the opportunity to finally be near the man she'd looked for all her life and once finding him---loved him wholly yet had been separated from him until this very day! "How very appropriate"—she thought rapturously--- t'finally be togethah on a Thanksgivin' Day---along with his family an' ouah friends!"

Upon reaching the church, they entered a dim private world of quiet reverence. Once inside the door, Hawk touched holy water to himself then to her---as they entered the sanctuary itself. He pulled down a kneeler and side by side, they knelt as a golden Thanksgiving sun shone through the fine stained glass windows bathing the whole chapel with an ethereal majesty. The ambiance was one of being surounded by glimmering colorful jewels while breathing clean faint odors of beeswax and incense. Together they drank in this peaceful silence which waited to embrace all who humbly entered in search of repose---a 'safehouse' from a turbulent world just outside the door. Both Lizbeth and Hawk were familiar with that world.

As they knelt, Hawk accepted that these gilded moments had been offered them as a special gift. His thoughts raced to the day when he hoped they'd be married---if she still loved him---and he thought she did! Wondering at his silent thoughts---she suddenly realized she'd found the peace for which she'd searched over these many years! Here in this holy place, her innermost longings were being filled just as one fills a jeweled goblet by pouring in only the finest, most costly wine. During this visit, each of them in their own way, had been given a very special gift to hold and to remember during the uncertain days ahead when once more, they'd be separated for awhile.

Helping her descend the steps, he looked into those long familiar sea-colored eyes---"Ready to look for the path?" Lizbeth smiled as she answered softly---"Yes, Hawk." With her hand in his, he led her away from the steps--- across the way---and into the hills.

Presently, they came to the place where Hawk searched for 'the path'---and after several attempts---he stopped, motioning her toward him. Giving her a happy grin, he pointed---"There! You were right, Lizbeth---though somewhat overgrown, it's still here---waiting for us. And you're ready to follow it—no matter what?" She nodded while catching at his sleeve---"You are m'guide, an' Ah must follow you." His black eyes searched her face--- "Lizbeth, I'm going to take those words the way my heart heard them---and hope you meant them in the same way." Returning his gaze, he knew she understood---she always had---the few times they'd seen each other, they'd known each other's heart.

Just before arriving at the place he intended to stop, Joseph suddenly halted, put his hands on her shoulders and turned her to face him---'Lizbeth. There's some things I must say before we go another step." He sighed, waiting for the right words while looking up and around at the bare trees whose naked limbs intertwined and silhouetted sharply against a bright blue sunlit sky. All around them winter sun-rays splashed a gold wash of color over everything. Intuitively, while looking at him and observing some apparent misery on his face, she knew he was about to go into the events of that awful night! But, like him, she guessed it had to be discussed at one time or another---so the sooner, the better!

"Yes, Hawk,"---she gazed at him---"…what is it?" "This is hard for me to say.."—he began as his hands gently squeezed her shoulders---"…but once I start, please don't stop me. Let me get it out---it's been tearing at my insides for over two weeks now." Lizbeth nodded as he searched for the right words. "Okay."---standing directly in front of her with his head slightly bowed he then began---"I blew it. That's it in a nutshell. I was so hellbent on looking after you and keeping you out of harm's way---that I screwed up everything---it's a miracle you're still alive. Thanks to 'know-it-all' here!"

 She started to interrupt but his finger touched her half-open mouth---"Right now, I can't tell you exactly HOW I managed to find out that---well, that Mac might be 'dangerous'. But when I actually had proof of it---I knew he intended to harm you---it was like God put information into my hands for a good reason! I simply took matters in my own hands and---tried to do what I could about the situation." Finally, he paused, looked at her face, slid his hands up from her shoulders and held her face---"I did some, shall we say, possibly unlawful things to garner information I needed to protect you. And with 'some help from our friends'---things were going our way. The problem was, I didn't know exactly when Mac planned to carry out his crazed scheme---but I'd already come to the apartment, I planned to sleep there during the day and guard you each night until he made his move. From the moment Doc told me Mac was secretly walking---I knew you couldn't be left alone with him any more."

He watched her eyes trying to keep up with his rapid explanations---"Now, about that night. While you were in the shower, I came into the house, put a voice-activated recorder close to your bed then hid-out in that closet near the kitchen where I could watch your bedroom door. It seemed forever and I was about to 'give up' for one night when I heard a noise---took me a moment or two to realize it was coming from the window. As Mac terrorized you, I slipped up behind him and waited for him to say the right words that would fry his ass---sorry---words that would hang him! He was at the point I wanted him---he'd just verbalized everything on tape so I moved---I needed only one step to jump him---to get a firm hold on him---then the floor gave a loud, horrendous creak. He heard, whirled toward me---fired off a shot---and hit me! Lizbeth, I tried to stay on my feet! I wanted to wrestle the gun from his hands---or turn it toward him and blow him away! But---I couldn't stay with it---I could hear you screaming as I went down---I'm so sorry! It's simple as that. And Doc's idea about moving the bullet? It was a good one since it worked---at least diablo is on a 'wanted' list! Not to mention we have his 'arrogant confession' on tape---if it's needed."

"Late that afternoon---or evening---Doc said you wanted to see me---both he and Salle tried to convince me. But coward that I was---I turned my face toward the wall---and refused." Dropping his hands from her face, Hawk turned his back to her, placing his hands on his hips---"I, uh, was too ashamed and humiliated to face you! My dear GOD---I couldn't handle looking at you---knowing all that time when I lay on the floor like a dead puma---Mac was beating the hell out of you! I apologize, Lizbeth. I let my ego get in the way---I wanted you to come up, just so I'd know you were all right, if for no other reason. But after remembering the way you'd looked early that morning with your beautiful face all bruised, cut, bloody, swollen---and you felt so cold---your pulse weak! So, for failing to keep you safe----and stop the beating---can you forgive me? Me, the great warrior?" Suddenly he whirled back, facing her---"I almost got you KILLED, Lizbeth! Don't you know that?!! If it had ever crossed his mind to shoot you before Salle and Bill burst thru the door---it would've been MY fault. Nobody's but mine---and I don't think I could've gone on living with that." Hawk exhaled then went totally silent.

It took a moment for her to digest the entirety of his story! It went along with what Salle had told her, but his revelation had more depth---and she wanted to remember all she could! Without a word, she stepped toward her beloved Captain, took him in her arms and held him close---finally she felt his hands on her arms---she didn't know if he meant to push her away---or perhaps return her embrace. "Hawk, dearest one!"---she began—"YOU nevah 'almost got me killed'!! YOU had nothin' t'do with it except movin' heaven an' earth t'keep Mac from murderin' me! How can you even think of tryin' t'take th' blame foah all that happened?" She reached up and held his face---"Have you been tormentin' yoahself all this time? Oh, m'dear! NO!" Her face was ablaze with concern as she thought---why he'd most likely not only been blaming himself but had been filled with false shame as well! "You mustn't! Ah won't have it---you heah me? No one is at fault but Mac---an' him alone!" She looked up at Hawk then tilted her head to one side as amusement played around her mouth---"..or maybe that creaky old board! One day we'll go ovah theah, rip th' damn thing out---an' burn it right up!"

A deep sigh escaped his lips as he pulled her close to him. Finally he whispered against her woolen scarf---"You're a mighty generous, forgiving woman, Miss Lizbeth." A small chuckle escaped her throat as she retorted---"When a woman is lucky enough t'come upon some fine man who wants t'take good care of her---she bettah have sense enough t'be somewhat forgivin' an' generous t'him! Don'cha think?"

The afternoon was passing much too quickly! The sun seemed to grow heavier as it dropped lower toward the western horizon. There in his chosen spot, they'd sat on a thick soft carpet of warm, dry leaves sharing each other's life story while rocks shielded them from a nippy November wind. In the warm sun, he held both her hands in his and watched her face as she told him about her early life and family---how she'd come to meet Mac, their married life together, her discovery of his Klan connection and her growing fear of him. She spoke of how---out of loneliness for her family and kept almost isolated from other people--- she'd written her book, hiding it away from Mac. Then destiny stepped in and to her surprise, the manuscript was accepted by a publisher who 'pushed it' as a possible best seller---which it came to be. She discussed her puzzlement over Mac's rage at her for writing the story. Had it been a simple case of his jealousy over 'her moment in the limelight'---she explained, she could've lived with it. But much worse---he was certain she'd written him up as 'the heavy'---a totally fictional character with a bad marriage! Not to mention the fact she'd woven into her story, an interracial couple from the early 1900's! Thus in his eyes, almost each fictional word she'd written, became total 'reality' and to him, she'd betrayed him, in every way! Afterwards, she said quietly, he retreated even further into his own dark world---his already strange behavior becoming more secretive, manipulative and abusive than ever. Though lavishly spending money from book sales, his resentment against her and ill treatment toward her continued to grow until she no longer recognized him as the man she'd met back in Georgia.

Finishing her story, she whispered---"..finally, he came
t'hate me---such was ouah relationship when we came heah.
Ah thought th' change might be 'good' foah both of us.
Howevah life only grew moah unbearable---then came Rita-
--th' letter---his accident. An' you already know th' rest."

While she'd talked, emptying herself to him, her white
hands held fiercely onto his strong brown ones. Alternately,
he'd pressed both her hands between his own his fingers
tracing her palms---afterwards he'd kiss them. The touch of
their intertwined hands poured strength into her soul,
encouraging her to speak aloud the unpleasantness she'd
kept locked up for so long. She loved Joseph beyond any
'normal' understanding. No human could explain the
loftiness of a 'predestined' love---or a true 'soul-mate' sent
by God. She'd heard it said that a soul-mate was 'a
connection for whom one feels a mutual affinity which
cannot be expressed through words'---thus had been her
experience with Hawk and one could only accept it---for
there was no 'explanation'!

Afterwards Hawk told her about his own life from earliest
memory through the present moment. But he saved his
childhood dream/vision until almost last because for the rest
of their short time together today---he wanted to savor her
reaction to it.

Finally he came to the afternoon he'd met her! How he and
Doc had driven away from her home and their subsequent
climb half-way up South Mountain where he told Doc the
story of his youthful dream/vision---which involved the
appearance of 'a white woman with reddish hair and sea-
colored eyes'. Now with those same sea-colored eyes only
inches away from his own black ones, he smiled while
sharing Doc's reaction after hearing how in the vision, the
woman offered the gift of a 'box'! A box that had a picture

of 'a tree' on it's top! And how it was only after supper that Doc would even go into the 'book part'---explaining who wrote it---then show him it's cover design!

His tale of that treasured afternoon and evening did not fail to bring the hoped-for response from Lizbeth. A blissful look of total amazement on her face with accompanying silence told him what he wanted to know. He confessed that he'd read *'The Post Oak Tree'* that first night---at least until he fell asleep with it in his hands. He'd then kept Doc's autographed copy to re-read over and over---- memorizing the sections about 'Gramma Parnell' and 'the first Lance'.

"And why did you do that?"---she asked, her eyes on his, hoping she already knew the answer. "Because."---he replied quietly---"Because when you looked at me that first day and saw me already staring at you. You knew 'who' I was---and I knew 'who' you were. Even though at the time, to you, I only seemed someone you'd written about--- however for me, I had 'seen' you before! In my vision, I loved you---and when I finally met you twenty-something years later---I still loved you. After reading the book, I only loved you all the more. Finally,"---he slid the woolen scarf from her fiery hair and held it around her neck while touching his lips to her warm, soft forehead---"…when you and Salle brought lunch to the cutters---and you and I sat together in the jeep? For weeks, I'd been sick with love for you! Inside, I was torn apart because you were married--- but I didn't know the whole story on that---Doc kept it from me for a long while---I think it scared him as to what I might try to do if he told me all the truth. Since the night Doc and I had our talk and I read your book---I wasn't able to sleep at night---my mind was too filled with thoughts of you. During those endless days which followed, I couldn't seem to 'find my place' any more. All that time---I was

certain that my misery was one-sided---that you couldn't
possibly care for me! But came that day in the woods and
the Omaha/Sioux in my blood told me to believe you loved
me as much as 'Mrs. Parnell' loved her 'First Lance'. Was
I wrong, Lizbeth? Am I over reacting to any of those so
few but precious, golden moments that we've shared?"

His lips lingered close, barely touching her forehead as his
lustrous, long, black hair softly fanned over her face---it's
back and forth movement hypnotized her. With him now so
near, she couldn't think---she could only wonder at how his
hair had grown since that first day! How handsome was his
new appearance---wearing leather, turquoise and silver,
jeans, boots---and sometimes a rolled bandana around his
head with that extrodinary hair streaming over his powerful
shoulders! "Lizbeth?"---his voice had a hint of anxiety as it
broke thru her swirling, meandering thoughts---then she
realized she hadn't answered his questions!

Never in her life had anyone ever considered her 'forward'
or 'bold'---but after all these months since meeting Joseph,
her hands now ached to carress his face, smooth his hair!
Just to touch him, making sure this was real---and not a
beautiful dream! As a proper 'southern lady', she
considered what he might 'think of her'—but as she
'thought on it'---her hands simply took action on their own!
Gingerly catching his face and guiding his eyes to meet
hers, she looked squarely into them then swallowing at her
nervousness, she spoke quietly---"Since first you saw me,
you have loved me---yet by displayin' gallant behavior in
this society of new barbarians, you've barely put your hands
on me an' Ah'm humbled by such lovely consideration.
But most of all yoah bravery an' willingness to save m'life--
-all put togethah, why you simply astound me! Without
you, Ah would not be heah now, m'love. Mah parents
would've already laid this body t'rest in th' family cemetary

253

back home---an' no one would've been th' wisah. Mac would've killed me then gone scott-free. An' while Ah owe mah very life to you---an' Ah'll forevah be in yoah debt foah that---Ah find those things actually have very little t'do with mah feelin's foah you---feelin's that have been theah since th' day Doc brought you t'me! Can you imagine me lookin' up an' actually seein' th' man Ah'd written about--- a man with whom Ah'd fallen in love! Isn't that th' limit? Fallin' in love with one of yoah fictional characters?!"

Her eyes had been brimming with tears from the beginning of her little 'speech'---now the tears dripped down her cheeks---"In answah to those questions? Captain Joseph Wintahhawk, you nevah ovahreacted---nor did you misinterpret any nuance between us! Aftah meetin' you, Ah regularly tormented mahself thinkin' th' love Ah felt foah you was probably of the 'unrequited' variety! Until that day in th'woods when we sat togethah---an' today you told me th' Indian in you told you Ah loved you---so, too, foah me, yoah eyes and behavior told me you loved me---or either you were a handsome Indian brave talkin' a white man's line! Foah days aftah our lunch, Ah was crazy-happy---just ask Salle! Poah thing, she had no idea what was wrong with me! Ah was so 'wild' with joy that Ah think Ah scared her half t'death!"

"Th' coffee cup you drank from th' day you and Doc came by..."---she swallowed as tears continued to flow—it was so good to sit close to him and finally empty her heart! "...Ah nevah washed it. Ah took it to m'room, placed it beside m' book an'each night befoah bed, Ah'd talk to you in mah heart---then kiss th' cup wheah yoah lips had once been. It's against m'nature bein' this bold but had you NOT loved me---soonah or latah, Ah would've died foah love of you."

He'd hoped she would reciprocate, he'd PRAYED she did care for him and possibly 'love him a little'---but never in his wildest hopes, dreams or prayers did he believe she'd respond so honestly! Her forthrightness filled him with such ecstasy that it took away his breath! Now, it was his turn to sit speechless---the Indian in him had taken flight and at present was soaring some place even higher than he'd flown in any military plane---OR in his vision!!

At some point, not even conscious he'd even moved closer toward her, he'd begun to kiss the tears on her face and whisper to her---and she was looking up at him in a way that he'd not expected! He knew at this point, she was no longer 'seeing' with her eyes---she only had 'feelings' and like him, she was 'blinded', all awash with emotions! Smiling tenderly at her, he cuddled her against him, holding her, protecting her---as he'd always desired. Once again as on their walk toward the church, they were quiet---no words to spoil the moment. And for now, it was enough for him to simply hold her and not just dream of doing so---as he'd been forced to do. For both of them, the past few months had been a time of much uncertainty and pain, he fully understood that now.

All too soon the time had come to start back but before they stood to leave, there was something else---"Lizbeth, all this business with Mac isn't over, we both know that---Doc, Logan, my family, everyone---they all know Mac must be caught and punished. But now I must ask you for something---which if you give, will carry me until we can be together again." Her finger gently touched the pulse at the base of his neck as she whispered---"Anything, m'love, what is it?"

Taking her hand away from his neck, he held it tightly--- "Please let me hear from your heart that you love me! Not from your lips, my own, but from your heart---tell me that you love me." Her hands reached up, held onto his arms as she replied softly---"Ah'm not certain Ah undahstand what you mean---exactly." Catching her eyes steady with his and never wavering, he eased her down to lie in the leaves and slowly unbuttoned her coat then the three top buttons of her woolen shirt. Finally, brushing his hair to one side and laying his ear upon her bosom, he said---"Now tell me that you love me---I shall listen not to your lips but to your heart as it speaks truth to me. This moment and this truth I'll carry---until these uncertain times just ahead are passed! Then, I will come to you---belong to you, free and clear. Then shall begin 'our time' together...."

Her heart had never pounded like this before in her whole life---could such a love as theirs cause one's heart to explode or stop beating altogether?! But---that was unimportant---she didn't care---it didn't matter if her heart exploded or stopped beating! Never had she experienced any emotions that rivaled these! Forceful, strong, powerful, raging, taking her breath away---like the wind tearing away large oak trees, snapping them as though they were tiny twigs! Or perhaps more like an earthquake---she'd never been in one---but right now either she or the world around her was quaking, rocking crazily! She wanted to speak--- but her vocal cords wouldn't co-operate! "Lizbeth."---she heard his voice---"My dream, tell me---say the words I have to hear from your heart."

At last her voice returned, at the same time her hands pressed his head closer to her bosom as she spoke---"Oh, yes---yes, Ah love you! Wholly, completely---in spirit, soul, heart, mind and---a-and body---Ah adore you. Dearest one---Ah love you. Since childhood, Ah daydreamed an' waited---searching at every turn, longin' t'find you---an'

now we've found each othah! It's you I love, Captain---you
and you alone ---now, forevah, eternally."

Her answer set his mind to rest and while he felt
incomplete, he was as satisfied as he could ever be at this
point. To move his head from the warmth of her flesh was
agonizing but the time had come to leave their 'hallowed'
ground. Raising his ear from her and turning his face
toward her body, he gently placed his warm lips upon her
bosom---then slowly and deliberately, he buttoned the shirt
then the coat until it was snug beneath her chin. Gazing
into her eyes, he realized he'd stirred her beyond herself---
so he whispered---"When our time has come, my love---
only then will I ever touch you as I wish to now. Even this
favor I would never have asked of you if we were as other
couples—but we still have a time of separation ahead of us-
--so until later, I had to hear your heart--- it's words will go
with me. I had to take advantage of the moment, my
Lizbeth, should it not soon present itself again."

Taking her hands in his, he pulled her to her feet---then held
her to him as his voice trembled with emotion. "My Indian
blood, my body---my whole being clamors to be with you---
wanting to keep you here---to be alone with you before you
change your mind---or something concerning Mac separates
us. The thought of being away from you even for a short
while fills me with deep darkness because you, my Lizbeth,
are the light of my life and I must treat you as 'light'---my
gift from God---The Great Spirit."

He sighed, shaking his head---"Here I'm taking you for
granted already! In my mind, heart, body and soul---I've
thought so much of you being my very own---I guess I've
forgotten to ASK you if you would become mine. Lizbeth,
my love.."---he asked---"...how do you feel about
interracial marriages?"

Her joy was complete---in a few minutes, she'd float off the earth---he was proposing!! Again her eyes flooded with 'silly tears' that she couldn't seem to stop---"If yoah proposin', Captain Wintahhawk, Ah have only one thing t'say! Th' heart knows nothin' of 'color'---of race---th' heart only recognizes it's reflection mirrored in th' heart of anothah which is like unto it! Love then responds to it's own kind an'---you are MAH kind. Ah'm delighted---and th' answer is YES!" Lizbeth began to giggle softly---"Ah thought you'd nevah ask!" He grinned then lifted her high into the air, spinning her body 'round and round'!

Setting her down again, he took his army-ranger ring and slid it on her thumb, closing her fist over it. Lizbeth lay her head on Hawk's chest---"Ah must confess---Ah need yoah help in bein' careful of---of m'feelings! It's an embarrassment t'say this—but---honestly, Hawk, tho Ah've been married many yeahs---Ah---well, it's nevah been this---befoah. Mac was an aloof man---in—in all ways." Once more she lifted her face toward his---"Do you undahstand?"

"I do---even more than you could know. So, beginning now---past things are swept away, gone---only a dim memory that even at this moment is fading into nothingness. Soon, when all is settled, I will see that your life is different from that point on." Slowly he carressed her cheek, kissed each eyelid softly as a butterfly then whispered---"I will make you happy, my dream love, in every possible way---indescribable discoveries await us---count on it. Maybe when you occasionally think of me, you might even look forward to joining me in said-discoveries as well?" Lizbeth blushed furiously as he seemed to have the ability of looking deep inside her and knew each emotion she'd felt course through her!

Turning to retrace the path back homeward, he remarked---
"My darling, sometimes you remind me of an innocent
child---yet you are a strong, confident woman. I've seen
you hurt, abused---yet remain unmarked by it all. I've
admired you, longed for your company, countless times I've
sat with my hands gripped tightly together to keep from
dialing the phone---hoping for the sound of your voice! But
looking at you now, there's a brand new sparkle in your
eyes! And I must admit to feeling some bit of male
arrogance that I might be the one who put it there!" He
grinned---"Or am I only getting ahead of myself again---
over-reacting, misinterpreting and all that?"

Both broke out in hoots of laughter---for the first time,
Hawk heard Lizbeth laugh as she had while driving the jeep
back home after taking lunch to the wood-cutters---when
poor Salle thought she'd 'lost it'! What a joy to hear such
light-heartedness coming from the woman he loved! He
thought perhaps she was carefree because their very first
lengthy, uninterrupted conversation had lifted some heavy
emotional burdens from both their shoulders and their
hearts! But what he found most amusing---was how she
laughed like a man---loud, honest, robustly and straight
from the gut! "Lord,"---he thought---"It's possible she
could turn out to be more than a handful! But how I'm
gonna LOVE it! Every minute of it!"

Chapter Forty-Two

Doc carried Lizbeth's few belongings up to Hawk's old
attic bedroom while Ida and Lizbeth set Mary's gift of
Thanksgiving left-overs out on the table. Ida's eyes took in
Lizbeth's clean but faded jeans, flannel shirt and the dusty
walking shoes she'd worn that afternoon then remarked,
"Lizbeth, we need to buy you some new things, dear---I

never saw such a small bag of clothing! Besides, it's
growing colder each day, you'll need heavier apparel!"
Lizbeth looked down at her duds---"Yoah're probably right-
--stayin' heah with you an' Doc will be different than
stayin' with Mrs. Wintahhawk---out in th' country an' all.
Ah wouldn't want t'embarrass you in front of yoah friends!
Y'think we could get Sheriff Logan t'accompany me out t'
th' ranch---it'd be foolish buyin' new things when Ah
already have plenty---all's needed is t'pick them up!"

Doc dug into his anticipated left-overs---"Don't see why he
wouldn't! He'd probably LOVE another chance t'poke
around th' scene of th' crime! I'll give 'em a call soon as I
finish my grub!" Lizbeth nodded and took up her fork---
"Ah wish you'd arrange t'ride along, too. Ah don't know
Sheriff Logan very well. He---kinda makes me nervous."
"I'd be more'n happy t'accompany you an' Logan.
Wouldn't mind pokin' around th' scene another time
myself!" Lizbeth nodded then remarked---"Uh, look---you
all don't need t'worry about heatin' up that attic room foah
me! Ah LOVE cold bedrooms---fact is, Ah always leave
mah window up some---except when it's cold enough
t'freeze th' pipes." She smiled---"Just leave it all nice an'
chilled---Ah'll sink up beneath those covahs---an' be happy
as a bug! Ah'm a country-girl---not used t'heated
bedrooms."

"Some more milk, Lizbeth?" Lizbeth shook her head---"No
thank you, this is fine. Maybe a cup of hot tea b'foah you
an' I go t'bed, Ida?" "Certainly---we'll do that when
'doctor' here sneaks his nightly portion of brandy! Not that
he fools me a bit---but it obviously does him good to think
he's pulling something over on me!" "Tee-totalers!"---he
snorted---"All her church group---a bunch of teetotalers!
Nothing wrong with a nip, Ida. Our Lord, Himself, drank

wine----an' probably danced a jig or two in His time on this miserable earth!"

"Doctor!"---Ida looked at Lizbeth then spoke of Doc in 3rd person and in absentee---"He's Irish, you know. I do believe all Irishmen love their 'little nip'---AND their tall tales NOT to mention their morbid fascination of dabbling in the lives of others! Watch these men, my dear, don't be choosing an Irishman---he'll steal your heart away, just like the song says! His Irish eyes will smile at you---and 'whacko'! You've been hit right in the heart by the little green people---and you'll never be the same!" "You haven't been the same since I came into your life, m'dear?"---Doc questioned. "No!"---she retorted---"You changed my entire life!" He looked at her, scrapping up the last of his food---"For better or worse? Or is this th' wrong time t'ask that question!" "If I didn't like you---I would've been gone long ago and you know it!"---finishing her milk, Ida daintly dabbed her mouth---"Now, you go and call that pompous sheriff-friend of yours while Lizbeth and I fix up some 'Thanksgiving' for your old dog out there!"

"Yes, Dear." He stood, bent and kissed her hair---"Ah, but you're still a fair lass, m'dear---a fair lass." "Get out of here, you old blarney-stone!"---she gave a sweep with one hand.

In the kitchen they could hear Doc's voice rising as he talked to Logan---Ida looked at Lizbeth remarking--- "Wonder what all THAT'S about! With them, you never know! It could be anything from the latest scandal to crime---or hunting and fishing!" "Think it could be about--- uh, Mac?"---Lizbeth looked at her. "My dear, I'm sorry! I just didn't think!"---Ida touched Lizbeth's arm---"I'm so used to living with that man---sometimes I open my mouth before my mind's in gear! We'll see---soon as he hangs up---we'll ask!'"

A tiny shadow flickered momentarily over Lizbeth's memory of her joyous day---the best day of her life, other than the afternoon when Doc showed up at the ranch with an army-ranger in tow. "Well."—Lizbeth sighed —"Maybe it won't be about Mac! Maybe it'll just be man-stuff they're getting all head-up about!"

Soon Doc returned with the 'news'. "Guess what, Ida---Lizbeth!"---adding relish to the 'old tale' Hawk had told him late yesterday, he rubbed his hands together---"They've located th' gun!" Ida gasped---"You mean 'THE gun'---out at the ranch?" "Yes ma'am!"---Doc crowed---"Been right there all this time---just discovered it late yesterday!" Her face pale, Lizbeth asked---"Who found it? Ah thought nobody had been lookin' around out theah lately!" Doc picked up his 'tale'---"Would you believe, Bill found it?! He an' a couple of his friends had gone t'put out hay at your ranch---as they turned in th' driveway, something shiny caught his eye. Reckon with th' sun shinin', that chrome reflected a bit of a flash---at least enough for Bill t'investigate. Y'know, Lizbeth, this is a REAL break---or a miracle! Imagine, those guys bein' there at just th' right time t'see an object off there in th' grass glimmerin' like a mirror!? Why---what if th' sky had been overcast---Lord, it's possible nobody woulda found it f'ages!"

Lizbeth stared at him---"Wheah was it? Why on earth didn't Bill SAY something t'me about it last night!?" "One question at th' time, m'dear. It was lying in th' tall grass---in th' far front yard just beside th' highway! Like I said, a pure miracle---coulda lain there f'months---years even, just rustin' away! Now they can match th' gun to th' bullet---old Mac's goose is cooked, m'dears---'roasted' like that turkey we just devoured!" "But Ah can't believe Bill nevah mentioned this!"---Lizbeth wouldn't give it up! "Now, now."---he cajoled---"This is a bit of news Logan didn't want gettin' out just yet! He has real good reason orderin' Bill t'keep his lip buttoned! Now---!"—pointing his forefinger, he cautioned both women---"You two didn't HEAR this, you got it? THIS, ladies, is classified information---from 'high up'! It is NOT to be bandied about over backyard fences or church bazaars---clear?"

Both nodded---Lizbeth then asked the inevitable---"Did Bill tell Captain Wintahawk?" Realizing the two had spent the better part of that afternoon together, Doc tested the air---she sounded a mite tart---he must 'remind' her that Ida was sitting there---"Mmm, probably not. If Bill didn't share it with you---he didn't tell Hawk either---after all, what does Hawk have to do with it? He wasn't even here!" Doc decided it best to guide the conversation toward another course, he certainly didn't want Ida to put Mac's gun and Hawk's 'injury' together---"As for m'self, man, I can't wait until tomorrow gets here! Surely Logan'll have more news by then. Oh---and by th' way, Lizbeth---Logan said we'd ride out t'get your clothes after lunch tomorrow, is that a good time for you?"

She nodded but her face looked worried. Ida noticed her expression---"Anything wrong, dear?" Lizbeth breathed a small sigh—"Ah just thought of somethin'---wondah how Ah'll feel goin' back---it'll be th' first time since---since all this happened. You know, Ah don't let mahself think much about Mac or wheah he might be---it upsets me too much. Reckon deep down inside, Ah know foah certain he'll be back---an' it scares me not knowin' when or wheah he'll show up!"

Dr. O'Barr wished he could tell Lizbeth everything but---
he'd better not. Only th' Almighty Himself knew how glad
he'd be when none of them had 'secrets' from the rest! So,
to calm her fears as best he could, Doc went over and
utilizing his most polished 'bed-side' manner said---"Listen,
m'girl. I give this thing two more weeks at th' most---now
don't be askin' me 'why'---'cause I don't know! I just feel
by then th' law will have him---an' if I'm not badly
mistaken, he'll be lucky t'escape th' chair! Th' very least
he'll get is life without chance of parole! All well an' good-
--after th' things he's done!!"

"But Doc,"---she whispered---"What if his father has
'friends in high places'---in th' judicial system 'round here,
I mean!? Couldn't they 'get him off'? Every time Ah used
t'mention 'divorce', he always threatened me by sayin'
things like that!" Doc snorted--- "With all they've got on
him?! Gettin' him off would be a travesty of justice,
Lizbeth! That won't happen here---also if Logan an' th'
judge are smart---they'll see to it he doesn't get a change of
venue either!!" "What's that?"---she looked at him. "Oh,
his lawyers might ask t'have th' trial held in some other
county similar t'this one. A good thing our little newspaper
an' television didn't make a big deal outta what he did
t'you---that counts when a venue request is made. In this
particular case, you having less publicity---was th' better!
This way his attorneys can't holler that any local jury would
be 'tainted' or prejudiced by too much pre-trial publicity!"

Before going upstairs later that night, Lizbeth pleaded with
Doc to take the shot-gun from his truck, bring it inside and
put it beside his bed! Almost to the point of tears, she
begged---"Ah couldn't bear it if---if Mac broke in here—an'
hurt th' two of you! Just humor me---please---an' get th'
gun inside th' house!" Doc nodded, patted her shoulder and
did as she asked. As he left the room, Ida whispered---"An

excellent idea, Lizbeth! We'll all sleep better each night knowing that gun's in here with us!"

Carefully and discreetly, Lizbeth examined each door-lock in the O'Barr house. Then when she was sure the couple had retired, she crept quietly back downstairs, making certain each door and window had been locked to her satisfaction.

Finally, after her shower, for the first time in ages---she stood peering at her face in the bathroom mirror and thought of skin creams, moisturizers, tweezers---but she'd brought none. Thoughts of Joseph immediately brought to mind her 'appearance' and vice-versa! Tomorrow, she decided, when they went to the ranch for her winter clothing---she'd bring back all her skin care products---and make up! After brushing her teeth and her hair, she slid Hawk's ring back on her thumb and climbed into the 'chilly' bed, then lay thinking of him as a dark-haired, beautiful child with sparkling eyes and smooth skin.

Suddenly remembering a gold neck-chain she once wore, she made a mental note that tomorrow the jewelry box must come along as well! In the darkness, she recalled shades of high-school days when the mark of a 'steady' couple was the girl wearing a chain around her neck with her fella's ring on it. "How many years has it been since those times?"---she smiled tenderly—"...seems all of that b'longs in somebody else's life, not mine. Like when readin' a book or watchin' a movie---just bein' a by-standah, events that're reality in othah people's lives---but not yoah own." Closing her eyes, she thought---"When this is all ovah an' done with, Ah'll ask Hawk t'take me home again---maybe Ah can regain some parts of m'self that've been lost foah a long time."

Her thoughts once again turned to the ring there on her thumb. What a comforting warmth it would bring hanging around her neck, it's weight resting there on her bare flesh at the spot where he'd pressed his ear then planted a kiss! Before arriving back at Mary's house late that afternoon, they both agreed to keep the ring a secret---until 'later'. Thus for now, it would remain temporarily hidden from everyone. Both of them were overly aware they could in NO WAY publicize their relationship—not until Mac was found, had his trial and been sentenced! Once caught and brought here to await trial, should he hear even one breath or whisper about Hawk and herself---and somehow or other, he'd hear---he'd have his attorneys 'make a big deal' out of it, compromising the reputation of two innocent people! Then only God knew what his lawyers might do to their rare and precious love---possibly Mac'd end up branding them a couple of 'adulterous lovers' planning HIS murder! It'd be just like him to do that---IF he could! Though Doc said it couldn't happen 'here', she wasn't so sure. For the time being, it seemed Doc, Salle and Bill, Hawk and herself must continue living with their bag of secrets.

The day Doc moved everyone away from the ranch then shuffled their living quarters like a deck of cards, he'd impressed upon them that even Ida didn't know Mac had shot Hawk! She thought he'd got a bullet in some 'secret, covert fracas', obviously 'not far away'---either Mexico or Central America---and naturally it couldn't be breathed to a living soul, not EVER! Even Mary must not know! If there was one thing Ida respected, it was the CIA, FBI---or any 'Fed'!! Nor did Ida know about the 'love-match'! Lizbeth knew she must constantly be on guard in conversations with Ida---she'd managed pretty well with Mrs. Winterhawk--- hopefully, she could do the same with Ida. Whatever it took for hers and Hawk's love to come through unscathed--- that's what she'd do! But tonight, in order to sleep---she'd

put out of mind Mac and everything connected to him.
And like Scarlett O'Hara, she'd 'think about it tomorrow'---
but tonight, she'd relive only this most blessed of days!

 Sleep found her turning Joseph's ring round and round on
her finger, mentally reliving this day from early morning
until almost dusk when Doc's truck drove them away from
the Winterhawk home as everyone waved 'good-bye'.
Already she missed them, but more than that, she now
missed Hawk's loving touch---his deep, resonant, accented
voice, his gentle strength. As had been the case since the
moment they'd met and as Hawk stated this afternoon---
today might have to last a 'long time'. But she could do it---
-she'd done it before---he was more than worth the wait!
Even if it was 'forever'.

Chapter Forty-Three

Thanksgiving at the McDougals was not quite so peaceful or
happy! Mac's arrival had caused no small stir in the
household as well as among local klansmen who kept the
phone line busy 'welcoming' him back! As to questioning
his foolish, high-handed but short-sighted son---the elder
McDougal was biding his time. And 'his time' finally
arrived late Thanksgiving afternoon---just as the sun was
setting.

 Along with their families, several Klansmen had come for
lunch and continued their visit on into late afternoon.
Mac's mother now passed on---was not there to cook and
serve, but his father had remarried thus life went on as
usual. No one actually missed the first Mrs. McDougal---a
'sick, ailing wife and mother'---who for years, had only
been somewhat 'in their way'. Frances, the second Mrs.
McDougal, was big, raw-boned and tempermental---taking

no nonsense off her husband---and had no intentions of taking any off this brash, up-start son of his either! In short, she was not pleased about Mac's return---she foresaw trouble coming down upon them because of it!

All afternoon Mac basked in the attentions as well as the conversations of his 'fellow klansmen' from earlier days--- and dressed in his new suit, he played it to the hilt. After standing on the front porch seeing off the last of their visitors---Mac and his father returned to the living room. The elder McDougal spoke---"Sit down, boy." Mac had heard THAT tone many times before—it meant that serious talk had been delayed long enough and the moment of truth had just arrived. "Now,"---the old man began—"...tell me agin about this boilin' pot ya stirred up back there!"

"Dad,"---Mac began---"---several times, I told you on the phone, nothing's changed since!" "Well, by th'cross, I wanta hear it agin!"---the old man snapped---"Let's have it frum th' beginning! Start with thet accident o'yourn!"

"What else do you want to know about it? I just fell and thought I'd never walk again---at least the fool doctor came to that conclusion. Though he DID happen to mention, in time, maybe the nerves would heal themselves. Several months later when a tingling began in my legs, I recalled what he said---that's when I forced myself to at least give it a try, secretly! And I can tell you ---it wasn't easy!" Mac's voice took on a lofty tone---"My body ached from head to toe---I pushed myself far beyond anybody else's point of endurance---all those late hours of exercising, dragging around on the floor like a damned reptile! But it paid off! I can walk---as you can plainly see!"

"Ya said on th' phone last spring, this here woman ya married had axed fer a divorce---how come?" "Well, I was

268

a little careless..."—Mac lifted a shoulder—"..I left a letter
from Rita in my pocket—Lizbeth was doing the laundry and
found it. That's all." "Thet's ALL?! This 'wife' ya tried
t'murder knows 'bout us, boy! Didn'cha think at some
point she'd get mad as hell then blab off to th'authorities??
This ain't no good time fer us t'be brought under public
scrutiny---'bout ANYTHING!" The old man's face began
turning fushia---"Th' niggers are marching---th' slant eyes
are warring an' killing our boys---college brats rampagin'
like th' buncha little sluts an' bastards they are---th' whole
country is about t'burn down t'hell---but YOU can't seem
t'git that thru your thick skull? Drawin' attention t'yerself
right now?! DAMN! You can be SO stupid---jest like ya
always was---dumb an' stupid!"---the old man spat---"High-
tempered little fool!"

Then he jumped up, stalking about the room! "Must'a took
after yer Maw! Shorely didn't take after me!!" Shaking a
finger at his son, he blasted---"If ya'd a listened t'me years
ago---you'd a been a 'dragon' by now---but oh no! You
knew best! Mister Know-It-All BIG-SHOT! Always
knowed everythang, didn' cha!? Couldn't listen t'nobody---
nobody but yer ignerent self! Now look at'cha! On th' run-
-with th'law after ya—nowhere t'go but back t'good old
Paw here! Go on, y'idiot, why didn't she git th' divorce?!"
Angrily, the elder McDougal ripped off a cellophane
wrapper from a big green cigar, bent over, lit a piece of
kindling wood at the fireplace, puffed the cigar to life then
flopped back into his easy chair!

Mac swallowed---the old man was madder than hell! Okay.
He knew the drill, the bellowing fit had begun---it always
did---that's the way it'd been when he'd sent him to
Lizbeth's hometown—after he'd knifed one of 'their men'
and the law was sniffing about. He'd tell him AGAIN---
over and over---he'd always been that way, the old man.

269

"We had a fight---I slapped her---she picked up a poker and whacked me twice before I knew what happened. See, she'd never come back 'at me' before---sorta surprised me. Anyhow, I took the poker away from her---chased her to the kitchen where she grabbed up a butcher knife and told me to get out---that she wanted a divorce. Then she ran out and blazed off somewhere in the jeep---I'd already planned to kill her---so I went out to the barn where the 'artillery' is hidden to get my .38. My intention was to kill her that night---but I fell before I got to the gun. I told her, the cop and the doctor when I fell that I was on the roof---not just inside the barn at the end loft opening. Figured that'd keep anybody from poking around inside the barn and maybe uncovering our little arsenal!"

The old man blew out several smoke rings---"So. When she found ya was crippled, why didn't she leave---eh?" Mac answered---"I told her I'd not sign a divorce---and if she went to court---'our' attorneys would make her out to be everything but a lady and I'd get everything we had! So she stayed on to cook, clean and look after me---which I made troublesome as possible." He erupted in hard cold laughter---"I gave her hell, Pop! You should've been there to see it! Little Miss Georgia Peach had all she could do about 20 hours a day there for several months! I kept her little back-field in motion---on the run. Had it not been for her somehow convincing me to let those damned Indians work for us---well, she'd be six feet under right now..." In the silence that followed, Mac realized his highfaluting manner had not impressed his father, not in the least---because in the end, in the old man's eyes---he'd failed---again! One more 'failure' to chalk up!

Ex-dragon McDougal pursed his lips blowing on the fire-end of his cigar watching it glow---"But she ain't six feet under, is she? B'sides a body has t'give her credit fer not leavin' ya, boy. Not that I, personally, give a damn---I never liked her---she wasn't 'like' us. Although more a southerner than us, she acted uppity---like born an' bred yankee-trash! And thet damn book---interracial romance!! UNGODLY!! Y'sunk low in th' Klan's eyes, boy—real low! Anyway, how come ya never let 'er know ya could walk?"

"That was my plan, Pop."---Mac saw a chance to redeem himself somewhat if he didn't get diarrhea of the mouth again---his father was always impressed by underhanded, sly, long-range planning. "Don't call me 'pop', boy."---he groused ominously---"I don't like it! Sounds damned smart-alecky---too mucha thet around a'ready!"

"Yessir, sorry! I'll remember that. Anyhow, I'd planned to keep this sudden recovery a secret from everybody around there---except Rita---who lives in the next town. I'd told Rita on the phone that I had a big surprise for her---and that I'd be seeing her soon. See, Lizbeth always left her bedroom window up a ways---I was going to climb thru that window, kill her---then go back to my room and hide the piece. The Indian would find her next morning---and I'd have my alibi! I couldn't walk---everybody knew that as a fact---also I'd planned to leave the kitchen phone off the hook---thus I couldn't call for help from my bedside extention! So, that day, I got her and them redskins off the place by sending them to town---I went out, got my pistol out of the barn---hurrying just in case anybody came by--- and I took it to my room and waited. The next night, I crawled in her window, got on her bed and was about to finish the 'job' when---uh, I heard a noise---and uh, I fired off a shot! Then I began beating her---first thing I know, her Indians come busting through the back door---I jumped out the window and ran! I stayed in some hills across the road till I saw the law arriving---then I figured I needed to send for Rita. She came, picked me up and you know the rest." Mac HOPED this would suffice BUT the old man was more thorough than that.

"There's some thangs not quite clear t'me, boy. Some pieces left outta th' picture. That shot ya fired---I'm assumin' ya left th' damn bullet?" Mac stared at him---"Of course, how could I find time to dig it out when I didn't know if the Indians were armed! Who'd ever thought they'd come a' running soon as they heard the shot---most niggers and redskins just stay away, minding their own business when they hear gunshots!"

The elder McDougal stood, fastened a glare on his son--- "And th' gun---I'm assumin' ya brought THAT little piece of evidence along with ya—back here---right? I mean, it's up in yer room?" Mac swallowed trying to think fast but he wasn't 'fast enough' for the old man! "I axed ya a question, young Mister McDougal! Would ya kindly answer it--- a'fore t'morrow?"

"Uh---no, no Dad. I--uh---hid it---before I left the area! You see, I didn't want to have it ON me---that'd sign my warrant if they'd found me! You always told me THAT--- never 'get caught' with a hot gun in your possession! Nobody'll ever find it, not where I—uh, hid it!" Mac suddenly realized he was nodding almost constantly and immediately ceased the nervous give away---"Naaa, nobody'll ever find it, Po--er, Dad."

The old man was silent---his face had enlarged like a reddish purple party balloon---the veins at his neck bulged out like half-inch box cording! Mac wanted to flee the room---but where'd he go!? So far, he still hadn't made clear to his father that Lizbeth had sworn he'd shot at HER and not at the man there in her room---he couldn't tell his father THAT!

Like a large stone statue, the elder McDougal now stood before the fireplace, his back to his son. Finally, he turned and began his dreaded summation---"Let's add all this up now. Ya git yer gun outa th' barn an' later climbed in yer wife's bedroom winder---yer're startin' t'beat up on her, you hear 'something' an' fire th' gun! Ya then foolishly continue th' beatin' before puttin' a bullet in 'er---these here hired Injuns suddenly rush in while YOU rush out! So, seems t'me, th' sum total of yer ignorance is as follers! (1)--Ya left a bullet with YORE name on it, sommers' in thet room! (2)--At some 'safe' location, ya took it inta yer ruinious head t'hide th' gun thet shot th' bullet! (3)--While YOU, th' 'cripple', are missing frum yer bedroom! (4)---This wife identified ya not only as her assailant but ya got an attempted murder charge hung on, as well! (5)---We won't even mention them Injun witnesses! DAMN!! Any other pertinent facts I need t'be aware of as I think on this here comedy a' errers ya jest presented me with?"

Mac hung his head, staring down at his shiny new black shoes---"Don't reckon, Dad. I think that's all." Suddenly the old man flung his half-smoked, mid-priced 'Anthony and Cleopatra' cigar into the fireplace, stomped in front of Mac and loomed over him---"Did ya fergit, ya fool, thet all them firearms ya left back there in yer barn back are STILL 'hot'?! You got a short memory, boy! Them thangs been used in three states---an' th' feds have long files---not t'mention LONG MEMORIES! An' up until YOU turned over this barrel a' slop---they had NOTHING t'go on! NOTHING! They KNEW nothing, had no clue WHERE t'find whut they needed t'put us away----cause if they did, they'd a come after us years back!"

Mac hastened to assure his father —"But they STILL don't have a clue, Dad! Nobody'll ever find the 'goods'---I hid 'em like an expert!" "Yeah, so you bragged right after ya did it!"—his father snapped---"But whut YOU don't seem t'grasp is---with any kinda 'search' a'tall in thet barn--- some smart turd could uncover them guns an' we'd ALL be up t'our ass in a hornet's nest!"

A familiar uneasy quiet now fell over the room---crackling firewood resembled .22 shots. Suddenly, the ex-dragon exhaled loud enough to be heard three counties away, stood ramrod straight then grandly pronounced in his 'quiet' voice---"I'm givin' ya a chance t'do right by me, boy. You're goin' back---I'm sendin' ya in a new camper-back pick-up---it's been paid fer, got all papers in th' dash, it's insured an' tagged in yer new ID. Come Monday morning, yer leavin'---I want thet woman AN' them two witnesses dead! I want thet pistol, th' slug from it an' all them guns in yer barn picked up! Everythang! I want thet whole place cleaner'n Methodist communion linen! In th' camper, there's a special wood floor built with a false bottom---put the 'pieces' in it, close it up---then pack a coupla huntin' guns, some campin' junk and a bedroll on topa everything! I want each 'piece' brought back here t'this very house--ya got that?! I'll not have ya makin' a' fool a'me no longer! This here de-backle o' yorn could put YOU away fer a time but it'd make me, ex-Grand Dragon McDougal, th' laughin' stock of th' entire KKK!!" His arms waved wildly about, his face and neck still distorted—"All across this country, th' men would be laughin' at me---an' I won't have it! Y'hear? I jest won't HAVE it! Worst a' all, if'n they search an' find them guns—we'll all be dead!"

This was the time---Mac had to ask---he'd never have the courage to bring it up again! "Dad. The Klan's lawyers--- uh, should I get caught---should worse come to worse and I go to jail---can they make bond for me? And IF I go to trial---will they defend me? I can't go to prison---shut up for life---Daddy, I just can't! You GOT to get me some kind of help---promise you will! I'll beg---I'm beggin now---you want me on my knees?" Mac slipped to the floor and took the position---"Honest, I thought everything through, Dad! Every angle was covered before I even started this thing! I swear it! I just don't know what happened---it's as though somebody or something read my mind, had it all figured out ahead of time---then caught me in a trap! You gotta help me!"

"Git up off'n th' floor, y'babblin' coward! Y'disgust me!" The voice was rising again--"Fer my own name's sake—I'll do whatever I can! But I ain't promisin' nothing, ya understand? This ain't nothin but one big over-turned dung heap—an' I don't know if even WE can git ya outta it! Not only ain't thet place not one of our best 'states'---it ain't even 'our county'!" Suddenly his voice lowered two octaves then snarled---"Git outta m'sight, boy, before I lose m'temper! I don't wanta lay eyes on ya fer a goodly spell---hopefully not b'fore you drive thet truck outta here this comin' Monday early!"

Mac stood and walked away---at the door, he paused---partially raised a hand to his father who stared coldly into his eyes without moving. Mac clenched his jaw, lightly tapped the door-frame with his unaccepted hand then turned and went up to his room.

Later as shock began turning to shame and shame to angry humiliation---Mac felt all the rage of a lifetime turn on his father and wondered if, one day, he could kill him! An accident, of course. A farm was a good place for an accident--"God! How I'd love to see that miserable old SOB lying stiff, cold and dead---in his coffin, lowered six feet down then covered with dirt!! I'd volunteer to throw in each shovel full! All my life, he's treated me like some ratty animal he inherited but didn't honestly want! And I'm thru, I just won't put up with his big, fat, loud mouth and overbearing ways any more! I'll use him to help get me off—oh, I'll crawl, grovel, lick his damned shoes, whatever I have to until I'm outta this. Then I'll see to him."

Chapter Forty-Four

Mac didn't come down for supper, when Frances asked where he'd disappeared off to, the grumpy elder McDougal replied---. "Mind yer own, Frances. Now ain't th' time fer discuss'n it." She shrugged and looked at her own three children by another marriage---"Whatever, Mr. McDougal, he's YORE son, thank God. Not mine."

After the household had retired for the night, ex-Grand Dragon McDougal sat beside the fire and lit another green cigar then put his feet up on an ottoman. "This here time,"---he thought---"I'll enjoy it in peace an' quiet." Utilizing a crude attempt at eloquence, he slowly and deliberately sucked in his jowls, puffed the fat rolled tobacco cylinder then drew the cigar away in an exaggerated manner, imitating George Raft in a movie, so long ago---finally he exhaled then gave a couple of short coughs.

He sat weighing the pros and cons of his maladjusted son's chronic stupidity. This unenviable spot had been brought about by Mac's decision to murder his wife---a decision which had put him on a 'wanted' list! And now, after their 'talk', there seemed a strong possibility the Klan could be drawn into it as well! Even with his scheming, cunning mind, the ex-Dragon could come up with only two possible plans of action! He had to admit the time had come to 'do

276

something' about Mac---"This son a'mine has turned in t'a
li'bility fer everone a'us! Th' question right now is—'will
he brang us down with him'---if so, th' truth is we can't
afford 'em any longer! Th' brothers have never let even
one 'questionable' man live long enough t'cause
investigations by th' authorities. Either local---or fed'ral."

"But th' REAL shame of it is—all this trouble wuz
unnecessary! If ever once, th' boy'd a listened t'reason! I'd
allus thought he'd grow up t'take my place---God knows, I
took 'em everywhur we met---t'each rally---each burnin'---
had a little cloak an' hood made up fer 'em!! But in spite of
everythin' I did---he turned inta a cowardly little 'snot'
a'fore he was fifteen—a loud-mouth little braggart!
Getting' inta fights alla time then come a'whinin' t'me t'fix
it fer 'em! If'n thet principal hadn't been favorable t'me---
Mac'd still be in high school! Later on gettin' into a fight
with one of our own men---half killin' him with a knife!
Never drempt when I sent his ass t'Georgia, he'd marry up
with a mealy-mouthed, sirup-drippin' woman frum th'
foothills! Allus thought twas an agreement he'd marry up
with Tom's little Leah Ann---but oh no! Mac didn't
'agree'---an' Mac allus did things his own way---no matter
th' outcome of his choices---he expect'd me t'be there---a
cleanin' up after 'em! He knew long as I was 'Grand
Dragon', I'd do what I hadta---fer appearances sake,
assurin' m'position! So—here he is, now---up t'his pea-
brain in big trouble! So whut do we do? Has th' time
unfortunately a'rived f'some untimely accident on his way
back t'pick up them 'pieces'---an' send somebody else on
t'pick up th' stuff? Er do we let 'em alone an' see if he can
do ONE thang right in his life?!"

He took the last coveted puff off his cigar, looked
regretfully at the small stub then tossed it onto the bed of
coals in his fireplace. "No man wants t'do away with his

own blood. But I recused m'self---not castin' a vote. Th' decision's now in th' hands of our local brotherhood. When Mac drives away frum here early Monday mornin'---it might well be th' last time I ever see 'em alive. Or he may have thet one chance. The elder McDougal rose from his chair, covered the few live coals with ashes and left the room. Above him, Mac lay awake consoling himself with fantasies of his father's death---and the various clever ways it could be brought about.

Chapter Forty-Five

Early Friday morning, a sleeping Joseph was unceremoniously awakened as both Rammah and Jerri bounded into the living room, turned on the television then pounced upon their uncle, rooting-in beside him, seeking the warmth they knew waited beneath those covers! The sofa-bed frame creaked ominously. "Uncle Hawk!! Look, it's a 'Tom and Jerry' cartoon! That's ME!! JERRI! SEE?!"---her little girl voice pierced Hawk's ear---he felt as tho someone had sounded 'reveille' three feet from his head! "SHUT UP, JERRI! Can't you SEE Uncle Hawk's still asleep??! You DUMMY!"---Rammah's head quickly bent down beside Joseph's face to check him out---two bright eyes stared into his uncle's squint as the boy reiterated---"You ARE asleep--aren't you? Huh?!" For several moments the two little people wriggled about under his covers, accosting not only Joseph's eyes and ears, but his body as well! They jerked the covers about, tugging and twisting them first this way then that! All the while their elbows and knees pummeled him but it was their chilly noses, fingers and feet that shocked his senses totally awake!

Joseph took in a deep breath then let loose with a full-volume war-cry while grabbing the kids, one in each arm! Pulling them to him in bear hug, he yelled---"OF COURSE I'M ASLEEP!!! SEE? I'M HAVING A FEROCIOUS NIGHTMARE! ALL ABOUT TWO CHILDREN WHO WOKE ME UP!" He pretended to bite at each of them, while growling in a loud, scary fashion! Beneath the three wrestling, struggling bodies and with such unusual activities thrust upon it---the old sofa strained past it's limitation! In the midst of the hullabaloo, Hawk heard a terrific loud twanging noise—quickly followed by some ear-splitting 'POPS'! Several springs had broken!! Slowly but steadily, the 'mattress' descended downward while all three bodies sank---half-sitting, half laying---all cupped together into one huge sofa-bed 'sinkhole'!!

"OH! MY LORD!"---Dottie was first to reach the living room where, by that time, Hawk and Rammah were hysterical with loud hoots and roars of laughter! And there, sitting half on and half off Hawk's shoulder, was poor Jerri---a terrified expression frozen on her face! When their mother saw what had happened, she began to giggle then joined the unrestrained merriment! Mary, Salle and Bill arrived at the door and stood staring at the demented group---then joined the laughter!

Accessing the 'damage', Hawk remarked to the rest who were standing about, staring helplessly at the now 'deceased' and oddly shaped sofa bed---"Guess that's one way to start the day with a 'bang'...,"---he began to laugh again---"...OR was it more of a 'twang'!" Suddenly he found himself snorting, then laughing so hard he could barely talk anymore---and collapsed onto a chair! When he could somewhat control himself, he put his arm around Mary and remarked---"Mama? Bet you can't guess what your EARLY Christmas present is gonna be for this year!"

279

Once they 'caught on'---everyone nodded, murmuring their
approval. "Been a long time in comin', I must say."---Salle
remarked dryly. "At least no one was hurt!"---added the
always cautious Bill. "Poor Jerri,"---Hawk picked her up,
holding her to him---then he began to laugh. After
'snorting' again---he managed to say--- "Every time I think
of the expression on this poor baby's face---I break up!"
Then he whooped---"I can't STAND it!" He laughed
longer, louder than he had----in years! And like the old
sofa, years of military discipline had collapsed----'levity'
finally came to Joseph Winterhawk!

After breakfast, Salle pulled Hawk aside and whispered---
"Look, I'm gettin' together with Dottie---you, too, if you
like---the three of us can 'fix up' the whole livin' room ---
our Christmas gift to Mama! One day this week, when
she's at the church---we'll go to town and pick out the right
sofa! How about it?" Hawk nodded—"Long as you 'make
it soon'---where am I gonna sleep!? This wornout sofa is
wrecked!" Then he began to laugh again as Salle
commented---"We'll rent you a roll-away bed—you can
sleep on it out here in the living room." Joseph sighed,
looking at her, he whispered---"I just GOT OFF a roll-away
bed over at Doc's!" "Well?"---she hissed—"You crabbin'
that it don't rest good or somethin'??" "No. I'm not
'crabbin'---I'm just saying---aww, nothing, Sis. Just forget
it---it's a joke anyway." Salle rolled her eyes at her
brother--"Okay, so it's all set then---a new sofa and other
pretties for Mama's livin' room as her gift?" He nodded---
"Sure, she deserves at least that."

Suddenly Salle saw her brother wince slightly---looking
quickly toward the kitchen where Mary sang as she put
away the dishes—she put a hand on his arm---"You okay?
You didn't hurt your fool self with th' kids earlier, did you?

I'd almost forgot about your 'problem'---you looked so
good when you 'came home' yesterday! After all this
time—you BETTER NOT have done damage to your
innards!" "It's all right, Sis---it's just been awhile since I
tussled---OR laughed." Salle fretted---"You looked at the
wound? There may be some blood! C'mon, nutcase, I'll
check it for you!"

He followed Salle toward her bedroom. Closing the door,
she watched him remove the faded long-sleeve flannel shirt
he'd slept in. "Well?"---he asked---"Any fresh blood for
the vampire!?" Pulling the dressing somewhat away from
his body, she peered carefully around the exit wound area
just above the elastic pajama bottoms, she finally answered-
--"Guess it's like it's supposed to be---there's no blood
but..." She paused then went on---"Fact is, when Doc had
me put that towel around you to stop the bleedin'—after
you were shot, I noticed your back looks---looks like you've
had a bullet more than once! This why you never talked
'bout your job in the army?!" "M'gosh, Salle."—he
responded---"All soldiers get hurt one way or another---it's
just a fact of military life---not to worry. Just so THIS
wound heals---real SOON. Today is Friday---and I got
things to do the first of next week."

Salle's face took on a pinched expression---"Exactly
WHAT things?! You can't mean what I think you do!
Joseph, you CAN'T get back on any pow-wow highway out
to that ranch---not until old 'white-eyes' is caught!"
Meeting her stare, her brother stated---"And they haven't
caught him yet! Somebody has to find him---before things
'begin to slide' down at the sheriff's office. Anything over
48 hours leaves less chance the perpetrator will be found,
Salle. And honey---this miserable, racist scum is NOT
going to be forgotten---at least not by me! Take it any way
you want, but he's NOT getting the opportunity to do more

harm---not while I'm living and breathing! In order to find him---I've got to stay involved! And this time I won't make the mistake of 'going by the book'! Sis, you KNOW as well as I that you can't compromise with evil! You put your foot on it's neck...," ---Hawk looked away as he finished softly---"...then you destroy it."

Joseph's words missed their mark as Salle argued---"But what if he's hidin' at the ranch---he could be any place --- the barns, the house---even our apartment! Bill got all our stuff moved out the afternoon we left---man, like he couldn't WAIT to get away! I'm afraid for you to go back."---she looked pleadingly at her brother---"Promise me you won't! For Mama's sake---if not for mine! Even for Lizbeth's sake!" Hawk picked up his shirt---"It's for her that I'm going---'wherever' I have to, Salle." "Joseph, it's plain you two are absolutely 'head-over-heels'...any dumb jack-ass would know that!"---she paused to reason ---"But what'll she have if you get yourself killed? It'd break her heart to lose you---why, that woman would just up and die! Don't you REALIZE that? And not one of us could help her---without you, she'd simply 'will herself' to die. I think she has that kind of power---reckon you could say she has some of our blood---in some odd, unexplainable way."

Joseph looked at Salle's troubled eyes and commented gently---"Well, silly me. I wasn't aware that mine and Lizbeth's feelings were so 'clear' to everyone! Does Mama also possess this wonderful knowledge?" "I don't think so."---Salle responded, then added—"But there were times yesterday---when---well, I thought she might've felt the 'static-electricity' in the air---and actually approved! I couldn't say for sure but Mama's no 'dumb-bunny'—she's Indian, too, y'know!"

Sighing, he gave Salle's face a pat---"I'm glad you know---
about Lizbeth and me, I mean. But don't discuss it with
Mama, let her have her own thoughts then express them if
she wishes. Hopefully she'll never have to know I've loved
'a married woman' since laying eyes on her. Maybe I can
manage to have her think it all began yesterday---when I
came back and Lizbeth was still here. But to the business at
hand, I have to go after 'white-eyes'---if I don't 'take care'
of him---he'll be back and 'take care' of her---then I'd be
the one who'd dry up, willing myself to die. And you're
right---no one could keep me alive either---not if he
managed to kill her." Salle took his hand and held it
between hers and exhaled---"All right, Joseph. And if I can
help---just tell me what to do. I'm on your side, so's Bill.
And Doc---he's ALWAYS on your side."

"Salle, take this..,"---he handed her a piece of paper---
"...it's a short melody I wrote late last night. Get Mama to
play it for you on the flute until you can hum it---then I
want you to go see Lizbeth and Ida. Get Ida out of the room
on some pretext then hum the melody to Lizbeth until she
learns to play it on that wreck of a piano! Tell her when the
time is exactly right---she'll hear someone playing the song.
And for her to remember that only I can play it---because no
one else will know the music. Explain I've written it for her
alone and when she hears it being played, she'll know it's
me---and it'll mean the time will have come for us to be
together." Salle looked down at the piece of paper with her
brother's hand-written notes---tears blurred her vision.
"How very 'Indian' of you, brother-san. No matter what's
happened in your soldierin' during the past 20 years, you're
still nothin' but a 'romantic'---and you got the heart of a
good husband-to-be. I'll make certain Lizbeth learns your
song---and it's 'Indian-meanin' as well."

He nodded and gave her a grateful smile---"Check and see who's in the bathroom---if it's vacant, I'll take a shower. I might need your assistance with a new bandage, okay?" Salle found the bathroom door open---"Come on, have your shower, just call me when you're finished. Mama's already left for church."

Chapter Forty-Six

Just around noon, the day following Thanksgiving---Sheriff Logan, Doc and Lizbeth rode out to the ranch in Logan's 'official' car. Behind the grill, Lizbeth sat looking out---her face blank---her eyes not really seeing the countryside fly past the side window. Joseph. He was never far from her ---it was as though he lived inside her, knew her thoughts, felt her heart beat and moved when she moved. Glancing quickly toward the back of Logan's head, she flushed, scolding herself---"Thank God no one can read yoah mind, girl! 'Specially th' sheriff! This whole thing would shock th' poah man t'death---especially th' part about Joseph! He'd probably believe Ah tried t'kill Mac just t'get rid of him---n'stead of th' othah way 'round!"

The sheriff had picked up her 'glance' and responded--- "Mrs. McDougal?"---his head tilted slightly back toward her without taking his eyes from the road---"I wanted to ask if you might've remembered anything else either about that night---or previous to that night---some small thing you'd forgotten then maybe remembered while you were away these past two weeks. Even after we'd talked on th' phone---something could've come to mind."

Her eyes moved to the rearview mirror between him and Doc---Logan was looking at her. Pretending to 'think'--- Lizbeth quietly 'meditated', pressing her lips together---

slightly frowning---she then shook her head slowly and finally replied in her best 'soft, helpless southern-belle' voice---"Ah don't believe so, Sheriff. T'tell th'truth, Ah tried NOT t'think much---until Ah came back an' find m'self once again faced with it! But..,"---she looked sincere---"..if Ah DO remembah anythin'---Ah'll call you right away---or have Dr. O'Bahhr call you---an' we can discuss it." Logan nodded, seemingly satisfied.

They turned off the highway and started up the driveway when Logan suddenly slowed down and pointed off to the left, announcing---"Over there, you two! See that small yellow flag down next to th' road? That's where Bill found Mac's gun!" Feigning interest, Lizbeth peered in the direction he pointed. Then she leaned forward, put both hands on the wire separating her from the two men and pleaded---"Sheriff? Now, you watch when you step out of this cahr! It's possible Mac could be heah---if Ah were you, Ah'd make certain that gun stays right handy! Mind now--- an' be careful!" Flattered by her obvious concern for his safety, Logan nodded, replying—"We've kept a good eye on th' place, Ma'am. Don't think he's about---but if he is and wants some action? Well, I'm th' man that can give it to him!"

Switching off the big 455 horse engine, Logan turned toward Doc and Lizbeth---"You two stay put a minute and let me at least walk around th' house---just check all th' doors and windows---makin' sure nobody's made a forced entry. Sit tight but if you hear any shots---Doc, you crank this thing up, back out toward th' highway an' call in. You know th' call letters---get some help if it comes t'that." "Sure thing---you certain I can't go along with you right now?"---Doc inquired. "Naaah, this is law-enforcement work---not civilian responsibility."---Logan opened the door, stood and reached inside for his scatter-gun.

Readjusting the weight and balance of his gunbelt, he
unsnapped the leather strap holding his pistol in place then
finally shifting the .357 to an easy 'grab' position---he
closed the door and strolled away.

Lizbeth whispered---"Doc? You think Mac's returned?"
"T'be honest, I don't believe so."---he replied. "It's my
thinkin' he's off with some KKK people---but our mutual
'friend' is sure he'll be back---when he thinks th' coast is
clear an' some of th' heat is off. But th' heat's gonna last
for awhile now that his gun's been found an' matches th'
bullet." Lizbeth leaned closer to the wire---"Doc? You tell
me th' truth now---you think, uh, anyone will evah find out
th' story behind that bullet? If they catch Mac, you KNOW
he'll tell a whole different story than m'self---about an
'intruder' in th' room! Won't they all come swarmin' back
out heah an' begin scrutinizin' anew---lookin' foah
'something' amiss in that room? Th' thought SCARES me,
Doc!" He sighed quietly, confessing---"I've thought about
that myself, Lizbeth. But---for right now, let's just think
positive---and cross that bridge 'if' and 'when' we come to
it! Okay?" Unconvinced, she nodded just as Logan
rounded the house, waving them out of the car.

Doc and Logan searched the entire house from attic to the
small 'root' cellar before allowing her to begin gathering
her things. There were no signs anyone had been around or
in the house, it was just as they'd left it.

As she began packing items she thought necessary during
the coming weeks---Doc took Logan off to her living room
to show him the grandfather clock and his own favorite---
the grand piano. But once Logan's eyes fell on the open
door to Mac's bedroom---which had been left as it was
when Mac crawled out his window---the sheriff lost interest
in the living room contents. His department had 'gone

over' Mac's room and made casts of his footprints beneath the window which led to Lizbeth's window then out again, they'd taken photos and fingerprinted both rooms---but Logan's slightly unabated curiosity still lingered. Now was a great time to perhaps sniff out something that heretofore had eluded him!

"Doc,"---he nodded toward Mac's room---"...let's go in there a minute. Since she's still busy in yonder, I want another look around while I'm here." "What you lookin' for?"---Doc followed the sheriff into Mac's room. Logan grunted, shook his head but didn't answer as he silently began poking about. His boot-toe lifted the chair-ruffle then suddenly, he removed his gun, lay it on the dresser then tossing his hat onto the chair, he lay down on the carpet and began running his hand beneath the chair. He proceeded doing the same to the bottom of each piece of furniture not setting flush on the floor---lastly he pulled forward each piece of furniture, scanning the backs. Taking out all drawers from the dresser and chests, he felt the bottom and back of each drawer---but finding nothing, he replaced them. A mask of concentration covered his face as he approached the bed then lying back down on the floor, he played the beam of his flashlight about beneath the bed frame.

"C'mere, Doc!"---his muffled voice called out---"Take holda this stuff I'm handin' up---an' throw it on th' bed!" Before 'the stuff' was in his hand, Doc had the distinct impression Logan had discovered Mac's store of KKK literature---and hopefully notebooks or something in writing---anything! The fact was, all along he'd thought Logan's men had found the KKK material that day they'd gathered 'evidence'---he figured it was all downtown tucked away with everything else removed from the house!

287

But obviously, he'd been mistaken---thank God Logan got 'nosey' today!

After thoroughly cleaning out a hidden wire-rack fastened to the slats beneath the mattress, Logan stood---brushed at his uniform and carped---"Can you believe?? My men missed all this---goes t'show, you want something done right---do it yourself! Would you LOOK at that?! This stuff DOES belong to him---don't it? I mean, why would it be hidden beneath his bed if it didn't!" "Hmmm."---Doc picked two books, slowly perusing them as well as the others lying on the disheveled bed---"Y' know, Logan, I used t'see him reading these very books---who could forget th' covers?! I'd come t'check on his condition---an' he'd either be watchin' television or readin' these big books--- an' some smaller ones as well. Never thought much about 'what' was inside the covers---figured if his readin' habits were anything like his mind, it wasn't anything I wanted t'see. But I DO remember eyeballin' just before he'd either push them beneath th' sheet or his pillows."

"Here," Logan instructed, "let's get this stuff in some grocery bags or something and out t' my car! We'll stow it in th' trunk and when I get back t'my office, I'll put it with th' rest of our 'evidence' and start working on it right away! Now, by gum-shoe, maybe I got one of th' leads I been needing ever since this thing happened! Reckon why SHE never told me about this? Surely, she knew!" Doc looked at him and replied quietly---"I can tell you 'why'---she was and still is afraid of him, not only for herself---but in th' past, he'd used his KKK connections t' threaten her family-- -IF she left him and went home! She might know a little bit, Logan—but not much, I'd venture. Bein' attacked the way she was, this stuff might've temporarily slipped her mind and she simply forgot t'tell you---never connectin' his readin' material t'his attack on her. But it's true, you do

need t'talk with her about his association with th' Klan---
she may know something important and not realize it.
Y'think you could wait until maybe tomorrow---an' give
her a chance t'get over being out here for th' first time?"

Logan shifted his weight from one foot to the other and
replied---"Well, I'd sure like to do it today!" "Another
day'll do fine---b'sides,"---Doc shrugged---"...what on
earth could change before tomorrow? You got your
'evidence' here in your hand---talkin' can be done
anytime!" Suddenly, Doc had a lightening strike of an idea
and laid it on Logan before the moment passed! "You don't
suppose---nawww---surely not."---he thought 'aloud' then
deliberately 'clammed up'! Logan took the bait---"Don't I
'suppose' what?! O'Barr! You know something else?!
Whadda I have t'do---solve th' case all by my lonesome?"

"Now, Logan."---Doc soothed---"You know I don't have
any experience in these matters! But YOU, now, bein' th'
experienced lawman---I was only about t'ask if----well, if
there were---or might be---say some 'other things' hid out
here on th' place!" "What kinda 'things'?!"---the sheriff
snapped! "Heck, I dunno."---Doc shrugged as he
continued to 'think' out loud---"Just seems t'me that IF he's
'one' of them---I'd be askin' myself this question---'is it a
lone-wolf thing' or a lifestyle he 'inherited'? By that I'm
wonderin' did he come from a Klan family---I'm talkin'
blood-relatives. IF so, some detective work 'bout past
activities---unsolved crimes an' such---and by jove---even a
premise search might not be such a bad idea!!" "Well, I'll
be cat-haired!"---Logan slapped his empty gunholster---
"Damned if you don't sound like a regular plainclothes
detective! You're absolutely right! Man, this could be th'
lead that'll take us as far as we need t'go to have McDougal
locked-up for good---get him outta this woman's life, give
her some peace!" Grinning to himself, the sheriff sent Doc

for the paper grocery bags as he slid the gun back into its holster and picked up his hat.

***

Still in her bedroom and making the most of the opportunity of being alone, Lizbeth pulled the chest away from the wall---she stared at the wall and with a harsh intake of breath, almost immediately picked out the bullet hole! "Maybe it's b'cause Ah know what I'm lookin' foah an' wheah---but we must do somethin' about this! Th' first possible minute---Ah'll get Doc, Salle an' Bill---we'll remove this board from behind th' chest an' put it behind mah bed---then use one of those boards left-ovah from remodelin' t'fill in b'hind th' chest!! Ah can't let them find out Hawk was in this room---Ah'll protect him even if Ah have t'tampah with evidence an' perjure mahself t'boot!" Placing the framed print back in place, Lizbeth began to drag her luggage toward the kitchen---the men heard her and immediately hurried to assist.

Soon everything was in the Sheriff's car---all except the scatter-gun and two small boxes on the kitchen table. Doc smiled at her and made a request---"Before we leave, Mrs. McDougal---I was wonderin' if you'd favor us by playin' a song or two on your grand piano? For old times' sake? Logan says he's never heard anybody play a 'grand' before and I told him you placed beautifully." "Oh, Dr. O'Bahhr, yoah just prejudiced!"---then remembering the boards in her bedroom, she batted her eyelashes slightly at the sheriff and said demurely---"Dr. O'Bahhr's trouble is, when he'd visit Mac? Ah'd always play these lil ol' ditties foah him---usin' mah own 'by-eah' method."

Doc looked at Logan---"She's played many a time for Ida an' me! Now, you sit right down here---and play my

special song---'The Waltz You Saved For Me'! Maybe
even a little 'Beautiful Dreamer'---'San Antonio Rose'---
'Danny Boy'---'When Irish Eyes Are Smilin'---a bit of
'Beer Barrel Polka'!" "DOCTAH!"---Lizbeth pretended to
'scold' him---"That'll take an hour! Ah'm certain Sheriff
Logan is much too busy foah some silly amateur piano
concert."

Feeling elated over his 'find' in Mac's room, Logan
immediately announced he was 'free'---for a while longer---
'at least long enough to hear' the requests! "Please do play
for us, Ma'am! Y'know, I haven't heard those songs in
years! Nobody plays 'em anymore---now-a-day, we just
hear a little 'country' or that fool 'acid rock' and 'protest'
folk musicians!" She sighed, looking from one man to the
other---"Well. Don't see how Ah can say 'no'---you both
such fine gentlemen---an' been s'nice helpin' me out!" She
went to the piano bench, sat down and played a medley of
Doc's requests.

On the way back to town, Logan found himself humming
some of the songs she'd played---Doc soon joined in---
before long they were happily harmonizing---off-key!
Putting fingers over her lips to keep from smiling, Lizbeth
looked out the window as the countryside once again flew
past. She felt better---maybe on the way out, it'd been
'nerves', the thought of going back 'home' for the first
time---AFTER that awful night! In the front seat, the older
men made her feel safe, as safe as possible without Joseph!
Then with Hawk back in mind, she determined—"Those
boards must be swapped-out---and soon! Logan knows that
Mac and I were struggling when the gun went off---so
that'll explain any odd-angle of bullet entry."

Chapter Forty-Seven

After his shower, Salle put a fresh bandage on Hawk.
"Thanks, Sis." ---he murmured, fingering the wide tight
band, then pulling on a thick flannel shirt he announced---
"You were right---I'm relieved our fun didn't do me
damage this morning. That lousy McDougal almost put me
through the 'vanishing point' with one lucky 'blind shot'!
But---better me than Lizbeth!" Looking back at his sister,
he shook his head---"And to think, all of it crumbled
because of one creaking board! Now I gotta start over
again---new plan, new maneuvers, new weapons---but the
same enemy!" Suddenly he was remembering days when
he hid his dog-tags between his boot-tongue and laces---and
how a rightly-filed hollow-point bullet from a sniper's gun
can take off your head at 900 yards. For some odd reason,
'lady luck' and chance had been with Mac that night---
while he, with all his training, almost became a victim! Not
to mention Lizbeth as well!

Noting his short sentences and complaints, Salle figured he
was almost well and straining at the traces to 'get going'!
Her instinct was that he wouldn't be sitting around the
house for long and was, in fact, ready to walk out soon as
his boots were on---she just didn't know WHERE he was
headed! And Salle being Salle---she wanted to know!!
"After all,"—she thought---"Bill and I have t'protect him
for Lizbeth---as well as FROM himself! Stubborn man!
Got a permanent case of 'tunnel vision' on his target---
hangin' on like a 'jack-bull' once he gets his teeth into
something!"

"I'm getting a few of the trackers together---," he began but
she broke into his sentence with—"But his trail's cold,
Hawk! What in th' world can you 'track' by this time?"
Her brother frowned at her---"Girl, if you'd just let me

finish my thought here?" "Oh. Yeah. Sorry, Hawk."---she sighed---"Go on about 'the trackers'." "As I was GOING to say---my war party won't be 'tracking', they'll be in the woods surrounding the house and out-buildings. They'll have radio contact with Bill---I want to know the minute they see ANY person---ANY vehicle---even a horse out there." Hawk sat on the bed and handed her his boots. "And you?"—she finally blurted out as she pushed while he pulled the boots on his feet---"Where you gonna be all this time? I'm warnin' you one last time----you better BE careful, Joseph! Since Bill found th' gun, th' high-sheriff and his men drive past there more often than they did before! They even go up to the house, checkin' to see if anybody's been around---lookin' for tracks, broken windows, locks or any signs of 'life' at th' place! What if one of them SAW you pokin' about?!" Joseph nodded his 'thanks' for helping with the boots---and for the concern--- then left the room.

Salle hurried after him---"Joseph! I am tellin' you NOT t'go out there!" "I'm not going 'out there', Sis. Not unless 'white-eyes' shows up!"---he shrugged into his coat then with one hand on the front door knob, he set his western felt-hat on at an angle. "But,"---she persisted---"...what'll you do if he DOES show up? You need help with your own boots yet! You keep sayin' he'll show up---and when that time gets here—WHAT are you plannin'?! You're not able to fight him---not right now! But I know you got somethin' up your sleeve---so what IS it!?"

Hawk opened the front door---"Salle, honey, if I could tell you—I would. Just trust me on it---and..."---he gave her a stern look—"...don't say a WORD to Mama. If she wants to know where I am---just tell her I'm 'out'!" Salle gave him an exasperated look, so he gestured with one hand--- "Tell her I'm meeting an old army buddy and may be gone tonight and tomorrow! Which is real close to the truth! Okay?" "OKAY."---she snapped---"Go on and gaze at the winter moon tonight! It's gonna be YOUR funeral---not mine." Hawk looked at her, shaking his head---"Tsk-tsk-tsk---when you gonna learn to trust me, Salle." "I did,"--- now her voice was rising---"..and you almost got your fool self KILLED! But for God, that 'white-devil' would've killed you dead!! And it bein' right there in his wife's bedroom! NOT to mention that illegal radio equipment in OUR bedroom closet!!" With Mary now away from the house—Salle let go her frustrations, her voice rising to full cry as she stamped one foot, her arms flailed about the air--- she wailed at him---"OH MY GOD, JOSEPH!"

He figured not only was his sister somewhat 'steamed'---at this point, she was REALLY cranked up, so he politely waited until she finished! "---and IN HER bedroom!!! What a riot THAT would've caused!"---she raged—"Poor Mama---poor ALL of us---Bill and me in jail---with you all laid out, military funeral and all---your spirit off huntin' th' stargate t'heaven! Don't do it, Joseph, don't do this to th' rest of us!" Noting her ravings meant little to her brother and that he was already several steps away, Salle again stamped her foot in frustration then sent one final blast toward his now wilted ears--"Try to remember you're not 'Geronimo'---no legend---NOT QUITE YET!" Successfully, Joseph retreated but called back to her---"And you're not infinite, nor a fortune-teller, 'Pocahontas'---so don't be burying me before I'm dead!"

Chapter Forty-Eight

As soon as Sheriff Logan dropped off Dr. O'Barr, Lizbeth and her luggage, he drove away leaving them in the carport.

Ida's car wasn't home so Lizbeth immediately voiced her
concern about the boards---then insisted they call Salle,
telling her what had to be done! Later this afternoon, they'd
all go to the ranch---at a time when Doc, who was familiar
with the sheriff's routine, thought Logan's weekend crew
would be patrolling another area! "It won't take long, Doc!
All we need is a saw, a crowbahr, some old second-hand
nails, a hammah---and a piece of good luck! Plus a broom
an' dustpan!"

"Lizbeth, honey!"---he looked closely at her---"You not set
on doin' this t'day, are you?" Swallowing quickly, she
nodded---"Soonah the bettah, Doc! Monday begins a new
week an' only God knows what a difference it might make
if we just go ahead an' do this today! Y'know, while folks
are still thinkin' Thanksgivin' weekend---with ballgames,
etc.---then travelin' home Sunday aftah lunch!! If we wait--
-let's just say Mac decides Monday would be a good day
t'return! Accordin' t'wheah he is, in an hour or two, he
could show up an' hide secretly in th' attic---or anyplace
close by---then he'd SEE us when we came! If an' when
they catch him---he'd TELL them he saw us---AND what
we were doin'! THEN he'd give his 'version' of th'
shootin'---don't you think Logan---or somebody---would
'smell a rat', go back t'the ranch an' take mah bedroom
apart??! Waitin' is too risky, Doc! T'day---we must do it!
We can't wait!!"

"And,"---she set her jaw, tilted her head and went on---
"...should one of Logan's men happen by an' see us, we
can always say we went along with Bill an' Salle, t'help Bill
put out extra feed since rain is on th' way with cold air
behind it! Tell them Ah insisted on comin' along t'make
certain 'Maggie' would be protected in th' barn--- that none
of you could dissuade me, that's when YOU decided t'come
along as well! Safety in numbahs, y'know!" Lizbeth raised

her eyes at him---"An' of course, bein' Logan's buddy, all
of us KNOW that latah on, aftah th' fact, you were plannin'
t'mention that we went back! Please, Doc!" Before she
was finished, he knew he couldn't say 'no' to something
that might save not only Joseph, but their story as well---so
he gave in.

***

Later that afternoon, dark gray tinted clouds began rolling
in across the mountains---heavy rain was forecast by
nightfall followed by a cold front clearing the whole state
by next morning. It would herald the end of autumn and the
beginning of winter.

Appointed as 'look-out' while the 'work' went on---Salle
kept shifting her vision from watching for patrol cars back
to the darkening cloud cover. All the while she wondered
where her 'fool brother had gotten himself off to'! True to
his word, he'd probably be gone all night and tomorrow!
"Now,"—she fumed—"Mama'll be worried t'death when
he doesn't drag his butt home---especially with this rain an'
cold comin'! Stubborn! All his life, he's followed where
the eagle cries---one day those 20 years of military war-
mongerin' will catch up with him! Then God knows what'll
happen!" Heaving a sigh, Salle stared at the highway and
waited.

Once the boards had been exchanged, the molding back in
place---everything matched so well that not one of them
could tell anything had been done to either wall!
Meticulously, Lizbeth began cleaning up any microscopic
signs of 'disturbance,' putting everything into a paper bag---
she then ran her vacuum over the whole room, hall and
kitchen. After sending Doc and Bill to the back porch to
'flap-off' the bed sheets, the covers, the pillowcases and

shams---she finally made her way back to the bedroom and brush-vacuumed all the furnishings, baseboards, window ledges, picture frames---anyplace that had a surface. When she was completely satisfied, she removed the vacuum bag and put it in with the other 'signs of disturbance', set in a new vacuum bag---then put the machine away.

"If anyone should evah inquiah---tell them except foah Mac's room, Salle and Ah kept th' whole house fairly clean foah fear of rats, roaches, etc. Aftah all, every piece of evidence was removed weeks ago---an' nobody told me I couldn't keep th' place clean!" She looked at Doc and Bill---and asked---"Right?" They nodded.

Thus early dark found their 'deed' successfully carried out and the almost silent foursome on their way back to town. By the time they were half way to Mary's house, a sullen cold drizzle had begun falling---the rain made a frying sound beneath the tires as Bill drove along. Suddenly Doc remembered he hadn't told Lizbeth about Logan's KKK 'find' earlier that morning! She'd knocked that bit of news plumb out of his mind when she insisted on coming straight back out here. Oh well, he'd fill her in later. Seemed to Doc, events of the past three days had been somewhat positive for 'good ole their side'---maybe, just maybe the scales of justice were beginning to tip in THEIR direction--- at long last! He felt it was high time---and somewhat 'over-due'!!

Along with rain, a fog also came rolling in. Bill's careful eyes were glued on the road and for a change even Salle seemed exceptionally quiet. Across from him, Lizbeth sat with her arms around her knees, pillowing her head against them as the 'trash-bag' rested safely between her feet. "You okay, Liz?"---Doc asked quietly. "Yeah."---she murmured---"Just kinda tired. Life's been heavy an' burdensome a little too long, Doc,---foah all of us." He nodded in agreement.

It was then that he realized this unusual 'quiet' might be the result of pure relief flooding thru all four of them! Now with the KKK into th' picture, a new investigation wouldn't be Logan---it'd be th' state men—or even th' FBI! Thank God, Lizbeth verbalized a very legitimate concern---then insisted on fixin' it---at once! She was right,"---he nodded to himself, looking straight ahead---"Now with any luck--- who knows---maybe this time next week---!" He'd voiced THAT before, but this time the thought had a real, honest ring of truth that he'd not felt when saying it earlier!

Chapter Forty-Nine

"So! This is the 'fabulous' Rita---at last!"---Hawk watched her coming out the back door then head toward a row of 'community' mail boxes fastened on a metal beam. Automatically, he wrote down the box number as she retrieved yesterday's Saturday mail and stood scrutinizing each piece. "Is she maybe expecting mail either for or from Mac?"---reaching for the binoculars, he zoomed in on her, memorizing her features. The brown 'frosted' hair was chin-length---fluffed, 'permed' and somewhat frizzed, her eyes looked an odd gold color or maybe it was just an optical illusion of reflected light. At around 5 ft. 8 in., Hawk estimated her weight close to 170 lbs. and said to himself---"One healthy looking gal---almost big as old Mac 'himself'!"

It was Sunday, Joseph considered a weekday. "Unless,"— he looked at his watch--- "…she attends church." Laying aside the binoculars he concluded---"And, if she does, she'll be leaving---almost any time, now." She'd disappeared back in the house as he continued his vigil.

While still recovering at Doc's, Hawk had made arrangements to borrow a 'specialized', completely over-hauled commercial-type van from 'an old military buddy' who lived almost a thousand miles away and who'd agreed to meet him at a half-way point where they'd exchange vehicles for awhile. After the exchange had taken place and the rain moved out, Hawk stopped at the first isolated, well-hidden area---slapped on a quick temporary blue and white 'wash' which left a dull matte-finish over the shiny cream colored van. After changing out the plates he proceeded to wipe clean a small peep-hole built into a floral decal painted on the van's exterior. Before driving on, he unlocked the glove compartment making certain that a proper ID was at hand---also the promised army issue 9.mm automatic along with a permit and box of ammo. Quickly he 'dropped' the clip, seeing it already full---he snapped it back, replaced the firearm and locked the compartment.

It was Sunday early when he arrived back at the town where Rita lived. Straight away, he searched out the street address supplied earlier by his best tracker---a man who had 'Indian' connections in Rita's area and who'd located her residence only a couple of days after the shooting. Across the street from her house, Hawk parked in a grocery store and billiard parking lot. After locking the van doors, he slid a false wall behind the driver's seat to one side, crawled back into the rear then set the 'wall' back in place. For the past 3 hours, he'd watched her house thru the small round one-way glass that looked part of the decal and which from the outside was practically invisible. Finally, Rita had appeared, walked to the mailbox then went back inside. Before long, he saw her exiting the house wearing a full length coat---she locked up the back door and headed for her car. Immediately, he opened the false 'wall'---slid into the driver's seat and prepared to follow her.

She didn't go to church but to the restaurant. "Why didn't I think of work---they told me she was a waitress!"---he scolded himself---"Everybody has to eat---even on Sundays!" Through the binoculars, he made certain she was inside wearing a uniform and taking orders at the tables. He waited 15 minutes then drove to an alley behind her house. Earlier, he'd driven through a few times, assuring himself that several business trucks, vans and assorted vehicles were parked there for the weekend. He backed into a park, locked up his van then set off for the back of her house. Wearing the brown parka left in the van for him, he pulled the fur-trimmed top over his head and tied the drawstring--- which hid his long hair. A pair of clear glasses and mustached beard changed his appearance a great deal---thin gloves covered the pads of his fingers. He took one last careful glance as he stood at her back door manipulating a master-key---then he was inside---silently closing the door behind him! Standing motionless for several moments, he accustomed himself to the sounds in what he hoped was an empty house!

The grumbling refrigerator had a rattle in it's hum, further past the kitchen, he could hear a clock ticking---also the echo of a drippy faucet. Easing toward the latter sounds, he discovered the house had only four rooms plus a small bath where the faucet was plopping water-drops straight down into the pipe. "Wonder how she sleeps with THAT going on!"—he thought. From her bedside table, a framed picture of McDougal glared at him but no one was home.

"The mail."---he said to himself after checking out the closets and finding nothing---"Where does she keep her mail?" Soon, he located two untidy piles---one on the living room coffee table, which he gathered in one hand and went toward the kitchen where on the end of her cluttered kitchen table, lay the rest. The envelopes and sales papers lay amongst her stash of restaurant condiments heaped next to a bottle of ketchup, a half-empty soda bottle, a jar of instant coffee and an empty napkin holder. He'd noted several dirty dishes and glasses on various flat surfaces through-out the house---now he saw others in the sink as well. Quickly, Hawk shuffled both piles of mail--- discovering two phone bills, he took them---one letter from Indiana that he figured might be from Mac, so he took time to read the signature. It was signed---'Love, you-know-who'---Joseph breathed---"Has to be him." Even though it had no return address, he tucked it inside his jacket along with the phone bills---he'd read all of it later. On the kitchen counter beside the wall phone, he saw her small red directory of personal phone numbers---he stuck that inside his coat as well.

Looking around in the kitchen one last time, he figured he had everything that could give him any pertinent information on Mac---seemed the viper was clever enough not to leave as much as a shirt or sock behind. Before going outside, Hawk stopped at the windows, scanned the area then let himself out, relocking the door. Not far away, children were playing---two dogs barked at each other---one adult kept shouting for 'RANDY!!' Cars rattled past on the front street as Hawk stepped quickly to the back alley and disappeared around the corner.

The letter proved basically useless---but the postmark was important. Now he knew where Mac had gone---unless he'd driven to another town to mail the letter. But upon opening the telephone bills, he hit closer to the jack-pot! The oldest billing showed several collect calls from Lizbeth's home phone to Rita's number---the latest billing showed calls made to her---but placed from the same town as the letter postmark! Hawk considered a call to the number and asking for Mac, maybe he could find out more---according to who answered! But it would be wise to place the call from a booth here in Rita's town---just in case McDougal found a way to trace it back. That way he'd be none the wiser---and probably confused. Hawk grinned to himself—the thought of any thing he could do to 'confuse' Mac, no matter how small, pleased him! He considered— "Is there any particular reason to wait and call tomorrow, Monday?" He had to choose! Today! Just as soon as he saw the next phone booth.

A few minutes later, Hawk stood feeding his coins into a pay phone. He listened as 'his party' rang several times---then a woman's voice answered---"Hello." She sounded grumpy! Doing his best to rid his own voice of any accent, he replied---"Hello, Mrs. McDougal?" "Yeah. Who's this?" "Well, Ma'am---I hope you remember me! Your husband, Mr. McDougal, introduced us once at a---you know, at a meeting? My name is Rollins---Sanford Rollins. I'm from Ohio." "Don't recall meetin' no Rollins---then agin, sometimes I fergit. Met too many strangers since I been with m'second husband---can't remember 'em all. Who you wanta talk to—m'husband?" "Actually, I needed to get a message to his son---Mac? We, uh, had the word, he was home---for a spell. Think I could speak to him?" A few moments of silence---Hawk held his breath---then she said, "Well. He's gettin' ready to---uh, go on a little trip. He had some last minute visitin' to git in---so he ain't chere." "When's he leaving, Ma'am? It's vitally important to us that I speak to him----you know, before he gets on the road!" "Well, he's leavin' in th' morning---real early. Take all day to git back there. Gimme a number---I'll see he gits th' message." The operator broke in---"Your time is up, Sir. Deposit $3.25 please." Hawk took advantage of the moment to ring-off---he shouted---"I'll call back later!"--then hung up the phone.

"So, he's coming 'back'---probably to Rita's, and so SOON! Something must've 'gone down' with the Klan---wonder what it was? I gotta get back and quiz Doc!" Hawk cranked the van and headed toward the highway that would lead him right past Lizbeth's ranch---then on to town. While he was away to pick up the van, he'd been out of radio-range but the trackers had radioed Bill yesterday morning, informing him that Logan, Doc and Lizbeth had gone out to the ranch house. When they left, they took some luggage and some grocery bags which Logan stashed in his car trunk. Before hanging up the phone, Bill had then informed him, in code, that mid-afternoon the 'four of them' had gone back out to the ranch house to take care of a 'possible problem'. Hawk needed to know about the 'possible problem'---so once he drove into 'local phone territory', he planned to stop and call Doc. They could meet at his office to share any latest information on the case---especially from Logan's point of view---as well as the 'possible problem'!

Chapter Fifty

Once back in town and still 'incognito', Hawk parked among a couple of dozen other vehicles whose owners were attending the local movie house. Exiting the van, he gazed across the street at the flashing marquee which proudly announced still another run of 'The Blue Max'. Hawk recalled he'd enjoyed the film himself---especially the aerial 'dog-fights'! Then he turned away and hurried toward Doc's office for their meeting.

303

After the two discussed Hawk's mustache and beard in uncomplimentary terms, O'Barr filled him in on the ranch happenings when Logan drove them out for Lizbeth's things. Especially how Lizbeth, after taking time to examine the bullet hole, fairly had a fit until 'the four' went back and took care of the 'possible' future problem. Doc then reported Logan's unexpected discovery of Mac's literature---which he confessed thinking was already in the evidence bucket! Coupled with Hawk's phone call to the McDougals, they felt they'd hit a fairly rich mother-lode of info---especially after their long 'dry spell', so they took a moment to revel in delayed successes. Joseph gave Doc a superior grin---"Lizbeth's pretty sharp, being so meticulous about details! Not to mention her beauty and charm---she's not only a 'woman after my own heart'---she already owns it!" Taking in Joseph's slightly tilted shiny black eyes above those carved cheekbones and the silly grin on his generous mouth, Doc retorted---"There IS more news---that is IF you can get your mind back on business again!"

Hawk cleared his throat---"Yessir! Kemosobe, SIR!" Leaning forward, gently tapping his forehead, Hawk whispered---"This 'mind' is a steel-trap and it's right here with you! So, keep on truckin'!" Doc gave an exasperated snort but continued---"While you've been doin' your 'thing'---this morning, I decided t'ease around an' see if I could catch Logan at th' restaurant---I did an' we had coffee t'gether. Now, get this---first thing he said t'me was 'O'Barr! I been hopin' I'd see your lazy self around today! I got some news for you---and most of it came outta that little drive yesterday!" Doc let out a deep breath, put a hand on his chest---"For one awful moment, Joseph, I thought he was talking about 'LATE' yesterday when th' four of us went out an' changed those boards! M'heart 'bout jumped outta my chest, I don't mind tellin' you! But it seems after Logan saw that KKK literature, he got real busy an' called

up th' BIG BOYS!" O'Barr's eyes were blazing with
excitement---"An' they've worked nonstop since yesterday,
pullin' out all stops t'connect not only Mac to those
unsolved crimes but his father as well---along with some
other Klansmen! After Logan found Mac's literary crap, I
sorta 'prompted' him with the idea that IF Mac was KKK---
it was possible 'other things' may be hidden at th' ranch!"
Exhaling, Doc gave his finishing touch---"They'll find those
guns at th' barn!"---he stuck up a finger---"And in the event
THEY fail t'search th' barn, one of us can make an
anonymous call! Hawk, I can see th' end of this ugly
thing!"

Amazingly, Doc didn't get his anticipated result from the
man sitting across from him. There was no excited war-
whoop nor exclamation, ---no verbal exchange---only a look
that could be described as something between a stare and a
glare. Doc regarded the strong handsome Indian---"Good
Lord, Hawk! Thought you'd be ecstatic over this turn of
events---a lot's happened since I last saw you on
Thanksgivin'!" Hawk gave a half-nod, raised his eyebrows
in a sort of resigned expression then replied softly---"Looks
like!" Standing, he began to pace about.

"So what the hell IS it?!"---Doc demanded! Joseph rubbed
the back of his neck with one hand---"Don't misunderstand,
Doc. Absolutely, I do want that whole nest of snakes
caught---for the sake of the victims, their families and for
the sake of justice! Not to mention for Lizbeth's sake---and
everything McDougal did to her for ten years! And yes, I
DO want these criminals to have their day in court---then
get sealed away for life---or 'fried'! Hopefully the latter!"
"Then..,"---Doc pleaded---"...what's wrong with you?
Why don't I believe much of th' stuff you just said about
everybody's 'sake'?" The older man squinted at Joseph's
face, observing the black, angry eyes. "I have to get my

305

hands on 'our' McDougal,"---came the quiet, omonious answer--"…before they do."

"I don't believe m'ears!"---Doc slapped his hand on his desk and swore---"Here you almost got yourself killed tryin' t'get 'court-evidence' as you called it---remember?! An' now, th' law has almost everything they need t'pull in a net---arrests within 24 to 36 hours---an' you act like Standing Bear at his trial??! All this tripe about wantin' justice for th' victims an' their families—naaaw, it's YOU wantin' your own 'justice', Winterhawk! That's what this is all about---you know it as well as I do!" Doc pointed at him---"And don't mention how you never did like McDougal---cause we're even, son, neither did I! He treated th' woman you fell in love with like hell then tried t'murder her---but, my friend, now they've as good as GOT him! They have in their hands almost ALL evidence needed t'hang this bunch! If you'll just wait a few more hours, why they'll have th' whole sorry shootin' match in jail!" Doc paused and flung out one hand in a pleading gesture---"B'sides, what CAN you do? If you insist on hornin-in t'take your blessed 'piece of flesh' outta Mac--- well, odds are---you'll screw up everything! The arrests, the trials, the damned evidence---you wanta DO THAT?! Hey, each citizen has civil rights an' they have t' be respected these days, no matter WHAT their crime! It's gotta be 'line upon line', every 't' crossed and 'i' dotted! Look, Hawk, I know you got a big interest in this---but don't go off half-cocked messin' things up at this point! Th' end is IN SIGHT, m'boy!!"

Hawk sat, crossed his arms then leaned back in a chair trying to consider the worth of Doc's words. He knew Doc was right about the justice system! But his 'being right' didn't satisfy Joseph---these particular 'judicial means' didn't necessarily mean there'd be 'justice' in the end!

While McDougal was still alive, too much could go-bad. Simply 'being in custody', having a trial---hell, that was no guarantee he'd draw a decent prison term---it happened every day of the week in courtrooms all across the country!

Doc waited as his younger companion silently mulled things over---and over again. "Well?"—Doc finally asked---"Am I right or am I right?" Slowly unfolding his body, Hawk stood from the chair, leaned over the desk toward Doc and gave his answer---"It's true that you're right about most of it, especially about me---and I'm not arguing that part. But there're some things about the rest of it that trouble me greatly---and I don't like the way they make me feel!" Doc looked at him---"And exactly 'what things' trouble you---except maybe not gettin' in that little case of personal 'vengeance'??"

"All right, just get off your 'staircase' hear me out. The very terms you used..,"----Hawk flung out a hand---"...like 'as good as got him'---'almost everything they need'---I don't LIKE the sound of those particular words, Doc---and I especially don't like the percentages! McDougal's just the type to 'cop a plea' by turning states evidence on the Klan---could be especially he'd want to 'get even' with his old man---'the dragon'! Who knows, maybe he just never made Mac's life 'easy'. At least SOMEBODY had to turn him into the monster he became---sure as hell wasn't Lizbeth! Pardon my little psychological digression there, Doc, but I won't settle for the possibility he'll 'get off' on ANY technicality---so my friend,---like it or lump it, just get it straight---I won't let Lizbeth's tormenter 'walk'---I won't!"

Doc stood, glared at Hawk several moments, at last he replied in an exasperated tone---"Well, seems all of us have blurred th' lines of th' law lately!! So I reckon it makes sense nothing should change---not at this late date, I guess!

307

B'sides, why should I, mere small-town horse-doctor that I am, expect a man like YOU t'settle-down an' lead a normal life! Not after being taught how t'bend International Law for th' past twenty years!! Too boring---too much to expect, yeah?"

Without another word, Hawk turned and started toward the door. Doc yelled---"Where you think you goin' NOW?!" The Omaha/Sioux stopped, looked back at Dr. O'Barr and whispered---"Why, I'm going to get a few hours sleep then take a little drive---and in all likelihood, I might even go hunting! Actually..."---he considered in an exaggerated manner---"... I haven't made up my mind exactly WHERE I'll go hunting. You're welcome to come along---you never can tell, Doc, we might find some 'big game'---and in that case, the possibility looms large that we'll need each other's assistance---to legally bag it. Legally, of course."

Doc dropped back onto his chair---stared hopelessly at the impossible man in front of him---"Well, whatever you do--- I guess I'd better be there t'either bury you---or be a witness t'save your ass! What time are we leaving?" A partial grin slid over Joseph's lips as he spoke---"Oh, a little before daybreak sounds pretty good. Just drive out to the hiding place we used---behind the brush. I'll be waiting there for you." He'd already gone out the door when he halted, stuck his head back in and cautioned---"Now calm yourself, Doctor, get yourself all un-jazzed---and sleep well!" Then Joseph was gone.

As always when the Indian left his office---Dr. O'Barr heard those measured footsteps descending the stairs. This 'son' of his had left him with some very negative and mixed feelings---'fear, dread, alarm' to start the list! He could only pray Hawk never really had it in mind to kill McDougal---only beat the living daylights out of him then drop him off inside the city limits! So whatever it meant in Hawk's terminology, Doc reckoned he really must be too 'jazzed-up'---because sleep was now the fartherest thing from his mind!

Chapter Fifty-One

With Doc's truck left parked behind the brush, the two rode silently along in the bluish-white van. "I'm not even going t'ASK about this van, but it sounds like a cop-car—big engine, pipes and all---but I would like to ask our agenda?"—Doc glanced at the van's inside roll-bars then over at the driver. "Don't have a 'set' plan as yet."---came the answer---"Right now, it's by ear---or by the seat of our pants. There's two possible plans of action---one is to go and meet him up the country. BUT I have no way of knowing whether he's taking a regular run---or using side-roads. However, since he's 'wanted', my choice is the side-roads. The next plan is to wait on him to come to us---but snatch him before he gets inside Rita's house---that way she'll have no knowledge he's been waylaid." Doc sat several moments before asking his next question---"If you don't know which way he'll be comin' in---how you gonna 'waylay' him?" "We'll have to wait it out. I'm probably about 12 hours too early---but I didn't want to take the chance he might decide to get up at midnight and start 6 hours sooner than the hour Mrs. McDougal gave me. I just hope she told me the truth---the ideal scenario would be his arrival AFTER dark!" Hawk stared through the windshield, his eyes had a far away look---"On a mission, we'd sometimes wait for days to get exactly the right shot—one shot! If there's anything a Ranger learns to do well---it's 'wait'. And you could say we also learned not to trust the word of many people. If you have to depend on anyone's word, especially someone you haven't known for 30 years--

-let it be your own word. You'll live longer that way." Doc shook his head---"You ARE a suspicious one, Winterhawk." "Kept me alive, didn't it?!"---retorted Hawk.

They were nearing the town where Rita lived when Doc finally gathered the courage to ask Joseph the question burning inside him since last night. "Uh---tell me something, Son. Y'think old Mac will make it t'trial---or even lock-up? Or is he gonna just 'disappear' from this trip off in some God-forsaken 'hole' never t'be heard from---or seen again?" Hawk chuckled---"Why Doctor-man, how you DO talk! You honestly think I'd touch that one with a ten-foot pole?! Cut me some slack! Y'know I can't put you in that kind of spot! Remember the saying that 'what you don't know can't hurt you'? In this case, it's 'what you don't hear'! And should the worst come down---nobody can later put you on a stand and make you say things you don't want to say---about your friends--or family. I think of you as family---all the Winterhawks' think of you as 'family'. And as for today?"---Joseph looked straight at Doc---"All you know about today is that last night, we decided to 'do a little hunting' come morning---and that's what we're doing! However, since we made no real plans---we just decided to drive north---and ended up in these parts." Doc nodded, he knew Joseph was right---he shouldn't know the answer to that one. But he would like to know what they were going to do for the next 12 hours--- like a Ranger, he might learn something about 'waiting'!

He got a clue as they drove past Rita's house then circled the block, passing through an alley making certain that only her vehicle was there. After driving around to select the best parking spot, Hawk gave Doc 'camping' instructions-- -"We're going to have some breakfast---which is back there behind us---AND if you have to 'go potty', old buddy, there's a 'convenience' for that as well, naturally I've

provided tissue and a spray-can of deodorizer. I'll even
allow you 'to go' behind a blanket which I'll hold up
around you!" Doc began to laugh---Hawk joined him, his
white teeth flashing like South Sea pearls. "And before you
ask, Doc---'no—you can't just get out and go to a public
toilet'! We can't be 'seen' loitering about the
neighborhood---the van's one thing but two strange men are
another! There's water, food and blankets,"---Hawk
continued—"Also, I tossed in a couple of books for you
along with a small lamp---even a bedroll and pillow so you
could have your afternoon nap! We'll be shut-in for awhile
so IF you'd like a walk before we begin, I'll take you to a
less populated spot then drive a mile or so ahead and wait
for you. You interested?" "Naww, I guess not.
Somebody's bound to notice an old man stumbling along on
a cold, wintery morning then stop an' ask if he'd like a ride-
--if I said 'No'---they'd be sure t'remember it IF anyone
ever asks! I'd best stay in this thing with you---though
m'bones will stiffen up on me an' turn t'stone."

"Speaking of."---Doc asked---"How's th' wound or DARE I
even ask? Reckon you used some Indian salve remedy
after you got home---an' now it's all miraculously healed t'
perfection?" "Why I took special care, just the way you
told me! I avoided anything that was more strenuous than
holding Lizbeth's hand---I guess you could say the wound's
in good shape." "But how long is it gonna STAY that way-
--if you an' Mac get into it like a couple of ruttin' buck
deers! The way things stand with you, the moment you lay
eyes on him---I expect t'see a 15-rack set of antlers begin
sproutin' right on that hard Sioux forehead of yours."
Hawk joked---"How appropriate!! WELL-SAID! You
right sure you don't have Indian Blood, Doctor-man?"

Chapter Fifty-Two

Mac drove away from his father's country house a little after 3:00 a.m.---ex-dragon McDougal saw his son off then went back to bed. As much as 'the boy' had grieved, aggravated, disappointed and angered him for most of his life---the older McDougal found that once Mac left, sleep was impossible. He lay wondering if he'd ever see his immature, cowardly and violent off-spring again. He even considered calling up Dragon Harris to see how the vote had actually gone. But, the more he mulled---the less he felt like hearing the answer. Sooner or later, he'd know. At some point during the up-coming day, a vehicle would come up the driveway and he'd have his answer.

By then, he'd begun to toss restlessly about in the bed--- finally he reached over and shook his wife roughly--- demanding fresh coffee. Not feeling very amiable at 5:00 a.m., she snapped---"If its coffee yer a'wantin' at this here hour, Mr. McDougal, you kin jest git yer twitching body up outta this bed an' GO MAKE IT YERSELF! Sure'n hell yer NOT sleepin' none! As 'tis, ye've kept me awake fer half th' night---first it wuz a seein' 'little Mac' off---then ye come back up here a fallin' inta bed like a ton a'brick--- a'shakin' th' whole room---then all thet rollin' an' tumblin' fer two more hours! I'll NOT be a gittin' up outta bed till m'usual hour! Thank ye very much---away with ye!"

Cursing her beneath his breath, the elder McDougal jumped out of bed---unfortunately, he wasn't as young as he used to be and immediately felt a back-muscle jerk painfully! "DAMMIT"---he squawked---"YOU LAZY COW!! NOW LOOK WHAT'CHA DONE!" Immediately as though lifted by some unseen supernatural power, she rose off the bed and blazed back---"Y'OLD S.O.B.!! Y'CALLIN' ME

A LAZY COW? HUH?!" He roared back--- "Y'SEE
ANYBODY ELSE IN HERE, Y'OLD BAWD?!"

Taking great offense at his selfishness, not to mention his
and Mac's unwelcome invasion of her nightly measure of
'rest'---she began laying on him all the blame for Mac's
endless ill-behavior patterns! After a fifteen minute scream-
fest of name-calling, threats and fist-shaking---the old
dragon duck-walked from the room, holding onto his
throbbing back and slammed the door---thus knocking a few
prized 'what-knots' and ghastly glass trinkets off the wall!
Treasures, which his wife kept on a dainty shelf! Jerking
the door back open, she raged at him as he disappeared
painfully around the corner---"RECKON YER HAPPY
NOW! Y'OLD BASTARD---YE BROKE M'FAVORITE
'WHAT-KNOT' PIECE! NOW I CAIN'T SLEEP
NEITHER!"

Several minutes later, she appeared in the kitchen---face
still red as a tomato, her lips moving silently as she began
slinging pots and pans recklessly about! McDougal sat
painfully in his kitchen chair moaning about his back
'injury'---but she didn't hear a word as she drowned out his
complaints with a din of clanging cookware. Finally, he
yelled at her---"I CAIN'T HEAR M'SELF THINK IN
HERE! THINK Y'COULD MAKE A LITTLE MORE
RACKET??" "Y'OLD PISS ANT!"---her voice taking on
all the shrillness of a loud off-key trumpet player---"SHUT
YER TRAP---STOP ALL THET SNIVELIN'! Y'LL GET
OVER IT! TIS LIKE CHILDBIRTH, Y'OLD FOOL---
T'WON'T LAST F'EVER! Y'OUGHTA TRY THET
LITTLE ACT SOMETIMES!! BIRTHIN' A CHILD---
NOW, THET'S PAIN, MR. McDOUGAL!! THET'S
THERE'S PAIN!" He shifted uncomfortably about in his
chair while swearing under his breath.

Once they both had a cup of coffee, each had calmed
somewhat and were delving into their 'country-breakfast' of
fried sausages, bacon, cheese grits, buttered biscuits with
thick cane syrup and orange juice. But outside the kitchen--
-not only 'trouble' but the end of a life-style was
approaching the front, sides and back of McDougal's house!

Just as the elder McDougal took a bite of his second biscuit-
-both he and his wife were terrified out of their wits as the
front and the back door each shattered at the same time
whereupon innumerable male voices began yelling,
shouting at the top of their lungs as they poured into the
rooms---"FBI! THIS IS THE FBI! HANDS IN THE AIR!!!
HANDS UP----DON'T MOVE! STAY WHERE YOU
ARE! DON'T MOVE!!" McDougal dropped his biscuit---
then stood so fast his chair fell backward, his back painfully
rebelling at the sudden movement! "DOWN! GET DOWN
ON THE FLOOR! THE FLOOR! GET DOWN ON THE
FLOOR!" Mrs. McDougal hit the floor and lay there---her
husband couldn't 'hit the floor'---so he held his arms and
hands up in the air, trying to explain about his back! No
one listened to him and by then, within 20 short seconds,
not only the room but the whole house had filled with two
groups of men, some wearing business suits---others a type
of military gear---all armed to the teeth with various
weaponry! Like a nest of angry disturbed hornets, they
yelled, while swarming all over the place, kicking open
closed doors---knocking furniture about---jerking things out
of closets and throwing boxes on the floor then kicking out
the contents! The sudden terror and ear-splitting noise
cowed McDougal! He watched as they searched for an attic
opening! All the while, they continued waving their guns
about and hollering threats! One of them pushed McDougal
AND his ailing back toward the wall---"DON'T MOVE,
McDOUGAL! DON'T EVEN SWALLOW YOUR SPIT
OR I'LL SHOOT!" Two of the men jerked his wife up by

her arms then cuffed her---"McDOUGAL!!"-- she screamed---"MAKE 'EM QUIT PUSHIN' ME 'ROUND LIKE A CRIMINAL! I AIN'T DONE NOTHIN'!! Y'CAN"T 'REST ME!!"---she raged at the FBI---"ALL WE'RE A'DOIN IS EATIN' OUR BREAKFAST! WE AIN'T DONE NOTHIN'!!" "SHUT UP!"---McDonald managed to scream at her over the din---"JUST SHUT YER TRAP!! DON'T SAY 'NOTHER WORD! Y' HEAR ME, WOMAN?!"

After they found no one else in the house but Mrs. McDougal's terrified children by her first marriage---most of the men then fanned out over the barns and out buildings. By that time, McDougal had been cuffed and shackled---a man in a business suit motioned, two 'military' men plopped the old dragon down into his kitchen chair and slapped a stack of papers down on the table! "Here's our warrant. Read 'em their rights, Baker! By the way, where IS he, McDougal? The one called 'Mac'! We know he's here---and we know you've been hiding him! It might go better if you told us where he's located! If he fires on us--- we'll take him out!"

"What's m'son done fer you people---th' FBI---t'come after 'em? I know he got inta a mite a'trouble with his wife, but---th' FBI?"---the old man queried. "I'm asking the questions here, if you don't mind, ex-dragon. Now, where's your boy?" "I don't know! Who told ya he wuz here? Thet's a mistake---he ain't chere—as y'can plainly see!"--- McDougal snapped---"An' had ya jest knocked 'stead a'tearing m'house apart---I coulda told ya he wuzn't chere!" "Don't get smart-mouthed---'sir'! By this time---every Klansman who's even stepped on an ant is being arrested! So don't count too big on 'help' from here on out!" Sensing he would get no where with the McDougals while they were together on their own turf, he jerked his head toward some guards—"Take both of them out---put 'em in separate cars with armed guards while we box up all this stuff for evidence!" "But I ain't DRESSED---jest in m'robe an' slippers! I'll freeze t'death---I'll sue!"---Mrs. McDonald screamed!! "SHUT UP, WOMAN!"---her husband roared a last threat before they were both escorted out to separate waiting cars.

McDougal sat numbly inside the cold black car and watched at least three dozen men blundering about all over the house, yard, barns and general vicinity 'of'. Shivering from the cold and from disbelief, he wondered how his life could crumble so quickly! Why were they here---NOW?? Neither he nor Mac had been actively involved in any 'underground' activities for several years---what could they possibly want NOW?! After Mac's last 'job' for the organization, orders had come for both of them to 'retire' from that particular department of 'work'.

During his many years with the Klan, he'd paid no attention to earlier 'talk' that the FBI, CIA and other government agencies work years putting together a case so there're no holes! They did what they were ordered, they waited and worked---until there were no doubts! Then they pounced---suddenly and without warning. These things had never concerned McDougal---indeed, they'd been far from his mind. Unfortunately for him he was basically ignorant of how 'trouble' actually arrived on the scene! Now---he looked out at the 'carnage' going on all around the car---and for him, it looked like it was all over---finished in one fell swoop.

Back inside the house, 'The suit' directed another man wearing the same variety of charcoal suit, black topcoat and tie, plus sunglasses---"Go to their bedroom and get the old lady something warm to wear. For him, too. One full suit each---from the skin out---including coats, shoes, hats. Can't let them get sick and die on us! Too much at stake. Anyway, by tonight, they'll most likely let her go."

***

By this time, Mac was a couple of hundred miles down the road---still humiliated.---"Sure different than when I came up last week---seems like months ago. That night I felt like 'somebody' again---the 'Grand Dragon's son---'young Mr. McDougal' with all the amenities. Now, I'm driving a pick-up truck with no escort---no companion---very little money NOT to mention I'm 'wanted' by the cops! The least that old blow-hard could've done was SEND somebody with some firepower along with me!" He yawned, shook his head several times---"I'm missing some sleep---maybe I could just pull-over in one of these deserted stretches, grab myself a nap. There's no time schedule---I'm not punching a clock for my old man---nor the Klan. I make my own choices now that I've left them behind---but I'll be back, 'dad'---we've got a score to settle."

And with that in mind---he began looking for a place to rest. After several more miles, he pulled into the woods, made sure he was locked in then sprawled across the seat wearing his overcoat and was asleep in two minutes.

Chapter Fifty-Three

Hawk noticed what he assumed to be a 'fed', cruising Rita's house twice in eight minutes. The driver, wearing a suit and sunglasses, drove a dressed-down, black four-door with no 'extras'---when it passed, the tag proved Hawk to be correct! He looked at his watch, it was 3:00 p.m.---Doc was napping, they'd been there since sunup.

"Must be all that weekend 'OT' work Doc told me about that's brought the action! Have they picked up Mac---and waiting for Rita to come home from work to get a statement, maybe take her in for questioning? OR---has Mac eluded them and they're looking for him here. Oh HELL, if ONLY I knew the route he was taking! He's not here yet---but THEY must not know that! And if they raided the old man's place and Mac had already left on his way back, well---he's somewhere between here and there! Mrs. McDougal must've been telling me the truth because had he left earlier, he'd be here by now. Unless, of course, he decided to kill some time on the way." Hawk exhaled watching the black car creep past the second time--- "There's a lot of 'things' I'll do---but being a civilian and taking a prisoner away from a government agent just ain't one of those things!"

Feeling some confusion as to what his next move should be---Hawk continued to watch. Rita would be home soon--- he'd just have to wait it out, see what 'came down' with her and the agent. Around 3:15 p.m., her car came into the dirt driveway---she parked in the same place she had last time. Detouring by the mailbox, she then let herself in the front door. Hawk scanned the street for the black car. He didn't have long to wait, soon the auto appeared then eased into her drive, pulling close-in behind her car and stopped. The driver exited, walked to the front door and knocked. At that point, Hawk saw another two men approaching from the alley way behind Rita's house---they were agents as well--- he knew them on sight! They were figuring if Mac was inside and tried a back-door get away, they'd be ready for him! Biting on his lip, Hawk never took his eyes off the front of the house nor the two men standing near the back door. Suddenly, he caught a glimpse of two more dark unadorned cars---they stopped on the street in front of the

Shelby Jean Roukoski Clark

house---both had two passengers each! Sweat formed on
his face beneath the crazy itchy beard and mustache—
"Damn! I'd give anything to be up front so I could roll
down a window---! Nerves, Winterhawk! You're not in
control or in charge of this situation---and it makes you up-
tight, huh, 'Captain'! Watch it—be cool. You're not the
one drawing fire! Mac's not there---you'll get him first---
it'll work out right, it has to!"

Ten minutes had passed when the agent inside exited the
house along with Rita, who was wearing her coat, cap and
carrying her handbag. Opening the passenger front door of
his car, he helped her inside---then cranked up and drove
away. The two men at the back disappeared into the alley---
-the two cars up front separated, one made a U-turn and
came over to Hawk's side of the street and parked. The
other car drove around to the alley---it looked like they were
set for Mac. There were enough of them to work in shifts,
Hawk thought, but there was only one of HIM to work
shifts!

Joseph began to talk to God--- "I seem to be losing the
battle here at the last minute! Lord, give me some back-up!
Many years ago, You showed me a vision of my Lizbeth,
then when the time was right, I met her---later, when
Lizbeth was about to be murdered—You 'let me fly'---and
watch McDougal WALK when NO ONE knew about it
except You! I did all I knew to protect her the right way---
but I failed and that night almost ended in tragedy---now,
here I am again---doing all I can with what little I have! If
You tell me for certain Mac'll either serve a life sentence---
or get the chair, then I'll back off. Right now, my back's
against the wall anyway---my hands are tied! You know as
well as I that Lizbeth will never have a moment's peace if
Mac plea-bargains, gets a light sentence and is out in two
years or less! You also KNOW better than I that the

moment he's out---he'll come after her, maybe even Doc, Salle and Bill! Being God, You certainly know the heart of this evil man---much better than any of us! I'm asking you to please choose between us, if he's right then help him---- but if I'm right, PLEASE help ME! I'm not perfect, Lord, not by any means---but Mac is little short of insane---and a murderer in the process. Perhaps being emotionally involved has tainted my view of him---only You know the true answer to that statement. So, like Abraham of old, I'm proposing You and me strike a bargain! If YOU KNOW that, in the future, he'll harm Lizbeth or my family or Doc-- -then put Mac in my hands. I swear to You, I'll not deliberately kill him---I'll just sorta 'corner him' and offer him up to You! Then You can do what You want with him."

Doc roused---"HAWK!? You in here? Hell, this thing is dark as an Irish dungeon!" "SHHhh!"---came the reply--- "I'm here. It's getting dark outside---around 6:45 p.m. You missed the FBI picking up Rita---but not to worry, there's still at least six of them all around us." "WHAT?"---Doc gasped! "Don't pass out!"---Hawk chuckled---"I only meant there's six agents in three cars---one parked over just to the side of this van with two men---and the rest out in the back alley, I think. They have to be waiting for Mac. And I don't know where the HELL he is! Shoulda been here by now!" "What're you gonna do, Hawk!?"---the alarm in Doc's voice was more than apparent---"You can't take him away from th' FBI!! Promise me you won't even 'go there'!" "Soothe yourself, m'friend. I wouldn't do that--- truthfully, I don't know anything to do at this point---except wait! You know, if Logan was right about the 'net'---the feds may already have the McDougals hauled in custody, even Mac. But I don't believe so---otherwise, why're they still hanging around here after taking Rita!?"

"Don't ask ME! I don't know 'nothin' about these damned covert activities! You're th' expert in that field! But, f'all that's holy, Hawk---try not t'get us either shot or become permanent residents in th' basement of Leavenworth!? Okay?" "Do my best, Doc. Have yourself a snack---or 'go potty'."---Hawk teased to lighten the mood. "How can I find a snack---much less EAT or 'go potty'!! I can't even SEE the end of my NOSE back here!" "Okay, okay. I'll give you a break---let me cover my peep-hole here and we'll turn on your 'reading lamp'!" Doc heard something slide quietly---Hawk reached for the lamp and turned it on---"See? Hooked up to the lighter on the panel up front---now, do whatever you like---for awhile. I'm going up front and see if I can make out any more 'gov-cars' in the parking area---plus keep an eye on those in the street. Hawk handed the 'lamp' to Doc---"Turn it off while I go through to the front, ---have fun."

By that time, Hawk was already half way through to the front of the truck. Doc sighed, stretched his stiff muscles---'went potty' then wiped his hands with some pre-dampened hand-wash disposables. Rummaging thru the 'food-bag', he chose an apple---some grapes---a banana/p'nut butter sandwich and some milk from the thermos marked 'M'. Doc grumbled---"At least it's palatable and not dry, roasted horse grain---like before!"

***

When Mac awoke---it was after lunch! "DAMN!"---he swore as he bolted up from the seat---every muscle ached, his head felt swollen and achy---even his eyeballs were sore! Taking time 'to go' behind a tree---he then hurried back to the truck while zipping up his pants---suddenly he stopped and went to the rear of the camper. Taking out two hand guns, he loaded them then slid one in each side pocket of his top-coat---"Should've been almost there—or at least half-way there by now! When I call the old man to check in---he'll have a screaming fit. Oh well, it'll be good for 'em." Resentment began to rise up inside him again---then with a roar of the engine, he turned the truck around and spun off, leaving behind a cloud of dust, leaves and dead grass. After he was back on the highway---he reached and turned on the radio for the last leg of his journey.

Each time the news came on his chosen station, Mac would switch channels. "Nothing I hate worse than a damned news-caster! Always talking down their noses at law-abiding people---like we were all brain-damaged or some such!" He stopped on a station playing some snappy pop-tunes---the speedometer clicked off the miles as he hummed along, occasionally tapping the steering wheel with his hands, keeping time with the beat. Coming into a town about 100 miles east of where Rita lived, he'd stopped at a traffic light when the music changed---'protest' and 'hippy' sounds now poured from the speakers---swearing out loud, he turned the radio off and decided to eat and have some coffee. By this time, it was getting dark---of course, he could wait until he got to Rita's to eat---but he was ready for a change of scenery. "Don't forget to act like a 'parson', Mackey!"---he sneered to himself as he made certain his mustache and glasses were on straight. Setting his hat on his head and polishing at the 'clergy' pin on his lapel, Mac grinned and went inside.

He was just ordering an extra coffee to go when two men straddled counter-stools close by---"Well, it's about time somebody did somethin' about them killings! Think they got proof to put 'em away?" "I dunno. The top-dog was purty close-mouthed on the news, if they do have proof--- it's sure as hell taken th' whole kit n' kaboodle long enough to GET it! Shucks, all that happened---why, it's been several years ago now. I, for one, never thought they'd ever do anythin' about it!" "No, now you gotta hand it to the FBI---they can come up with some pretty strong stuff---that is, when they put their heads to it! Getting' em to do anything is th' problem!" "Yeah, if they cared as much about this as they did prohibition---hell, it'd all been done and done a month after the killings!" "May I take your order?"---the waitress interrupted. "Oh. I'll have coffee and a piece of that lemon pie over there! The wife didn't get around to making dessert t'night!" "And you, sir?" "Hmmm. Just give me some black coffee, the doc told me I had to lose a pound or two---'cholesterol', you know. My old man lived to be 95---and nobody ever talked 'cholesterol' t'him! Always somethin' t'kill a man's enjoyment of life! Right, Roy?" His companion nodded and their conversation went off on a health kick.

Feeling better now that he'd stopped, walked around a bit, eaten, had coffee---Mac was ready to get back on the road---and to Rita's. Having been routed out of bed early this morning, he was looking forward to a good night's sleep on a bed! Had things 'gone better' for him back home---he wouldn't have missed Rita at all. And sooner or later, he would've simply 'replaced' her because already he needed greener pastures, newer faces but he'd sort of 'promised' to marry her once he was free. However that was his father's dumb-ass idea---and still 'future'---and IF he was smarter than his father, he'd never marry her! She'd 'do' for the time being---besides she was 'crazy' about him and he could make use of that. "Still,"---he thought---"...if the old man had lost his knack for raising hell and making my life miserable, things could've been better between the two of us this time. BUT things were the same---now I know for sure that it'll always be that way. I don't need a damn brick wall to fall on me---nothing can change him!"

Near 9:30 p.m., Mac drove into the city limits and headed in the direction of Rita's house. Third shift workers at the power plant had left vehicles in the grocery parking lot across the street and carpooled to work. Mac pulled in among them, parked beside a van and sat looking at the house---she wasn't home! "Hell, she must be on second shift at the restaurant, maybe even third."---he complained. "Well, guess I'll walk over and see if my door key is still under that rock at the front steps. I can grab a shower then drive over to see her---that'll put me in good with her. Women are so damn gullible---lie to 'em, make 'em feel important, trash-talk 'em---and they'll love you forever."

He walked across the street, into the yard and up to the rock---squatting, he turned the rock over---the key wasn't there! He swore aloud, stood and angrily crashed the rock against the step then turned to go back to his truck--- suddenly out of nowhere, a man, wearing dark clothing approached him. Mac's heart raced, his hands shook, his mind whirled as he sought to calm himself---"What th' hell's the matter with you, you idiot! Don't let this damned fool scare you---coming outta no where like this! You got your guns---put both hands in your pockets right now---take him out if he tries to mug you!"

"Good evening, Sir."---the man spoke in cool, educated tones then suddenly beamed a flashlight in his face---"May I ask what you're doing here?" Mac blinked against the blinding light, swallowed and took a deep breath then answered politely---"Why, I'm a pastor friend of Rita's--- she attended our church a couple of years back and I thought to drop in on her—and say 'hello'. Might I ask who you are, my good man?" The agent flashed a badge--- "FBI, sir. Mind showing me your ID?" Mac's hands were trembling so he could hardly remove his wallet---handing it to the agent, he managed to ask---"Is anything---er, wrong here, sir? I mean, is Rita all right? My goodness, there's not been a crime committed here---at her house! Has there?" The agent didn't answer but shone the flashlight closely over the entire wallet---then finally answered---"No, Reverend, no crime committed here. Where was it you said you'd just arrived from?" "Er. I, uh, don't think I said--- but from---Indiana, sir. Just drove in."---Mac was shaking in his black parson's shoes---he couldn't even remember where the ID said he was from!!

"Oh God."---he thought and swallowed---by now his throat was almost closed up from sheer terror! They were after HIM---of course---but why? He could understand the local 'fuzz' after him about that Lizbeth-thing, but why the FEDS?! What'd happened??! Had she spilled her guts about the Klan? He needed to call his father!! He didn't know what to say or do---or how to act! He'd never faced anything like this before---his teeth chattered like castanets- --he clenched his jaw to still them!

Neither the agents nor Mac noticed as a light colored van in the grocery parking lot cranked up then pulled slowly out into the street. It drove two blocks north, made a block east then came back, halting just out of sight of the agents car at the house---and out of sight from the alley. The van parked at a corner and sat idling---it's big, special heavy duty 455 block purring like a testy mother panther.

"Reverend."—the agent stated---"I hate to detain you but we'll have to check out your ID. Please step across the street in front of me---I'll call in---then you can be on your way." Mac managed to whisper—"Of course, sir."

Standing in the street beside the FBI auto, Mac eyed his truck---he hadn't locked the door---he could make it--- maybe. There was one man inside the car---the other standing beside the open door with him---he could shoot both of them and make a run for it. The grocery store was closed, a few die-hard billiard players still soaked up beers and puffed cigarettes as they waited for closing time. There was almost no traffic in this area right now---Mac hadn't seen any people about---would it be possible to make a 'get-away'?? While he was considering---the agent asked— "While we wait on a reply, mind if I ask you a question, Reverend?" Mac shook his head and croaked---"No. I'll certainly give you the answer if I know it, anything to help out." "When you approached the front steps? You squatted down and picked up a rock---then threw it hard against the steps---and swore! It hardly seems the behavior one would expect from a man of the cloth---'sir'." "What're you saying, Agent? That even a parson can't----lose his temper---and curse once in awhile?" "No. What I'm saying is--- why did you pick up a rock? Were you planning to--- perhaps break a window and enter the house?" "WHY certainly NOT!"---Mac acted 'outraged'.

At this point, the radio began chattering back the report on Mac's ID and both agents became slightly distracted with the radio! Mac made his move---jerking both guns out of his pockets, he fired on both men---the one beside him went down on the street while the one in the car slumped over--- then Mac ran! Before the agents in the back alley could make it to the front street---Mac's truck was screeching out the back entrance of the parking lot! By the time the alley stake-out got to the wounded agents---Mac had disappeared into the night!

He didn't know where he was going---but automatically, he headed down the highway toward the ranch! He'd gone south about 7 miles out of town when unnoticed---off in the distance behind him---a pair of headlights began closing in. Mac had the accelerator of the truck pressed on the floorboard---the needle showed he was doing around 90 mph---and that was all she'd do! The engine was doing it's best, but she just wasn't made for a chase.

Chapter Fifty-Four

Hawk had noticed the truck when it eased slowly into the parking lot and stopped near him. In a small town, not many people were out and about at that hour---so Hawk closely scrutinized the driver when he exited the vehicle. He fit McDougal's general description but had a mustache, wore glasses and was wearing dark dress clothes with a top-coat. The driver paused for a few moments so near the van window that had Hawk rolled it down, he could've touched the man---for a moment, he thought about looking away in another direction but then it struck him! If he, himself, was using a false mustache and beard---and wearing glasses--- why not Mac?! No one in his right mind would expect a fugitive to show up looking the same as his wanted poster photo! "Okay, if you head toward Rita's----I'm gonna call you 'McDougal'---no matter HOW you look!"---Hawk never flinched from staring at the man---soon he realized the 'gent' had taken no notice of him whatsoever but was casing out the whole area. Finally, he began walking toward the street---Hawk gave a quick intake of breath---"It IS you! I recognize your walk from the day you shot me in Lizbeth's back yard! Of course---! DOC!!" Quickly Hawk reached behind him, pulling the false back to one side--- "Turn off your light and get up here! And put a move on! Our man just showed!"

Doc blundered across his 'bed' in the dark, then clamored--- as best a 60-odd year old body could 'clamor'---across to the front seat! Jamming his hat down on his head, he looked this way and that---"WHERE!?" Hawk nodded his head toward the street---"He's already in Rita's yard---there---see him? He's stopping by the steps---,". Hawk adjusted his binoculars---"Looks like he's picking up something. Uh oh! He just threw it down---and one of 'the boys' over here next to us is already on him! Can you see?" "Yeah."—Doc whispered---"Just barely---but I can make out some of what's goin' on! Hawk! What you gonna do?!" "Dunno. Don't talk to me right now---let me watch and think!"

A couple of moments later, Hawk cranked up the van and began to ease slowly out of the parking lot---making a right turn away from the area. "Why you leavin' NOW??! Ain't this what you been waitin' for?!"---Doc hissed! "Oh, not to worry---I'm not going far---but he's practically in their hands---at least temporarily. They'll be asking for his ID, then checking it out on the radio----that gives me a minute to reposition---and be ready for whatever happens! Yet be far enough away not to be noticed." Doc sat silently as Joseph circled around and parked one block north of the scene, leaving the high-powered engine idling. Hawk watched every move through the binoculars----suddenly two shots rang out!! "What th' hell?!"---Doc gasped, turning to stare! "Mac just shot the agents---both of them, I think! The son-of-a-gun suddenly had a pistol in each hand—like Wyatt Earp---I don't think they expected that! The rear stake-out won't get around front before he makes his get-a-way---probably in his truck by now---I can't see! I'm taking the chance that he won't come out the way we did---but use the rear drive! We gotta get moving so we don't lose him!"

Looking at Doc, Hawk started east while giving him orders---"It may get rough from here on, Doc. Now, I want you OUT of here---at the next corner---open the door and roll out! Go any place, find a restaurant and eat---if I don't

come back for you---call this number!" He waved a piece
of paper at his balking passenger---"It's one of the trackers
who lives close by---he'll come get you and take you to
your truck!" By now, Hawk had turned south, the van shot
forward as he accelerated---"When I slow for the first bend
in the road---be ready---I'll stop then you bail out, man.
GOT IT?!"

"HELL NO!"—a stubborn O'Barr shouted---"I not goin'
NO PLACE!! I'm here for th' duration---whenever THAT
is!" "LISTEN TO ME!"—Joseph's pleas rose over the
sound of the engine---"Even with the weighted frame and
under-carriage, I still may end up totaling this thing and I
don't want you IN HERE!!" "I don't give a rip what YOU
want!"---Doc roared---"I'm STAYIN'!" Hawk shouted
back---"And what about IDA??"

 By now, the van was following a set of red tail-lights off in
the distance---the speedometer registered 88 mph. "What
about YOU?!"---Doc shouted back! Joseph yelled---"If I'm
dead it's one dead Indian--that's ONE thing--but YOU'RE
something else!! I wouldn't injure you for the world!! So
when I slow and stop---GET THE HELL OUT---before
you're too far from town!" "Balls-a-fire, kiddo!"—Doc
laughed ruefully--"Life'd be too miserably dull with you
gone---I may as well hang on to th' bitter end!"

"LORD, GOD! YOU'RE SELF-WILLED AS ME!!"---the
Omaha/Sioux exploded in exasperation! "So you're telling
me to go ahead, floor-board this thing and maybe kill you?
You're giving me permission to possibly maim you for
life?! You wanta end up the same as McDougal---flat on
your back? And what if the fool draws both guns on us and
shoots you!!? I'd be willing to lay odds those aren't the
only two guns he has with him either!!" Hawk's loud
questions went unanswered until the older man finally

replied---"Whether thou goest, I will go---I think 'thy people' are already my people! This whole thing began th' day I picked you up in my truck an' carried you off where you met Lizbeth---so, together, we'll finish this episode in our lives! Drive on, James!"

Hawk took one quick glance at Doc, shook his head and shouted over the engine's loud reverberations---"You're crazy, I reckon you KNOW that, huh? HUH!!!?" There was no reply, only silence. "ALL RIGHT! Dear GOD!! HAVE IT YOUR WAY---although it might mean the both of us could go down! At least we've got built-in roll bars. MAYBE, God willing, we won't get killed!" The speedometer now read 90 mph---Hawk exhaled in frustration, his voice rising again—"I can see it now! Ida and Lizbeth spending the rest of their days together--- visiting the freaking cemetery every day---taking flowers to our final resting places!" "Shut up, Indian. Just drive--- catch your damned quarry! It's what you've wanted since day-one! This is your chance, so go get 'em! An' may God be on our side!" "I've already talked to him about that one, Doc!!"

Chapter Fifty-Five

O'Barr's eyes followed the tail lights ahead then called out- -"Why in heaven's name do y'think he's driving toward th' ranch Hawk? Don't he know that's th' first place they'll look??!" Hawk shook his head slightly as he concentrated on the road---"He's scared. The ranch is the only place he knows to go right now---unless he has another spot in mind. Time will tell, I guess!" Doc's eyes took in the fuel tank--- he knew the van had to be a high burner---"You gonna have enough fuel t'finish th' chase?" "Got mounted saddle-tanks.,"—Hawk replied---"...we can switch over any time!"

A half hour passed, they were nearing the ranch when
Joseph called out---"See any headlights behind us? I can't
make out a thing back there---not and drive at this speed!"
O'Barr watched the rear-view mirror for a minute or so---
"No lights of any sort! I still can't believe this idiot just
shot two agents then got away in what seemed like only
seconds! He's gotta know we're chasin' him, how come
you reckon he hasn't taken a shot?" Hawk's laugh was
harsh---"He's got all he can handle pushing his pick-up this
way! If he keeps this speed constant for too long, he may
find himself walking! That truck engine's not 'broken-in'
yet., I smelled heat from it when he parked beside us!"

Doc peered over at the speedometer---it registered 92 mph.
"You're not gonna get within firing range, huh!" Hawk
shook his head---"Not until we're at the end of this run!"

They were approaching the driveway to Lizbeth's house---
automatically Hawk let off on the accelerator---but Mac
kept to the highway! "Where's he headed!"---Doc yelled---
"If he goes too far, he'll meet up with Logan an' his men!
Surely McDougal knows the Feds have alerted every local
law agency in this state an' once Logan gets organized, this
is th' first direction he'll head out!"

A few more miles shot past and Mac seemed to be slowing
down just a little! Then Hawk saw the brake-lights
suddenly flash on---the pick-up skidded, swerved several
times as Mac made a left turn onto a gravel road and
'righted' up his steering with Hawk right on him! Gravel
flew from Mac's tires, pelting the hood and windshield of
the van! Joseph yelled---"This is Indian land! Why'd he
turn off here, for crying out loud!? There's an old burial
ground not far ahead!" "So what if there's a burial ground?
What's THAT got t'do with it?"---Doc hollered! "Well

now! It's just a place we 'Injuns' call 'sacred ground'---
hell, Doc, you KNOW about these things!" "Sure, but some
of what we hear, ain't most of it a lotta hokum? I mean---
nothing's gonna happen t'McDougal just because he turned
up this road!"---Doc stared at Hawk, then hastily added---
"IS IT?" "I can't divulge that information to you, white
man!"---the Indian teased—"But---you never can tell!"

Doc sat in silence---the engine alternately roared and
quieted as Hawk accelerated then braked while almost
'pushing' the van into Mac's rear bumper! "When's this
road gonna end, Hawk??! We're already half way up th'
hill!" Hawk took a close curve followed by a bump in the
road---straightened out then yelled---"I find it more than
extremely coincidental that this road leads right up to a
'certain' mountain---then continues on 2/3 of the way UP
the mountain before it suddenly ends---without warning!"
"What's so 'extremely' about that? Happens all th' time out
here!"---Doc retorted in a loud snort! "Not true in this case-
--THIS mountain is MY 'prayer-chant' mountain! You
know, where I've always gone to drum, play the flute,
dance and pray to God? Doctor-man! This is where I had
my vision---the day I saw McDougal walking!"

Doc whispered---"Oh my blessed LORD."---then closed his
eyes! He remained silent as once again he remembered a
disheveled Joseph Winterhawk turning up on his own
doorsteps with powder-burns on a wounded bloody hand,
insisting McDougal had shot him during a vision---when
Joseph had taken on the body of that hawk! At this point,
O'Barr decided there was nothing left TO say---maybe he'd
said TOO much already! Had he been too 'cavalier' stating
maybe burial ground legends were 'a lot of hokum'?! He
swallowed several times during the next few minutes---
hoping the 'ghosts' of every Indian whose body had ever
been brought here didn't all gather up and take some sort of

332

vengeance on HIM! Maybe being a reservation physician then having Joseph and all the Winterhawks for lifelong friends would help his case!!

Mac continued on the road---almost losing the truck on several turns but always managing to 'right' the vehicle before wrecking it! Each time Mac slid and spun, Joseph braked yet kept control of the van.

At some unknown point during the very recent few days, something in this 'barn-burner' non-fiction had changed---and in this 'change', Doc felt Mac would no longer out-maneuver Winterhawk---not any more! Since this whole thing with Hawk and Lizbeth and Mac began---and for a long time thereafter, it seemed McDougal got all the breaks---but for some reason, Doc realized the evil favor which earlier courted Mac was no longer there. He didn't know if it had ended because of some cosmic schedule, an eon's old plan designed by the ancients---OR if Mac's luck had ended when he turned on this gravel road leading him into Indian territory! How ironic that instead of turning into his own driveway---he'd driven straight onto property belonging to the very people he'd hated so much! And now he was driving up Joseph and God's mountain---Doc shook his head----definitely not a good choice for McDougal!!

After Hawk's astonishing statement, Doc believed he understood 'how' this bumpy road would end! He also understood that past events connected with 'God and Joseph's Mountain' might've dictated that 'fate, destiny or The Almighty' had entered this chase to make certain the end was a just one! Maybe Mac no longer knew WHERE he was going! Was it possible that something or some-ONE injected a compulsion into his brain forcing him to hasten toward the road's end!! Unexplainably, O'Barr was almost certain this road represented McDougal's life and at the end of it, his life would end as well---O'Barr could only pray 'the road' didn't also end for Joseph Winterhawk!

"You die over there, Doctor-man?!"---Hawk yelled above the engine plus the clank of gravel against the van---"You haven't been this quiet since you were 'in-utero'!" Dr. O'Barr stared at him between bounces, skids, swerves and jerks---"Inuter-what?!" "Before you were born! You know, in the uterus?"---Hawk jibed—"Didn't you study the human fetus---or did you sleep through that semester??" "How th' hell can you JOKE at a time like this??"—O'Barr bleated loudly—"Neither of us know if we'll even be alive in one more minute!" "You chose, Doc! Remember I tried to get rid of you---but you'd have none of it! Swore to 'die' with me and all that! This is NOT the time to be changing your mind, you know! Once I stop and exit this vehicle, I'll have to do it right---one shot, one kill---we don't have the artillery to pound our enemy and his truck to a pulp!!" Doc stared at the Indian---suddenly he seemed to be talking to his troops and not him! Hawk took a quick glance at him then hollered---"It's you an me, friend---we may as well talk---even joke a little, in case we 'exit life', huh?!"

"Shut-up, you fanatic!"---O'Barr roared---"Watch where you're going---I'm willin' t'die---but if I do, let it count f'something! Not because you weren't watchin' th' road!! Is this long grade that mountain you were just talkin' about?" Hawk nodded---"Not much further, half a mile or so---I'm gonna drop back just enough so I don't run over him and he can't get a pot-shot at us when he bails! Would you open the dash, take out the gun? When I cut the engine---have the gun there for my hand! According to what he tries---somehow I've got to draw his fire until he's out of bullets---he hasn't had the opportunity to reload---he has one bullet missing from each gun, probably. If he doesn't drag out some other weapons, he can be out-foxed!

You're going to hear shots---but don't worry and above all, don't---DO NOT---get out of the van thinking to help me--- you might catch a stray bullet! I promise you this, Doc--- much as I want to take-out this rotten human, I won't put a fatal bullet in him---nor will I knife him---I love Lizbeth too much to get myself put away until we're both dead of old age! Just try to believe that I know how to keep myself--- and you---alive!" "Then what CAN I do, Hawk?" "Lock the doors after me and stay in here out of the way! You've already done your part--- stay put!"

Chapter Fifty-Six

Mac's mind was running wild---he honestly didn't know where he was---it was only after entering into then immediately coming out of that small unexplained patch of fog that he realized he'd missed his turn to the ranch! He couldn't turn around and go back---the FBI tail was too close behind him now! Then after passing the ranch turn, for some crazy unknown reason, he'd turned onto an unfamiliar gravel road! In the past, after buying the ranch, he'd never spent time checking out old rarely used roads like some men.

Once more checking out the headlights still in the rearview mirror, he couldn't understand why his tail hadn't tried to 'take him' while still out on the highway! They could've at least made some attempt to stop him---but they hadn't! Why didn't they shoot out his tires?? Since he caught sight of their headlights in his rear mirror, all they'd done was follow along---and after he'd shot two of their men? It wasn't logical! Was it? He'd never been chased by the FBI before---he didn't know what they were allowed to do in a chase and what they weren't allowed to do! "And,"--- wrestling the steering wheel, he swore aloud then jerked off

the mustache and glasses---"Will this damned gravel road
EVER END??!"

The further he drove, the narrower it became! During the
spring and summer---grass, briars and bushes had grown up
between the tire trails---heavy frosts had killed them back
and now they beat, thumped and scraped against the truck's
undercarriage and exhaust system! Growing unchecked
from both sides of the road, countless scrub trees and
bushes seemed to encroach closer and closer---bare limbs
and sticks took on the appearance of claws reaching out---
hoping to pluck him from the truck! The same miserable
fog that caused him to miss his turn-off at the ranch, now
once again drifted through the dead trees toward him and
surrounded the truck---which, he noted, was beginning to
run hot! The higher up he drove, the more he wondered
about a local mountain of such height on the eastern side of
the highway! HELL! He wished he knew where he was
and which direction he was traveling---he felt LOST---but
how could he BE lost, he wasn't THAT many miles from
the ranch!!? Obviously, the idiot behind him wasn't going
to quit---sooner or later, he'd face another shoot out! With
much regret, he thought of the 'hunting guns' the old man
had made him put on top of the false-bottomed box back in
the camper! And now because they weren't in the cab,
there'd be no chance to get hold of them! Not with 'Elliot
Ness' back there on his tail!

Without warning, the trail turned into a narrow path---
heedlessly Mac forced the truck on---then almost crashed
into some large rocks that came out of nowhere and cut off
even the pathway! This was it!! The end of the road!!
Quickly, he opened the door, letting the truck lunge
forward into the rocks then stall out! All in one motion, he
grabbed up both pistols, bailed out and took a few shots at
the vehicle that was halting about 70 feet behind him! He

dropped to the ground, rolled through dead briars and undergrowth then headed for some trees---he could hear someone running after him---it sounded like only one---but he couldn't tell for sure! However this wasn't the time to worry about that! He needed to 'double-back' undetected--- he had to get away—he MUST!

Retreating from the truck headlights---he stopped for a moment, leaned against the dark side of a tree, trying to adjust his eyes to the night! If only one of the agents would be dumb enough to run between him and the lights---then he'd blast him! Mac stumbled further away---a sudden loud 'thump' sounded off to his left sending more adrenaline spraying through his body! Out of fear, he took two blind shots to the left!

Blundering forward, he continued about 200 more feet! Approaching what appeared to be a flat open area---he slowed---sure enough, above him was the night sky! Halting momentarily, he listened! Above his own racing heart and panting breath, he could hear them coming behind him---on both sides?! Now it sounded like at least five men tearing through the underbrush! When did one turn into five??! He cursed, fired off three more shots behind him then ran toward the opening! Once there, he heard a low menacing growl off to his right side---DAMN! Did he have to fight animals as well?! Hell, why weren't they off in their grubby holes---asleep?!

Mac squatted as a Lakota Moon, dulled by some atmospheric phenomenon, shown dimly around him. Attempting to catch his breath, he took stock of the area as best he could---suddenly the awful growl came again---only louder---more terrifyingly guttural this time---what if it was a mountain lion!!? At the same moment, a trampling and snapping resounded from undergrowth back where he'd just been---the noise grew to deafening proportions!! Rushing to the far side of the opening---he fell to the ground and rolled while firing several shots in the direction of his 'pursuers'!

As he lay waiting and listening, his heart beat so loud that he could hear nothing else---then he realized that was because all of a sudden, a total silence had descended! That damnable mist had followed---here it was all around him---thickening, forming strange blobs!! Where had it come from??! All day there'd been NO fog nor mist---no sign of any---until he was almost ready to turn into his own driveway!! Even then, he'd immediately come right out of it again! Yet from nowhere it'd arrived here at the clearing like a damned zombie---slowly but surely dogging his trail---all around, everywhere it was dropping down---swirling, rolling!

Then, faraway---off in the distance---his ears picked up a new sound---faint but identifiable groans, moanings, wailings---and what almost sounded like a kind of howling---whether it came from a tormented human or animal, he couldn't tell! An odd feeling now washed rapidly over and through each cell of his body---a sort of disoriented anxiety, his head wasn't 'working right'---he was certain some imminent complete disaster was just ahead! His sanity was slipping---it had to be his nerves---the long drive, his father's usual rejection of him, shooting the two feds! He'd gone through too much---whatever he was experiencing right now---it had to be some sort of horrifying delayed reaction---it'd go away! It HAD to 'go away'---else he'd lose his mind!! The faint sounds of agonized 'beings' became clearer, louder---they, whatever and whoever 'they' were, were coming closer! His heart raced---it's pounding beat became irregular---sweat poured off his cold, clammy flesh---he longed to tear the clothing from his body---he

was burning up---freezing at the same time! He felt bound--
--tied down!!!

"DEAR GOD!! WHAT NOW!"---still feeling 'bound', he
let loose a string of swear words---the loathsome fog was
now all but upon him---it pressed, pinning him down---and-
--OH HELL!! Those unidentifiable growls had begun
again!! Whatever THAT was, how close was IT?! Was this
some psychological game---had the FBI already surrounded
him and hidden by the mist---were they within arms' reach-
--would all of them suddenly grab him at once?? He'd been
afraid when he shot the agents---now his plain self-survival
'fear' had turned into something new---emotions like
nothing he'd ever experienced washed over him in nauseous
waves! Those inhuman noises, that infernal fog, the sounds
of being chased---followed suddenly by this unexpected
silence---all of it tore at his mind---clawing, ripping,
shredding at what was left of his sanity!! Water poured off
him as his breath grew more and more shallow! He was
certain his heart would tear into bits at any moment now!!
In fact, he was fighting to get oxygen---his lungs felt
paralyzed, he could barely breathe out---he felt needles
sticking into his flesh!!!

Something was going on---it was happening all around him!
But none of it was 'natural'!! It was this freaking location,
this damned mountain---WHERE WAS THIS PLACE??!
After turning off the highway, nothing had been quite real!
In less than two hours, his life had turned into a nightmare
of unprecedented proportions!

For one short moment, he thought he saw hell opening it's
gates---while souls of the wicked dead poured out---many
of them drifting toward him there in the mist---wailing,
screeching---it was residents of hell making those god-
awful crying noises that rang in his ears! Mac scrambled

away on the ground and taking refuge behind a large rock, he cowered there flattening himself against the hard cold stone! Perspiration literally ran off his face---had he somehow driven off into another 'world'---into hades, itself? He'd heard about things like that happening to people---but he'd never BELIEVED it! Those devilish ghouls---were they coming to drag him to Hades---and him still alive!? He wasn't THAT evil!! NO!! NO, NO!! "Abaddon!"---Mac's memory clicked feverishly---"It was HIM---'the destroyer'---HE'D sent the mist---he'd sent 'THEM'!! O God Almighty!! Perhaps they'd already taken the agents as well because nothing around him seemed human nor of this world!" Above his complete mental confusion and clamor, Mac's ears now began to pick up the sound of a single human voice---loud, verbose---it was his father ranting his interpretation of the Bible---"...an' th' angel opened up th' pit of hell---an' demon-locusts poured out---black like smoke!! Thet's yer niggers!! Revelation Chapter Nine!! Remember it, boy!" The old man had been right!! Surely they were blacker than before death and now they were coming for him---they'd chain him and drag him bodily back to hell!

He could fight what he 'understood'---but his tormented brain couldn't cram this night into any experiential catagory---not one moment of it! From earliest memory, he'd chosen to be a 'loner'---but never before had he FELT so alone---and utterly abandoned! Among the entirety of humanity---he'd become a castaway---rejected by all beings in all realms—physical, human or otherwise! The earth had vomited him out---now it was opening up again to swallow him into HELL!!!

Suddenly Mac seemed to lose his last shred of control---the sly cunning that for decades had lived inside his own soulish flesh left him----he stood, mindlessly screaming

obscenities and threats then began shooting wildly in all
directions---until there were no bullets left! Click---snap----
click, snap, click---click---then from Mac's chest came one
single howl of human desperation---forlorn---hopeless,
filled with blackest despair.

Joseph heard the metallic snapping---the moment had
arrived! While Mac had been having his 'insane moment'--
-Joseph was removing his jacket and shirt, he laid them
aside, removed his 'disguise' then stuffed it into a shirt
pocket. Reaching inside one of his jacket pockets, he pulled
out a smallish flat metal container with several
compartments. There with the Lakota Moon shining down,
he painted his face, arms and bare chest with a specially
mixed phospherescent war-paint used for pow-wows and
ceremonial events. Finally, he wiped his hands on his
discarded shirt, loosed his hair and shook it! Laying the
9 mm. down on his clothing, he stood and walked into the
clearing---his mountain-top---his and God's! His feet
crunched across cold, hard black embers left over from
countless bonfires he'd lit during his lifetime---but
especially when he'd prayed and grieved over Lizbeth---and
Mac's treatment of her.

The same mist that hemmed Mac into his mental abyss
began to clear slightly, making a path for Joseph to walk as
he approached his now helpless enemy! The paint on his
face and body glowed eerily in the night light as Hawk
called out to Mac---"McDougal!! STAND UP!! Stand, turn
around toward me---and face me!!" Mac cursed at him and
spat---"GO! GO! GET AWAY FROM ME!!! Who and
WHAT the HELL are you!!?" Joseph approached further---
"I represent those screams you've been hearing---I'm
nothing more than a manifestation of your own demons!
Your evil has caught up with you---tonight, it is coming
forth, materializing for your physical eyes to see and your

ears to hear! Know this---you're at the end of the line, your sins have found you out---we've come for you, McDougal! You'll NEVER get away from us! You are only one and we are MANY. Stand---stand and look for yourself!"

With his eyes tightly closed, Mac pulled himself up and lay over the rock---waving his empty pistols about and screaming---"NO! NEVER! I'LL NOT GO WITH YOU! YOU'RE TAKING ME NO PLACE---YOU UNDERSTAND? I'LL KILL YOU!" Joseph said nothing simply took two more steps---Mac forced himself to open his eyes, then hissed in a shaky, hoarse voice---"You painted bastard, whoever or whatever you are---if you wanta keep on living---you better back your ass off!! I swear I'll shoot you DOWN! RIGHT NOW!" His chest burned and ached---his breath came in ragged, irregular gasps---but upon seeing what at least 'looked' somewhat human, some of the fight came back into Mac! His tongue being the first member experiencing revival!

"No."---Joseph said in a low confident tone---"You won't shoot me---don't you know that no bullet can kill me?! Try it! Pull the trigger!" Joseph approached further---Mac then stood, frantically clicking the empty chambers! "You're out of ammo, hero! You're a BIG man when it's women you mistreat, abuse and beat up---you're BIG when you got fire power!! But I'm no woman!"---Joseph tapped his glowing chest with one hand—"...And you got no fire power! So, it's finally come down to us---you and me! Now, let us make an end of it! Come on---COME ON! TRY AND TAKE ME!!"

Hawk began to circle Mac, goading him and motioning him with his hands, verbally daring Mac to come after him--- "SHOW ME YOUR BEST, YOU SCOTS' COWARD!! WHY YOU'RE NOTHING BUT A CRAVEN

MURDERER!! A MERE WIFE-BEATER! KKK
BIGGOT!! COME ON---GET ME! SHOW ME
SOMETHING, YOU HOODED MAGGOT!! BURN ONE
OF YOUR CROSSES---YOU CHRIST-HATER!!"

Mac stared at the glowing paint on the one who circled him,
encroaching closer---calling him names---daring him to
fight! "DAMNED INDIAN!"---he screeched---"You're
nothing but a miserable REDSKIN!! YOU'VE TRICKED
ME WITH YOUR INDIAN MAGIC!! WELL! SINCE
THERE'S NO REAL GHOSTS AND THIS ISN'T HELL--
-LET'S DO IT! C'MON---I'LL CUT YOUR GUTS OUT
RIGHT HERE!" Mac tossed the empty guns and patted his
pant's pocket---feeling for his knife!

"DON'T TRY IT, man!!"---Hawk snapped---"I'll take any
knife you got and ram it down your throat or up your
backside then I'll hang you on a meat-hook by your rear
end!! C'MON!!! CUT THE CHATTER---OR YOU
WANT ME TO START IT? THAT WHAT YOU
WANT?? I'm up to the challenge!! Want me to hit you
first, Macky??"

"I GOT NO GRIPE WITH YOU, INDIAN! YOU FBI??!
WHAT YOU DOIN' HERE, ANYWAY?? Don't you
know these woods are full of agents---and while they're
after ME---you could get YOURS as well!! One of their
stray bullets might get lucky and we'd have another 'good
Indian'---meaning a DEAD INDIAN!"

By then Hawk was close enough, like a flash---he reached
out with one hand and pushed at Mac---Mac stumbled
backward slightly then countered---but he was too slow, in
one micro-moment, Hawk had slapped his face hard—once
on each side---then pushed him again! Mac took a couple
of swings trying to land a punch---but Hawk easily side-

stepped his blows allowing Mac to stumble forward and fall sideways! Hawk reached toward the gravel, jerked Mac up by the collar then slammed him back to the ground and walked a circle around the fallen bully---waiting for him to recover!

Mac felt the breath rush out of him---this red-skin was beating him---he couldn't have that! His mind had returned---he was functioning---he had to get away---he drew his knees up to his chest, fighting to get air in his lungs! He had to LIVE---he had a mission! He must kill Lizbeth and those two Indians, get the bullet out of the wall, then take the guns out of his barn and go back to his old man! He didn't know where he'd lost the chrome .38---but he'd almost bet nobody had found it---nor ever would! He'd show ex-grand dragon, the old fool---and when he showed him he COULD do something 'right'---then he'd erase him off the face of the earth! Memories of belittlement and humiliations heaped on him by his father fueled Mac's rage afresh! He rolled across the ground then pushed himself up---the Indian didn't seem to be in a hurry---he'd make this Red-Skin, WHOEVER the hell he was---he'd make him sorry he'd interfered in things he knew nothing about!! He'd picked the 'wrong night' to mess with a McDougal!!

With his switchblade now in hand, Mac snapped it open and ran at the eerily glowing man! The Indian met him---lifted him up with his powerful hands, then slammed him back to the earth! Once again Mac found himself thrashing around on the stones and gravel---but held on to his knife.

Watching his enemy struggling to get to his feet---Hawk realized this was far from an even match---he almost felt sorry for this unreasonable, angry and wicked man! With his years of training, he could end McDougal's life at any

moment he chose and knew it! At once, Hawk understood
something! His 'journey' over the past several months was
strickingly clear---this 'enemy' struggling on the ground at
his feet had never BEEN a 'man'—only a pitiful shell---a
'something' that had in some way come to be without a
heart or a soul! And only God knew what or who had
brought him to such a sorry state. Why, he'd never known
what it was to feel love, pity or compassion for another
human being---likely he'd never felt close to anyone! No
living soul had ever 'touched' Mac---he pushed everyone
away with his incurable malignant hatred! Observing his
'enemy' writhing on the ground at his feet, Joseph
Winterhawk knew he no longer wanted revenge---no matter
what this individual had done---Hawk simply didn't want
to be the one to judge him---he'd not been sent to judge---
only to love.

Slowly, he walked back and forth waiting for Mac to get to
his knees---once on his feet, Mac then began backing in a
circle, looking for a chance to put his knife into Hawk's
body! Hawk watched him warily---ready to counter any
move on Mac's part! The move came suddenly----in the
misty moonlight, the blade made an almost inaudible
'swoosh' as it flashed close to Hawk, who in one fluid
motion, simply flung his arms upward, arched his
midsection back, jumped, whirled aside and away from the
long, super-sharp switch-blade!

In that same moment, the mist simply evaporated----it was
as though it had never been there at all. Mac continued
walking backwards in a circle, all the while turning his
head, keeping his eyes riveted on Hawk---then with a quick
intake of breath, Hawk saw how close Mac was to oblivion!
"McDOUGAL!!"---he shouted--"STOP GOING
BACKWARDS!! COME BACK THIS WAY! YOU'RE
ALMOST AT THE EDGE OF A CLIFF! I'll back away

from you---!" Putting out both hands in a kind of calming gesture as he stepped backward, he stepped backward lowering his voice to a quiet, calm tone---"See? I'm stepping away from you---come toward me before you fall. Please!!"

Mac's answer was high-pitched laughter laced with lunacy---flushed with what he considered a vicious triumph over 'the cowardliness' of this Indian, he watched Hawk backing away from his knife! "YOU RUNNING AWAY, YOU 'YELLOW-BELLY' GREAT GRAND-SON OF A SCALPING MURDERER?! YOU BEGGING ME?! BIG-TALKING, PAINTED-UP, THIEVIN' HEATHEN---YOU AFRAID OF MY KNIFE?! Now, now! Mustn't go away so soon, we're only getting acquainted!"---Mac chuckled as he taunted Hawk in a low hiss---"Didn't you just say it was 'you and me' and we should 'make an end of it'? What'd you mean by that anyway?! 'WE' haven't had any dealings before! Your voice sounds a little familiar---but I've never seen you!" Mac's feet paused---he ceased backing up— "However since you DO seem to have a problem with me--- guess what! I got THE answer to that problem---TONTO!"

Spreading his feet apart, he gripped the open knife, expertly waggling it----then pointing it out toward Hawk! He began slightly swaying from side to side, tossing the knife from one hand to the other---all of a sudden it came to him!! After using the name 'Tonto'---Mac remembered why this painted beggar was familiar---he was none other than that military up-start---Captain Joseph Winterhawk!! 'Dear' doctor's friend! What WAS this!!? A set-up? Was that old bastard O'Barr out there thrashing the brush with his Indian friend?? Were they after him because of O'Barr's liking for Lizbeth?

"DON'T BE A FOOL, McDOUGAL!!"---Hawk shouted---
"GET YOUR BUTT AWAY FROM THE CLIFF!" Putting
his weight on one foot and going down on the other knee---
Joseph held out a hand---a gesture of help to his enemy---
Mac cursed---"I'LL BE A S.O.B.! You ARE Winterhawk!
YOU FBI as well as RANGER??! Well, WHATEVER you
are---YOU'LL SOON BE DEAD MEAT!" Never blinking
an eye, he snarled angrily---"And O'Barr as well---IF he's
out there with you!! You two interfering pieces of dog-
dook---you'll never live to see another sunrise!! NEITHER
OF YOU!" He then stamped one foot forward then quickly
back while beginning a full-powered side-slicing motion
with his knife! In one flashing move, Hawk jerked aside---
went down balancing himself on the palms of his hands and
immediately bounced back to his feet, making ready for
another defensive move---but the offensive never came!

It happened so suddenly---one minute Mac was confidently
cursing both Hawk and Doc as he prepared to move his
knife into another slicing jab---but when he swung forward
with all his might, he missed his target and once into the
turning motion, couldn't stop the momentum! Being only
two steps from the cliff's edge---he miscalculated---
stumbled---grabbed at empty space---then went over the
edge! His loud, terrified screams filled the cold night air---
then grew fainter as he fell far below toward a large
formation of sharp, pointed stones! Hawk ran to the cliff's
edge but could barely make out the form as it hit the rocks,
bouncing like a rag-doll from one level of stone to another--
-sickened, Hawk sank to the ground on his knees! "I tried
to TELL you!!"---he whispered to the now silent night
around him---then louder he called out---"I TRIED TO
HELP YOU! WHY didn't you listen!? Did you EVER
listen to anyone in your whole life, Mac?" Bowing his
head, crossing his hands over his chest, he closed his eyes
and prayed, "Oh, God---God. Please have mercy on his

soul---in spite of it all." Joseph knelt silently for several minutes then said—"I'll have a mass said for you---for that part of you so filled with hate---and may you at least make it to the lower levels of purgatory."

Joseph felt someone lay a shirt over his shoulders then came a hand on his tangled hair---opening his eyes, he finally looked upward--- "I didn't kill him, Doc. I---truly tried to help him, I--I begged him to stop---but he wouldn't listen! He just kept on and on---like he was 'high' on something--- until he fell off the cliff!" "I know, Joseph."---Doc confirmed quietly---"I've been up here all along---I saw an' heard th' whole thing."

Doc offered a hand and pulled---Joseph stood, sighing---"I never thought it'd turn out quite this way. This afternoon, while you were catching some 'ZZ's---I made a bargain with God. I promised Him if He'd just let me know in some way that Mac wouldn't get off scot-free then come back and hurt the people I love---then He could take care of Mac, Himself. That whatever was meant to be---would, in some miraculous way, go on to happen!" Peering over the edge of the cliff, Doc spoke almost reverently---"Looks like He might've done just that, m'friend."

After a few minutes, Joseph looked at Doc and quietly dressed-him-down---"Thought I told YOU to STAY in the van. Just what're you doing way up here?" "An' where'd YOU be IF I HAD stayed in th' van? Exactly, WHO you think helped stir up all that racket in th' bushes---makin' Mac think he was surrounded?" Wearily, Joseph exhaled--- "O.K, man. I just can't argue with you right now." He felt empty---no 'high' from the demise of a man he thought he'd hated and had taken a vow to make certain the man paid for his evil. Making an empty gesture with one hand, Hawk asked---"So, is it possible he survived the fall, Doc? Do I need to go down, have a look---see if he's still alive, if we can help him?" The older man looked at the Sioux---"No one could survive that, Hawk, you know better---too much trauma, he's deader than th' stones he's lyin' on. Here, take this flashlight, let's go over th' area where you two tussled---just in case you dropped somethin'. Lucky for us, th' whole place is practically a mass of rocks---no footprints t'speak of, no tire tracks t'worry over!" He looked around in the dark then stated---"Th' whole mountain must be nothing but one huge stone!" Joseph nodded, replying--- "As they say, 'I'm beholden for all your help, Doc'. Not only tonight but---for everything since the day we met---and I tried to bite you for giving me that smallpox vaccination." Again, Doc patted Joseph Winterhawk's muscular back--- "All right! Come alive, Capt. Winterhawk---and let's get this area 'policed'!"

When they were sure the area was 'clean', Hawk headed toward his clothing and the paint---Doc followed. The two exchanged no words as they made their way back to the van, once there, O'Barr asked the pertinent question on his mind---"Y'don't think Mac got any of your war-paint on his hands, clothing or body?" Hawk took a towel and wiped at his hair, face, ears, neck, chest, arms and hands before replying---"No. Each time we made contact, I made sure I used my hands, legs or feet. He doesn't have any 'paint' on him." "Why'd you put that stuff all over you, anyway?"-- Doc asked, not sure if he'd get an answer or not. "Well. Since the day I met McDougal, I felt he was evil, an enemy---he hated Indians, along with most everyone else---and being who and what I am, I figured I might as well add a bit of theatrics. What do you think, Doc, was it effective?" He looked back toward the cliff—"Or did I over-do it?"

Doc shrugged---"Dunno. But somethin' drove him past his usual craziness. Who knows, maybe it WAS your war-

paint---you looked scary as hell t'me an' I knew who you
WERE! Tell me..."---Doc tugged at his ear---"...did you,
er, hear anything back there---before you confronted Mac?"
"Hear anything---like what?"---Hawk had already put his
shirt back on, shrugged into his jacket and was plundering
about in the rear of the van putting everything in it's proper
place. "You know damned well what I mean! I could've
sworn when that fog came down that I heard---well, some---
uh,"---he rubbed at the corner of his mouth---"...a sorta
wailin'---or somethin'. Far away, almost like echoes." "I
told you there was a burial ground back there...,"---Joseph
grinned to himself in the dark---"...and you made fun of
me! Remember?" "Hell!"---Doc expostulated---"I spent 15
minutes tellin' them ghosts I was SORRY f'sayin' what I
did! I even heard an unusual growlin' noise---never heard
no animal make a sound like that b'fore! Scary as th' very
dickens, too! Now answer me---DID you hear what I did?"

"Well now,"---Joseph considered---"...maybe I did---then
again---maybe I didn't! You ready to see if we can get
outta here---probably wear out the reverse finding a place to
turn around. Tell you what, give me the flash-light and I'll
walk---you back up the van behind me---and DON'T back
over me!" "There're times when you make me SO
FRUSTRATED!"---Doc snapped then mumbled---
"Miserable Sioux!" "Miserable Irishman!"---Joseph
retorted and began walking away with his flashlight looking
for a place that wouldn't leave any noticeable clues when
they turned around and drove away.

Later, upon reaching the highway---a closed metal gate
blocked their way off the reservation land!! Doc sat and
gaped at it---"Where the dickens did THAT thing come
from?!" Even Hawk's mouth hung ajar---as he answered a
question with a question because he didn't know the
answers himself---"What 'thing'?" O'Barr blinked at the

Indian---"You don't mean t'tell me you don't SEE that damned GATE!!" "Yeah. I see the gate. What about it?"---the Sioux commented matter-of-factly. Totally exasperated, Doc flung open the van door and determinedly stamped off toward the gate---upon close examination, he saw it was neatly fastened with a chain---it wasn't bent, hadn't been knocked off the hinges or anything---in fact, it was in perfect condition! After standing there 'bumfuzzled' for several minutes---he felt Joseph walk up behind him--- "All right, Indian!"---he barked and gestured toward the gate---"Where'd the gate come from----you know as well as I do that it wasn't even HERE when Mac slid off the highway an' blasted through here like a house afire! Talk t'me!! I'm stiff---I'm worn-out an' I've had about enough of this 'crap'----this---this supernatural tomfoolery or whatever it is!" Hawk slid on his leather gloves and opened the snap---pushed the gate open then motioned for Doc to drive through.

Once back on the highway and headed toward Doc's truck, Hawk looked over at his mentor---"Doc, believe me, please! Like it's not that I don't want to TELL you---I just don't got no answer for you, man. Usually there IS a gate---but like you said---it clearly wasn't there when Mac went through--- otherwise we'd have not only SEEN him hit it but we'd have heard it, too---why, there'd be pieces of it scattered all over a 100 ft. diameter. Could we just chalk this one up to---to destiny, even helpful ancestors or something?" "For real?"---Doc stared at him. Hawk exhaled and nodded seriously---"For real, man. For real."

After a goodly silence had passed, the physician asked--- "So, what's next, Hawk? I mean---all that's left now is for some law enforcement agency t'search Mac's barn an' find th' guns! Wonder when his—er, 'remains' will be found--- do y'think his parents will make a big 'bru-ha-ha' over his death? Y'know I feel like th' Klan used Mac hidin' them guns---an' things bein' th' way they are right now---they'll likely want as little trouble as possible." Hawk nodded--- "Probably right, Doc. But first things on my agenda are the following: I'm going to wash this van down---it's really not this blurry blue and white, y'know---it's a shiny cream color. Next I want a long, hot shower, some sleep then tomorrow I'll clean the inside of the van. After that, I'll take it to the man who loaned it to me and pay him for a new paint job where the gravel pocked it---as well as any other damage. Finally, I'll drive my own 4-wheel drive back home---and sleep for an entire week!"

"You left something out."---Doc stated. "What?"---Joseph looked at him. "Rather you left someONE out---Lizbeth! You comin' t'see her at my house? Least until this thing gets straightened out by th' law, you know you can't be seen with her!" At the mention of her name, Joseph's countenance changed---he smiled over at Doc---"Yeah. If you'd invite me over---I think I just might---kinda accept. Think Ida would---get suspicious?" "Maybe if you're as clever as you THINK you are, she won't figure it out!! Until it's too late!"---Doc laughed aloud knowing Ida probably already HAD it 'figured out'---she just hadn't let HIM in on her 'secret'! How very LITTLE she knew about the depth of his own involvement in this whole thing---from the very beginning! And he wasn't sure he'd EVER tell her----after all, a man needed one or two secrets for taking to his grave!

Chapter Fifty-Seven

Doc had been right about '...in two weeks, everything would be behind them'. Things were indeed falling rapidly into place. After he arrived back home, Ida told him that

Logan had been calling all day---she then demanded to
know why he and Hawk stayed away so late---that she'd
almost worried herself to death thinking they'd had an
accident. He attempted to soothe her by relating tales of
large bucks with huge antlers, of having to replace a burned
spark-plug wire, change one flat tire---finally to really seal
his case---he did the unthinkable, he 'admitted to getting
lost'! And 'THAT was the REAL reason they were so
late'! Silently, he hoped his 'clincher' would work on Ida's
overly-intelligent, razor sharp, rarely-foiled female mind!

She seemed mollified but verbally chastised him---"You
should've called me on that radio, Dr. O'Barr---how could
you allow Lizbeth and me to worry ourselves half to
death!!? How very thoughtless of you---and Joseph! I can't
believe the two of you could 'get lost'---after hunting
around here all these YEARS!? And HIM a Sioux!!" Her
eyes were still flashing so he hastened with further
explanation---"Oh, y'see, we took Joseph's vehicle so I
couldn't call you! We drove over 50 miles away from here,
Hon, but"---he managed a sheepish grin---"...we got lost
instead. Now, Ida, promise me you won't TELL anybody!!
A man'd rather DIE than let it be known he got LOST while
huntin'! Why, if you tell any of these old hens around
here—it'll get t'the barber-shop an' I'll never live it down!"
He threw up his hands dramatically---"We may as well
move away!" "Dr. O'Barr!"---she retorted---"You know I
never tell 'family-secrets'!!" "All right! That's all I ask!
Now, I'll call Logan and see what bee is in HIS bonnet. I
hope he doesn't keep me for hours, it'll soon be 12:30 a.m.-
--I'm dyin' for a shower---an' maybe a good hot egg or
two?" He cajoled, giving her his best 'pleading'
expression---"Please? I'm hungry enough t'fall over!"
Thinking of one last 'clincher'---he stated, hand over heart--
-"And I promise not t' go hunting for th' rest of th' season!"
She rolled her eyes---"Get on with it then! I'll scramble

your eggs, y' blarnified old Irishman! But best you
remember that promise!"

Logan was in a fair froth when Doc called, waking him at
his office---"WHERE TH' BLAZES YOU BEEN ALL
DAY AND NIGHT??!! I've called a dozen times---man, I
have NEWS for you and Mrs. McDougal!" He began
relating the tale of how the FBI raided Mac's father's home
just at daybreak---how the old man was arrested and being
held along with a dozen or so other Klansmen.

"An' Mac?"---Doc inquired---"Did they get him too---I
hope?" "Heck NO! I clean forgot about him! Now here's
a circus for you---can you believe that low-down so-and-so
shot TWO FBI agents??!" "You don't SAY!"---Doc
'breathed' into the phone—"Where? At his Dad's place?"
"You kiddin'??"---Logan chirped---"He'd left there earlier--
-the raid missed him completely---BUT get THIS!! He
went straight to that Rita's house and you know, O'Barr, the
stake-out almost had him! I mean, he was IN THEIR
HANDS---but somehow, that toad managed to shoot TWO
of them and got CLEAN AWAY!!!" "OH MY LORD!"---
Doc echoed---"LOGAN! You better send some men over
here t'protect Mrs. McDougal! He'll come after her f'sure!
Should we pack her up t'leave town---again?" "Right now,
I can't spare any men---the feds have every lawman within
a 500 mile radius out looking for McDougal! But.,"---the
sheriff replied thoughtfully—"I could swear you in as a
temporary deputy---think you could keep her safe? It'll
give you permission---if McDougal shows up---you just
blow him in half with your shot-gun! Don't give that
slippery murdering coward a chance to hurt any of you! I'll
come right over and swear you in---okay?" "Sure, come
ahead, use the back door---I'm in the kitchen."---Doc
answered then hung up, thinking---"If only you knew
Mac'll never harm ANYONE---not ever again."

***

Hawk drove the van into a shallow stream just off the highway, there in the cold running water, he diligently washed down the van. But with only the setting Lakota Moon for his light, he couldn't tell the real damage done to the paint job but it didn't matter---he'd gladly pay for all repairs needed. Changing the plates back to the originals, he wiped down the .9 mm., put it in the glove compartment and locked it up---grateful he'd never had to use it! Once home, he backed the vehicle into his storage building then made certain all was safely locked away the night.

Inside the house, it seemed everyone slept undisturbed. After showering, Joseph turned the washing machine on, tossed in the paint smeared towel as well as the one he'd used for washing the van---plus his special sneakers with no tread on the soles, all clothing he'd worn that day, from the skin out---head to toe. After adding some soap, he briefly leaned against the wall, took several deep breaths, allowing himself to go limp as he listened to the machine's agitator begin making it's muffled 'thump-thump' sound.

Later after replacing the paint-box in Mary's pantry, he sat down at the table, resting his head in his hands. And just as after a military operation---once the tension, danger and action was over---it seemed the weight from a whole mission---from beginning to end, suddenly sat down upon every soldier who'd made it safely through! Once their 'ride' had picked them up from the operation and their minds were somewhat numb with relief, they'd huddle silently together, usually on the floor of a 'Huey', their ears filled with the deafening engine's roar and the loud popping-banging rotor-blades. From that point on until they vacated the chopper, it was the job of the rescue gun-ship's

355

pilot and the gunners to protect them! So, with the 'fire-power' of their rockets and those brave gunners riding shot-gun, sometimes sitting in the chopper doorway, their feet braced on the skids---everyone would soon be 'home-free'---they hoped---they prayed---all of them.

And now that Lizbeth's safety was assured, he realized how bone-tired and drained he truly felt---the word 'burn-out' didn't really do justice to his weariness. Sitting there at his mother's kitchen table, his head in his hands---he wondered at the quietness---that there was no popping rotor-blades, no loud rapid-chatter repeat of chopper guns or the whizzing blast of rockets being fired!

Pressing his fingers against two tired burning eyelids---he realized that through the medium of 'sound', his thoughts were temporarily slipping back to other memories---a sure sign of sleep deprivation. It was the washer agitator that had for a moment, taken him back. He sighed then folded his arms on the table and lay his head down. Much as he'd despised McDougal and all he stood for---still, earlier this evening when it was 'all over' for the man---he felt some regret that his demise had come in so gruesome a manner. Now, all he could do was wait until the body was discovered, let the law take it's course and fervently hope that one day soon---he and Lizbeth could 'find their place'---along with some well deserved peace---in a more permanent life!

Mary stood silently in the kitchen doorway looking at her handsome son---he was suffering some kind of trouble but she didn't know what. Unless it was---could it be as had come to her mind during an occasional moment---could it possibly be---Miss Lizbeth?? Although he'd given no outward sign of affection for her before they took their afternoon walk on Thanksgiving---even that being at her own suggestion! Still, she couldn't forget how during their lunch, he never took his eyes off Mrs. McDougal. She had to know---and felt sure if she asked---he'd tell her the truth. He was a good boy.

Walking over to him, she put a hand on his shoulder---he looked up---"Mama! What on earth you doing out of bed at this hour?? Hey, I woke you, didn't I? Sorry Doc and I were so late getting back." She looked down into his eyes---"You have trouble, Son?" "Yeah, sure did. We---well, we went hunting in a place we'd never been---and---we got off on some bad roads!" He apologized again---"I didn't mean to wake you up." "Bad roads not kind of problem I mean. You seem to carry weight of world on big broad shoulders! Tell Mama what is trouble---will understand." She pulled up a chair beside him---urging---"Tell Mama."

He managed a smile for her---"Guess I'll never be able to fool you, huh." She shook her head and remained silent waiting for him to go on. "Okay. For one thing, I'm at loose ends after retirement---at the beginning, I had enough to keep busy for months. Now, everything around here that needed 'fixing' is 'fixed'---but I don't have a job. Mama, I need something to do." He gave her a forced smile---"An Indian can't hunt and fish any more---not like in the old days. Even my little 'business' a few weeks back was temporary. Maybe tomorrow I'll talk to my old army buddy and see if he thinks I could join the reserves---or even return to active duty." "NO!"---she cried---"No active duty!! Promise me you will not do this! Buy own land--- you have money from army years! Or get job on ranch somewhere close by---must be somebody need good, smart man, who works hard---yes?" Rubbing at his burning eyes, he sighed---"We'll see. I can't promise---y'know, Mama, sometimes we just don't have the luxury of choosing."

"You hungry, son? Like to have left-overs? Like when hungry teen-ager?" He nodded---"I'd like that but---you go to bed. You need your rest and I'm certainly no longer a teen-ager, I can warm it up." Mary stood---then without warning, she took Hawk by his 'tailfeathers'---"Son. You love Miss Lizbeth?" Shocked at her question, he turned and stared at his mother---"Mama! Whatever made you say something like that? And out of the clear blue!" "Mama remember being in love---acted like you act now! You thought Miss Lizbeth attractive---Mama not blind---could see THAT much." "Ma!"—he protested---"You only saw us together one day!" "Still,"---Mary spoke wisely--- "...love sometimes comes in one blink of the eye. Maybe your blink-of-the-eye came months ago---first day you saw her! You love her?"

It was by now 1:30 in the morning! He'd been through hell since he'd arrived home from the army! All those months of anguish and uncertainty because of a sudden, unexpected but sure love for a woman married to an evil, abusive man! His love-sick condition only worsened after he'd finally come to believe she loved him as well! He'd prayed, crying out to God to help him find some answers---some peace! God's answer was the flying-vision ---he and he alone--- among humanity---knew Mac could walk! It was God's gift of discernment working with his own skillful instinct which let him know that 'the walker' would actually harm his wife---possibly that very night---or the next! That 'flying-vision' had begun some hasty scheming for keeping Lizbeth safe---yet allowing him to stay hidden from view! Immediately he'd carried out a plan as best he knew ---yet not bend the law too far in the process! The night Mac chose to kill Lizbeth---in order to get evidence needed, he'd been forced to listen to Mac's assault on Lizbeth. Finally, in a circumstance beyond his control, Mac had shot him--- he'd fallen, hearing her screams as he slipped into

blackness! Mac had gotten 'clean-away' or so it seemed
while he, himself, tolerated a short recovery period---and
for propriety's sake---continued to keep away from Lizbeth!
Finally feeling physically up to the task, he'd driven almost
2,000 miles during the last three days and nights, then put
into action his plan to find Mac---catch him---and execute
his own brand of judgement on him! But that, too, had
changed---thanks be to God! It'd been a long, difficult
three days with little sleep or rest---now, it had ended only a
short while ago with Mac's death. He couldn't fight any
more battles with anyone---not tonight---he couldn't pretend
to his mother that he didn't love Lizbeth. Now was as good
a time as any to find out how Mary felt about it!

Scraping back his chair, Hawk stood, turned to her, took her
in his arms and lay his cheek on her hair. "Yes, Mama. I
love Lizbeth. One day I will marry her and we'll have little
red-haired 'Indians'. Now, my mother, be at peace---go
back to bed." Mary hugged her 'always wonderful' son and
asked---"Your choice has been made then?" "Yes, I have
chosen." Mary started back to her room---but stopped at the
doorway and looking back at her son, smiled her gentle
sweet mother's smile---"Your choice is a good one. I
approve." His answer satisfied her. It was as she'd
thought---and in the end, all would turn out for the best.
God and her prayers would make it so.

Chapter Fifty-Eight

Lizbeth knew very little of what had gone on between Doc
and Joseph since Thanksgiving---but she watched her
tongue with Ida---still, she felt the woman knew more than
she let on! Not giving up 'her cover' however, Lizbeth
utilized her 'dumb'---'innocent'---very 'southern belle-ish'
silliness and before long, even Ida wondered if she could've

been imagining what she thought she saw in both Lizbeth and Joseph's eyes on Thanksgiving afternoon---after they returned from a very LONG, extended 'outing'!

Not that she 'minded', really, but interracial relationships were---well, still not generally accepted in 'good society'. However, she considered, Joseph WAS several cuts above the usual white men---and he was a fine, good person---a strong fearless man and would be a good provider. Perhaps he just MIGHT make a good husband for Lizbeth---that was IF she ever got around to divorcing that wretched beast, McDougal!

"Whenever Joseph comes around---I'll keep a close eye on the couple."---Ida mused to herself as she considered a possible 'interesting situation'---"And IF there's 'anything' between them, he WILL come around! THEN I'll know!" Smiling to herself, she thought---"Ida, you may be a mite older---but you still haven't lost your intuition when it comes to signs and symptoms of this thing called 'romance'!!"

Lizbeth hadn't seen 'her love' since that Thanksgiving afternoon but his ring, now on a gold chain, lay hidden beneath her clothing. Warmed by her flesh, it never left her neck, it was a part of him---he was always 'within touch'. She knew that one day they'd be together---no doubts clouded her mind---so much so that she found herself spending time 'planning' some of their future years as a couple! It'd been SO LONG since she'd allowed herself to experience 'hope'---'anticipation'--- most of all, 'love'!

 Salle and Mary had arrived one afternoon in December for a visit. After the four 'filled each other in' on any late breaking 'Mac-news-flashes', they went on to general local happenings. Finally, Ida and Mary began the usual annual subject of how to create their own Christmas decorations and up-date favorite holiday recipes. Soon they exited to the kitchen for further meal planning while Salle and Lizbeth stayed in the living room for some 'girl-talk'!

Lizbeth told Salle how much she'd missed her since coming to stay with the O'Barrs. "Not that they aren't absolutely wondahful people, y'see---but I became so---so fond of you, yoah Mom---an' the rest that I sometimes find m'self wantin' t' borrow Ida's car an' drive out foah a visit. But...,"---she shrugged, looking down at her hands---"..till this situation is a closed book, Ah doubt Ah'll be 'out' very much." Salle fussed over her then exclaimed about how well Lizbeth was looking these days. "You look just like you used to when I first saw you! Your hair's so shiny and pretty again!" Touching the soft shiny red-blonde hair, she went on---"And your skin's all soft and glowing---why, you're even wearing make-up! I would ask WHO's the 'lucky man'---but I think I already know!" Lizbeth blushed scarlet---then Salle pressed a folded piece of paper into her hand---explaining about the song Hawk had written for her.

Lizbeth was elated---she was touched---she wept copiously while Salle gently admonished her! "Now, you stop that! Everything's going to be fine---they'll catch Mac and you can pick up your life again!" Taking a small packet of tissues from her pocket, Salle offered one to Lizbeth--- "Here! Wipe your tears and come over to Ida's awful piano. I'm gonna hum this melody you memorize it then learn to play it so you'll be familiar with the melody and be able to recognize it! Now accordin' to Indian-lore, one fine day---or fine night---you'll never know where or when--- that's part of the romance and mystery of it---you'll hear this very tune being played on a single flute! And it'll be Joseph! Let me see if I can remember the right words describin' this special event. You'll be 'delighted' by his

love-song he's written---just for you alone. Y'see, no one
else will know this tune nor recognize it as a signal between
the two of you!" Lizbeth was overcome---"Oh, Salle!
What a lovely tradition! Ah feel most fortunate---t'have
Hawk---an' you---th' whole family! Not t'leave out Doc
an' Ida! Oh, mah life IS changin'---really changin'---at
last."

After a few quiet moments to 'gather herself together',
Lizbeth turned---looking back toward the kitchen, she then
leaned toward Salle and whispered---"But Ida has a nose
like a bloodhound! Ah d'claire, she just about put two an'
two t'gethah on Thanksgivin'! It's taken me all this time
t'lead her off in a different direction, gettin' her away from
mine an' Hawk's trail!!" Lizbeth grinned then added---
"An' she doesn't give up easy!"

Salle began snickering---"You've turned into a regular
'actress' durin' the past several months, Lizbeth! I swear---
I wouldn't want to pit myself against you, Joseph and Doc!
What a team the three of you turned out to be!" "Shhhh!"---
Lizbeth shushed while shaking her head madly---"Not only
does she have th' nose of a bloodhound---but she has eahs
that heah thru th' wall as well!" Both giggled as they
headed for the piano.

Chapter Fifty-Nine

Christmas crept closer, both Joseph and Doc HOPED Mac's
body would be found not only for a 'decent burial' but so
the case could be stamped 'closed' and Lizbeth could
finally have peace of mind. But before closure could come
for any of them, the remains must be discovered. Neither
Hawk nor Doc could step forward with such news, this must
come from other sources. Then perhaps the seasonal

promise of 'Peace and Good Will' would become the true order of the day.

Two weeks before Christmas, Doc suggested Ida invite Joseph over for supper---afterward the four of them could drive around in Ida's car, taking in the Christmas lights. Being 'ready' for his suggestion of bringing Lizbeth and Joseph together, she exclaimed---"A fine idea! You come up with a tree and haul out that mountain of decorations--- I'm sure you can talk Lizbeth into helping you with the decorating while I cook for our guests! I think I'll invite not only Joseph, but his mother and the whole family over for a little 'do'!"

Doc stared at her---"B-but.."---he stammered, quite unprepared for this most unusual generous offer---"…w-we can't all get into your car!" She turned, staring him down--- "Why, Dr. O'Barr, how silly you are! OF COURSE they can't all get into my car---but we could arrange something! Joseph has a nice vehicle that would haul several people! By your expression, one would think you didn't want the WHOLE Winterhawk tribe visiting us at once! I would've thought you'd jump at the chance to have all seven over for a Christmas romp through the house! You can buy gifts, then dress up and play Santa!" Doc looked around---casting his eyes sideways toward Ida---the woman always seemed to have an upper hand! "Well."---he swallowed---"That's exactly what it would be, y'know---a 'romp'!" Picking up steam, he plowed on to discourage her odd suggestion--- "You remember how 'exuberant' Dottie's two are---they were 'wound-up' at Thanksgiving---just think how they'll be this close t'Christmas! Why!"---he blustered---"They'd tear your neat, lovely, well-ordered home t'shreds!! They might even run into a table or cabinet an' break some of your treasured antiques!! They---." She cut him off---"All right, as you wish, we'll invite only Joseph---maybe as a dinner partner for Lizbeth? A foursome?" She arched her eyebrows at him---he began shifting his weight from one foot to the other, shrugged a shoulder, stretched his head awkwardly from one side to the other. "Something wrong with your neck, Doctor? All of a sudden, here you are acting like a wet blanket." Clearing his throat, he began--- "Ida. You forget Lizbeth's a---a married lady! If you can call th' likes of McDougal a 'husband'!"

"Goodness, I haven't forgotten that, dear! But, after all, Mac may never show his face to his wife again---not with the countless crimes he's piled up all hanging over his head! He's probably in South America by now anyway. And Lizbeth, the poor dear, is a lady of quality---she needs a gentleman 'partner' around on special occasions. That way she won't feel like an old maid aunt at the table or on the dance floor." He wondered what she meant by THAT--- who mentioned dancing?? They hadn't been dancing in AGES! Sometimes he wondered if ANYONE of their generation danced anymore.

He didn't know how to reply---Ida stirred the contents of a pot on the stove then blandly commented---"You might suggest that she divorce Mac, y'know. She'd listen to you---I'm certain she leans on you as a father-figure." "Th' idea HAD crossed my mind, Ida!"---he huffed---"But I figured--- well, I oughta keep m'nose out of her business." He came a step closer to her---"You really think I should speak t'her about a divorce?" Ida slapped the lid firmly down on the pot---"Of course I do. Neither she nor Joseph are getting any younger, you know! And he isn't a BAD catch, even though they're not of the same race---he IS a decent sort, well mannered, quite handsome! And.."---Ida turned to her husband, tapped her fingers lightly up his arm, smiling coyly---"...he needs someone! We know them both, so who, better then you and I---could play 'cupid' so well!?"

364

Doc stood astounded---speechless! His sometimes overly-clever wife never ceased to amaze him! Since it began between Hawk and Lizbeth, he'd have bet his life Ida would respond negatively---in fact, his idea had been that 'negative' would be the 'good' part of her reaction! He was certain she'd be more than 'difficult' about an inter-racial couple!! Sighing, he guessed this was the way it was supposed to be---a clever woman kept a man guessing---all their married life. NO matter how long a man thought he knew a woman---he'd never REALLY know her! They were so apt to change their mind---so often---and worse yet, on the spur of the moment---and always just when a man thought he had one figured out! Well, he knew he couldn't hang around in the kitchen as she might change her mind! He practically raced from the room to call Joseph and 'invite him over'!!

***

A week and a half before Christmas holiday vacation began, Logan was in his office sifting through papers when suddenly his band radio came to life, squealing out his call-letters. He answered and as the voice on the other end squawked away---his facial expression changed from one of general nothingness to surprise and total interest! Early that morning, it seemed a private plane with two hunters had been flying around an area north of town when they spotted something down on the rocks---something that greatly resembled a body! But not being certain, they called in their location to the airport official who notified the FBI. Agents still in the area carrying on a thus-far fruitless search for Mac were ordered to meet in Rita's town---along with state troopers, investigators as well as Indian law enforcement.

Later, once they got a visual sighting so far below them, a few men were assigned to stay and investigate Mac's truck and the entire cliff area while the rest took a lower route. Once down there, the body was then somewhat above them so climbers were sent up for a closer look. Sure enough, it was a body---and since it was in Logan's county, he was called in to help identify the remains. Upon signing off--- Logan immediately telephoned O'Barr's office.

Soon the two were bounding up the highway in Logan's car---it's siren screaming, the big engine roaring---Logan's foot had the accelerator pressed to the floor! "Slow down, Logan!"---Doc ordered---"You're gonna kill us both before we get there! How we gonna help identify a body, if we die in a speedin' accident?!" "Sorry!"—Logan replied--- "After all this time and nobody finding a clue to his whereabouts---I was almost certain Mac had escaped the net and was long-gone! Hell, it's been well over TWO weeks! Reckon it's him?" Doc shrugged---"Dunno. Where'd you say th' exact location is?" Logan repeated the directions and Doc murmured---"Knowin' th' area fairly well---that sounds like it's between th' McDougal ranch and th' reservation! What would he be doin' there?? I'd have thought if he was in this vicinity, he'd find a deserted hunter's lean-to an' hide out there---or maybe hang out on his own land!" "Beats me!"---the sheriff replied---"I never knew much about this jerk---didn't see him that often! I just got his ugly face imprinted on my mind from looking at his 'wanted' posters all this time! Look! Here's the road we take...,"---without much deceleration, he slid into a turn, spewing dirt and gravel as he righted the steering---"...we'll soon know, old buddy, we'll soon know." Doc gazed back at the metal gate that someone had opened and pulled back out of the way----recently, his mind had begun to doubt the existence of the damned thing---but there it was!! Big as life---he'd never know the answer, never.

As Logan sped down the bumpy road, Doc held onto the harness around his body and mentally prepared himself for the ID---he'd never liked helping to identify a body that had been 'out' too long. Early in medical school he found out he wanted no part of   forensics! But this was something he had to do---Logan would've thought he was acting peculiar had he not raced over to join him on this errand! After all the info they'd passed each other on this case? He must do his best to appear both excited---but very, very dumb about the location of this as yet 'unidentified body'! Suddenly an untoward idea flashed across his brain---what if it WASN'T Mac!!???

Up ahead, they recognized the black cars of the FBI, the state trooper cruisers, the reservation police 4-wheel drive vehicles—and some of his own men who'd been in the area when the call came thru. Overhead a helicopter hovered about----conversation was buzzing---bits and pieces about the case---about Mac's father's arrest and the KKK. As he stood leaning against Logan's cruiser---Doc saw the climbers coming toward the group of men---they were carrying a body-bag on a stretcher. He coughed, cleared his throat, spat then joined Logan to approach the scene.

A climber unzipped the body bag and stepped back. Doc pulled on latex gloves as he and Logan went closer---looking down, they could see the remains---to Doc's relief it WAS Mac---and due to the cold weather, he was in 'fair condition'! "What'cha think, Doc?"---Logan whispered. Quietly and diligently, Doc 'took his time' viewing Mac's body and 'touching it'---as would be expected of any decent physician doing a job like this. "Well."---he finally spoke—"This definitely IS the McDougal that I knew---as a patient." He looked at the agents and Logan then stepped

367

slightly toward the body, took a longer look then nodded to the men---"It's him."

Doc heard the heavy-duty zipper on the body-bag make a final slide---turning toward the sound, he saw Mac was once more hidden from view. "The FBI agents identify him as the man who shot their men?"---Doc whispered to Logan who replied---"We'll see. C'mon over, I'll introduce you to these guys---at least the ones I know."

After an hour, they drove away. It was quiet for a moment then Logan stated---"Well, O'Barr, it's over---at least for old Mac. Those two empty handguns they found are almost certainly what he used to shoot the agents! Don't know what'll come of the trial with his father and the Klan over there in their home state. We'll be have a hearing at our courthouse, then the case will be closed. Lizbeth will have to testify---also Bill and Salle---probably you---since you were his doctor---and also took care of Lizbeth after the beating. And of course, my men and I will have to give testimony about our findings at the ranch----the crime scene, etc." Doc nodded, grateful the body had been found.

The car turned onto the highway back to town. Doc waited a couple of minutes then ventured---"Th' cause of death? I mean, I can almost bet he fell---but without a coroner's examination---I couldn't swear to it! Do they suspect 'foul-play' or did you hear?" "Much too early to tell---stuff like that takes awhile, I'll keep you posted though. However, I don't think 'foul-play' will get honorable mention! And I did talk to the FBI about searching the barns and out-buildings there at the ranch---thanks to you. Course I couldn't tell them you brought it up...,"---he frowned and gave Doc a 'knowing' look---"You know how close-mouthed law-enforcement folks are supposed to be with 'the public'! You and I know the truth---but I can't let them know you and I have sorta---been 'in cahoots' on this one!"

Relieved over the entire morning, Doc laughed and responded---"Oh, that's okay, High Sheriff, I understand these things. Sure wouldn't want you t'get reprimanded because of some silly suggestion I made during one of my Walter Mitty 'private investigator' states of mind! Rest assured, it'll be OUR little secret! I've been wonderin'--- you believe th' Feds will want t'go over Lizbeth's house again? After th' shock of findin' out her tormentor is dead an' all that---before long I know she'll want t'know when she can live in th' house again. She and Salle go out occasionally with Bill and some men, she's seen to it that it's been kept free of mice and roaches but she's been too scared to live out there! I know your men were thorough--- but will the feds insist on their own report of his attempt on her life an' th' beating he gave her?" "Aww, if they do--- it'll be short and swift! Believe me, it won't be the attempted murder of Mac's wife OR the beating he gave her that'll be 'the deal' in their case against Mac! After all, he shot two of their OWN! That'll seal his fate---far as they're concerned, he's guilty and not much else matters! And if they find anything that vaguely reeks of KKK hidden out there on that ranch---they may not even CARE about the house, except for Klan evidence! But, like I say, I'll keep you posted! Tell her I'll let her know when she can go back to the ranch and live there again."---Logan shook his head then added---"Some Christmas present, huh!" "Yeah."--- Doc nodded and looked at the road ahead---"Sure is."

***

In three days and with a little help from Logan who'd had help from Doc, the FBI uncovered all the cleverly hidden guns at the ranch---and tied them to the KKK---which tied

369

Mac, his father and other Klan members to those past unsolved crimes and murders. So at least one part of the case could be closed---in their minds anyway. They could rest knowing the guns had been picked up, the investigation carried out and 'over' as far as Lizbeth, Doc, Bill, Salle--- and Hawk were concerned.

Upon completing his examination, the coroner released Mac's body to 'the family' for burial. However, no family members arrived, instead they had Mac's remains sent home on the train. Other than a brief visit to further ID the body, Lizbeth never saw Mac again. She didn't travel to attend the funeral nor did she speak with any of his family or friends. Once the train carrying 'the remains' gathered speed, passed the city limits and went out of sight---the years that had been filled with misery, pain, loneliness and regret in Lizbeth's world---all these went along with Mac, forever closing that period of her life.

Only one time did she look upon her deceased 'husband' to give further ID to the authorities. She'd held onto Doc's arm and gripped Ida's hand as the coroner opened a metal door, slid out the shelf then unzipped a bag and folded back a sheet. There in the cold lower floor of the mortuary, she viewed Mac for the last time. His body was covered with only his face being shown to her. After nodding toward the coroner, Logan and an FBI area chief, she whispered--- "Yes, that was my husband." Then the trio left the room, walked back up the stairs, down the hall to the front door--- then out into the cold winter sunshine. Lizbeth felt the tears that had begun blurring her vision start to run down her cheeks. Once inside Ida's car, she wept. "Poah, poah soul,"---she whispered aloud in her grief for him as Doc and Ida clucked appropriately.

Doc and Ida left her 'be' for a few days---then she began
exhibiting some signs of being her usual self. They nodded,
smiling at each other and quietly allowed her to start
becoming the 'real Lizbeth' once again.

Chapter Sixty

Christmas was almost upon them, bringing with it many
special church programs and extra meetings. All the
activities left little time for too much moping. Besides,
being busy was good for Lizbeth. There was Ida's choir
practice for the cantata and drawing names among her
ladies circle then choosing a gift for the name she'd drawn.
There were gifts to buy for Doc's nurse and receptionist, for
the Winterhawks, friends and a few patients. Lizbeth and
Ida baked feverishly for several afternoons one week---then
took one day to help Mary and Salle. The grandparents of
Dottie's late husband would be picking up the two children
for a holiday visitation with them. In town, a small local
Christmas parade escorted Santa down the street as he threw
handfuls of wrapped hard candies to all the children who
danced about---whooping, screeching and running after his
'wheeled' sleigh that was pulled by several aged horses
accustomed to boisterous children!

Lizbeth enjoyed the many visitors who dropped in at the
O'Barr home---their laughter, the Christmas decorations,
the tree and the lights lifted her spirits as nothing else could
at this point. 'Only Hawk could've made everything
perfect', she thought so many times as she stood at the edge
of the merry making then insisted upon doing most of the
serving and cleaning up afterward while Ida and Doc
entertained their guests. Lizbeth loved being useful to the
O'Barr's---they'd done so much for her---she could
NEVER repay all of it! Without Doc---without Joseph---

without Salle and Bill---she knew she wouldn't have been ALIVE when this Christmas Day finally arrived---she'd be the one dead---not Mac! A slight shiver would pass over her, she'd put it out of her mind and go on with her work--- time would heal it all.

Ida's friends dropped in for hot spiced tea, coffee, cookies or cake----but in the case of Doc's friends, there was cake with hot Irish Coffee---or salted nuts and a stiff drink of choice---sometimes more than one 'stiff drink'! The 'merrier' they became, the 'louder' their laughter---Ida would look at Lizbeth, shake her head, roll her eyes wondering just how the obvious 'extra' bottles had found their way into the house! Lizbeth would chuckle, pat Ida's back and herd her off into another direction---to do something more constructive and useful.

The night before Christmas Eve was the evening Ida chose to invite Joseph for supper---for her anticipated 'foursome'! First, they'd dine in the little-used formal dining room, then while she and Lizbeth cleaned up----the men could enjoy a warm fire in the living room. Afterwards a drive around town taking in the lights would put everyone in even more of the 'seasonal spirit'! Upon returning home, they'd warm themselves by the fire and have a mug of hot chocolate--- hopefully to warm the younger couple to each other---as they'd only seen each other once on Thanksgiving! THEN, Ida thought---by then I'll definitely know for certain if there's any 'sparks' between Lizbeth and Hawk! "Unless, of course, respect for her late 'husband' puts a damper on their 'feelings'. Even with that, they'll not fool me for a minute! I can read expressions, eye contact---and no matter how Dr. O'Barr tends to dissuade me away from the possibility of attraction between them, I still say it's there! Dead husband or no!"

***

At home, Joseph nervously dressed for the 'occasion', it was the first time he'd be seeing Lizbeth since she and Ida came one afternoon to help his mother with some Christmas cookery. His mother knew about the two of them---but Ida wasn't SUPPOSED to! However, that afternoon, he had the very distinct feeling that she suspected 'something' as her subtle side-glances toward each of them clearly indicated she'd extended her 'romance-antenna' out to it's last section! In years past, she'd tried to 'fix him up' a couple of times with Indian girls she'd met through Doc---now she had that same look on her face! Hurriedly, he made his excuses then vacated the premises leaving Ida with a slightly puzzled and 'let-down' expression on her face!

Tonight, he stood looking in the mirror and carefully brushed at some non-existent lint on his suede jacket. Ida had SAID this was an 'informal' occasion and that he should wear something 'comfortable---but nice'. He hoped she considered his apparel 'nice' enough for her dinner. What would he do if she answered the door wearing some bejeweled, after-five creation and find him standing there wearing suede and tweed!

Salle had insisted on pulling his hair back and making one long, shiny, black braid---she'd fussed over it for an hour and now he wondered if maybe he should've had all his hair cut! "Too late, Winterhawk."---he thought---"You're an Indian---so just be an Indian. If Lizbeth loves you and your hair---doesn't matter what anybody else thinks---right?" He nodded at himself in the mirror and left the room.

Mary, Salle, Bill, Dottie, Rammah and Jerri were expecting Joseph's grand entrance into the living room just before the kids other grandparents came by for them. Mary, Salle and

373

Bill sat quietly on the new sofa-bed---Dottie lounged in the new recliner while the children sprawled in their bean-bag chairs. All waited to check-out Hawk's 'change of habit' from the usual jeans, scuffed harness boots, flannel shirts and thick plaid woolen jacket---to what? The kids were certain he'd wear his ranger camouflages with paratrooper boots and beret---after all, that was the height of Uncle Hawk's being 'dressed-up'!! He'd been a warrior---what else would he even consider wearing some place special where he'd have supper?! Besides, he might have to stop on the way and make 'war' with some secret enemy!! Mary hoped he'd wear his turquoise and silver jewelry---Salle was concerned he'd sneaked in and unbraided his hair--- after all the trouble she'd gone to! Smothering a giggle, she'd forgotten to tell him if he undid his braid, he'd have crimped and kinky hair for his 'big occasion'! But then, she guessed he knew that from having sisters in the house!

Suddenly he came through the door and stopped short--- "My Lord! What's going on? I knew the house had grown silent as a tomb---what're you guys sitting around in here for? The TV's not even on! You meditating---or expecting Santa one day early?" Everyone started talking and exclaiming at once---the children were soundly disappointed in his tweed slacks, suede casual shoes, woolen sweater over a dress shirt and tie---even the suede jacket was a 'let-down'!! Mary noted with quiet pleasure that he did wear his turquoise and silver---and Salle saw his hair was still neatly braided.

"You smell great, bro!"---Dottie teased---"Wish I had some great looking, good-smelling guy to come have supper with ME!" Hawk smiled then gestured---"Guess I'll have to dig one up for you---does it matter how old he is or his skin color?" She shook her head---"Nope. Just let me know when you 'dig one up'---I'll try and lose a few pounds before you introduce us!"---she bit into another chocolate cookie. "Okay. Do I pass muster?"---Joseph turned around once. Everyone agreed he passed with high marks.

Once at the O'Barr house, he rang the doorbell and stood taking deep breaths. Soon Ida answered the door and beneath her ruffled apron, she was wearing---a tweed skirt, silk blouse and cashmere sweater! Removing his hat and handing her a box of chocolates, he smiled at her---relieved he'd obviously chosen correctly. "Right on time, Joseph! Come in! My!"---she gushed---"Don't you look nice---like a picture in a man's magazine!" She took his hat and coat, then pointing to the living room---"Go right in, the doctor is relaxing a bit before we eat. Lizbeth just went upstairs to change---she'll be down in a minute. Make yourself at home while I check on the meal."

Doc grinned as Joseph entered the room---"Merry Christmas, Captain! Sit down, Bird-man, take a load off an' tell me what's new!?" Hawk took a chair, grinned back at Doc---"Not much going on, doctor-man! It's pretty quiet right now---how about yourself? You still sharp as a ground-down rock?" "OH yeah!"---the older man preened---"Not much gets past me. It's not th' years that's slowed me too much! Fact is, th'past several months have taken more outta me---than th' earlier 60 years all put t'gether!" Joseph laughed---"I take it, you had a bad autumn and early winter then!" "Reckon you, of all people, would know somethin' about th' answer for THAT one!"---Doc leaned toward Joseph and said in a low voice---"Let's make a New Year's resolution t'gether---you an' me! Let's resolve t'have a nice, quiet, lethargic year---th' whole year long! Not get in any sorta trouble, not poke our noses in anybody else's life, not break any laws, have no secret night-time investigations or illegal goings-on, no messin' with th' feds, no detective work, no getting' shot, no 100 mph-plus auto

375

chases, no flyin' around in th' air like birds---whadda y' say?"

Hawk had been chuckling all through the litany ---"You mean no more work for the Lone Ranger and Tonto? Man! How boring---you DO know all this high-burning lifestyle is addictive, don't you? I expected to come over here tonight and find you in a state of 'withdrawal'---like it's been too quiet lately? And here you are---all loose as a goose, sitting by the fire---mellowed out to the gills. What's the matter with you?!" "Just promise me that you'll marry this girl who's been livin' in m'house, move her some place far away from here for awhile---an' leave me t'carry on m'quiet, small-town doctor life then get old t'tell about it. B'fore I forget it, that coroner's report is back--- Logan says it's 'death by misadventure'. NO sign of 'foul play' at all!" Hawk pursed his lips, blew out a relieved breath and leaned back in his chair---then said quietly--- "Thank GOD, Doc, thank God."

Then the stairway gave a familiar squeak---Hawk's eager eyes turned immediately toward the door. Doc smiled to himself then called out---"LIZBETH? That you? Come in for a minute---our guest is here an' wants t'say 'hello'!" She appeared in the doorway---Joseph's eyes met hers as he stood---Doc had melted into the woodwork---the two of them were alone in the world. The red-haired 'vision' in front of Joseph was wearing a yellow sweater with black satin blouse beneath---the soft black wool skirt swirled slightly as she approached him---"Good evening, Joseph. Merry Christmas to you." He bowed his head slightly in a nod and answered—"And to you, Lizbeth. May this be the best Christmas of your life." There in the room, their eyes never left each other---just as their hearts had never left each other from the moment they'd met.

On her way to call them for dinner, Ida had stood in the
shadows for a moment and observed Joseph's face as
Lizbeth approached him---"I was RIGHT!! I KNEW IT!
He is utterly 'gone' over her!! I haven't seen a man look
quite so taken with a woman---not in a long time!" Giving
it a couple of minutes, Ida then lifted her head and walked
briskly into the room---"Dinner's ready, everyone! Let's go
into the dining room before the food gets cold!"

Dinner was another of Ida's many successes---the drive was
exhilarating and the lights beautiful---the hot chocolate
warmed their bodies while the fire warmed their feet.
Conversation was alternately quiet then animated---Ida
decided there was too many 'sparks' in the room---too
much static 'electricity' for her and Doc to stay up too late.
And presently, she 'yawned'---"Oh my, please excuse me!"
Her glance fell upon the doctor---"I believe the heavy
holiday food and this fire has made a dullard of me!
Doctor? How about you---we've had a long day and
tomorrow's Christmas Eve! Beginning early, I've things
for you to do, m'dear!"

Joseph looked startled---"Oh. Mrs. Doc---I didn't realize
the hour! I, uh, do thank you for the delicious meal, the
lovely evening---it's time I should go!" He stood and
stammered---"Santa will have to make at least a couple of
trips into town tomorrow---even though I've been promised
that everything 'is ready'---it never fails that something's
been left undone." Ida could barely hide her smile of being
'proven correct'---he didn't want the evening to end---that
was obvious! He was NOT ready to leave but for the sake
of good taste, he was making a disjointed attempt at
'goodnight'. "Oh no!!" Ida crowed---"Not you two young
people! PLEASE, Joseph, you must stay and keep Lizbeth
company for as long as you like---I feel she's a bit lonely
for people her own age what with only Doc and myself for

company! She's been cooped up here too long with us
'older folk'! You can listen to Christmas music---watch
television---or.."---she shrugged cleverly---"...put another
log or two on the fire and---just talk."

Lizbeth looked gratefully at her---then at Joseph---"Please,
Joseph. Do stay an' visit with me awhile---you can tell me
what th' children and th' family are gettin' foah Christmas."
"Thank you."---he replied softly---"I'd love to---uh, stay
and visit. Thank you." "Well---goodnight then!"---Ida took
Doc by the arm and hurried him from the room, calling---
"Drive safely going home---and we'll see you and the
family tomorrow afternoon!" "Yes ma'am!"---Joseph
called back. The stairs squeaked again---Lizbeth and
Joseph were alone to enjoy the lighted tree, the fire, the
season---and at last, they could enjoy each other's
company---at least semi-privately!

Much later after he'd closed the glass over the fireplace---
locking in the remaining glowing coals, Joseph gave her one
last lingering kiss and bade her 'goodnight' at the door.
Climbing the stairs, Lizbeth felt light as a feather---as
though she'd lift off the steps and float to her room. Once
inside the door, she closed it tightly and looked at the
sparkling diamond ring----Joseph had slid it on her finger
and after her tears were dried, they made an outline for their
future plans.

Once the hearing was over, she'd told Joseph she wanted
Salle and Bill to live in her ranch house and run the ranch
while she went to visit her folks back in Georgia. He
suggested that he stay on here for awhile---then tell
everyone that he had a job traveling overseas for a year.
Instead, he'd come to Georgia---meet her family. They'd
get married in her church then he'd take her on a long
vacation---any place her heart desired! Perhaps during the

early fall of next year, she'd return to the ranch. After a few weeks, he'd come back home also---they'd start 'seeing each other'---and later be re-married in the reservation church---and then the rest of their lives would pass softly--- like autumn leaves drifting lazily to the earth's waiting arms.

As she sat on the bed where Hawk always slept when visiting Doc and Ida---she was too excited to even think of sleep! He'd only been gone 20 minutes but she missed him already---pulling her robe over her flannel pajamas and wriggling her feet into her fuzzy slippers, she went to the window to look out for awhile. Outside, the stars twinkled in a midnight blue sky---it was so quiet, so still and peaceful! Just like another Christmas so long ago. Careful to be very quiet, she slid the window open---just for a few minutes---she HAD to breathe in the fresh air and the beauty of her special night---the night she'd become engaged to Joseph Winterhawk!

Then she heard it! A very soft, subtle sound---it was---oh, her heart raced! It was a flute---and it was slowly playing her very own melody! Leaning far out the window---she looked and looked---but saw nothing! Where was he?! She waved and waved---but there was no one to be seen, only the music told her he was even there! Finally, the quiet, almost imperceptible haunting melody faded away---then he suddenly appeared seemingly from nowhere! Standing in the yard just past the porch roof---he opened his arms to her, then crossed them over his chest and bowed his head over them---then he threw her a kiss and disappeared into the night.

The earth had turned many times since his first vision of her then decades later, without any warning at all, the vision

Joseph's Visions AKA "Hawk"

became reality! Joseph's visions had become her visions and now the time had finally come for them to be together.

The End